D1713596

Ravenous horror from the past returns to stalk the residents of Lawless, British Columbia, and this time, it's got company...

CLAW
RESURGENCE

KATIE BERRY

ENTER TO WIN!

Become a Katie Berry Books Insider; you'll be glad you did. By simply sharing your email address*, you will be entered into the monthly draws! That's right, draws, plural.

Each month there will be two draws: one for a free digital download of one of my audiobooks and the other for a free autographed copy of one of my novels delivered right to your mailbox.

There will be other contests, chapter previews, short stories, and more coming soon, so don't miss out!

Join today at:

https://mailchi.mp/756d0cbb50ea/subscribe-page

*Your email address will not be sold, traded, or given away. It will be kept strictly confidential and will only be used by Katie Berry Books to notify you of new content (or perhaps that you're another lucky winner of the monthly draws).

ACKNOWLEDGEMENTS:

Special thanks to Paulina, Jen, Bob, Betty, Gary and Michael. Your time and attention are most greatly appreciated.

PREFACE

Welcome! I'm glad you decided to pay another visit to Lawless, British Columbia. The residents have been hard at work, repairing the town from the earthquake in January and trying to get back to some semblance of normality, or as close as Lawless can ever come to that.

What you now hold in your hands is the story of what happened next. You'll reconnect with your favourite characters and meet some new ones as they encounter further trials and tribulations around the valley. Just as they try to put the last year behind them, they discover that what lives in the caverns on Gold Ridge is not quite done with them yet and that new horrors await.

I had a wonderful time as I revisited Lawless over the last several months and hope that you will, too. So, without further ado, sit back, get comfortable and prepare to enjoy this tale of hidden fortunes, rampant greed and ancient horrors.

-Katie Berry

September 7th, 2021

To the past, and all the wonders and terrors it contained.

CHAPTER ONE

Wind-driven snow skittered past the tall windows of the Lawless City Hall, rattling at its aged panes as if seeking entry. Austin Murphy was about halfway up a tall step ladder which stood next to a towering blue spruce in the lobby. He looked out at the winter's day and shivered slightly. It had been bitterly cold and snowing heavily for the past couple of days, just like the weather office had forecast. With a shake of his head, he turned his attention back to the task at hand.

"Don't drop this star—and don't fall, either!" Christine Moon said from below, stretching up and holding out a multi-pointed Christmas star toward him.

Reaching from the ladder to retrieve the proffered ornament, Austin smiled down at Christine. "I'll be careful, Chris, thanks. I have done this on a couple of different occasions over the years, you know." With Christine steadying things from below, he carefully negotiated his way back up to the top of the ladder, placing the silver star firmly atop the apex of the pungent spruce. Despite being in a pot, the magnificent tree was quite tall and voluminous. Initially, the conifer had been planted during a city hall remodelling many decades before and was now so large that there was talk of having a tree topping service come in to prune it.

"That's good. I wouldn't want the new mayor of Lawless to fall and hurt himself just before the holidays," Christine responded with a grin.

With Mayor Bob Nichols missing in action, along with Councillor Ray Chance and Chief Reggie VanDusen, a new civic by-election had been held in the spring. After the earthquake damage in January, the town had had its metaphorical hands full with the number of critical systems and structures that needed to be fixed and upgraded. Just getting the damage repaired on so many buildings around town had been an enormous undertaking and Austin was glad most of the work was now done. Thanks to his City Works crew, along with help from the valley's citizens and their hard-working, ready-to-tackle-anything attitude, almost everything that needed doing had gotten done just before the first snow of the year.

Austin had been working so hard on everything that Christine had joked that he should run for mayor. That had gotten him pondering things, and after a bit, with some additional egging-on from Trip, Austin had put his name into the mix. Since his desire was to get the small mountain town up and running again as quickly as possible, he'd made that his platform. With Trip's help, they'd planted numerous signs around town that said, 'Murphy for Mayor! Let's Get 'er Done!' After that point, he hadn't canvassed door to door or anything like that. In fact, he'd almost forgotten about it, so busy as he was just doing what needed to be done around town. Then, during an all-candidates debate, he had a particularly good showing after reiterating his pragmatic principles. During the subsequent election, it seemed that his organisational and managerial skills, along with his hard work, had not gone unnoticed by the local residents. When all the votes were finally tallied, Austin had won by a landslide.

Shaking his head in disbelief as he thought about his new position, Austin stepped carefully down to the lobby floor as Christine continued to steady the ladder. "Yeah, breaking my neck would put a damper on things, that's for sure." He smiled in thanks for her assistance, and his heart suddenly skipped a beat.

2

His feelings for Christine had grown stronger and stronger over the past several months. She had been there each day, working next to him every step of the way, and they had grown quite close. Her job as ladder-steadier complete, she was currently focused on poking through a box of Christmas decorations at the moment, looking for just a few more ornaments. The way she wrinkled up her nose as she poked around the box was just the cutest thing Austin recalled seeing in quite a while. He nodded slightly to himself and smiled again. Yes, he was definitely falling for this woman and wondered if she felt the same.

"Hey there, Captain Kirk!" Christine said.

Austin shook his head, bringing himself back from his flight of romantic fancy. "Sorry, Chris, what was that?"

"You looked like you were way out in space there for a second."

"Oh, yeah," Austin said with a sheepish grin. "Just thinkin' some thoughts."

"Good ones, I hope," Christine replied with a smile, then handed a couple of ornaments destined for the tree to Austin.

"Always," Austin replied, temporarily mesmerised by Christine's smile. Moving back to the spruce tree, he found himself holding two red glass globes, one in each hand, and began looking for some empty branches. This cherished tree had survived the quake unscathed, one of the few things to have been so lucky.

The damage to the city of Lawless last winter had been phenomenal, and many people were still recovering from its effects, both physically and psychologically. Then, just last week, the town had been put on edge once more when another, smaller trembler occurred, centred along the north end of the valley, near the Kootenay Glacier like last time. Fortunately, this new jiggler had only rattled the windows around town, unlike the 7.8

magnitude shaker back in early January.

Wondering if he should be concerned for the town's residents, Austin had checked with his geologist friend down on the coast, Jerry Benson. Jerry had been quite reassuring and said that what they'd felt was most likely some delayed subsidence—just the ground settling, which it sometimes did after a major quake, often many months later. So technically, Jerry had concluded, the shift in the ground was a very minor quake and likened it to Mother Nature getting comfortable and settling in for the winter.

And that is what many people were doing as well, including Christine. Though busy with her own conservation office tasks despite the falling snow, she had volunteered with Austin to decorate some of the public-owned buildings around Lawless. So far today, they'd managed to decorate the interiors of the Community Health Centre and the Lawless Police Department. Thanks to Christine's assistance, they were almost done. It was less than a week before Christmas, but this was the first chance they'd had to have anything resembling seasonal normalcy around the small mountain town since the incident.

At their backs, a gust of wind and snow blew into the lobby, and Trip Williams rolled through the revolving door. He was finally back from his errand, a white shopping bag bearing the Home Hardware logo draped over one snow-covered arm. This no doubt contained the new string of Christmas lights Austin had requested. Slung over Trip's other arm was a clear wide-bottomed plastic bag. A box was nestled inside, the kind that usually contained a dozen doughnuts, many of which were no doubt honey crullers awaiting immediate consumption. In his hands, he held a cardboard tray with four Tim Hortons coffee cups inside.

"Hey, guys! Look what I have!" Trip seemed excited to be the bearer of tasty treats and Christmas cheer. He held them out to Austin and Christine and looked down at the tray, saying, "There's a dark roast double-double in the mix, so don't anyone take it by mistake. It's for Willy Jr.'s trial by fire tonight.

"Thanks, big guy, I appreciate it," Austin said, being careful to take the cup with 'DD' written on top and not the 'DRDD' for Willy. While he was there, he grabbed the shopping bag of tree lights from Trip's overloaded arms.

Christine removed a cup labelled 'ST', which contained her steeped tea. With a large smile, she said, "Thank you, Trip, but you didn't have to go and do that." Trip smiled back, appearing to blush his usual beet red beneath his beard, just like he did every time he interacted with Christine. If it wasn't for the tops of his cheeks peeking through, nobody would have been the wiser.

Trip placed the doughnut box and his coffee on the information desk for a moment. As he brushed the snow from his shoulders and shook out his toque, he said, "The tree looks good, guys. And nice job with that star, Mr. Mayor." He picked the doughnuts up and flipped the lid open, offering them to his friends.

Christine declined and held up her tea, saying, "I'm fine, thanks."

Austin took a Boston cream and said, "Thanks, Mr. Public Works."

Trip had been promoted to head of the public works yard in Lawless after Austin had been elected mayor. And although Austin missed the everyday hands-on nature of his old position, he knew the functioning of the town was in good, if slightly sticky hands with Trip now running the show.

Shaking his head, Trip lamented, "You know, I just gotta say, it's not the same anymore without you down at the yard, Boss. Willy Wilson Jr. just isn't as funny as you are."

"Well, thanks, buddy. It's nice to know my fantastic sense of humour is appreciated. I'll try to drop by more often to keep things lively around there for you."

"Speaking of the yard and stuff that still needs to get done, Mr. Mayor," Trip said, now sounding serious. "We've really gotta get things moving on the Sinclair building."

Until the January quake, the heritage newspaper building had been in the early stages of renovation by the city. Thankfully, it had been constructed of more sturdy materials like city hall and the hospital, and it hadn't suffered much during the shake-up. Located across the street, the Bank of Montreal, unfortunately, couldn't make the same claim. Despite its own heritage status, the bank's building had to be condemned due to structural instability issues, mainly because of its sinking three metres into the ground during the quake.

The Sinclair building was a beautiful old brick and stone structure that the city-owned, having been bought in the early eighties after the Sinclair Corporation's bankruptcy. The Lawless Heritage Committee had wanted to save the old newspaper building if they could. Some renovation of its structure had already been underway, but after the quake, the foundation had needed some additional corrective procedures before anyone could use the building again. Once everything was completed, the city had planned to use it for office space rentals below and condominium apartments above. Several interested tenants were already lined up to occupy the building once it was completed, and now, it just had to get done.

One of the issues plaguing the town's reconstruction had been the recent report from the city comptroller's office. It had pointed to many instances of financial irregularities over the last few years regarding the town's budget. Apparently, this was due to ex-Mayor Bob Nichols and his cooking of the town's books. Thanks to his numerous embezzlements over the years, the post-quake renovation budget for the city had to be severely reduced. As the new head of city works, Trip now had to ensure that the remaining things were done ASAP and as economically as possible. With the snow on the ground now and fog in the air soon, most outdoor renovations were on hold for the next several months until springtime. And so, it was now time to get inside jobs like the

Sinclair building done.

Fully aware of all these facts, Austin asked with interest, "Okay, so how're things going at the Sinclair, anyway?"

"Not bad, but I had to pull Willy off working cleanup at the place so Larry and I can have some time off from plowing that mess on the roads out there. Anyway, I need to hire another body to help out with some grunt work for a week or two until just after the new year. Someone to move old cartons of newspapers and other paperwork up from the basement to go to the shredders, along with throwing out old office furniture and stuff like that. So, I was wondering if you knew of any young fellas out there that could use some more money, especially with the holidays coming up and all?"

With an appreciative nod and smile, Austin replied, "Thanks, Trip. I'm sure Alex will appreciate the work since he has a lot more expenses now, what with his new ride to fix and a girlfriend to boot." Alex had just bought himself a used 1995 Toyota Tacoma off a neighbour of theirs and had been looking for another part-time job to provide more of a financial 'fix' to his new automotive 'habit'.

"That would be great! Even if we can just get that basement cleaned out before this year is over. I've already got a dumpster in the alley behind the building that Alex can use to throw out the basement crap."

Austin glanced at his watch; it was almost three o'clock. "Alex might be wanting to start today after school if you text him now and ask him."

Glancing out the front doors at the gusting snow, Trip agreed, "That's a great idea, and there is no time like the present. I'll text Alex from my truck before I head back to the Works for a bit. Willy is ready for his first solo shift on the Citrus Express this evening, and I want to make sure he's up to speed on everything before he pulls out."

At Trip's behest, Austin had hired Willy Wilson Junior at the public works yard several months before. Trip had told Austin that he felt sorry for the kid, what with his dad getting eaten and the fact that the young fella didn't have anyone else in the world. Austin suspected it was also because of Trip's own life, living as he did with the stigma of being orphaned at an early age himself. Though Willy wasn't the fastest learner, Trip said he was honest and a hard worker, and just needed a little guidance, now and again.

And so, Willy had been hired on through a work-training programme offered through the Province of BC. The programme paid half of his wages for the first six months—which had been more savings for the cash-strapped city. Fortunately, Willy worked out fine and had recently gone full-time at the yard as Trip's assistant. Tonight was his first shift driving the Citrus Express around the town for the evening, sharing the shifts with Trip and Larry and giving the other men some extra time off at home each week over the holidays.

"All right, tell Willy I said, 'Hi'. And thanks again for the coffee."

"You bet, Boss." Trip flipped open his doughnut box and offered it to Christine one more time. She demurred and held up her tea, saying, "This was great, thanks, Trip."

Giving a quick thumbs up to Austin and Christine, Trip said, "Catch you guys on the rebound," then revolved out the door with his remaining doughnuts and coffee.

After a sip of her tea, Christine turned to Austin and said, "Are we still on for dinner tomorrow?"

"Of course!" Austin replied, excited to be taking Christine out somewhere, just the two of them. He'd asked her out to the newly reopened Frostbite Fred's for a meal now that the place had been fully renovated and repaired from the damage of the bear attack and the quake. Over the last ten months, things had seemed non-stop, and although Austin had wanted to get to know Christine better, he just hadn't had the chance. So now, with things slowly getting back to normal, he looked forward to the opportunity. "Listen, do you have a second?" he asked.

"Well, I was just going to pop out to Geraldine Gertzmeyer's place to check on how she's doing. What's up?"

"Follow me." Austin led her to the office of the mayor on the second floor of the building. It was a lavish affair, covered in rich cherry wood panelling that absorbed most of the light and made the room seem quite dark and mysterious. Even with the drapes pulled back, revealing the brilliant whiteness of the blustering snowstorm outside, it still seemed dim inside the office.

"So, what did you want to show me?" Christine asked as she took in the ornate room.

"Well, it was in here." Austin moved to a painting on the wall and swung it open like a cupboard door, revealing a small safe with an electronic keypad on the other side.

"Cool. How did you figure out the combination?"

"I Googled it, of course!"

"Googled it?"

"Sure, I found the name and model number."

"And you got inside, just like that?"

"Well, not quite. I found that there was also supposed to be a bypass key." Austin pointed to the top drawer of the desk and added, "Found it right in there next to the paperclips, with the drawer unlocked as well."

"Ah, yes. High security in small-town BC at its finest, huh?"

Christine said with a smile.

"It's a regular Fort Knox around here." Austin inserted the key into the wall safe and pulled out a bundle of old newspapers tied together with twine.

"Those were inside?" Christine asked incredulously. "Who keeps old newspapers in their safe."

Austin handed the bundle to Christine, saying, "Apparently, the ex-Mayor of Lawless did. Oh, and I found this in there as well." Austin reached into the safe and pulled out eight tall stacks of bills.

Christine's jaw dropped, and she said, "Oh my, are all of those hundred-dollar bills? How much is that?"

"Comes to a nice tidy eighty grand."

"Wow! What are you going to do with it?"

"I'm going to have the comptroller list it as a city asset and put it into the town's coffers since we need the money."

"That's very boring but very responsible. Good call," Christine said with an approving nod.

"Thanks, I thought so. Not to mention the fact that most of that money presumably belongs to the city anyway, thanks to Mayor Bob's financial shenanigans."

Christine pulled the leather office chair out from behind the desk and asked, "Before you give it all away, may I sit at your new desk, touch your stacks of cash and check out some of those papers, Mr. Mayor?" She batted her eyelashes and smiled demurely, adding, "I've never seen that much money in one place before."

With a hard swallow, Austin tried to reply casually, "Oh, of course! Any time." Inside, he was dealing with an accelerated heart rate but hoped it didn't show too much on the outside. Christine's piercing blue eyes were almost hypnotic as they regarded him. He was on pins and needles at the thought of their upcoming dinner date. After the dinner portion was over, he planned on taking Christine to the Winter Solstice Smackdown. That was the town's name for their new winter festival, which ran all weekend starting tomorrow. Austin and the rest of the city council had wanted to have something to celebrate the grand reopening of Lawless, and the Winter Solstice Smackdown had been voted into existence as just the ticket.

Turning on the green banker's lamp situated off to one side of the expansive mahogany desk, Christine sat down and untied the bundle of papers. More than just newspapers, it also contained several letters. Holding them up, she queried, "Love letters?"

"Well, you'll love to read them, that's for sure," Austin replied but would say nothing more.

Christine looked briefly through the newspapers and noted that they were all from 1895. "Wasn't that the year when the gold rush started around these parts?"

"Yes," Austin said, then added, "That's the year it really took off. But it turns out it was also the year when the big fire happened, amongst other things."

"Fire?"

"Yup, almost the whole town burned to the ground."

"Really? I never knew that!"

"Neither did I, and I've lived here my whole life. However, I do remember that my grandmother mentioned once that her father had told her there had been some very dark times in Lawless many years before, but would never say what they were, exactly."

"That's curious. So, they covered up this fire?"

"Seems that way."

"But who were 'they'?"

"It could have been the company that used to own the building that Trip is now renovating."

Christine returned this news with a momentary blank stare, then said, "The Sinclair Building?"

"Yes, the Sinclair Development Corporation owned a surprising number of things in this town up until its bankruptcy in the 1980s. Remember that big disappearance I told you about a while back that always fascinated me?"

"The one that happened on New Year's Eve back sometime in the early '80s near Entwistle, right?"

"Yes, that's the one." For some reason, he'd always been fascinated by things like the Roanoke Colony, the Mary Celeste and, of course, the Sinclair Resort Incident being among some of the better-known ones. He added, "In addition to owning the ski hill, they also owned the local newspaper and several other businesses before they went bankrupt after the lawsuit."

"Something like a million or two per person, plus damages, wasn't it?"

"It ended up costing the company everything it had, as far as I know."

"A college friend of mine is going to be looking into that, actually."

Austin's eyes widened in interest. "Really? You'll have to fill me in on all the details sometime. You know how I am about learning what happened there."

"Don't worry, I'll keep you posted."

Tapping the papers on the desk, Austin said, "Regarding Lawless, I find it interesting that the same company that couldn't cover up a mass disappearance like in Entwistle, was able to cover up a fire that destroyed an entire town, as well as other assorted oddities that occurred here a century and a quarter ago."

"Other oddities?"

"You'll have to borrow those and read them at your leisure. There's lots of good stuff inside."

"Such as?"

"Such as, supposedly, parts of what is currently the Sinclair building survived the fire, and the newspaper business established there was built up around it. Before that, it was one of the West Kootenay's biggest saloons, the Golden Nugget. And they were big enough to influence whatever they wanted in this town, such as covering up the fire." Austin added, "As you know, if enough palms are greased..."

Christine continued his thought, "Or if enough people were permanently silenced." She shook her head dolefully, adding, "And it's not like it can't happen in real life. Look at what almost happened to me!"

"All too true. Well, I won't keep you any longer. I've got some paperwork I need to take care of before the holidays start. You'd better get going. I don't want you to suffer the wrath of Geraldine Gertzmeyer."

"Thanks. She was expecting me this afternoon, and daylight is wasting." The snow outside the window now appeared almost horizontal, and it scoured across the glass from the wind. She looked back into the room and said, "And besides, I wouldn't want to miss out on any of her cookies."

"When you get back, you'll have to grab a mug of cocoa to sip on while you learn some of the forgotten history of Lawless."

"I'll have to do that. Have you read all of these?"

"Enough to get the gist of them."

"And?"

"Burying secrets around this town is not a new thing."

CHAPTER TWO

The snow was getting heavier than ever, and the wipers on Christine's Dodge Ram were losing the battle to keep the windshield clean. Gusting winds that rattled at the truck added to the excitement, making the drive out to Geraldine Gertzmeyer's a little more challenging than usual. Still, she mused, it was nothing like the snail's pace she'd have to drive if this were fog instead of snow. Then again, that would be the case in the valley soon enough. Just after the new year, the fog would probably be back and sock-in the valley for more endlessly drab months. At least, that's what the locals said, and after last winter, she believed them.

With a smile, Christine realised it was just part of living in the beautiful West Kootenays of British Columbia, and she was more than happy to put up with it. This was especially true right now since she was feeling part of the local community around Lawless more and more, finally getting to know the residents. During the reconstruction, Christine had repeatedly witnessed people going out of their way to help neighbours in need. Just seeing everyone pitching in where they could to get the town up and running again after last winter's horrors was a beautiful thing. The way the people came together, as they did around these parts, made her proud to call the small mountain town of Lawless her new home.

Another gust of wind rocked the truck, and Geraldine Gertzmeyer's laneway suddenly came into view. Christine had been lost in thought, and due to the blowing snow, she hadn't noticed any of Geraldine's friendly little signs along the way. Since the January quake, the elderly woman had added another sign to her collection, this one attached to the towering oak tree at the entrance to her property. Mostly obscured in snow right now, it was still legible, however, reading, 'Private Property: Nothing is Allowed Here - Just Go Home."

"You know how to make a girl feel welcome," Christine said, smiling. Knowing the elderly woman as well as she did now, she was always surprised by how friendly the senior was, despite her unfriendly signs. When she'd asked her about it over cookies and tea a while back, Geraldine had replied, "Gotta keep up appearances, dearie." Apparently, Norbert, Geraldine's late husband, had been a bit of an old curmudgeon and liked the privacy that their acreage afforded them. He'd never been particularly friendly to strangers over the years, unlike Geraldine, who had always enjoyed opening her house to visitors. Christine suspected it was especially so now, after Norbert's passing a few years back. However, for a woman as mature as Geraldine, easily in her mid-90s, she was as spry as some sixty-year-olds that Christine had met over the years, showing no sign of mental deficit. She was still quite independent and required minimal assistance from the outside world.

Christine had formed a close bond with the woman over the last few months and regularly took her into town to grocery shop since Geraldine didn't drive, and apart from Trip William's, she had very few people to help her after her husband's passing. Geraldine invariably repaid Christine's kindness by treating her out to lunch at the Burger Barn. And Christine, being a sucker for a good cheeseburger, couldn't refuse.

The house came into view through the blowing snow, and Christine slowed to a crawl, marvelling at the lights. "Good job, Trip!" As if the man wasn't busy enough around town with the reconstruction going on, Trip had found enough spare time to renovate some of the damage to Geraldine's porch and help her decorate for the holidays as well. The bedazzling array of lights on display, while not quite the level of Clark Griswold, was still an impressive sight to behold. String after string of almost every coloured light imaginable was on display, blinking and twinkling away. She shook her head in amazement—it must have taken Trip dozens of hours in his time off to do this much.

Pulling the pickup truck around the circular laneway, Christine brought it to a halt in front of the wide porch steps that led up to the front door. The steps looked to have been swept a short time ago, but the snow had already filled in most of Geraldine's work. At the top, a broom stood propped against the thick wooden porch railing that ran along the front of the house and wrapped around both sides. Christine took the broom and brushed the snow from her uniform pants and boots first, then gave the steps a quick sweep as well. She knocked on the door using its heavy cast-iron knocker, currently framed by a green wreath of pine boughs and holly, then turned the knob and pushed the door open. A frail voice called out, "It's open, dearie!"

"It's Christine Moon, Mrs. Gertzmeyer. Sorry I'm…" She trailed off, her jaw dropping open. She was almost tempted to turn around and see if she was in the correct house since it certainly didn't look like the same place she remembered from when she was here only a couple of weeks ago. Christmas now ruled the Gertzmeyer household. Dozens of wreaths, resplendent in their greenery, were on almost every wall. They intermingled with bough after bough of berry-covered holly, which peppered the walls like an indoor climbing vine gone crazy. Strings of Christmas lights graced the crown moulding that capped the top of each wall, making the room a delight for the eye wherever a person looked. A large fir tree stood in the centre, glowing brightly with dozens of strands of lights, its branches laden with hundreds of antique china ornaments. On top of everything else, the house smelled heavenly, the scent of gingerbread filling the air, giving Christine an overwhelming sense of happiness tinged with just a touch of sadness. Though it was wonderful to see a person who enjoyed the season so much, at the same time, it made

Christine feel a hint of melancholy for her own family Christmases that were now long past.

"I'll be right there!" Geraldine called.

While Christine removed her boots, a rumbling sound came from the hallway, and Geraldine Gertzmeyer wheeled her tea cart into the room, using its handle in lieu of her walker at the moment. "Merry Christmas, dearie!" Geraldine's face lit up, and she held one arm up in the air while the other one held the cart, signalling to Christine she would like to hug her. Christine complied and enjoyed the elderly woman's comforting embrace, missing her own grandmother more than she had realised.

"Thank you, Geraldine, the same to you." Christine hugged back, but not too forcefully since she didn't want to harm the small, thin-boned woman. She was surprised that Geraldine got as much done as she did. Over the last several months, it seemed more and more that a strong gust of wind would carry her away. Christine was concerned she was getting enough to eat. She knew from experience that her own grandmother had become a very fussy eater when she'd turned eighty and lost many pounds before the doctor had gotten her on a regime of nutritional drinks to boost her own lacking diet. "How've you been? Are you eating regular meals like we talked about?"

"Yes, I am, thanks! I had a bowl of Chunky Chicken Noodle Soup for lunch. Now, why don't ya take off that heavy parka and sit down; you're makin' me hot just looking at you." A tall wooden coat rack stood just outside the parlour. Christine removed her conservation-issue parka, hanging it on a peg next to a huge fur hat.

"Don't worry about Mongo there. He won't bite!"

"I'm sorry, Mongo?" Christine asked, turning and smiling.

"The hat, a course. I know it looks intimidating, but it's as warm as all get out. Used to belong to my late husband, Norbert, you know."

"Oh, yes," Christine said, "I remember you wearing it last winter. I'm sure it must be toasty inside with all that fur."

"Yup, it keeps my thin-haired old melon from freezin' when I'm out and about! Sit down, dearie, have a Christmas treat and a hot cocoa! I know we normally have tea, but I felt rather extravagant today and decided to get out the cocoa mix. After all, it's Christmas!"

Christine had never seen Geraldine so animated. It truly seemed that Christmas was the woman's time to shine. But that wasn't surprising since Christine had a friend in Calgary who set up her Christmas tree the day after Halloween. Some people just love the holiday more than others for some reason, she marvelled to herself.

The tea cart appeared overflowing with every Christmas delicacy a person could imagine. Nanaimo bars, mincemeat tarts, shortbreads and sugar cookies all fought for a place on the overcrowded platter. Christine could almost feel her insulin spike just looking at the goodies spread out before her.

"I'd offer your mug of chocolate to you after I pour it, but I wouldn't want to trust my shaky hands not to scald ya in the process," Geraldine said as she poured the cocoa into a couple of mugs sitting next to each other on the trolley. With a glance behind herself to verify she was aiming her derriere in the right direction, she sat down with a slight puff into an oversized wingback chair. Once settled in, she reached out and carefully grabbed her mug of cocoa with two hands, bringing the piping hot liquid to her lips so she could blow on it. Christine's heart jumped into her throat as she watched the steaming chocolate beverage sloshing around unsteadily in the mug as Geraldine moved it toward her lips.

"I appreciate your concern for my safety, Mrs. Gertzmeyer. Thank you." Christine carefully took her own mug from the trolly and had a sip of the hot cocoa. It was creamy and delicious—everything that store-bought chocolate was not. She closed her eyes and inhaled the dark chocolate richness of the quality cocoa.

"A course, dearie. I wouldn't want you gettin' burned. If you want, grab one of those skookum napkins for your fingers that I picked up at the dollar store." There were several differently coloured festive napkins to choose from, and Christine took one with a snowman on the front.

Taking a sip of her chocolate, Christine recalled the bundle of papers that Austin had given her to read. Though she'd hardly had half a chance to look through them yet, this seemed like an opportunity too good to pass up. After all, who better to ask about early life in the valley, she reasoned, than a long-term resident like Geraldine? Taking a nibble from a small, rectangular shortbread that almost oozed butter, Christine asked, "Geraldine, I was wondering what you knew of this area, particularly the gold rush that happened here around 1895?"

Peering over her mug, Geraldine said with pride in her voice, "Well, dearie, though I look as old as Methuselah, I'm not actually a hundred and thirty years old."

"Oh, my, I am so sorry! I didn't mean to imply that you were that old!" Christine was mortified.

Geraldine smiled, a twinkle in her eye, and said, "I was just havin' ya on, dearie! As I like to say, even though I'm pushin' the wrong side of ninety, at least I'm still on the right side of the grass!"

Feeling relieved, with a slight laugh, Christine said, "That is always a good thing. But, in all of your years around this valley, have you ever heard of a fire that ravaged the downtown here in 1895?"

"Well, I knew they rebuilt the downtown around then since it was originally a bunch of wooden structures, and they wanted more permanent buildings to show the area's wealth. But I never heard it was because the town burned to the ground." Geraldine looked stunned.

"From what I recently heard, they had something major happen around here that they tried to cover up."

"Tried to cover up? I'd say they did a pretty damned good job if I never heard about it after all these years here in the valley!"

"Well, this new information that has come to light is highly classified. So, what we've just discussed here is hush-hush."

Geraldine leaned forward conspiratorially, saying, "You don't say! Well, trust me, dearie, I won't blab to anybody since anybody I ever knew is already dead."

Christine almost choked on her chocolate when she heard that remark but nodded, and after she recovered a little from her coughing, she gave a thumbs up.

"Land sake's girl! Be careful with that cocoa; it's powerful stuff! None of that Dutch-processed stuff around here, no siree!" she added proudly.

"Thank you," Christine said, wiping her mouth on her snowman napkin.

In a more serious tone of voice, Geraldine said, "I know you like to check in on me out here every few weeks, just like today, and I greatly appreciate it since I so enjoy your visits. But I must add, I am particularly glad you could make it out here this afternoon." With the steaming liquid sloshing dangerously, she lifted her mug to her lips and sipped her cocoa again.

"Well, thank you, Geraldine." Christine nodded in acknowledgement. "But why are you particularly glad I came out today?" She took another sip of her cocoa and then reached forward, taking a gingerbread man off the huge platter on the cart between them. This particular gingerbread man had tiny gumdrop buttons running down his green and white-frosted shirt and a winning smile sure to be popular with the gingerbread ladies.

Leaning forward again, Geraldine said, "I'm having some of my family up from the coast to visit this Christmas, and I'm a little concerned for my great-grandkids that are coming to visit. They're only four and five, and I wouldn't want anything to happen to either of the little munchkins. They're so adorable." Her face broke into a beatific smile as she thought of her two grandchildren.

Tilting her head slightly, Christine asked, "Anything happen to them? What do you mean?"

After another sip from her mug, Geraldine clarified, "I mean, there's something out there leaving prints around the property like before. And whatever it is, it's gone and run off all my little Norberts again!"

Christine's heart jumped into her throat for a moment, fearing the worst. She recalled the wild turkeys, or Norberts, named after Geraldine's late husband, which had been slaughtered back in January by the giant racoon, and she was hoping to not have a repeat of that.

"Afore ya get too ahead of yourself, it's not the same as before, these tracks are smaller than that consarned bear, but still, they look off. And I can't show you any outside right now since they're covered in snow. I hope what was left of my Norberts made it to safety.

"What do you mean, they're off?" Christine leaned forward.

"They look like a dog track but much bigger."

"How much bigger?"

"Well, the only thing I can compare them to would be

Ichabod's tracks, and these are substantially larger than his."

"Ichabod, as in Crane?"

With a gentle smile of remembrance, Geraldine said, "That's right, dearie, just like in the story. Mind you, he was our dog, not a schoolmaster."

"I figured as much," Christine said with a laugh. Then she became serious again, asking, "But what breed was Ichabod? He must have been bigger than a Chihuahua, I presume?"

"Oh my, yes, dearie! He was a Saint Bernard!"

Christine was dumbfounded. "Bigger than a Saint Bernard?"

"Yes, that's why I'm a little concerned. Ichabod was almost two hundred pounds of hairy lovin'. But those tracks I saw are bigger and deeper than his ever were."

"Did they look like your turkey gobbler's tracks from January? Perhaps it's another one of those?"

"No, dearie, it's bigger than that. My grandson sent me one of those new-fangled cell phones in the mail. With it, he included step by step instructions on how to turn the darned thing on so we could do something called 'Facetiming', whatever that is, before they come up. But that's not the point. What I wanted to say is it turns out this phone has a camera for still pictures! Can you believe it? And it's a pretty good one, too! What'll they think of next!"

With a nod and smile, Christine said, "That is an added bonus." Hoping to hear an answer in the affirmative, she asked, "So, did you use that camera to take a picture of the prints?"

"A course, dearie! And I have to say, even though I was never much of a photographer, this phone's camera is the bee's knees!" Geraldine pulled a slightly battered looking iPhone 6 from a pocket in the cardigan she was wearing and turned it on. She scrolled through her pictures for a moment and then handed the phone to Christine.

Rather than a print from an unknown animal, Christine was presented with a young family beaming happily away at the camera. The man and woman wore red and white Santa hats, and both of the children sported a lovely set of antlers on their heads. The little girl was smiling broadly, but the boy was frozen forever in the middle of one of the saddest, most tear-filled, wide-eyed pouts that Christine had ever seen, making her want to both laugh and go, 'Aww…' at the same time.

"Sorry, I just wanted you to see my grandson, granddaughter-in-law, and great-grandkids first. Aren't they the cutest little buggers?"

Christine smiled broadly, looked down at the photo once more, then said, "They are that, and more."

Satisfied she'd done her due diligence showing off her great-grandkids to her guest, Geraldine said, "The picture of the print is right next to the one of the kids. It was the first shot I took once I figured out how to get the darned thing turned on!" With a nod to the phone, she concluded, "You just need to swipe it with your finger, dearie, to get to the next picture."

With a small laugh, Christine said, "Thank you. I've used these a couple of times over the years, but sound advice is always appreciated."

"Oh, a course, dearie. Being a young whippersnapper like you are, I'm sure you're more up on these techno things than I am."

Christine didn't remember the last time she'd been called a whippersnapper and smiled and nodded. She swiped to the following picture, and her smile faded quickly away. The photo was taken next to Geraldine's snow-booted foot to show a size comparison for the print. It was large, bigger than the raccoon from January, but not as large as the incredible Angus had been. At first, she thought it could have been a coyote or a wolf, and she'd seen her fair share over her ten plus years in the BC Conservation Officers Service. But this was unlike any coyote or any wolf she'd ever seen. The comparison of Geraldine's foot next to it made such a thing an impossibility—it was far too large.

"I made sure to get my size eights in the shot so you could see how big those prints are."

"I see that. And thank you for the comparison; it really helps. But tell me, when did you first see these tracks?"

"Sometime last week."

With a nod, Christine said, "Listen, can I have a copy of this picture?"

Geraldine nodded her head in agreement, saying, "Sure! If you can figure out how to do it!"

Christine nodded and smiled, saying, "I think I can figure it out." She clicked the share icon on the screen and typed in her email address, sending a copy of the print to her Provincial conservation account. She munched on her gingerbread man, then took a sip of cocoa from her mug while she waited for the link to go through. She was glad she hadn't tried to send a copy of the picture to her own cell phone since she would have been there all day, thanks to the spotty reception in the valley. Since January, she'd kept an eye on her budget at the conservation office, hoping to see when she could afford to request another high-speed satellite phone. Her first one, brand new though it had been, was now buried under millions of tonnes of rock and snow up at the cavern on Gold Ridge.

"Listen, I have to run, Geraldine. I would like to thank you so much for the cookies and cocoa!" Christine needed to get back to the office and see if she could figure out what this thing was. It could mean a call to Zelda on the coast for assistance, but she knew that wouldn't be a problem; her zoologist colleague was always more than willing to help identify tracks and prints that Christine sent to her. She stood and moved to the elderly woman's chair to save her from getting up, but Geraldine stood, nonetheless. Giving a gentle hug, she said, "Just in case I don't see you beforehand, "Merry Christmas and a Happy New Year, Geraldine."

"Why, thank you, dearie. Same to you." Geraldine hugged back quite fiercely for such a frail woman. When she finally loosened her grip on Christine, she added, "If you want to stop by and say 'Hi' to my grandkids, feel free! And if you don't have any place to go for Christmas dinner, you're also more than welcome to come up here and join us!"

"Well, thank you, but actually, I am joining some friends here in town for dinner over Christmas, but I'll see what I can do if I'm free. In any event, I hope you have a fabulous time with your family when they arrive. And I will definitely check into this print and try to see what I can find out."

"Thank you so much, dearie." Geraldine's voice was heavy with emotion. "I wouldn't want to see anything happen to my two little reindeer." She smiled wistfully as she mentioned her grandkids once more.

After another round of quick hugs at the door, Christine exited Geraldine's with an armload of festive baked goods and climbed into her truck. She started it up but didn't drive away immediately, wanting to let it warm up a bit first. As well, she wanted a chance to study the copy of Geraldine's photo a moment longer. Though it was almost entirely dark in the truck, Christine didn't turn on any interior lights. She didn't need them since her cell phone's screen was more than bright enough. The picture's link awaited her when she loaded up her email, and she clicked the link. Before forwarding it off to Zelda Wolowitz on the coast, she wanted to see the photo again. After waiting the requisite couple of minutes for the picture to be fully downloaded, she studied it intently.

Christine felt a strong sense of deja-vu, and unfortunately, it wasn't the good kind. She shuddered briefly as she put the truck in gear and pulled away, looking into the swirling snow that surrounded her with newfound unease. What was out there? Was this just a coincidence that when Geraldine first spotted these tracks, it just happened to be about the same time the slight earth tremor had run through the valley earlier this month? Shivering, she turned up the heater and put the truck into gear. Her mind was running a million miles a minute as she moved off into the darkening, snow-filled afternoon, her eyes constantly returning to the nearby forest as she drove.

CHAPTER THREE

Willy Wilson Jr. over-revved the motor on the Mack, its turbo whining painfully inside the cold engine and sounding very unhappy.

With a wince, Trip said, "You don't need to rev this baby to warm it up, Willy. I've told you before, just let it idle to warm up and do its thing." A gust of wind kicked up a cloud of snow, obscuring the truck in front of Trip, even though there was only a metre between him and the orange steel.

"Got it, Boss," Willy called down through the driver's side window of the Citrus Express. The plow had been so named by Larry, the regular driver of the large neon-orange truck, due to its similarity in colour to a bottle of Tropicana orange juice, which was also one of his favourite beverages.

Giving a serious look, Trip said, "Well, I hope you do. We can't afford to replace the engine in this puppy."

Willy grinned sheepishly, saying, "No, we want to keep letting it warm up and do its thing."

"Good answer," Trip said with a nod. "All right then, kiddo, you're on your own out there tonight. No more Larry or me holdin' your hand while we show you the ropes."

"Yeah, I know. And I'm excited to start my first shift, but scared shitless I'm going to do something to the Citrus Express here."

"You'll be fine if you keep it low and slow," Trip said. That was the mantra that anybody being trained to use the Express had drilled into their head. Having the blade placed almost all the way down to the asphalt and a slower speed was the best practice for keeping the roads drivable around these parts in the winter. Not to mention, there'd be hell to pay if Larry found out anybody was pushing his baby too hard. The maximum anyone was to drive the truck was sixty kilometres per hour if they were throwing snow. Anybody caught exceeding those bounds would suffer the wrath of Larry—all six feet, six inches of him.

"Okay, Boss, I'm outta here." Willy flipped Trip a surfer 'shaka' sign with his left hand out the cab window, then gave a brief blast of the horn and put the truck in gear.

Giving the kid a thumbs up, Trip watched as Willy pulled out of the yard. He smiled, still finding it strange to have someone calling him boss for a change after all the years of calling Austin the same.

The snow was coming down almost sideways now, and Trip was buffeted repeatedly by the bitter, howling wind and biting snow. He pulled his toque lower on his head with a shiver and moved toward the cinder block building that housed the offices of the City of Lawless Public Works.

The building also happened to be the current whereabouts of Clara Carleton, office manager of the Works yard. Since Austin had moved on up the totem pole to Mayor of Lawless, Clara had had her hands full. In addition to her regular duties, she also had to make sure the paperwork that Austin used to assist her with still got filled out correctly. At the same time, she was trying to show Trip the ropes so he could learn how to help out with its completion. It had been an uphill battle for her thus far, unfortunately, since Trip discovered there was one other thing in life that he hated more than walnuts in his brownies, and that was his new nemesis, paperwork.

Trip moved through the darkened garage and pushed open the heavy metal fire door which led into the shop. At the far end of the corridor, the top of Clara's greying head was just barely visible through the glass door. She was sitting at her desk, head down, most likely filling out some more forms and paperwork. Upon seeing Clara labouring away on his nemesis, Trip jogged sideways into the room that held the dog kennel to check on Spider, hoping she hadn't spotted him. If she did, he knew what would happen—more paperwork.

Spider was a small tan-coloured, wiry-haired dog that Trip figured had to be purebred Heinz 57. He knew it the moment he'd found the little guy rummaging through a dumpster at a lookout near the top of the Golden Mile Pass last week. The dog didn't have a tag, and Trip presumed it had wandered away while a family was taking a break, and they had left without it. That's what Trip liked to tell himself, at least, since the alternative was too heartbreaking.

He'd seen his fair share of abandoned pets over his years working animal control. Everything from kittens in burlaps sacks tossed into the river (thankfully saved before they drowned) to puppies that were a Christmas gift but no longer wanted after the new year. And then there was the classic manoeuvre of negligent pet owners the world over: drive out into the forest or over to the next town and leave your dog at a rest area or the middle of the woods and then drive away.

Trip had always had a soft heart for any four-legged beast that came his way, especially of the canine variety. He'd had a dog that had passed away several years ago, but he'd resisted the urge to adopt another since he was so busy with his work for the city and didn't think he could give it the full attention it would need. However, if no one claimed the tiny furball in the other room, he might just be forced to break his rule and adopt the little critter before he had to do something that would break his heart. If they couldn't find a home for Spider, he didn't think he could bring himself to have it put down by the SPCA over in Castlegar—the little bugger was just too damned cute.

Before Trip could flick on the light in the small kennel room, he heard a rhythmic tap-tap-tap coming from the darkness. With a click, the lights illuminated their current guest. Spider was sitting patiently inside his hotel suite and looking out at Trip, his ears perked and tail thumping happily away on the floor. It had been Clara who'd come up with the idea of calling the four small, individually heated cubicles 'pet suites'. This, of course, meant that any dogs or cats who temporarily called this place home were now its 'guests'. With a smile, Trip figured that made him the concierge.

"How is your stay at the Hotel Lawless this afternoon, Mr. Spider?" The dog responded with an 'Erf!' and began wagging its tail even harder, the tap-tap-tap even louder now. Trip held a finger in front of his lips and went, "Shh!" In a low voice, he continued, "Happy as a clam, are you?" He knelt on one knee and popped the gate to the cubicle open. The small dog sprang out of the door and into Trip's lap, knocking him backwards so that he now sat on the concrete floor. Though Spider was a small dog, he still weighed around ten kilograms, which was more than enough to bowl a person over if they weren't prepared.

"Whoa there, big fella! Give me a chance to brace myself the next time before you launch, okay?" Still sitting on his butt, Trip now had the small dog's paws on his shoulders while it gleefully licked his nose and bearded cheeks. He laughed and scruffed the dog's head, at the same time marvelling at the pattern on the animal's chest fur—almost a perfectly shaped hourglass, just like a black widow spider, except the marking was brown rather than the classic red. Because of that marking, Trip had decided on the name Spider for the dog rather than Black Widow, especially since the hyper little furball looked nothing like Scarlett Johansson.

Spider continued giving Trip a thorough face washing, which now included behind his ears, just for good measure. "Okay, okay, little buddy, I'll spring you again tonight after work, just like last night. But I have to wait until Clara goes home for the day because I'm pretty sure she'd frown upon my fraternising with the 'guests'."

From the open doorway at Trip's back, a voice said, "You are correct; she does frown upon you fraternising with the guests."

Trip jolted and turned with a laugh to see Clara Carleton standing in the doorway, a large bundle of papers held in her arm's embrace. She had snuck up on him once more, using those stealthy knit slippers that she liked to wear when at work. "Clara! You're like a ninja in those things." You need to make more noise when you walk!" Spider agreed with an 'Erf!'.

"I'll see if I can get my arthritic joints to grind a little louder when I walk. How would that be?" Clara replied semi-sarcastically. Looking over to the dog, she added, "And I don't need your two cents worth, mister."

With a slight whine, Spider started to lie down, putting his head on Trip's lap. "Sorry, boy, I gotta get up." With a grunt, he stood and faced Clara. "I was going to mention this to you when I made it down to the office, but you beat me to the punch."

"Uh-huh, sure you were." Clara smiled. "You, more than anyone, should know you're not supposed to get attached to these little visitors at the hotel, right?"

"Yeah, I know, I know. You're preaching to the choir here."

"Then why are you breaking your own rules?"

"It's Christmas?" Trip suggested. Spider 'erfed' in agreement.

With a shake of her head, Clara turned and moved back toward the office. Over her shoulder, she said, "You have two messages waiting from Christine Moon."

Following behind Clara down the corridor to his office, Trip asked, "Chris? Did she say what it was about?"

"Nope, and I didn't ask. She just said it was important and then called back an hour later to see if you'd gotten in yet."

"Sorry, I must have had my ringer off. I was out back seeing Willy off on his maiden voyage. I wanted to make sure he was ready to roll. Told him I wouldn't want him making any dents in Larry's pride and joy."

"True, Larry would be devastated if anyone dinged the Express."

"I know. But I think it should be in good hands. Willy's a responsible kid."

"Hopefully more so than the new head of Lawless Public Works who breaks his own policies."

"Did you hear that, Spider? You're a broken policy." The dog tilted his head and regarded Trip for a moment. He made a slight whine and then reached up and began licking Trip's fingers. Trip laughed, "Well, that makes up for it then." Still chuckling, Trip turned to Clara and said, "I'll take Chris's call in the office. And thanks for your vote of disapproval." Spider let out another 'erf' in agreement.

"Oh, before I forget, I am officially reminding you to take your mess of paperwork home to sign tonight when you leave." Clara thrust the stack papers into Trip's unwilling hands and marched back down the corridor to her office at the front.

Trip called out, "Thanks, Clara," He looked down at the thick bundle of papers in his hand, then added a somewhat muted, "I guess." With a sigh, he walked into his office.

Several rings later, Christine Moon picked up the phone at her office, and Trip said, "Hey Chris, what's all the hubbub?"

"Trip! I'm glad you called. I'm just on the other line with my zoologist friend at SFU. Can I call you right back?"

"Sure, Chris, I'll be here doing some paperwork." Christine thanked him and hung up. Feeling sudden warmth near his snow-booted feet, Trip looked down to see Spider curling up underneath the desk and settling in for a nap. He smiled and reached down to scruff the dog's head for a moment. As he did, he glanced dolefully at the stack of paperwork towering in front of him.

Tonight, a Vancouver/Calgary NHL game was playing on TSN at the newly renovated Frostbite Fred's. Trip wanted to christen the array of large-screen 4K TVs scattered around the pub, particularly the one situated right over his little table in the corner. He also wanted to try their new line of IPAs on tap. What were the odds of him not being at Fred's tonight because he had to stay home to do some paperwork? He shook his head in wonder at the very thought—the odds of that happening were so slim they were anorexic.

Trip's slight head shake morphed into a guilty glance over his shoulder, and he poked his head into the hall toward the front office. Clara seemed busy typing up a final report before heading out for the night. Trip slowly opened the top desk drawer over his knees. With another surreptitious glance, he placed his arms around the pile of papers and slowly pulled them into the drawer and then ever-so-gently closed it once more, grimacing as it squealed slightly.

Trip began to breathe a sigh of relief, a smug smile forming on his face. It vanished in an instant, however, when Clara called to him from the other end of the hall, "Don't forget to take those papers out of your desk drawer with you before you go home tonight!"

Shaking his head, Trip pulled the papers out of the drawer and made his way up to the front office. Pushing the glass door open, he asked, "How did you know?"

Clara stood near the front door, each of her knit slippers hanging from a separate peg on the coat rack on the wall. "You realise you're not the first person to sit at that desk, right? Your old boss tried to pull the same thing on me all the time. Trust me, it's not worth it." With that, she waggled her fingers goodbye at him and slipped out the door.

"I can see that. Thank you, Clara." Trip said as the front entrance slowly clicked shut. Another sigh of inevitability escaped his lips. Walking back to his office, a small smile formed when he realised he could always 'miss' a few sheets and do them tomorrow.

Suddenly, Clara popped her head back in the front door and called out to the shop, "Oh, and don't 'accidentally' leave any of your papers behind." Trip cringed once more.

The phone rang, and he grabbed it on the first ring, "Chris?"

"None other," Christine chimed musically from the handset, then laughed lightly.

Trip smiled. Christine's voice was one of the most pleasant things to listen to, especially when she laughed. "Hey, what's up? I heard you left me two messages."

"Yeah, I did. So, bear this with a grain of salt, but I think we may have another 'anomaly' out there in the forest around here."

"An anomaly?"

"Yes, you know, like the two-tonne anomaly that you shot with your howitzer in January?"

"Are you saying we've got another bear?" Trip almost stood

out of his chair as he asked the question.

"No, nothing like that, but there's something out there, and it's leaving some strange tracks. I wanted to let you know to be ready for something that looks a little bit out of the ordinary wandering around town. Maybe have your plow guys keep an eye out."

"Okay, I'm game, an eye out for what?"

"I don't know for sure. I sent a photograph of a print to my zoologist friend, and she said it wasn't something from anywhere around here, at least not during this millennium. But that was all she could say for now. She's going to get back to me a little later."

"Could you keep me posted if you hear anything?"

"Will do. And I'll let Austin know since I know he'd want to be in the loop as well."

"Great, thanks a million, Chris. I'll let Willy on the plow know to keep a lookout tonight. I'll talk to you soon."

Christine hung up, and Trip sat staring at the phone on his desk for a moment and then glanced upward. On the windowsill of his office, silhouetted against the blowing snow of the darkening December afternoon outside, sat the shell casing from the howitzer he used to bring down Angus. Thoughts of hockey and beer were suddenly crowded out of Trip's mind as he began wondering if, just to be on the safe side, he'd better start packing another shell.

CHAPTER FOUR

"I told you I didn't have a good grip on it," Trudy said with a pout.

With a sigh, Alex said, "Sorry, I didn't hear you." He bent over to pick up the pieces of broken glass that had spilt from the garbage bag when it had slipped from Trudy's fingers. When he'd dropped the cracked windowpane into the heavy-duty bag, he'd assumed she'd been holding the bag tightly. But it seemed now that he'd been incorrect in his assumption.

Alex had received a text message from his Uncle Trip just before he got out of school this afternoon, asking if he wanted to earn some extra cash over Christmas. He'd replied with an enthusiastic, 'Yes!' since it would be a great way to prop up his dwindling finances. Along with the expenses of owning a vehicle and paying for gas and insurance, Alex had discovered that having a girlfriend was a significant financial drain, and his savings account had been haemorrhaging money pretty fast over the last few months. Although he also had a part-time job at the local Pharmasave drugstore, it only gave him less than ten hours a week—definitely not enough money to do more than pay his gas and insurance. Too many dinners out at the Burger Barn, along with the new light rack he'd purchased for the top of his truck, had put his ailing savings account on life support. Fortunately, Trudy also had a part-time job over at the local Gas 'n' Gulp, and she liked to pay her share when she could afford it. Despite that, when Alex took her out, he wanted to do things like play mini-golf or have a burger together, covering the lion's share of the cost himself since he liked to treat her special. He and Trudy had been going out for about six months now, but it wasn't like he had any thoughts of marrying her at the moment, though he really liked her. "Hey, ya never know," his father had said at one point and then reminded him that he and Alex's mother had met in high school.

When he checked messages after school got out, he'd immediately replied to the inquiry Trip had sent. Seconds later, Trip had texted him back the code for the lock-box next to the building's front door so that he could get inside and start work as soon as he wanted. Considering his financial situation, today had seemed like as good a day as any to do so. He knew some friends at school operated under the 'procrastinate until it's too late' mantra, but not him. Like his dad, he liked to tackle things right away instead of putting them off. He'd asked Trudy along, thinking she might be a bit of help in the cleanup or at least provide some company. Unfortunately, she was now creating more work than she saved, thanks to him having to stop and clean up this new mess on the floor.

Trudy shook her head as she looked around, her bright blue ponytail bouncing back and forth as she did. "I didn't think this place would be so messy." She watched Alex pick up the sharp fragments, saying, "Watch your fingers, honey."

"Thanks for the advice," Alex said, standing and dusting off his hands. He towered over Trudy. When she stood next to him, Alex's Tolkien nerd friend, Izzy, said, "It looks like a Hobbit standing next to an Ent." At four feet, eleven inches tall, Trudy Boseman was petite enough to stand in Alex's shadow when they were out in the summer sun, and she could stay cool all day long. She affectionately called him her 'shade rock', thanks to his honed, muscular physique. Brushing his hands off once more, this time on his jeans, Alex asked, "Are you ready to get dirty?"

"Aren't we already doing that?" She glanced around the basement of the Sinclair building in distaste. They'd been in this dusty dungeon for a couple of hours now, and Alex could tell she was ready to call it quits. That was okay; he would take her out for a burger, and then after he dropped her off, he would come back here for some more cleanup. Seeing as he was getting paid by the hour, Alex wanted to work as much as he could, as fast as he could, in order to get some of the promised cash before Christmas. Then, he'd be able to afford Christmas gifts for everyone.

"No, we're only getting started. There's another whole set of rooms to go through," Alex said. Trudy had been supposedly moving a small pile of cartons to a waiting cart that she could take to the dumpster. But she'd also brought her cell phone, so in reality, she had spent most of her time Snapchatting with her friends and watching TikTok videos. While she was occupied, Alex had gotten rid of a pile of garbage bags from the hallways upstairs and taken them to the alleyway dumpster, exploring around the old building at the same time.

Trudy sighed and said, "Can we get some food soon? I'm fading away here."

Alex didn't say anything but just smiled, amazed at how well he knew his girlfriend after less than six months together.

Smiling herself now, after a moment, Trudy said, "So, what do you figure?"

"Huh?" Alex asked. He leaned down so Trudy could repeat herself. He'd been lost in another personal fantasy involving the beautiful girl standing in front of him and had missed what she said.

"Never mind," Trudy said, standing on her tiptoes. She kissed his forehead lightly, leaving a faint outline of purple lips in the centre between Alex's eyes.

Alex shook his head and smiled as he stood back up, saying, "Thank you," a slight red hue blooming on the tops of his cheeks. He took Trudy's hand, saying, "Come here, I want to show you something," then led the girl down a short hall toward the other storage rooms further back in the labyrinthine basement.

In the first room, a row of wooden file cabinets lined one wall, their drawers empty after the old newspaper proofs had been removed. Several retired mimeograph machines sat piled high in a far corner. Next to them, a row of teletype machines lay forever silent, dust lying thickly upon their antiquated keyboards. The second room, across the hall, contained hundreds and hundreds of cartons of old newspapers destined for recycling.

"Gah!" Trudy said, "Do we need to move all those tonight?" She seemed aghast, holding her hands to her chest as she spoke as if she were a southern belle having a case of the vapours.

"No, this is for next time." Alex had just wanted to see Trudy's reaction and hadn't been expecting her to do any work in the room. Her reaction was everything he'd anticipated. Satisfied, he decided he might as well just take her out for some food at the Barn right now and then drop her off like he planned and come back here.

Just as Alex was turning to leave, Trudy asked, "What's that over there?" She pointed to a drop cloth covered object in the far corner, away from the cartons.

"I don't know, a ghost?"

"Don't say that!" Trudy swatted his arm. Unlike her aversion to manual labour, the girl was into all things paranormal and supernatural in a big way, forever reading werewolf and vampire novels. She also loved horror movies but somehow found them a little too scary to watch alone. As a result, Alex had now seen all five of the Twilight movies thanks to his girlfriend, having watched a marathon session of them with her one rainy long weekend several months ago. Despite that experience under his belt, Alex still couldn't understand the franchise's appeal.

Grabbing hold of the age-yellowed sheet covering the thing in the corner, Alex gave a grand, "Ta-da!" then whisked the covering off in a cloud of dust that set them both coughing and sneezing for several seconds.

"Thanks for that!" Trudy sneezed again, wiping at her nose with the corner of her cardigan.

"Bless you," Alex said with a sniffle, "When I saw this earlier, I thought you might find it interesting, but I didn't realise the cloth was so dusty. My bad."

"You got that right," Trudy said with a cough as she looked at the object from beneath the cloth with wonder. "But thanks for showing me. This thing looks awesome! Does it work?"

Hidden from sight in the corner for untold decades underneath the cloth, a one-armed bandit resplendent in its antiquated oddness gleamed brightly as if still ready to take their money after all these years.

"Why do you think it's down here?" Trudy wondered. The machine wasn't overly large and sat on a wooden pedestal. The top of it, sporting a brass name-plate tiara, declared the machine to be a product of the Liberty Bell Slot Machine Company. Along its face, three reels depicted diamonds, hearts, spades, horseshoes and bells (the Liberty kind, presumably).

Alex shrugged his shoulders, saying, "I don't know, maybe they needed to repair it at one time, and it got left down here and forgotten instead." He tugged gently on the machine's brass handle, but nothing happened.

"This looks like it's from back in the gold mining days."

"Well, my Uncle Trip told me a while back that the Sinclair building here was also a Saloon at one time a little over a hundred years ago."

"You mean like with dancing girls and all that old west stuff?"

Alex looked at the machine more closely, then said, "Yeah, something like that. Trip said when the rush ended, the company that owned the Saloon got into the newspaper business, amongst other things." Though the slot said it only took a penny to play, he could see through a glass window in the side of the machine that it was unlike any penny he'd ever seen; it was so big. He fished around in his pocket for a moment and then stuck his hand out and asked, "Do you have a Loonie, Pumpkin?" Pumpkin was the pet name he had bestowed upon Trudy after discovering her enjoyment of all things having to do with Halloween.

"Whatever for? It says it takes a penny."

"Just humour me, please?" Since Canada no longer made a penny as large as the old machine took (or any penny for that matter), Alex thought the current Loonie looked to be about as close in size as they were going to get.

Trudy reached into the small back-pack style purse slung across her shoulders and fished around in the bottom for a moment. "I don't have much money since payday isn't until Monday. But let's see… a quarter, a dime, couple of nickels and…" She dug about a bit more, then looked up with a smile and dropped a Loonie into Alex's waiting palm, saying, "Don't spend it all in one place."

"Thanks." Alex dropped the coin into the slot on the front, and it rolled down into the machine. Pulling the small brass handle once more, this time, the reels spun around and around, finally settling on a horseshoe, diamond and a heart. "Well, so much for my gambling addiction." He gave the pedestal a swift kick with his snow-booted foot and was rewarded with something other than money. "Did you hear that?" he asked Trudy.

"Hear what?"

"That click when I kicked this thing."

"Wasn't that the machine just resetting after taking your money? Come on, let's go; I'm starving!" Now jonesing for some food, Trudy tugged briskly at Alex's bomber-style jacket.

"Hang on, hang on." Alex persisted and looked around to the back of the machine. "I thought I heard something back here. He pushed on the side of the slot to slide the machine a little, meaning to turn it to see if a panel had opened so he could check out the coins. Instead, the entire machine moved to the right as if it were on wheels. "What?" He pushed harder.

Trying to see around Alex, Trudy asked, "What did you do?"

"I think I won the prize," Alex said, his head still peeking behind the antique gambling device.

"What's that?" Trudy asked, tilting her head.

With a forceful push of the machine further to the right, Alex said, "I just won a hidden room!"

"What?" Trudy stood back as Alex manhandled the machine.

Alex pushed again, but the slot machine wouldn't budge any further. It was jammed, perhaps coming off its track from the shifting of the building during the earth tremors around Lawless. "Here, give me a hand." He leaned all his weight against the side of the machine, but it wouldn't move any further.

Trudy didn't weigh more than ninety-five pounds soaking wet, but she tried to assist anyway and pushed as hard as she could.

With a squeak and a groan, the machine slid a little further, and Alex said, "Okay, stop. I think we have enough of a gap." He tried to squeeze his large frame through the small opening, but it wasn't going to happen. "Not enough room for me. Why don't you see if there's something on the other side blocking this thing?"

With a dramatic sigh to signify how weak and hungry she was, Trudy took the flashlight supplied by Alex, saying, "Fine." Thanks to her petite size, she squeezed through the narrow opening without a problem.

"Just be careful," Alex advised.

"Don't you worry about me. I'm a big girl, sort of," Trudy replied as she clicked on the flashlight and disappeared from view.

After a moment of silence, Trudy said, "Oh, wow!"

"What is it? What did you find?" Alex tried to get his broad shoulders into the gap to see but was blocked by his bulk.

"You're not going to believe this," Trudy said in a low voice.

"Well, try to see if something is blocking the door, and then I'll be able to see and decide for myself if I believe it," Alex said, pushing on the slot machine again.

"Hold on there, King Kong," Trudy said from the other side. "I think I found the problem. There was a small crash on the other side of the door, and Alex said with concern, "Are you okay, baby?"

After another pause, there was a grunt, and Trudy said, "I'm fine. I was trying to get something moved aside. Try it now."

Alex pulled gently on the machine, and it slid easily now as if on well-oiled tracks. "What did you do?" he asked, stepping through into the hidden room.

"Some boxes of stuff had fallen down and were blocking where the machine was supposed to roll on this side, so I moved them," Trudy said, shining the flashlight at the obstruction and sounding quite satisfied with her accomplishment. "And look what's behind you!" She spotlighted a row of old-fashioned switches on the wall at Alex's back with the flashlight's beam. There were four switches altogether, each consisting of a round white button overtop a black one and set inside a brass faceplate. "I think they're light switches. You should see if they work."

Pressing one button after the other, Alex said, "Let me brighten your day." Several bulbs flickered to life inside of old fashioned drop-down hooded fixtures, but many did not, leaving several sections of the large room in darkness. With his illuminating duties done, Alex turned around and grabbed Trudy, saying, "I'm glad you're okay." He hugged her hard.

After a moment, Trudy said, "You're cutting off the blood flow, Hunny Bunny. Could you loosen up on your impersonation of a boa constrictor?"

"Huh?" Alex hadn't realised he'd been squeezing Trudy's delicate frame a little too strongly for her liking. "Oh, sorry, baby. I don't know my own strength sometimes."

"I know. You're like a superman, and you're all mine." She stepped onto her tiptoes once more and gave Alex a quick peck on his cheek.

Alex smiled and touched where she'd kissed him, then touched his lips, saying, "You missed."

"Well, if we get out of here at a reasonable time, maybe we can have some kissing practice at my house before my parents come back from doing their gambling up at the casino."

All thoughts of coming back to do a few more hours of work this evening had flown from Alex's mind the moment Trudy mentioned the words 'kissing and practice' together in the same sentence. He cleared his throat and said, "Okay, let's take a quick look around here before we go and…" Alex turned around to look at the room for the first time and stopped talking all at once. After gawking for a moment, he added, "Oh, wow!"

Trudy grabbed Alex's hand, saying, "I know, right?"

The room before them was huge. It seemed that another sub-basement had been fashioned into the foundation of the Sinclair building. Under decorative plaster ceilings, rich wood panelling lined the room, with dusty hardwood floors beneath. Dozens of tables and chairs were dotted about the space as if waiting for patrons now long since deceased. Apparently, the basement of the Sinclair newspaper building had been used for more than just papers. On the far side of the room, behind a long wooden bar, a large mirror ran along the wall. It was backed by several shelves that were mostly empty now. Most of the bottles that had been on the shelves looked to be in pieces scattered over the back bar. Whether that was by man or by nature after a recent quake was anybody's guess. Across the room, a roulette wheel sat off to one side, cobwebs draped across its spokes. Two doors exited the room, both now closed, one on each end of the bar.

The Canadian Government introduced what became known as the 'Temperance Act' in the early years of the 20th century. Through this act, local officials could prohibit alcohol sales for the 'greater good' of the public in various municipalities and cities across the country. During the First World War, it had been adopted across Canada as law, with the United States following suit with its own 'Prohibition' in 1920. However, only a few years later, Canada repealed its Temperance Act. This proved to be a huge financial boon for Canadian bootleggers, who then began running cheap whiskey across the border into the US.

"It looks like a hidden saloon!" Trudy observed as she walked around one end of the bar, being careful of where she stepped. Broken glass lay thick on the hardwood floor where some of the bottles of alcohol had tumbled.

"They used to call this kind of place a 'speakeasy'. At least I think so, from what I remember seeing on the History Channel," Alex said.

"Say, I wonder what's back here?" Trudy moved toward the closed door on the left side of the bar.

"Hey, where are you going?"

"I thought we were exploring here?" Trudy said, pushing the door open into the next room.

"Yes, but wait for me," Alex said, catching up to his girlfriend.

"You snooze, you..."

Before Trudy could finish, Alex yanked her back from the room as a roof beam came crashing down on the other side of the door. It would have crushed Trudy had she stepped blindly into the room. "You've gotta make sure the room is clear of obstacles before walking in blindly," he said in exasperation, then added, "Didn't you ever play Tomb Raider?"

"Sorry, I missed that one. But thanks for the save." She hugged his waist as she shone the light about the darkened room beyond the door.

"I think we should presume this room is unsafe. What do you think?" Alex didn't want to risk their lives and decided to curtail further exploration in that direction for the moment. With his arm around Trudy's shoulders, they retreated to the bar.

Together this time, they moved to the door at the other end and peered cautiously inside. It looked to be a storage room. "There's nothing in here, just empty shelves," Trudy said, sweeping the light into the semi-darkness.

Alex almost agreed with her assessment, then called out, "Hold on!"

"What is it?"

"Shine the light back in here once more."

Perhaps it was the carrots for which Alex had an affinity helping his eyesight, but his sharp eyes picked out a discrepancy in the wall of shelves along the back of the storage room. They looked 'off' to him, somehow. "Can I borrow the light?" he asked Trudy.

She passed the light over to him, asking, "What is it?"

Alex didn't respond and shone the light toward the ceiling, looking for any signs of weakness before going any further, but things seemed fine. He moved into the room for a closer look at the shelves. They were hanging down slightly to the right, but not because they had collapsed. It almost looked like they were on a hinge, like that of a partially open door. Alex pulled the shelves gently toward himself, and they swung further outward on their hinge, revealing another door behind.

"Whoa," Trudy observed, "A secret room inside of a hidden room! This is too cool!"

"I agree." Alex turned the handle and pushed the door open, revealing more blackness beyond. Shining the light around revealed a small room with a desk, chair and cot, but not much else. "Looks like someone used this as a little hideout within the hideout." The light bulb in the ceiling had no discernible way of turning it on, with no switches evident on any of the walls.

"Hey, we're in luck," Trudy said, holding up an old lantern. "Got any matches?"

Alex took the lamp from her and shook it slightly. It was bone dry. "Have any kerosene?"

"Umm, no."

"Then I guess we're out of luck." Alex continued to examine the room with the light. An old survey map was pinned to one wall, with several locations around Gold Ridge marked with Xs. Next to each of the marks, a note had been made. All of them said, 'NG'.

"What is this? A prospectors map?" Trudy asked.

"Or a treasure map. Maybe the person hiding out here was looking for some buried gold, like in Treasure Island, and the parts that are crossed off and labelled NG means there was 'No Gold'.

"Ooh, I see. How exciting!" Trudy looked more closely at the map. The two spots left were not yet marked with Xs and apparently unexplored for this possible gold. She snapped several pictures of the map with her cell phone, saying, "A few photos can't hurt. And they're much easier to carry than a musty old map anyway."

A small, red leather-bound journal lay on the desk. After gently brushing the dust off, Alex opened it, revealing tightly packed writing on both sides of the pages throughout most of the diary. Together they quickly flipped through the journal, discovering a hand-drawn map near the back. Most of the pages afterwards had been torn out.

"Maybe," Trudy surmised, "they were using this journal to try and locate the gold along with the big map up on the wall?" She turned to the last page, then asked, "Is there a name in this book anywhere?"

Alex picked up the journal and flipped through to the front, quickly finding an answer for Trudy. Looking stunned at what he saw, he said, "Yes, there is."

"Well, who does it belong to? What's the name?" Trudy asked excitedly.

His voice hushed and eyes wide, Alex Murphy said, "My great-great-grandfather, Caleb Cantrill."

CHAPTER FIVE

Unlike his name, Angel Oritz was anything but. He'd spent most of his life in and out of prison. It was almost a year ago now since he'd heard from his brother, Manny. They'd been particularly close for most of their lives. Back home in Barcelona, Manny had been the youngest of the four brothers, and Angel, being the oldest, had looked after his little brother when he was a kid. He'd helped get Manny started in the 'business' showing him the ins and outs of the drug distribution underworld with which he'd been involved at the time. A few years back, his younger brother, Juan, had died in Mexico during some Cartel violence in which he'd been engaged, and his second youngest brother, Carlos, had been shanked in Barcelona in an El Modelo Prison riot back in 2012.

Fortunately for Angel, for the last ten years, he had been incarcerated in the Lower Mainland near Vancouver at the Kent Institution rather than El Modelo. Today was a day of celebration and mourning for him. It was his first day out in the real world again. He was free and clear, having served his entire sentence, and he had no parole officer to answer to or any parole to worry about violating. This was a good thing because he had a score to settle. But not regarding his prison term, however, as that had been legit. No, he knew something had happened to his brother while he'd been in prison, and he needed to find the parties responsible. And that meant he might have to step outside what the law would allow, just a little.

Angel had just finished retrieving his messages from the discrete email server, which no one else knew anything about, at least not on the legal side of the world. It seemed little brother Manny had left him an email earlier this year before heading to the town of Lawless. He stated he was going on a 'secret mission that involved great wealth' but wouldn't or couldn't say what it was.

Over the years, his brother had worked for a pair of crooked casino owners in the interior as an on-again, off-again enforcer. Angel had tagged along on a couple of occasions, so he knew a little bit about the small town from firsthand experience. He recalled that Manny had always been proud to say that though his T4 from Chance listed him as a mere security consultant, he always made much more than was ever claimed on the government form. In the email, Manny had listed some of the more salient details from conversations with both Mayor Bob Nichols and his business partner, Ray Chance, and the obscene amounts of money they had offered him for his upcoming job. Once he'd figured out what was going on, Manny said he would send another message to Angel when he got the chance. However, Manny had never gotten that chance, and that email had been the last time he'd ever heard from his brother.

But there was a second message on the server that was even more interesting. It was sent from an unknown individual using Reggie VanDusen's email account. The message was short and sweet and pertained to what his brother was getting involved in up in Lawless, with the sender claiming to have inside knowledge of the whole affair. It also mentioned that the great wealth to which Manny had alluded had, in fact, been gold, and lots of it. That had gotten Angel's attention fairly quickly. The sender had also listed a name and address at the bottom of the message, stating that the person at that address had extensive knowledge of the golden cavern's location. It was something that Angel would be sure to check on very soon once he was done here.

Angel now stood inside the 'fish market', a shipping container he and Manny had purchased together many years before. It was so named because they'd always felt like sardines whenever they were inside the shipping container and also because of the damned smell. Though never used for fish hauling that they knew, the container still reeked of the ocean despite the passage of the dozen years that he and Manny had owned it.

It was not something that many people knew about, and that's how the brothers wanted to keep it. Inside the container, Manny had stocked numerous items for his blackmail trade and other criminal enterprises, including a nice selection of false IDs. A small smile played at the corners of Angel's lips as he briefly leafed through a collection of police and security IDs that sat in a box on one of the metal shelves lining the shipping container. He picked a couple out and stuffed them in his pocket. Though not identical in their appearance, the brothers were similar enough physically that Angel could almost pass for Manny in many of the ID photos.

However, Angel was more interested in what sat on the shelves next to the IDs—stacks and stacks of extra cash for emergencies. Angel figured because he hadn't received another message from Manny in almost a year since the last email, this was an emergency worthy of borrowing some of their hard-earned cash. When he'd walked out the door of the prison this morning, he'd had only twenty bucks to his name. Now, several thousand dollars were bulging in the front of his pants, and he looked like he was extremely happy to see someone. In a way, he supposed he was, happy that he would find out what had happened to his brother and that whoever was responsible would mourn the day they were ever born.

With his cash problems solved for the moment, he moved to the weapons and ammo section of the locker. The Glock 17 he picked up felt strange to hold in his hand after so many years behind bars, but it also felt good to be packing once again. Angel and Manny shared many similarities, especially in their love of firearms. Angel loaded up several dozen clips in a backpack he found on a nearby shelf, along with some other goodies that he threw in 'just in case'. These goodies included some C4 and detonators they'd 'bought' many years before. He also threw in a handful of psychotropic drugs Manny had used on some of his blackmail victims over the years. You never knew when you'd need to dope someone up, Angel reflected with a crooked smile.

Manny had been the kind of man who liked to ask questions. And he would often pump his victims full of drugs in order to ask them and then blackmail them afterwards. On the other hand, Angel had always been more headstrong and liked to jump into things feet and fists first. This method wasn't the best, unfortunately, and for the rare time when he did need answers, he eschewed the use of drugs and was more than willing to extract the information from people in some of the most unpleasant manners of which he could think. No, when Angel questioned someone, it would most likely be the last question that person answered, ever.

Though brother Manny had always been the kind to steal a car when he needed one, he'd also liked to have a nice reliable ride whenever he wasn't doing 'business'. A stolen car for a job was one thing but driving a hot set of wheels around on a regular basis wasn't one of the brightest things to do. Manny had been crazy, but he hadn't been stupid. Angel smiled as he looked at the black, late-model Lincoln Navigator parked just inside the front end of the storage container. It was big, heavy, and mean-looking, just like him—the perfect thing to transport him into the interior. He wasn't a man who enjoyed flying as his brother had. Despite his name, Angel had no wings, and could not/would not fly, even if his life depended on it. No, Angel always preferred to keep both feet on the ground, or at least one foot on the accelerator and the other on the brake. He'd rather trust his fate to his own driving ability and not the airline maintenance department since you never knew if they were having an off day, especially during your plane's routine servicing.

The storm that was currently blowing across the province made the matter moot since there were no flights presently going in or out of Vancouver, or Lawless, even if he were inclined to fly. And though it was raining here, he knew once he got through the Coastal mountains outside of Hope, it would soon turn to snow. Over sixty centimetres were forecast for the Cascade Mountains of the West Kootenays tonight.

Fortunately, the Navigator had a very aggressive set of all-season mud and snow tires, and Angel figured they should do the trick. Weighing in at just about three tonnes with full-time four-wheel drive, it was a vehicle that would stick to the road like glue. He climbed into its black leather confines and started the SUV, then drove it out of the container. Latching the container door closed, he locked it back up with the heavy-duty Master combination padlock that kept it secure. It was one of those expensive locks that he'd seen paranoid people pay a thousand bucks for. There was not much left inside the shipping container, but Angel didn't want to let anything happen to the assorted odds and ends left behind, just in case. Who knew, maybe he'd still find Manny alive, and they'd want to start a new fake ID business together.

Rain mixed with wet snow lashed the windshield, and he put the wipers on high as he drove out of the industrial park where the container was located. He didn't plan on rushing up to Lawless on the snow-covered roads. After all, it wasn't like he was in a huge hurry. If his brother were truly dead, there was no sense in Angel getting himself killed in the process of travelling somewhere to find out who killed Manny.

Manny had been a rotten son of a bitch, and there were numerous people who wanted to kill him on at least five of the planet's seven continents. But of the many things in life of which Angel Oritz was sure, one of them was the fact that his brother would never have died from natural causes. He didn't doubt that whatever had killed Manny must have been of human origin and that someone in Lawless had some 'splainin' to do. Angel was going to make absolutely sure he found out who they were and what they'd had to do with Manny's disappearance. And while he was there, he'd make sure to get his hands on some of the gold that had been promised to Manny; because he figured whatever had been owed to his brother was also owed to him. With a slight smile, he drove toward the downtown core before he blew town. He patted the pocket that contained the fake IDs and the Glock reassuringly—there was still one more crucial stop to make before heading eastward into the coastal mountains, and he'd need them both.

CHAPTER SIX

"Man! it's wicked out here tonight."

Another gust of windblown snow buffeted the Citrus Express as Willy Wilson Junior plowed his way down the valley highway. He'd already plowed the Golden Mile pass and was now coming back down the hill, ready for his first run up the other end of the highway to the Golden Nugget Casino. The mountain road that led up to both places usually got hit the hardest whenever it snowed, and it needed the most attention first. Fortunately, the city of Lawless itself was reasonably level, with only a slight slope from the uptown portion to the downtown. It was usually plowed last after the high accident areas were tended to. The way the snow was coming down, he knew all of his hard work wouldn't last long tonight, and he'd have to go back and forth between the two alpine extremes the whole evening while plowing the city streets in between.

The plow blade scraped against the pavement as Willy motored along. A bright shower of sparks chipped off into the surrounding snow and were quickly extinguished. He sneezed, his nose irritated by the orange-scented air freshener hanging from the CB radio. While he plowed, he'd dug through some of the music that Larry kept in the console between the seats, all of it on cassette tape. Unfortunately, Willy had never used a cassette in his life. So, as he'd motored up the hill to the resort, he ended up listening to an entire side of the tape already in the player, which turned out to be Trisha Yearwood's 'The Sweetest Gift'.

On the return leg, Willy decided it was time for a change of music. Much to his dismay, it appeared the music, much like the sound system, was just as vintage as the rest of the Citrus Express. It was from a time before he'd ever been a glimmer in his dearly departed daddy's eyes, and most of it was Christmas albums to boot. With a sigh, he randomly fished another cassette out of the console and quickly glanced at the title, 'Beyond the Season' by some guy in a big black hat named Garth Brooks. Willy was about as much up on Christmas country music as he was on magnetic media. From what he could see, it appeared that Larry had stopped buying cassette tapes around 1995 for some reason. Willy sighed again, a retro evening it was going to be.

The snow had gotten thicker, and he decided to devote more of his attention to the winding road in front of him for a moment instead of trying to rewind the cassette tape currently in the deck. It was tricky enough manoeuvring the huge truck back down the last few switchbacks with its long metal blade sticking partially out into the other lane of traffic, and he didn't need any more distractions. And, of course, there was the wildlife to watch out for as well. He'd seen quite a few deer on the way up the hill to the Casino tonight and narrowly avoided hitting several of them. Altogether, there must have been over a dozen in about three different groups leaping left and right in front of him with careless abandon. It seemed they just didn't give a shit if they lived or died sometimes. His dad used to call them 'rats of the forest', and Willy agreed with that assessment. They seemed to be everywhere you looked. And for some reason, they were much more active at this end of the valley than at the other end near the Golden Mile Pass.

Hitting a straight stretch once more, Willy ejected Trisha Yearwood and grabbed for the tape wedged between his legs, prying the case open with his right hand while driving with his left. It seemed Garth Brooks was going to be the man of the hour for the next little while. A loud 'clunk' came from the tape deck as he slid the cassette inside. Unsure if it was supposed to be that noisy, he hoped it would be okay. He didn't want to screw up any of these tapes since they didn't look very durable. Quickly glancing down, he saw 'Play' flashing in green LED letters on the tape deck's small display, and he felt relieved it was working at the moment. 'Go Tell It on the Mountain' began to drift from the speakers in the doors. He sighed, disappointed. His quest to find a tape containing neither Christmas nor country music would continue once this tape was over, but he wasn't holding his breath.

Glancing back up at the road, Willy's heart leapt into his throat. A whitetail deer bounded from the shoulder directly into the path of his oncoming truck. Fortunately, it was far enough away that there was no danger of colliding with the animal. But man, was that thing booking it! They usually never moved that fast, not unless something was chasing them.

In the milliseconds it took for the thought to germinate in Willy's head, a grey-black blur streaked through the glare of the truck's high-intensity headlights in pursuit of the deer, narrowly missing the edge of the plow blade. His foot covered the brake for a moment, just in case anything else appeared.

Suddenly, a second grey-black blur shot past in pursuit of the other animals. Unfortunately, this creature did not clear the front end of the Mack and collided with the right edge of the plow blade, making a sickening 'crunch' as it did. As the creature became airborne, it took out several of the cab's marker lights in the process. The chains on the truck's tires jingled musically as Willy stomped on the brakes and brought the rig to a juddering, skidding halt at the shoulder of the road. At a loss as to what else to do, he shouted, "Shit!" at the top of his lungs. This wasn't good. Larry was going to be pissed.

Throwing on the four-way flashers, Willy then flicked the strobing light atop the truck to maximum brightness. As an afterthought, he hit the high-intensity backup lights as well so he could hopefully see what he hit, then killed the engine. A six-cell

Maglite was attached magnetically to the truck's roof, and he grabbed it as he stepped down out of the cab to survey the scene. From a quick glance at the front of the truck, it seemed that apart from a couple of broken lights, the damage was minimal. "Thank the Lord," Willy said in a hushed tone.

Biting wind and snow gnawed at his face, and he held his arm up in front of his eyes to shield them from the sting. Hopefully, whatever he'd hit would be dead and unmoving behind the truck. The last thing he wanted to do was execute a wounded animal at the side of the road tonight. Shaking his flashlight, he felt frustrated that it was doing minimal good and only made the blowing snow a diffuse white mess all around as he shone it about. He moved back into the darkness, wondering how far the creature had been thrown. He'd seen it fly over the plow blade, but after that, it was anybody's guess. Perhaps it had bounced down into the ditch?

Willy scanned left and right as he moved, looking for more than just the creature he'd hit. He was also looking for the creature's mate or sibling that had been chasing the deer with it initially. If that animal saw its companion was down or injured, it might break off pursuit and decide to circle back and pursue his little-old defenceless ass instead. Willy had been around the proverbial block a couple of times, hunting the local forests with his dad, and he knew how things worked.

Superfine ice pellets carried along in the snow scoured across his skin, and he felt as if he were being sand-blasted alive and was having a tough time seeing anything. But it looked like he was in luck—something was lying in the middle of the freshly plowed road just up ahead. Whatever it was, it didn't seem to be moving. With a feeling of relief, he smiled slightly.

However, within seconds, his smile melted away into an expression of open-mouthed incomprehension. The Maglite's stark white beam cast the crimson of the creature's bodily fluids into sharp relief against the virginal white of the road that surrounded it. He stared at the beast like a slack-jawed yokel at the zoo, seeing a lion for the very first time. Because of the animal's speed, at first, he'd thought he may have hit a winter starved wolf, but as he got closer now, he saw that definitely wasn't the case—this was no wolf. Not only was the colour all wrong, but the thing was bigger than any wolf he'd ever seen. With a poke of his boot, he began his roadside post-mortem.

Along with its caved-in skull, one of the creature's forelegs seemed to be missing, no doubt sheared off by the Mack's plow blade. The beast was coal black with dark-grey patches intermingled in its pelt, and it also appeared quite muscular. Trying to categorise the beast, part of Willy wanted to say it was a dog, but that was wrong, too. No, this thing was bigger than any dog. His Auntie Bee had a Spotted Great Dane when he was a kid, and that canine would stand and look directly into his little eight-year-old eyes without any problem. Now, a dozen years later, he was staring in disbelief because the creature laying at his feet appeared tall enough to look into his adult height eyes.

Willy began casting the light into the swirling snow around him. His mind snapped into self-preservation mode when he realised he had been mesmerised by what he'd hit with the truck. Here he was, standing defenceless in a raging snowstorm on a mountain road in the middle of nowhere while not knowing where this creature's companion was. Perhaps it skulked just out of range of his almost useless flashlight? Willy whipped his head left and right but saw nothing. He looked back to the carcass on the road and knew he couldn't leave the animal lying there. Ever so slowly, he backed toward the comforting glow of the Mack's high-intensity lights. There was a rope in the truck, and he decided he wanted to truss the creature up and take it back to Lawless. He was pretty sure that nice conservation lady, Officer Moon, would be interested in seeing something as unique as this.

The wind tore at him with unseen claws as he made his way back to the truck to retrieve the bundle of rope from the cab. While he was there, he decided to back the truck up a little closer to the animal since he wasn't about to drag the thing through the snow for a dozen yards to the back of the truck. Doing so would be dangerous as it would make him extremely vulnerable.

With the backup lights already engaged, he threw the truck into reverse and moved it as close as he thought he could safely get without squashing the creature. Once he had the animal lashed to the steel platform, he'd get the hell out of Dodge as quick as he could. He left the engine running as he jumped down out of the truck.

It was a struggle, but he managed to get the heavy beast onto the steel deck. The thing had to weigh at least a couple of hundred pounds and then some. After much groaning and cursing, Willy managed to get the animal secured as best he could, its head hanging down off the back of the platform as if sniffing the ground.

Willy walked slowly around the truck, almost certain he saw something moving with him in the snow as he moved, just beyond the light. While he'd been tying the body to the deck, he'd felt pretty sure something had been circling around him, and he'd kept looking over his shoulder the entire time. And now, for some reason, he'd chosen the truck's passenger side to walk around instead of the driver's side. He moved past the front of the tall plow blade, shining his light on the bare metal of the scoop as he passed. Bright red gore was streaked across the entire front of the blade, solidly frozen into the sub-zero steel.

The lights illuminated everything down the entire driver's side of the truck from the cab back, and it looked clear of anything with teeth or claws, thankfully. He was almost starting to look forward to some more of that Christmas with Garth Brooks that he could hear emanating from inside the cab. About to pull the truck's door handle open, he heard another noise nearby.

At first, Willy couldn't figure out what the sound was—some sort of deep groaning noise came from the rear corner of the truck. He hoped it wasn't an issue with the differential or something else resulting from his collision. As he approached, the noise rose in volume until it became a howl of anguish. Willy stopped walking and decided he might just want to drive away without seeing what was making that noise. He'd begun to turn when a dark creature suddenly rounded the rear corner of the Express, its eyes shining in the truck's lights. It was Willy's worst nightmare made real, and he froze in his tracks.

The beast was as tall as the one lashed to the deck, possibly taller and so very lean, it almost looked anorexic. Yet, at the same time, it also looked dangerously muscular, and if it were starved, there was no telling what it would do. The animal uttered a low, visceral growl, its mouthful of pointed teeth gleaming in the light. Willy giggled hysterically for a moment, wondering if the creature had been inspecting the job he had done securing its packmate to the truck. The beast howled again. From the sound it made, Willy realised the creature was more than just a packmate with the dead one, it was its lifemate, and he knew he was in the middle of some serious shit.

After his father's fatal attack, Willy felt like he'd been suffering some form of PTSD from the nightmares he'd had every night since. No matter how tired from work, and no matter how much alcohol he drank trying to blot out the images of what happened, the nightmares still came. Every night, he woke up in a sweat, a scream on his lips as he relived his father's slaughter in the cavern. And yet, somehow, though that horror at the cavern was now dead and gone, a new and different one stood before him. A mate to the creature he'd lashed to the plow stared unflinchingly back at him. It was a wolf, but not a wolf. A dog, but not a dog. He knew it couldn't be either of those animals because this beast was the size of a mule, and that wasn't possible. A small river of saliva washed from the creature's parted jaws, and it began slowly stalking toward him.

Not taking his eyes off the creature before him, Willy backed up as the beast moved forward. The leather creaked across the knuckles of his work glove-covered hand as he loosened the fist he didn't realise he was making. His panic-stricken fingers pried at the Mack's Silver door handle, trying to get it open. The door latch released with a small metallic click, and then the cab door

62

was torn open by the wind. Garth Brooks blasted out 'The Old Man's Back in Town', his southern twang battling against the howling storm that had suddenly redoubled its assault.

The creature paused for a moment as it heard the loud music, and it tensed its sinewy body. The bitter wind whipped the animal's shaggy pelt this way and that, caressing it like a pet that was about to get a treat. Satisfied Garth Brooks was not a threat, the beast lowered itself into a crouch, its powerful muscles clearly visible through its wind-ruffled fur. A ravenous look burned in its eyes, a look that Willy knew all too well. Images flashed through his mind, and he suddenly saw his father scooped up with a swipe of razor claws by the beast in the cavern. And then it had feasted and feasted, oh dear sweet Lord how it had feasted. His father had been eaten alive before his very eyes, and Willy had been forced to flee for his life.

And now, here he was again, looking into another set of eyes with that same kind of hunger. He didn't/couldn't/wouldn't take his eyes off the creature as he very slowly reached for the chromed hand railing used to haul a person up into the cab. Willy tensed his arm, preparing to haul his ass as fast as he could into the cab before the beast could launch itself toward him. He thought once more of his father's death, and a sudden surge of adrenaline coursed through his body. With a shriek, he tossed the Maglite into the cab and then hauled himself upward with every ounce of power, straining his arm almost out of its socket as he tried to move faster than he'd ever moved before.

The beast launched itself as Willy began to twist his body and pull hard with his other hand, dragging himself upward to the beckoning warmth of a Garth Brooks Christmas, now only inches away. Willy's steel covered work boot swung up and out as he spun up toward the cab. It connected solidly with the beast in the side of its throat, and it howled in pain as it crashed into the side of the cab below the door instead, momentarily stunning itself. Willy used that brief time to his advantage and succeeded in throwing himself into the cab, with only one foot now sticking out.

Scrabbling its talon-sharp claws on the snow-slicked road, the animal stood up again and lunged toward Willy. It managed to catch hold of his exposed boot, which was just now being retracted into the cab.

Fire erupted in Willy's foot as the creature's teeth tore through the side of his leather work boot. With a shriek of rage, pain and loss, he grabbed the heavy Maglite on the seat next to him and swung it hard. A satisfying crunch came from the beast's snout along with a pained howl. It let go of his foot, dropping down to the frozen ground outside.

A small whimper of fear escaped Willy's mouth as his fingers skittered across the door handle to pull it shut. He pulled so hard, he thought he may have ripped off part of the grip from the handle at the same time but was too panic-stricken to care. The wrath of Larry couldn't possibly be as bad as the savage fury of the beast outside the truck. There was a thump against the steel as the animal howled and jumped at the door, trying to get inside. Willy jammed the complaining truck into gear and tromped on the accelerator. He needed to get back into Lawless, talk to the boss ASAP, and maybe go to the hospital. Shifting and grabbing higher gears, he was pretty sure he felt blood pooling with the melting snow around the accelerator pedal, and he was pretty sure that wasn't a good thing.

CHAPTER SEVEN

Austin sat behind the desk of the mayor of Lawless and surveyed the room around him. He shook his head in disbelief for the umpteenth time that he'd actually won the mayor's seat and was trying to decide how it made him feel. Although introspection was not something in which he usually indulged, since winning, he'd done it several times over the last few weeks. Typically, he was used to overseeing a place consisting of three or four staff members. But now, with the entire city staff answerable to him, as well as being responsible for the care and well-being of almost eight thousand souls in this small city, it seemed like a daunting task indeed. But with the support of his family, friends and the vote of confidence from the townspeople, he felt up to the task.

The snow was falling fast and thick outside the window with no sign of letting up. His smile faded a little, feeling sorry for Willy tonight, his first night on the plow and battling one of the worst snowfalls of the year. It was typical of the caprices of nature and how its unpredictability affected mankind for better and for worse. He recalled his first shift on that very same plow many years before, encountering an evening just as challenging as this.

Young Austin had only been with the public works department for about a year at that point. His maiden voyage on the Citrus Express had gone smoothly despite the dump of snow that had accompanied it. So now, on his second shift, he was feeling like a seasoned pro, and he'd carried on as he had the night before.

However, the temperature had become gradually milder as the day had elapsed thanks to a pineapple express headbutting its way into a stubborn arctic front stalled over the province's interior. It had all been pretty standard stuff on the way up, and Austin had made sure the Express was throwing down a wide spray of sand. But in the half-hour it took for him to come back from plowing the other side, things had changed dramatically. The light snow falling had turned into a deadly shower of freezing rain, and the road ahead was like glass. As soon as Austin touched the brakes to slow for a corner, the large orange Mack suddenly started to go sideways and then backwards down the hill. Fortunately, the tires bit into the edge of the road where a patch of gravel had been scraped through, and just as suddenly, he was facing down the hill once more. He'd lost traction several more times on the way down but had stayed closer to the edge of the plowed road and the grippy dirt that lay underneath its icy crust. No, he didn't envy Willy, but at least the boy didn't have anything as bad as freezing rain to worry about tonight.

Last week, he'd dropped into the Walmart over in Nelson and purchased an excellent Christmas gift for Alex. He'd hidden it in the closet of his mayoral office, next to the present he'd already purchased for Christine. Austin impulsively decided that he needed to see them right now. He wheeled over to the closet in his office chair without bothering to stand, enjoying the quality casters on the chair's legs as he rolled across the short-knit wool carpeting. He peeked inside and made a sigh of exasperation. Alex's gift, a socket wrench set for his new truck (so he didn't have to keep misplacing Austin's when he used them), had fallen over and knocked up against Christine's gift, a pair of cross-country skis. He'd picked them up back in October at a yearly ski swap held down at the Lawless Community Complex. When the wrench set knocked into the skis, it had caused a domino effect, and the tall pair of skis were now leaning against the closet's back wall. He sighed again as he stood and moved inside the closet to straighten things up.

Touching the tip of the skis, he did a double-take. Had the corner of the wall moved ever so slightly just now? "What have we here?" He pushed gently on the small gap, and it became ever so slightly larger. "Bob, you sneaky little devil, you had a secret room at the back of your closet." The door behind the panel swung inward with a harder push, revealing a small room that contained a large secret.

The windowless hideaway had to be an original part of the city hall when it had been rebuilt after the fire of 1895. Was this an antiquated safe room, in case the mayor needed to hide from a lynch mob, perhaps? Or did the city founders have something they wanted to hide from prying eyes? Several burlap sacks sat in a corner. Austin poked one with the toe of his boot, asking, "What's in here?" Whatever it was, it was solid—like it was full of rocks. But why would Nichols be storing rocks in here? He unravelled the tie on the closest bag and found the answer to his question. Twenty-four sacks of lustrous gold ore gleamed beneath the weak light from the single bulb in the centre of the room.

Austin shook his head in amazement and said, "Nice! Now we have some more money to help fix things up around this town and make up for Bob's indiscretions." He'd heard Christine's tales of what had happened to her in the cavern on Gold Ridge, and she'd mentioned that the gold up there was beyond belief. Never an overly greedy person, Austin had always found his pay from his job more than sufficient for his and Alex's needs. However, looking at the sacks of gold, he could understand how such a significant find of the precious metal could mentally affect a person or persons and trigger their avaricious side.

And it seemed that the room contained one more interesting secret. A book sat open on a small table in one corner. Austin picked it up and leafed through it, his eyes widening as he did. It was a record of names with dollar amounts listed next to them. Were they payments of some sort? But payments received for what? And why was it hidden in here? The front of the red leather-bound book was of no help and only said 'Ledger'. Some of the names Austin recognised, others he did not. The listings were chronological, and it appeared that the newest entries in the book were written by a different hand. Austin flipped back toward the beginning. Whoever started this book did so back in 1895, the year of the town's founding.

"What were all of you paying for?" Austin wondered aloud. Perhaps it was blackmail money to conceal crimes or other little dalliances of which the people in the ledger didn't want others aware? Or were they paying back money for a debt owed? This book appeared meticulous in recording the payments made to its owner, whoever they had been, but not what they had been made for. Leafing through the pages, he noted that the handwriting changed every twenty or thirty years as another generation of debt collectors took over the record keeping. However, it was the latest entries in the book that interested Austin the most.

According to the ledger, over the last dozen years or so, the initials of the person collecting the money had been 'R.V.' "Well, that certainly doesn't stand for Recreational Vehicle." That only left one other person that Austin could think of with those initials—the town's late but not lamented Chief of Police, Reggie VanDusen. And then, a new collector with the initials 'F.P.' had been added to the book just over the last year.

Continuing his train of thought down these mental tracks, Austin realised that only left a single possibility: the new hire made to the police department during last year's budget increase for an extra officer, Reggie's nephew, Franklin Pearce.

Through Christine relating her experience and his learning of the crooked ways of the ex-chief and his cronies, Austin knew that Pearce may have knowledge of the internal workings of the town's previous corrupt management. And if he were involved in the gold extraction operation, he may have also been involved in the other shenanigans going on up there. Though Franklin was most likely employed as a low-level lackey, there was a possibility there could be more to the story than he realised. Christine said they had tossed poor Carl Kuehn, the previous conservation officer, down a lava tube to keep him quiet about their discovery. So, who knew what else they might have been capable of and what other crimes they may have actually committed with Franklin's assistance?

After the events of the last year around Lawless, and with these new discoveries in mind, Austin Murphy suddenly realised that not everything in his quaint little town was what it seemed.

CHAPTER EIGHT

Peering over the edge of his black, horn-rimmed glasses, Chief of Police Fred Paulson regarded Constable Franklin Pearce through his partially open office door. Franklin was currently lacing up his Sorels before going out on his evening patrol. Fred watched him for a moment and wondered. Even before Chief Reggie VanDusen had gone missing back in January, Fred had begun to have serious questions about the morals of the other officers at the LPD.

As the front desk sergeant, there hadn't been much Fred could do about it, however. That was, until the results of the Civic elections had come in, and he discovered he'd been appointed to the position of Chief of Police by the newly elected mayor of Lawless, Austin Murphy. Fred hadn't been sure at first if he'd even wanted to accept the position, but after a long discussion with the new mayor, he had acquiesced. He said he would be willing to serve as police chief until they could find a qualified candidate who was a little bit younger than Fred's sixty-five years. In the meantime, he wanted to dig a little deeper and learn more about the other officers, especially after what had happened, because things ran deeper here than they seemed.

But in the meantime, here he was, sitting in this office as the new chief of police. As a long-time member of the force, Fred had never had too much desire to advance in ranks and had been more than satisfied with his lofty rank of sergeant. Of course, that was partly because it had been impossible to advance within the force over the last couple of decades with the previous management running things in the town of Lawless. Bob Nichols, being mayor, had appointed his hand-picked chief, VanDusen, who, in turn, had been in charge of hiring new constables. And some of them were questionable choices, as far as Fred was concerned.

Over the years, Fred had had his doubts about Oscar Olsen but had known that despite being a sycophant, there was some tiny shred of integrity still remaining behind the man's badge. As for the rest of the force, he wasn't sure how far he could throw any of the remaining officers, apart from the one laying at his feet. K-12 snored softly underneath the desk near his chair, kicking out a paw every now and again as he heroically chased down yet another perp in one of his numerous doggie dreams. Fred reached down and scratched the aged canine's head, and it grunted softly at his friendly touch.

Mariana Silva sat a couple of desks down from Franklin, currently in charge of the dispatcher's radio. She was one of three members who alternated at the dispatching duties. Friendly and eager to help, she'd been with the force about five years and was generally well-liked. Fred considered her one of Reggie's better choices. Jimmy Johnson was one of the other officers, and tonight, he was out on highway patrol. Jimmy was a little on the slow side sometimes, and Fred didn't think he had the capacity to be deceitful. Oscar Olsen had also been part of this cycle of patrol and dispatch, and with his loss, Franklin had been thrown into the mix. So now, Fred needed to worry about hiring more members in case anyone actually wanted some time off.

There were only seven members on the force in Lawless, and the chief's position, along with the police dog, were two of them. With VanDusen's disappearance at the cavern and Oscar's demise at Geraldine's, they were now down to five officers. Fred knew that Franklin had worked closely with Reggie just before his disappearance. So much so, in fact, that Fred thought Franklin may have been trying to weasel in and take the number one bootlicker's job, which at the time belonged to the late Constable Oscar Olsen. Fred had also known that something was afoot behind the scenes between VanDusen and Olsen, and he suspected that Franklin had been involved in those monkeyshines as well.

Despite Reggie keeping Oscar close by on a daily basis, it had seemed that Reggie had been grooming Franklin to someday be the town's next chief of police. At least, until his untimely disappearance along with the mayor and Chance, that was. Of course, a lot of VanDusen's favouritism could have to do with the fact that Franklin was also Reggie's nephew. From everything that Fred knew of Franklin, he sincerely doubted he'd recommend the man on any level if he had anything to say about it, which he now did as chief. Pearce was lazy, rude, and obnoxious. All in all, he would have been a fine successor to his uncle Reggie had it ever come to pass.

Fred's line of thought was derailed when a change in air pressure moved his office door slightly due to someone coming through the main doors out front. He sighed, missing his old public relations duties sitting at the desk in the lobby. In his new office, he never saw who was arriving at the station anymore.

With a blast of fresh air, Clara Carleton blew into his small office. During the reconstruction, she'd been in regular communication with Fred, who was then acting as interim police chief until he'd been appointed full time by Austin. As things had wound down, Fred and Clara had chatted more and more over the phone from their respective offices, and both realised they were in similar situations; two widowers with holes in their lives left behind by the passing of loved ones. Clara's husband, Riley, had passed away almost a decade before from a heart attack. Fred's wife, Lydia, had passed on after an intense battle with cancer three years ago, and he had been feeling the emptiness in his life since. Though he still loved Lydia, wherever she was, he missed the feeling of companionship and of sharing his life with someone worthy. He felt that Clara Carleton was that person, and she seemed to feel the same way about him. They had been seeing each other for a few months now. He smiled broadly at Clara as she entered the office. "Clara, my dear, how was your day?"

"It was good, except for all this fluffy white crap messing up the roads!" Clara dusted off the coating of snow from the shoulders of her winter coat.

"I bet your boys will be busy for the next few days with clean-up, that's for sure." He started to stand from his desk, being in the presence of a lady and all.

"Keep your weary old bones where they are." She moved around his desk, then bent over and gave Fred a kiss on the top of his short-cropped, white-haired head, saying, "Yes, they'll do their usual great job, I'm sure. Of course, here it is, one of the worst storms of the year, and we have a rookie out on the roads. But I know Trip taught Willy Jr. well, so he should be just fine. So, how was your day, Honey-bear?"

"Just more of the same, dear. The paperwork never ends," Fred said with a sigh.

"You're preaching to the choir! I know all about it. After years of getting your new boss trained in the fine art of paperwork, he goes off and becomes mayor. Now I'm left trying to train his replacement, Mr. Trip Williams, as you know."

"Ah, Trip. How're things working out for my doughnut-eating friend?"

"He'll be fine at the job once he figures out he can't hide from me, at least when it comes to paperwork."

Fred laughed, saying, "Well, he has a lovely, wonderful teacher." He stood with a slight grunt and pushed the office door partially closed, then, once he was sure the coast was clear, briefly kissed Clara on the lips. He didn't want the men to see him playing smoochie-face so early on in his relationship with Clara. They were already talking about it enough around the precinct that he didn't need to add fuel to the fire. He stepped back and looked

Clara in the eyes, saying, "Are you hungry?"

"Famished, but are you sure you want to drive out to Fred's with all that crap on the roads out there?"

With a small smile, Fred replied, "Well, I think the chief of police should be able to handle a bit of a storm. After all, tonight's special."

K-12 stood from beneath the desk and stretched. He looked at Fred and Clara with a tilt to his head and woofed lightly at them as if to ask, 'what about me?'

With a smile, Fred said, "Yes, you're special, too. But you, sir, will be getting dropped off at the house for a delicious can of Alpo."

A half-hour and one can of dog food later, Fred discovered the roads were as bad as Clara had said, and they definitely needed his full attention as he drove them toward Frostbite Fred's. After the double-whammy of the bear attack on the building and the earthquake, renovations and sorely needed repairs at the pub were finally completed. With everything back up to speed, they'd officially reopened just this week after undergoing a soft opening over the last month or so.

Tonight was a special occasion since it was the anniversary of Fred and Clara's relationship, and they were officially celebrating three months together. He'd been surprised when she'd suggested they should celebrate after such a short time. But as Clara observed, the older you get, the more you have in common with dogs; every three hundred and sixty-five days feels like seven senior years. So, frequent celebrations were a necessity.

They'd debated about going up to the Bonanza buffet at the Golden Nugget Casino on the hill, which had also recently had a grand reopening. However, their shared love of Frostbite Fred's prime rib had made the decision for them.

A gust of wind rocked the LPD Chevy Suburban. They were approaching the first major curve of the Valley Highway before it began to wind its way up to Frostbite Fred's and eventually the casino beyond. It looked to have been plowed, but not recently. Clara peered through the windshield and said, "What's that kid doing? He should have been back and forth along this stretch a couple of times by now."

Almost on the wrong side of the road, the Citrus Express came flying around the curve.

"Holy Toledo!" Fred slowed their momentum and watched as the highway truck blasted by.

"What in the name of Pete has that kid's panties in such a bunch?" Clara asked in surprise.

Fred hit his light rack, saying, "I don't know, but I think we're going to find out. Hang on!"

Clara double-checked her seatbelt and said, "Give 'er hell, Hunny-bear!"

Cranking the wheel, Fred spun the SUV around on the slick road surface, the Suburban's tire's kicking up a plume of snow, then accelerated away in pursuit of the Citrus Express.

CHAPTER NINE

Trip shook his head and sighed. He'd decided he'd better be a little more responsible in his new job as head of Lawless Public Works and had stayed late at the office to catch up on the paperwork a little. If he missed out on some of the hockey game as a result, so be it. A small whimper came from near his feet as Spider had yet another dream. Trip smiled, enjoying the companionship of the tiny creature and wondered if the dog were chasing rabbits. He reached down and scruffed the animal's ear, his smile fading when another thought popped into his head. Perhaps the little guy was reliving some moment of abuse by his previous owner. He frowned, hoping that wasn't the case.

Spider awoke from his dream and let out a small 'Erf' in a questioning tone as if asking, 'What's up, big guy?'

"Hey there, sleeping beauty, how's it going?" Trip scratched the dog's ear a little bit more, then sat upright in his chair. He'd only been around the animal for a couple of days now, but he was damned if the wiry little hair-wad wasn't growing on him. If he wasn't careful, he might just end up adopting the little bugger. "Well, my small friend, I think we are going to call it a night." He looked at his wristwatch. It was 6:52 P.M. He'd only missed part of the first period so far. If the roads were okay, he'd be out to Frostbite Fred's and tucking into a plate of juicy prime rib just as the second period of the game was getting underway. Yeah, he could live with that. "I think I'm going to put you back in your suite at the hotel here until I get back from Fred's. I can't bring you inside the pub, and I don't want you freezing to death in my old truck, so your heated suite is where you're going to spend the next few hours." Trip realised if he took this little life form under his wing, it would necessitate a bit of a lifestyle change. In the past, he'd always made fun of doggie parents who, whenever they were out, invariably felt the need to rush back home to their fur babies at the first opportunity. Then he smiled again, realising he might possibly be one of 'those' people sooner than he thought.

Just as he flipped off his office lights and prepared to move Spider into his accommodations for the evening, the radio in the front office crackled to life. Willy's panicked voice said, "Boss! Are you still at the yard? It's Willy! I had something happen out on the road and thought I should get back as soon as I could!"

Trip had made his way to the front with Spider in tow, arriving just as Willy finished. Visions of a mechanical issue with the plow blade was the first thing to cross his mind as he picked up the mic and said, "I'm here, Willy. I hear you. I was just getting ready to leave. Is everything all right?"

"Boss! I'm so glad you're there! Everything is far from all right at the moment. I hit something with the Citrus Express. And before you ask, no, there's no damage, except for a couple of the spotlights."

"And are you all right, Willy?"

"Sort of, but I think I need to go to the hospital to get something done about the blood leaking out of my boot."

"What? Blood?"

"Yeah, it's slowed to a trickle now, I think, but I should probably have it looked at. Anyway, I'm almost at the yard; I'll see you outside."

77

"Roger that," Trip responded. He turned to Spider and said, "I don't have time to put you back in the kennel, so you'll just have to hang out here, okay?" The dog gave an 'Erf!' in agreement. Trip jogged down the corridor into the shop, the dog close on his heels. Turning to his small companion, he said, "Sit," in a commanding voice. The dog stopped sniffing the edge of the outside door and looked up at Trip, a tilt to its head. "Sit!" Trip commanded again. The dog sat down this time with a slight whine. "Good boy! Now stay!" The dog acquiesced and lay down on the rubber mat near the door with a small grumble.

The wind tore at the door as Trip opened it, trying to pry it from his fingers. Snow whipped through the opening and dusted the little dog slightly, and Spider curled into a tighter ball. Trip pushed the door closed, pulled his toque down over his ears, and walked out into the snow-filled yard. What had happened to Willy? He'd said his foot was bleeding for some reason. What did the kid do, drop the plow blade on it?

Lights from the Citrus Express appeared as the truck came around the corner and turned into the yard. Trip's eyes widened as he saw the large, orange Mack quickly followed by the chief of police's blue and white Suburban. The truck pulled to a stop, and Willy killed the engine, then flipped on the rear floodlights. The chief's Chevy pulled in next to the Express. Now Trip was panicking a bit. What did the kid do, hit someone?

Willy swung one leg out of the cab with a groan. The tan leather of his boot was covered in bright crimson that dripped down into the snow below the open door. Trip had a sudden flashback to the campsite where he and Austin found Jerry Benson at the beginning of the year, but there had been so much more blood there. With a shake, he brought himself back to the present and asked, "What happened, Willy?"

Willy Wilson Jr. sucked a breath through clenched teeth as he stepped down into the snow and said, "It wasn't my fault, Boss. Honest!"

"Nobody's blaming you for anything, Willy. But you need to tell me what happened."

Standing illuminated in the Express's high-intensity lights, his hair a silver halo around his head, Fred Paulson said, "Tell 'us' what happened."

Clara Carleton stepped out of the passenger side of the Suburban and joined Fred near the truck. With concern heavy in her eyes as she saw Willy's foot, she said, "Good gravy, Willy, what did you go and do to yourself?"

With a grimace of pain, he limped toward the brilliant lights at the back of the Citrus Express, saying, "It's not what I did to myself. It's what something did to me." Now at the back of the Mack, he gestured toward something tied down with rope on the truck's steel platform. It was currently encased in a thick layer of snow blown up by the Express as it moved down the road.

"What in tarnation is that?" Fred queried as he approached the snow-covered blob.

"Careful, Honey-bear," Clara advised.

"I'll be safe," Fred reassured.

Trip moved past Clara for a closer look. As he passed, he queried with a grin, "Honey-bear?"

Clara scowled back at him but said nothing. Trip envisioned extra paperwork waiting on his desk tomorrow morning, judging by the severity of Clara's glower. After a small sigh, he said to Willy, "I take it, you hit it with the plow?"

Gesturing toward the light rack at the front of the truck, Willy replied, "Yeah, but fortunately, it just took out a few lights." He looked back to the platform and continued, "I don't know what this thing is. First, I thought it was a wolf, but now I'm not so sure. It looks too big for that. And so did its mate."

Hearing this, Trip's heart sank, and he said, "There's more than one of them? That's just great." He shook his head dejectedly. He'd been hoping and praying that they had seen the last of the creatures from beyond time. However, after Chris's phone call and now this, it seemed he hadn't been praying hard enough, and the past had caught up with them once again.

Together, Trip and Fred chipped away at the encrusted snow. After a moment, a large black triangular-shaped head was revealed. Pointed ears stood out on either side of its grey-black furred skull, and a long snout revealed a mass of wickedly sharp teeth. It was something Trip would not want to see alive, drooling and snapping in front of his face, not now or ever. And it did indeed look a bit like a wolf but painfully thin and on the verge of starvation. Every lethal aspect of this animal's physiology had been cranked up to eleven, from its teeth to its ripped musculature and its massive, claw-tipped paws—this thing looked to be death incarnate. Shaking his head, Trip said, "This is no wolf, at least not like anything local I've ever seen."

"I'd agree with you, Trip," Fred said. "No way this is from around these parts. I would have seen it at some point over the last six decades or so." Like Trip, Fred was an avid hunter and long-time outdoorsman.

Moving next to Willy, Clara said, "Okay, fellas, now that we've established that we don't know what this thing is, we need to get this boy to the hospital before he bleeds to death."

"You're right, and he probably needs a tetanus shot after that thing biting him, too," Fred added.

"Rabies, as well, I'd imagine." Trip interjected, adding, "Don't know where this thing came from or what kind of diseases it might have.

Shaking his head, Willy said, "Gee, thanks, Boss. Are you

trying to make me feel better?" With one of his arms around each of their shoulders, Fred and Clara began to limp Willy back toward the police SUV.

Trip called out, "I'll call Chris Moon from conservation and have her come down and check this thing out. And then I'll get out there and plow some of these roads."

"I should be able to do it after I get patched up, Boss," Willy called back.

"With a couple of injections in you and a sore foot, you'll be in no shape to pilot the Express for the rest of the night, at the very least. Call me in the morning," Trip shouted over the storm, then turned back to the snow-crusted creature, his mind spinning a million miles a minute.

Was everything starting again? He looked out into the falling snow at the red and blue lights of the LPD SUV as they faded into the night. What other horrors lurked out in this storm, waiting for a chance to strike, he wondered? With a sigh, he figured first things first: he'd call Chris Moon before he did anything else since he was sure she'd be more than interested in seeing this and wouldn't mind the interruption.

CHAPTER TEN

The palm leaves rippled in the early evening breeze.
Unfortunately, the air current from the large ceiling fan did not
reach George MacKay's position, currently inside the small
mechanical room of the Lawless Memorial Arboretum. Sweat
dripped from his forehead into his eyes as he finished up replacing
the seal on one of the water pumps that helped regulate the
irrigation system. With a puff of air from his pursed lips, he sat
back and extracted a handkerchief from a pocket in his work shirt.
He wiped the sweat from his brow and then ran the hanky over top
of his shiny, bald head for good measure.

The Lawless Community Complex had suffered structural
damage like many buildings in and around the city. In addition to
the large domed tropical enclosure, the complex also housed a
swimming pool and skating rink, and all three recreational areas
had needed some major repairs. However, after many months of
work, they had finally gotten everything up and running once
again. The pool had reopened last week, and the rink was opening
tomorrow, along with the arboretum. It was all just in time for the
town's first annual winter solstice celebration. So, he was feeling
a little pressure, but things seemed to be almost ready to go.

Originally built in the 1950s when the town was still riding
high on the tourism brought in by the ski hill, the arboretum had

also been a major tourist attraction in its own right. In fact, several decades ago, the town had started advertising it as 'BC's Interior Tropical Paradise'. George MacKay had been maintaining this unique indoor garden for almost forty years now and loved every day he spent in its confines. Not that he was thinking of retiring, especially not in the middle of winter. Just the fact that he got to spend his day in a tropical paradise in the middle of winter in the Kootenays was the icing on the cake for this job as far as he was concerned.

With several banana trees, palm trees and hundreds of other exotic plants, the arboretum was a favourite of the townspeople and especially popular in the winter once the snow and fog rolled in. It regularly brought visitors from nearby communities such as Silvervale and Castlegar and as far away as Kelowna and Cranbrook. During the January quakes, numerous panes of glass had been broken, along with part of the geodesic dome's structure, and repairs had taken a while to complete. As a result, most of the plants had seen damage to their delicate foliage from the cold that had seeped in, and many had died. Sourcing more tropical plants to replace the dead ones had been a challenge, but the city had succeeded in procuring some from the coast, and everything had just been replanted in early fall. Now, after several months of careful tending and loving care, George had the glassed-in paradise nearly ready for the public once more. His goal was to have it open over the holidays so that people could come and get their warm-weather fix and see some of the new plants and trees they'd added to the arboretum.

Except there was a problem. Something had gotten into the arboretum through a ventilation access panel and had been breaking down some of the more delicate plants. He figured it could be racoons or coyotes but wasn't sure. Whatever it was, it was very stealthy and had rather large feet, judging by the paw prints he'd found. He was going to have to call animal control if it kept getting in here. The arboretum was quite sizable, and there were several places an animal could hide, but George thought he had checked them all, as far as he knew, and couldn't find any sign of the creature.

While the structure was being repaired and the glass replaced, several propane heaters were brought in to help keep things moderately warm inside during the chillier fall temperatures, especially at nighttime. Against the outer wall were a couple of unused thirty-pound propane tanks that needed to be returned to the propane company for a refund. With a grunt, George picked up one in each hand and humped them over to a door that led to a service corridor. Just as George placed the canisters onto the ground with a clang, a knock came at the exit.

Opening the door, George was presented with a friendly smiling face and a huge slow-roasted pulled-pork sandwich. It was Pattie from the food court. One of the draws to the Lawless community centre was its concession stand. Unlike most eating areas at other multipurpose arenas, this one was open even when there weren't any hockey games or other civic events going on; the food was that good.

"Burning the midnight oil tonight, George?" Pattie asked.

"Yeah, just making sure everything is ready for tomorrow."

"Me too. I was just locking up and getting ready to leave for the night after getting everything prepped. But I had a little bit of trimmings left over from shredding the pork roasts, and when I heard you clanking around over here just now, I thought you might like a sample, so I threw this together," Pattie said with a smile, holding the giant foil-wrapped sandwich out to him. George accepted it with a huge grin of his own, thinking that was one of the things he enjoyed about working here—the fringe benefits, just like today. When he'd seen Pattie earlier this morning, she'd commented that she was prepping several pork roasts, which she planned on cooking throughout the day today, so she'd be ready for the festival tomorrow.

George sniffed the sandwich through the foil wrapping, inhaling the scent of barbequed porky goodness. "Oh, I thank you so much, as do my tastebuds and stomach. You are a generous and lovely soul, Pattie."

"You're quite welcome. I know it's not as good as it'll be tomorrow since letting it sit in the fridge overnight does wonders for the cooked meat—something to do with the collagen and connective tissues, apparently. Anyway, I didn't think you'd mind a pre-sample," Pattie said. She gave George another quick smile and a nod, then turned and headed back across the service corridor to her kitchen to finish locking up.

MacKay sat down on a bench underneath the pair of banana trees, taking a breather for a few minutes to enjoy the peace and quiet along with his sandwich. The bun was pillowy soft, and the pork was so tender that he hardly had to chew, with the barbeque sauce at the perfect level of tang and sweetness. Pattie had her own secret recipe that she used for her pork, and she guarded it closely, saying if she wasn't careful, Max Renaud out at Frostbite Fred's might hijack it. But it was not as though she was direct competition to Fred's. After all, Pattie only offered slow-roasted barbecue pork, not all the other smoked items like Fred's did. And although George loved to eat at Fred's, now that it was finally open again, Pattie's was still delectable and sold a considerable number of sandwiches each day to people who didn't feel up to driving out the valley highway to the pub.

A second huge bite of his delicious sandwich was currently in progress when George heard something nearby. He finished chewing, then tilted his head for a moment, trying to discern what the sound was as well as its origin. After a moment, he heard it again, high-pitched and plaintive. Perhaps it was the animal that had been sneaking in here, and it had gotten trapped somewhere? He placed his sandwich on the bench and moved slowly in the direction of the noise. At first, he thought it might be a bad bearing in a compressor motor in the mechanical room, but as he approached that area, he realised the sound wasn't coming from there. And it wasn't just one noise—it was coming from two separate sources.

He moved through colourful beds of exotic flowers and past

the fig trees, soon finding himself in the section which housed the Robusta and Arabica coffee plants and the magnificent Amazon lilies. He looked up at the gently waving palm leaves being stirred by the fan in the roof as he listened intently for another moment,. The noises were coming from the backside of this section, near the coffee plants, about as far away as one could get from the entrance to the building.

George had finally identified the sound—it was a squealing noise, like newborns or something, and it was coming from behind the bush just up ahead. "Well, isn't this just tickety-boo." He knelt and peered into a thicket of coffee plants. Hidden from view were two of the cutest little creatures he'd ever seen. "Where did you guys come from? Was it your mama that snuck you in here?"

The foundlings mewled and cried, and he reached in to pick one up. Tan and white in appearance, their ears were low to their heads and their eyes still closed. These creatures couldn't be more than a couple of days old. He examined the kitten he held; it was a hefty little thing with only a vestigial tail, making it look like it could be part bobcat. Either way, he knew he couldn't leave the pair of them here by themselves for the night, especially not knowing where the mother of these creatures was at the moment. So, he decided he would call animal control for the city and the conservation office, but not until the morning when they were actually open instead of leaving a message on the machine. With a shrug, he decided that for now, he might as well take them home for the night.

Placing the infant back down in the nest next to its littermate, George said, "Okay, boys and girls, or whatever you are, I'll go find you a nice little box and a blanket and take you home to meet Mrs. MacKay because she just adores cats, and it doesn't matter what kind."

CHAPTER ELEVEN

Roxanne Rooney held one hand out and examined her latest manicure job. The girl at the salon in town had done a fantastic job, almost as good as she could do on her own. It was nice to spend the money to have it done by someone else and not worry about being able to afford it or not. Her windfall after Reggie VanDusen disappeared had enriched her life in more ways than one. Upon learning of his demise, she had surreptitiously removed all the sacs of gold from his basement root cellar and moved them to a 'safe spot'; currently, her tool shed out in back of her tiny bungalow.

All in all, she'd moved thirty burlap sacks from Reggie's cellar before anyone had come poking around to settle his estate. The ex-police chief had been a fun diversion and a profitable one. Though she hadn't been particularly attracted to him, he was very attentive and showered her with gifts. That had made up for a lot. However, being somewhat younger than Reggie, she had always been on the lookout for other, more fit and muscular dalliances on the side. She had finally come to the conclusion that she would miss Reggie, but not too much. The wealth he had so conveniently accumulated in his basement, which was now hers, was something that would forever allow him a soft spot in some remote corner of her gold-digging little heart.

It turned out that Reggie had had his eye on Roxanne for quite a while. Her ex-boss, Ray Chance, had been too drunk to notice that she'd kept the intercom open during most of his 'private' conversations. As a result, she knew as much about the operation as did Chance himself, and of course, Chief Reggie VanDusen. Reggie had been a little more observant than Chance and had tumbled to her eavesdropping addiction after only a couple of visits to Ray's office. He'd made her aware of this fact and had asked her out to dinner and drinks. It was at this time he'd proposed to her.

However, Reggie's proposal had not been one of marriage but rather one of partnership instead. "I know that you listen to everything that Ray says in his office," he'd said as he'd shovelled prime rib roast from Frostbite Fred's down his gullet. During a brief pause for air, he'd added, "And don't deny it, cause I've noticed that the light on his intercom flickers on when I visit sometimes. Especially when you think you'll hear something particularly useful or juicy, ain't that right, little missy?" he'd asked.

Roxanne hadn't denied it and had just stared at Reggie for a moment. Despite his seeming a little slow on the uptake, she'd suspected that he usually missed nothing, and she'd been right.

Just as she was preparing to utter some sort of excuse, he'd clarified and asked, "Would you be interested in a little partnership? Cause I'd love to know what goes on between the two of them when Bob Nichols comes up the hill to visit Raymond, and you are most likely very knowledgeable in that regard, aren't you?" Reggie shovelled an entire Yorkshire pudding into his mouth at that point, followed by another slab of prime rib.

She'd been surprised that Reggie hadn't choked himself to death right then and there before her eyes. Fortunately, he hadn't, and she had agreed to his proposal in a heartbeat, especially once he added that he'd give her a percentage of the take. And then after VanDusen's unfortunate accident up at the cavern, well, that just made it all hers now.

With a small sigh, Roxanne stood and placed the gold nuggets that she had been fondling back into the burlap sack in front of her. All of that gold ore worth tens of millions of dollars was great to have, but she couldn't do anything with it without causing any suspicion. Reggie had bought her a fur coat, perfume and other jewellery bobbles, but that had been from his own money, not out of the gold cache. He had a strict policy on anyone involved in the operation spending any of their money too soon, not wanting to arouse suspicion. Though he'd had some of the other crooked members on the force help him bring the gold down the hill, they had never known where it had been hidden at Reggie's. But Roxanne had. After the gold had been left in his garage by his lackeys, she had helped Reggie hump it down to his root cellar, placing it behind the potatoes and other root vegetables stored there.

After Reggie disappeared, the first chance she'd got, Roxanne had popped over one dark night and moved it from his house to a safer location—namely, her place. And more specifically, a hidden space in the floor of her tool shed that she'd dug last spring. Though she felt like she'd given herself a hernia from the effort, it had been more than worth it.

But turning the bags of gold resting in the hole in the floor into a fat early retirement bank account was going to be a challenge. Finding someone to fence all of this was her next step. Large bags of gold ore like this were sure to raise some eyebrows wherever she took them. She needed a partner to help her with this aspect and was thinking she had an accomplice in mind, but first, she had to see which way the wind blew their moral compass, so to speak.

Roxanne slid the wooden cover back over the gold, then rolled a cart of gardening equipment on top. Locking the shed, she moved toward the back door of her house. Absorbed in fantasy as she was, she didn't see the idling police cruiser cloaked in snow sitting in the alley behind her property.

***

Constable Franklin Pearce wiped at the viewing portal he'd created in the side window of his ageing police cruiser once more. He'd really hoped he'd be driving the Chief's Chevy Suburban by now, but that honour had gone to another man. Franklin was still choked that he hadn't been nominated for chief of police, and instead, that old fart, Fred Paulson, had been awarded the honour. Pearce knew he was not the highest-ranking officer at the precinct. Still, he'd had his hopes set on advancing once VanDusen had retired or suffered a major coronary infarction, whichever came first. Reggie's disappearance at the cavern had been a welcome relief to Franklin, and he'd been looking forward to advancing up the ladder until the new Mayor, Murphy, had picked Paulson instead.

After going on shift this snowy evening, Franklin's first stop, as on many nights for the last little while, was to surveil Roxanne Rooney's house, along with several other suspects on his list. This was not police sanctioned surveillance but rather Franklin's own curiosity and greed.

Tonight, he'd arrived just in time to see her lock her shed and move back toward her house. He had suspicions that this woman had something to do with the fact that the gold he'd helped the chief store at his house was no longer there. He'd never known exactly where his uncle had hidden the ore in his house and had only taken it as far as VanDusen's garage. After the funeral was over, Franklin had torn the house apart, looking for it, but someone had beaten him to it and taken the gold. But now, he had a pretty good idea of who that might have been, as well as an idea of where the gold might be located.

Franklin had known his uncle was having a fling with the loose redhead before his disappearance. And she had seemed a perfect place to start his investigations into where the gold ore may have gone. He'd held off doing anything immediately after Reggie disappeared and had given things a few months to cool down. But over the last little while, he'd started doing some sleuthing about town and had formulated a plan. He'd still get his slice of the action, death of his uncle Reggie or not, now that he had an idea where to start looking. After all, why had she gone out to her garden shed in the dark of night in the middle of a snowstorm? Was it a pottery shed, and she was making cups and saucers on the side? Whatever the woman had been doing, he knew he would find out very soon.

"That's a big bingo, bitch," Franklin muttered under his breath. He turned his wipers on and slowly pulled out of the alley into the snow-clogged street, then drove off into the shifting white nothingness of the storm.

CHAPTER TWELVE

With a sigh, Jerry Benson snapped his suitcase closed. He hated packing almost as much as he hated unpacking. Quickly glancing about his small Yaletown condominium, he looked for anything forgotten. As far as he knew, he had everything he needed for his trip. He'd rented a small cabin near Lawless over the holidays, and now he just had to get there. Though he'd sworn to himself that he'd never set foot in the area surrounding Lawless ever again, especially after what happened to him and his friends, here he was, going on a vacation to that exact place.

It was part of the realisation Jerry had come to—that he needed closure regarding what had happened to Matt, Nick and Tyler. He thought he'd already had it since the beast which killed his friends was itself now dead. Apparently, he'd been mistaken and soon found himself wanting to do more. And so, he'd ended up giving away most of the half-million dollars that he'd been gifted by the elderly couple at the Golden Nugget Casino. It went to a worthy cause, and he felt good about that. Matt had never married, but Tyler had left behind a widow, as did Nick, plus two kids. The unexpected windfall of his gift had been greatly appreciated by both widows, and Jerry had been more than glad to give it.

It seemed he'd grown fond of the new friends he'd made over

the time he'd spent in Lawless. With a small smile, Jerry figured surviving a disaster together could help form strong bonds with one's fellow survivors. Realising he had a holiday break from his teaching job at UBC rapidly approaching, he'd been thinking more and more of coming up to Lawless over the break to say hello to everyone and reconnect. After the tragic deaths of his college buddies in January and being a single child with both parents deceased, Jerry had little reason to remain down on the coast over the holidays.

The valley surrounding Lawless had recently suffered another trembler, but it had been nothing too significant according to the sensor data that he'd seen, much smaller than the quakes back in January of this year. It opened up intriguing thoughts to a geologist like himself. Had this recent shakeup in the West Kootenays created another access point into the cavern of wonder, like the earthquake earlier this year had provided? Or did it still remain buried under millions of tonnes of rock, ice, and snow? That was the most likely reality, of course, but just the thought of access to that cavern and all of its wonders from beyond time was far too tempting for him to pass up. Besides, he'd become partial to sledding from his time in Lawless last winter, and it would give him a good excuse to rent a snowmobile when he was up there in order to check things out on Gold Ridge.

Heavy precipitation was being called for over the next few days thanks to two frontal systems moving in from the Pacific, the first of which was still going over top of them. And that meant snow and plenty of it in the province's interior. These two massive systems were what the Weather Network was calling 'The Storms of the Century'. Fortunately, it was supposed to let up in the next couple of hours, allowing a brief respite between the systems— just enough time to drive up to Lawless, in fact.

Although he didn't like the thought of spending between eight and ten hours on nasty snow-covered roads, when he'd heard that a break was going to occur between the two frontal systems, he'd decided to depart early to take advantage of it. This break in the weather was his best chance to make his way into the interior in time for his holiday reservations. And there was no other way to go because he couldn't fly up since all the airports in the interior were closed. Jerry had rented a late model Subaru Forester from a nearby Budget Rent a Car and needed to get a move on to get there before the agency closed for the evening.

He looked around, still feeling like he'd forgotten something, and then he realised what it was. With a grim smile, he unplugged the charger for his GPS unit from the power bar on his desk. The last thing he wanted was for it to run out of juice as it had in January. Unfortunately, he still couldn't find the lighter attachment that plugged the thing into a twelve-volt outlet in a car to charge it. But even without it, the GPS coordinates were burned into his memory, most likely by the trauma that had followed his discovery of the cavern.

He was looking forward to the vacation to help put things in perspective and hoped it would be an adventure to stay at the tiny rustic cabin. Of course, there was also that little part of his brain that was rubbing its hands together in glee at the thought of exploring further around the glacier on his rented snowmobile. If there was a way into that cavern, the scientific and geological bounty potentially contained within made it too much for Jerry to resist, and he had to know.

Being single and finally working as a tenured professor at UBC, his condo on Richards Street was long ago paid off, and Jerry wasn't scrambling financially, nor had he been for several years now. With his RRSPs paid to the max every year as well as a full pension when he retired from teaching several decades in the future, he figured he was all set, or at least, so he hoped. With all that in mind, he'd been toying with the idea of buying a small place in Lawless, one where he could pop up any time he wanted to explore around the countryside and not have to rent on a continual basis. In addition, there was also the investment potential of the Kootenays, both East and West. Many of the other towns in the region, such as Nelson and Rossland, were also busy and growing destinations, much like Lawless.

But Lawless had an edge, however—it was set to explode. If the riches in that cavern were ever to come to public light, the town would be swamped with would-be prospectors looking for a slice of the action. That had been the case over one-hundred and twenty-five years before when the town was founded, and he didn't think things had changed too much since. In fact, he'd been talking about that same subject with his friend, Austin Murphy, over the phone recently. The call had been to touch base about the quake as well as congratulate his friend on his win as the newly-minted mayor of the small mountain town.

After the monster bear had been put down and the secondary quake had brought most of the mountain down on top of the cavern, he'd thought that would have been it for his interest in the area. But now, with the most recent mini trembler occurring up there, he decided things might need further investigation. If he found another way into the cavern of riches and it contained as many valuable deposits of gold as he thought it did, he would love to share it with his new friends in the town of Lawless. The good he could do around the area would be phenomenal. And the impact he could have on his friend's lives could be just as great.

It was getting close to the end of the day, and the rental agency would be closing soon. Time had gotten away from him, again. He needed to get his but in gear and…

Pounding loud enough to wake the dead came from the other side of his front door. It was as if someone were trying to break it down. Jerry hurried through from his bedroom toward the door to see what was so urgent.

He squinted through the door's wide-angle viewing portal and saw a tall, dark-haired man holding up an ID that identified him as a CSIS agent. However, the picture looked a little off, as if the man in the photo were, in fact, the man's brother and not the man currently holding the ID in front of the door for his viewing pleasure.

The man pounded on the door again, "Federal agent, please

open your door, Mr. Benson." The man lowered the ID and growled, "Don't make me get a warrant."

That was enough for Jerry, and he cautiously opened the door, his security chain still engaged. "May I see your ID again?"

"Sure." The man flashed the ID up toward Jerry's face and pushed against the door, hard, all at the same time. The screws holding the brass chain popped out of the wood with a short squeal, and the man pushed his way into the apartment. Jerry was thrown backwards, slamming onto his back on the bare hardwood flooring that covered the apartment's foyer.

Stepping inside, the man closed the door behind his back. He was tall, muscular and had a slightly crazy look in his eyes that Jerry found particularly terrifying.

"W-who are you? What do you want?" Jerry felt disoriented from shock and surprise. He scuttled backwards on his bottom until he ran up against a wall.

The man stuffed the ID into his jacket pocket, then stepped forward, picked Jerry up by the shoulders and lifted him high into the air. He slammed Jerry up against the wall so that they were eye-level and said, "Jerry Benson, you and me are going on a little road trip."

CHAPTER THIRTEEN

Christine had returned home for an early dinner since she'd
skipped lunch today. Her dessert was supposed to have been a hot
chocolate and some of the baked goods from Geraldine. However,
as she sipped it, the hot chocolate seemed to be a no-go, and she
grimaced. Up until her Christmas extravaganza at Geraldine's this
afternoon, she had always considered the stuff in her mug
acceptable. She reflected that a person can never truly realise how
amazing something can be when all they've ever had their whole
lives have been mediocre versions of it at best. The mug of
chocolate bliss Geraldine had given her had been full-bodied, dark
and rich. The stuff currently in her mug was runny, light and
barely brown—it reminded her of something else that looked quite
similar and of which she'd rather not think while she was drinking
her chocolate.

Geraldine's home-baked cookies were out of this world, and
Christine couldn't even look at the store-bought packaged
gingerbreads that now sat off to one side on her kitchen counter.
And thankfully, she wouldn't have to since Geraldine had given
her plenty to take home. Her nonagenarian friend had said she
liked to get her Christmas baking done by the end of October, just
to be ahead of the game. And so, everything Christine had
received had been frozen, and that is the way everything was
going to stay since she loved eating her cookies, tarts and

chocolate bars frozen anyway. Currently, there were several Tupperware tubs full of various goodies in her freezer, such as buttery shortbreads, mincemeat pies, and some strikingly handsome gingerbread men, just like the one she was nibbling the head off right now. According to her latest calculations, she should be good for baked snack items until about spring thaw next year.

Spread out on the kitchen table were the documents from the safe that Austin had loaned her. Newspapers, a ledger and some journal pages. So far, everything she'd read from the newspapers had been exceedingly boring for an area with a name like Lawless. The ledger turned out to be a record of births and deaths, and it currently sat open before her on the table. It covered a period of ten years from the founding of the town in 1895 onwards. Each page was a long list of names and occupations with either the letters B or D noted with dates underneath each. However, on a single page dated July and August 1895 in the back of the book was a separate list, and each person on the list had a separate column next to their name, all filled in with the letter M. Since the rest of the book was births and deaths, what could this one be, Christine wondered? The only logical thing she could think of was 'M', for Missing. Whatever had happened to these people, it had happened in a very short period of time.

"Oh my, how many disappearances did they have around here that they needed a separate listing?" She scanned through the names. It appeared that people from all different walks of life, ages and genders disappeared during that long, hot summer in 1895. It didn't seem to matter who you were—residents, businesspeople, miners and travellers all went missing equally around the area over the course of that two-month period.

Something had been stalking the town's residents, something that had killed over two dozen people. That kind of slaughter made what had happened in present-day Lawless seem like a walk in the park. But what exactly had happened back then? And was it linked to what she'd experienced at the beginning of the year?

In a newspaper dated August 31st, 1895, it declared, "Fire Ravages Kootenay Town!" That was obviously the fire of which Austin had spoken. But why had it been covered up? Why didn't they want the world knowing that their town burned to the ground? It had happened to Boston, Chicago and San Francisco, and it was never hushed up in those cities. Then again, maybe it didn't need to be, or it couldn't have been. San Francisco's was a result of the earthquake the town suffered beforehand. Boston's fire was so massive that nothing could cover it up, mysterious though it was. And Chicago's fire was either Mrs. O'Leary's cow, too many dry wooden buildings, or a combination of both.

From the pictures she could see in the paper, Lawless of 1895 had had its fair share of close-together wooden buildings. However, it seemed other issues were occurring in town apart from that. In the summer of 1895, Lawless hadn't been called Lawless. As was prevalent throughout the province of BC and many other Canadian provinces at the time, if an area wasn't officially designated with a proper name, it would have one bestowed based on one of its standout geographical features or attributes. Proto-Lawless had been named after the ancient being that lived above them all back then, as it did now, the massive glacier, Natánik.

According to the Kootenay Examiner, the name of the local newspaper at the time, a contest was being held to officially rename the flourishing mountain town when it was incorporated the following year. The contest winner was to be announced at the first annual fall fair on September 1st, held at the brand-new fairgrounds. The Grand prize was a pair of round-trip tickets departing September 15th to Vancouver via first-class coach on Canadian Pacific, along with two nights stay at the Hotel Vancouver, all drinks and meals included. "I would love to have won that," Christine marvelled with a shake of her head.

One newspaper page of particular interest to Christine was from late July when things took a darker turn. The paper reported that there had been several disappearances in the area over the last month, starting just after an unprecedented late June swell in the

Kokanee River, which ran through the valley. Some had called the surge a tidal wave due to the amount of water that had coursed through the riverbed in the nascent summer of that year. Also on the page was an article on one of the town's founders, a man who had been instrumental in the burgeoning trade throughout this valley and much of the province's interior. The same man whose newspaper building was undergoing restoration in Lawless at the moment, Mr. Thomas Sinclair. Included in the article was a small, black and white picture of the wiry-haired, angry-looking man. Though small in physical stature, the man had been a giant of an entrepreneur with many successes to his name.

And Christine knew he was notorious for another reason apart from his business acumen. It was one that had fascinated Austin for his entire life as well as her own—the mass disappearance at the Sinclair Resort near the small mountain town of Entwistle, BC. In fact, her college roommate, Minerva Deadmarsh, had recently contacted her for a quick chat and had mentioned she was going to be investigating the resort with her brother, Lively, as soon as she was done at a job over in Ireland. Christine smiled as she thought of her friend and her jet-setting lifestyle; that girl was all over the place. However, she didn't envy Minerva because she wouldn't trade her fantastic conservation job in this little mountain town for all the money in the world.

But now she wondered, was the man who was fundamental in the building of Lawless also involved in the disappearances around town before moving on to bigger things at the Sinclair Resort Hotel? Christine flipped through the papers, looking for more.

Picking up the series of journal pages, she flipped them over and discovered a surprise on the back of one. Someone had copied down part of a map. It appeared to show Gold Ridge with a series of spots marked around the area. But spots to mark what, exactly? Were these spots where the owner of the map buried some gold? Always a possibility around here. Or were they merely gold claims or possible gold strikes, perhaps? There were also several other pages with cramped writing on them, and Christine tried to discern whose journal this was and why it was included in these papers. She took a moments to read a few of the entries.

***

July 4th, 1895 - Had a hard time today. The Gang has been all over town looking for me for the last couple of days. They want their gold back, and there doesn't seem to be any length to which they won't go to see it back in their hands. Sandy told me several of them tried to rough him up in the alley near the Nugget, but he taught them the error of their ways pretty quick. He told me Doc Brown had to set three broken arms, a leg, nose, and two thumbs after he'd finished with them.

July 16th, 1895 - Don't know why I thought I could get away with taking all of the gold for myself. But at least I hid it good. If they ever do find it, I'd be very surprised.

July 29th, 1895 - I'm heading back to the cavern today. Now that the gold from Red Deer is gone, I think it my duty to see if I can find me some more back in that cavern from hell up in the hills, but this time I'll go prepared. Thankfully my ankle is healed well enough now due to Miss Kitty's ministrations. Despite her choice of professions, she is a fine woman, and it is an honour to have her in my life. I think the reason for my decision to stick around this town is due in no small part to her. Who'd have thought an Irish lout like me would meet a lovely Scots lass in this remote part of the world no less. I figure if I can get a wee bit more of that gold I discovered at that cavern, then I'd be set for life—a new life with Miss Kitty Welch.

***

Christine smiled at the thought of the wild west romance that the two must have had together. But her smile faded as she wondered if this man was the one who had somehow unleashed horrors that stalked Lawless, both then and now? Could his actions have been enough to precipitate the blood and death that had been bestowed upon this unsuspecting town earlier this year and at other times over the last century and a quarter?

Several deeds to properties around town were included in the papers, presumably ones that had been foreclosed on. Along with these deeds were several promissory notes for loans issued by Thomas Sinclair to some people whose last names she recognised: Alistair Chance and Horace VanDusen being two of them. It seemed some of the descendants living in this valley were more intertwined in things than they first appeared. She wondered if their present-day counterpart's avarice had been hereditary.

"So, there was some back-scratching and glad-handing going on here as well? My, but this little burg has its fair share of greedy, closed-door dealings." She was thinking she was about done for the evening. However, as she began to put things away, a photograph wedged between two newspapers changed her mind. "A little bit of everything inside this little bundle of joy." She took a sip of her cooling hot chocolate by mistake and shuddered again.

It was a black and white photo taken outside of a tall western-styled structure. According to the sign on the front, it was the Golden Nugget Casino and Saloon. A group of men and women stood in front of the building, presumably, the owners or partners in the venture, along with some of their staff. A very stern-looking Thomas Sinclair stood in the centre of them all, glaring into the camera. The way the other individuals in the photo posed around him, it seemed as if he were a planet, and they were merely his satellites.

Next to him stood a very mysterious-looking woman with piercing dark eyes and raven-black hair. Even with the limited resolution of the black and white film stock from back then, her arresting beauty was almost as commanding as that of Sinclair's stern gaze. Behind her, several other women stood next to a blond-haired giant of a man who towered above them all in the background, like Natánik over the valley below. Sitting protectively in front of the entire group was a dog, one which looked to have wolf blood in its veins due to its size.

The sight of the large canine made Christine's mind jump to the tracks she'd seen in the photo at Geraldine's. These new tracks had looked familiar, but not because they were from the same creature that had last been in the area around Geraldine's. No, these new tracks were eerily similar to the ones she'd remembered noting on the cavern floor near the underground lake, which was just about when Ray Chance lost his head. Had that ferocious creature merely been an adolescent? The new tracks at Geraldine's were distinct in their own way as well, in that they were larger than the ones she remembered seeing before the attack, much, much larger.

Christine jumped slightly as her cell phone began to ring and vibrate on the table. The caller ID informed her that Trip was calling. "Hey, Trip, what's happening?"

"Chris! I'm glad I got ahold of you. Remember those strange tracks you told me about earlier?"

Her heart began to beat faster in her chest, and she said, "At Geraldine's, yes. What about them?"

"Well, I think I may have found what made them. I just finished untying its carcass from the back of the Citrus Express here at the yard."

"What? I'll be right there!"

"That's what I thought you'd say," Trip responded, but Christine was already off the line.

CHAPTER FOURTEEN

"So, I think we should do it!" Trudy said with finality. She picked up another french fry from Alex's plate and dipped it in a puddle of catsup remaining on her own plate.

Alex Murphy watched as Trudy slowly nibbled the deep-fried potato, mesmerised by his girlfriend's purple-tinted lips as they enveloped the golden-hued tuber. It made him feel hungry and horny, all at the same time. He had to mentally slap himself to pay attention to the words coming out of her mouth, not just her appealing, plump and pouty lips. Having missed the first part of the conversation, he said with surprise, "You think we should do it? Wow, finally!"

"Not that, silly. The map! We should take your truck up to the resort then head up to Gold Ridge. After all, you already have your sled in the back of your truck. Then, we can make like we're in Treasure Island and check out some of those spots on the map."

"Oh, that." Alex sounded somewhat disappointed, then added, "It's storming outside, just in case you hadn't noticed." He took a last big bite and engulfed the remains of his Triple Bacon Barn Burger with cheese.

"The weather office says there's a break coming in the storms in the next twenty-four hours. It's not supposed to snow as much for about a half a day or so, and then the second storm is supposed to come blasting through."

"Not snow as much, huh? That's reassuring."

"What are you, ninety years old? C'mon, live a little!"

Alex watched his girlfriend's lips as she spoke once more, this time paying attention to what she was saying. She had a point. He was far too cautious sometimes, especially so after the horror at the casino. But things seemed to have ended with weird wildlife around the area, and he needed to get back into things more. Plus, those pouty purple lips were another argument on the 'pro' side of things. He shook his head and said, "I don't know, Trudy."

"It'll be fun! Let's have some excitement in our lives!"

"I've already had plenty of that this year."

Trudy batted her thickly mascaraed eyelashes at Alex and said, "Maybe we'll find a nice little hot spring to soak in up there. We could skinny-dip, maybe."

The last of Alex's reluctance crumbled, and he said, "Okay, fine. When is it supposed to clear?"

"Sometime tomorrow."

"That's a little vague, but okay. Maybe I'll get some more time in pulling trash out of the Sinclair building before we go."

Trudy stretched up from her seat next to Alex and kissed his cheek, saying, "This is so exciting! Let's look at the map again." She pulled up the photos she'd taken on her cell phone and pinched and zoomed as she tried to examine them on its small screen.

"All right. Just a second." Alex reached down and grabbed the backpack he usually carried everywhere. Inside was a menagerie containing everything from his schoolwork to his post-workout protein bars, along with his iPad Air tablet. He pulled up the photo's Trudy had shared with him and set the tablet down on the table. "Here, check it out on the big screen," he said, nodding at the tablet.

"You are the bomb! Thanks, honey!" Trudy gave him a quick french fry flavoured kiss on the lips.

Someone, possibly his great-great-grandfather, had sketched out a reasonably accurate topographical map of the area. Alex supposed it was thanks to the man's time spent in the military before coming to Canada. He definitely had some questions he wanted to ask his father regarding his ancestors when he got home. Alex zoomed in on the map, flicking away a couple of french fry crumbs as he did. "Well, that definitely looks like Gold ridge."

"And it looks like there are two spots left to check since the other three on the map are crossed off." Trudy licked some remaining catsup from her fingers and poked at the map.

"One of them looks like the spot where we pulled Chris Moon out of the cavern." Alex shook his head as he remembered that day once again.

"So, what do you think? Is that other X a back door?

"Back door?"

"You know, into the cavern with the hot springs and gold."

Alex shook his head. "I don't know, maybe. Every place should have one, I suppose." He thought of back doors for a moment. One of them wouldn't have done them any good when the earthquake struck while he and his dad and Uncle Trip were eating here back in January. They could easily have been killed when things started to plummet from above. He looked up at the walls that surrounded them and saw that Ed and Marie Popov had been true to their words, and all of their gewgaws, whatnots and other memorabilia were now firmly screwed to the walls. Some heavier items sported cables to keep them in place should another quake ever strike the area. Even the cigar store indigenous person was earthbound after his recent swan dive into the deep fryer and now stood sombrely on a low platform in a corner overseeing the main dining room instead of a ledge two stories up.

"And why shouldn't a gold mine have one!" Trudy said in a loud whisper, although she needn't have bothered as they were alone in the restaurant. It had just reopened about a month ago, but apparently, the storm occurring outside its doors had kept all but the most dedicated customers at home in their warm, dry little houses. With a loud slurp, Trudy finished off the milkshake she and Alex had been sharing, then pointed at the map on the table.

Alex tore his eyes away from Trudy's lips on the red and white-striped paper straw and looked to see what she was pointing at. At the tip of her black-painted fingernail was a symbol. Alex squinted at it for a moment, then zoomed in on the marking. It was quite small, but from what he could see, it was one he recognised, and he said, "I know this symbol."

"Really?" Trudy studied it intently for a moment. At first, she thought it was a star but then saw it had other markings as well.

"Yeah, I saw it in the lobby of the Sinclair building."

"In the lobby?"

"Yeah, I'm pretty sure I saw it underneath an old bronze bust of one of the town's founding fathers, Thomas Sinclair."

"What? Cool! Let's go!"

"Where to now?"

"The Sinclair building, of course. We need to check that bust out—they're obviously connected."

"It's obvious, is it?"

"Sure!" Trudy snuggled up next to Alex and kissed him again, this time lingering for a moment on his lips.

With a smile, Alex reluctantly disengaged from the lip-lock and stood, towering over Trudy. He shook his head slightly; he was having a hard time saying 'no' to this girl. She seemed to know exactly which buttons of his to press, so instead, he said, "Sure."

CHAPTER FIFTEEN

The beast raised its snout and sniffed the air, smelling something it could not pass by. Bright light shone up ahead through the swirling whiteness. The light was almost as bright as daylight, though the creature knew night had fallen once more. Other tantalising scents were nearby as well, and it suddenly remembered how hungry it actually was. It was the same craving that had driven the beast from the warm sanctuary it had found, and the need to feed returned ten-fold as it smelled fresh quarry—raw, pulsating and no doubt tasty. Its stomach rumbled, and it let out a low growl of anticipation. As it got closer to the light, it slowed its pace and moved with greater stealth through the snowy night.

Up ahead, bright light spilled from a series of openings high on the side of a large structure. This brilliance was so unlike the darkness from which it had recently emerged after the shaking of the ground. Back in the darkness, it had fed on what it could grab from the lake with its long claws, but it had never been enough. But now it was free, and there seemed no limit to the prey. Its hunger raged anew in its belly, demanding to be fed. And it desperately needed to eat so that it could, in turn, nurse its young back at the warm place. The animal inhaled deeply and moved through the deepening snow toward the bright structure and its plenitude of quarry.

***

Virgil Raines stood in the small, open-air office located on a raised platform at the front of the building. He looked out onto the floor, watching the occupants of the large structure mill about. God, how he hated them. He regretted every decision he'd ever made that had brought him to this point in his life. The decision to move to the West Kootenays, the decision to buy a farm, and ultimately, the decision to invest his life savings in these stupid, stupid creatures. It couldn't have been chickens. No, that would have been far too easy. Small, cute, clucky little chickens laying their eggs and pecking about the place. Yeah, that was the route he should have gone.

But instead, he'd listened to Margo, his wife, as he usually did. And now, he was paying for it. The cost of the building alone was bad enough, but ever since, he had been here looking after these creatures three-hundred and sixty-five days a year. There were no vacations anymore, no weekends away with the boys, no Christmas day off, no nothing. These animals didn't take the day off or observe any national holidays. These creatures were a twenty-four-hour per day job where one day blurred into the next. How he despised the brainless creatures in front of him. He removed his toque and ran his hand through his thinning brown hair; the damned thing always made his head itch.

The thanksgiving holiday in October had moved some of his stock, and he still had high hopes for the upcoming Christmas and New Year's Eve celebrations. In the meantime, the occupants of the building gobbled, garbled and gurgled, making their inane sounds as they bumped into each other and shuffled about the inside of the barn. It was a large structure meant to handle many heads of whatever the farmer chose to shelter within its walls. Virgil had been stupid enough to decide on turkeys. And these particular birds seemed just as stupid as he felt. They had an entire turkey house in which to roam around, one that was over three hundred feet long and a hundred feet wide. But they didn't roam around this wide-open space. His current raft of nine-hundred and thirty-nine birds hardly filled a quarter of the building, and the entire structure looked ridiculously large and empty when all of the birds clumped up together as they were prone to do. And clump they did—they were insanely sociable creatures. Rarely did he find any of them outside of the large group. He supposed part of it was for self-defence where the outer birds kept a lookout so that the inner birds could feel safe and secure from predators.

For some reason, the birds were all gobble-gobbling their way down to the other end of the barn as he watched. There was nothing threatening in the immediate vicinity right now, only Virgil. And the turkeys had long ago lost interest in him. Was there something lurking around outside, he wondered? It had to be a coyote, most likely. He'd need to go and get his rifle from the house and then go on a little pre-Christmas coyote hunt this evening.

The little open office where he stood was located on a platform over top of a door leading to the mechanical room attached to the exterior of the building. He finished up a quick check of the bank of monitors that showed the turkey's latest water and feed stats. Everything looked fine. The building's state of the art heating system was currently keeping his gobbling gang of gonads at a comfortable sixty-eight degrees. With the storm currently occurring outside, he'd have to make sure to check in on them every once in a while this evening.

Virgil moved through the group of birds on his way to the exit at the far end of the barn. They parted for him as if he were Moses, and they were the Red Sea. He double-checked that the door was securely latched and locked, then turned and surveyed the barnyard around him. Another ten centimetres of snow had come down since lunchtime, and it looked like he'd need to get the tractor out to plow some of the crap into a corner of the lot. If he didn't, he'd be working twice as hard to move the snow tomorrow morning. With a sigh, he moved toward the house to get his rifle. First things first, he needed to check for coyotes. He'd had a bad time with a pack of them back in the early fall and suspected they might be back. The high-intensity LED lights that were atop the barn shone down into the yard. The snow was currently so thick he could hardly see two metres in front of himself. But he knew which direction the house lay and didn't think he could get too lost if he just moved straight ahead.

Biting wind nipped at his exposed cheeks and nibbled at his earlobes. He pulled his toque lower with a shiver. He'd have to remember to put his balaclava on for his coyote hunt tonight. Almost to the centre of the yard, he paused, peering into the snow. What was that? He could have sworn he'd seen something moving about in the snow just on the fringe of visibility—something large. But it could have been a trick of the light and the snow. He suddenly wished he'd brought the rifle out with him earlier and felt naked and exposed here in the middle of the large barnyard.

The lights from the turkey barn shone faintly but directly behind him, and he figured the house should be about a hundred metres straight ahead, but its lights were not yet visible. The thing he had thought he'd seen skulking around had been just out of the fading range of the barn lights where the snow and the night became one. He knew coyotes were never that big. Maybe it was a large dog? Suddenly, he felt a jolt of worry as the thought occurred that the thing in the darkness might actually be a wolf or a pack of them. It had been almost five years now that he and Margo had lived in the valley, and they'd never seen a wolf around their farm. However, it didn't mean that it couldn't be one—there was always a first time for everything, he supposed.

Virgil carried on in the direction that he thought was forward, the barn's lights no longer visible at his back. Gradually, the lights from the house began to resolve out of the freezing grey limbo, and he felt a tiny bit of relief. Once he got inside, he'd have to locate his balaclava, as well as his rifle. The last he'd seen them, both had been in the hall closet, and...

His thoughts were disrupted as something large moved quickly past his field of view just up ahead, hazily outlined in the heavy snowfall. It couldn't have been a wolf—it was far too tall for that, and it didn't appear bulky like a bear. From his brief glimpse, it seemed longer and leaner.

Unfortunately, he didn't even have a flashlight for protection at the moment since he'd left that at the house earlier this afternoon, in the same closet as he had the rifle and balaclava. For a moment, he'd toyed with the thought of going back to the turkey barn but then decided to carry on since it wasn't like he had a weapon back there or anything else with which to defend himself.

Suddenly, off to one side, he glimpsed the thing once more, but this time, it didn't disappear. It stayed just beyond the edge of the light as if tracking him and paralleling his movements as it stalked him. Virgil was usually a pretty chill guy, but at the moment, he felt he was on the verge of losing his shit, bigtime. He wanted to just bolt blindly toward the house. But he knew if he did that, he'd be brought down in a matter of seconds by whatever was out there. However, the thing was no closer as he got nearer to his house, and he was thankful for that.

Thrusting his gloved hand in his pocket, Virgil searched for his keys. Though he had no problem leaving the house unlocked when he was out and about on the property, Margo, on the other hand, did. She would have no doubt locked the front door just as soon as the sun had set. It was now long past that time, and he knew Margo would have bolted down all the hatches by now. She was probably already in bed to boot, having taken one of her sleeping pills.

With a small grunt of satisfaction, Virgil's gloved hand found his keys quickly. They were attached to the turkey-shaped key fob that Margo had given him for his birthday this year as a joke. He had used it daily just to spite her and was thankful now that he had it. The porch steps were just up ahead, and Virgil glanced to his side and saw the creature in the darkness had started to get closer to him, just a little bit, but it was noticeable. He quickened his pace, but he still didn't want to run and then have the thing break into full pursuit of him.

Finally at the house, Virgil climbed the three steps to his

porch, key held out in front of himself in a death grip. He was now only a dozen feet from the door, and he quickened his pace.

All at once, the creature must have decided it was done toying with him, and there came the sound of its claws scrabbling on the wooden steps as it charged toward his exposed back.

He jammed the key into the deadbolt, finding it locked as he'd expected. He turned the key so hard he feared he might break it off in the lock, but it clicked, and he twisted the doorknob with both gloved hands, thrusting the door open. He stumbled inside, then slammed the heavy door shut and leaned back against it with his full body weight. He let out a small gasp of air as he slid down the door and sat on his bottom.

On the other side of the heavy maple door, he heard something let out a low, feral growl over the sound of the wind. It scratched its long claws slowly down the wood at his back several times, and he was thankful for the thickness of the door. Expecting the creature to continue to scratch for a moment longer, he instead heard the animal padding away down the porch as it gave up on him and headed for his turkeys instead.

Virgil Raines stood and moved to his hall closet. He yanked the door open and grabbed his balaclava, his flashlight and his Marlin 336 rifle. The last thing he wanted to do was to go out in the storm again with whatever was out there still wandering around. But he knew he had to since their livelihood depended on it. Preparing to pull the front door open, he wondered if he was risking his life in the process.

CHAPTER SIXTEEN

Mayor Austin Murphy stretched his arms and swivelled around in the thickly padded office chair that Bob Nichols had left behind. He scratched his short-cropped brown hair, unused to not having a baseball cap on all the time like he used to. Managing the public works yard for so many years, the hat had been part of his identity. But now, he was expected to look presentable, and a sports jacket and dress shirt sans tie was his new uniform. But one thing that hadn't changed was the paperwork. He'd finally caught up on all the little things he'd meant to do at the office. Now, he wouldn't have anything to worry about over the holiday break.

His mind returned to thoughts of the corrupt ex-mayor and his equally corrupt partner, Ray Chance. It was fortunate for the city of Lawless that most of the town council's corruption had been eliminated in one fell swoop. However, taking into consideration his latest revelation about Franklin Pearce, he mulled over what he and Fred might actually need to do about the corruption still remaining in the police department.

Fred Paulson, the new interim chief, was as honest as the day was long. Austin had known the man since he was a child and remembered seeing Fred out on patrol in the old blue Ford Fairmont, of which the department had two at the time. Constable Paulson had always taken the time to stop and talk to both the big kids and little kids, if he saw them, generally keeping a good rapport around town with the local citizenry.

If there was any corruption left at the police department, he figured it had to be through Franklin Pearce. Austin hoped that whatever dishonesty he'd gotten up to with VanDusen, now with his uncle gone, Pearce wouldn't be further egged into any other untoward pursuits. But then again, Austin thought, knowing Reggie as well as he did, he suspected the apple didn't fall too far from the family tree sometimes, so he didn't hold out much hope for Constable Pierce.

Austin's own little apple was now an inch taller than him, healthy as a horse and built like a brick shithouse, as his grandad used to say. His son had kept his grades up despite everything around that had seemed designed to distract him. First, his mother getting sick, then her passing, and then, not quite a year later, the incident with Angus rampaging about the valley eating people left and right. Fortunately, it hadn't been as bad as it could have been if the bear had gotten inside the casino with the seniors, then it would have been a slaughter. And he knew without a shadow of a doubt that without his son's help, that most likely would have been the inevitable conclusion. But, thanks to Alex's quick thinking, along with Trip being in the right place at the right time, it had all worked out. But if it hadn't, and the beast had made it into Lawless... He shuddered at the thought. Well, thank goodness things seemed to have calmed down for now in the frozen monsters from hell department.

Despite all of the craziness, Alex seemed to thrive. His son had matured so much since everything occurred that he hardly recognised him. In a matter of a year, he'd gone from a boy unsure of himself and his place in the world to a young man who was focused on his future and gaining confidence in his abilities.

Austin had tried to talk to Alex a little bit after the whole experience was over, wanting to know more of how it had impacted his son, but the boy had been somewhat uncommunicative about the entire thing. Personally, he still had nightmares about what had happened. And though he tried to be nonchalant about the whole episode, inside he was just now coming to grips with things. Every time he looked at the howitzer gun, he felt triggered, no pun intended, he thought to himself with a slight smile.

A revelation came to him as the humorous thought popped into his head—and it was precisely about that, humour. It was always something he tried to utilise in any situation that was tense or frightening. In addition to trying to be calm and cool, he always tried to make a small joke now and again, depending on the situation. For him, humour in a tight spot seemed a natural thing to do. In fact, after joining the area's search and rescue last year, he discovered it was a common thing amongst many people in high-stress situations to indulge, including fire, police and EMS. After joining, he'd read several studies that had come to the same conclusion, stating that overall, the use of humour in stressful situations aided in decreasing the actual stress level of those experiencing the situation.

And yet, that was also part of his problem; he came across as so calm and laid back, people didn't think he had a care in the world. Everyone thought he was far more 'together' than he actually was. That was something he'd meant to discuss with Chris—how the incident in January had affected everyone's lives and mental well-being. The constant nightmares were something that he wished would end. He was pretty sure that it had affected her as well, though she seemed to be coping, but who knew what dreams or nightmares she might be having herself. Perhaps she was still trapped in that cavern each night with God knew what chasing after her. And he suspected the same could be said for his son after his own experience at the casino. The more he thought about it, the more he thought maybe all three of them should sit down for a group therapy session in the near future in order to deal with any underlying issues. Heck, maybe he'd bring Trip along, too and get a group discount. Well, he could discuss this topic with Chris at their upcoming dinner at Fred's tomorrow night, he supposed.

Austin was thankful there were no more council meetings until after the holiday break. He now had almost three weeks off without any formal structure to his days. Since he'd finally gone over various budget proposals and other minor city business that needed tending, he was free and clear. So much so, he almost felt he might need to find a hobby in order to occupy his time over the holidays. Leaning back in the luxurious old chair, it creaked loudly, as if reminding him of its age. Stretching once more, he thought about what he could do over the next few days, and a plan suddenly formed in his head.

Tomorrow was Saturday, and although Chris was on call pretty much 24/7 with her conservation job, she tried to take it a little easier on weekends, especially if she had some plans. The more Austin thought about it, the more he thought he would like to add to her plans. Although their date was supposed to take place tomorrow night at Fred's for dinner and drinks, he wondered, what if they started the date a little sooner? Perhaps get out a little in the backcountry on his snowmobile and enjoy all the fresh powder the storm would have left behind. They could even bring their snowshoes for some webbed walking in the winter wonderland. He'd recently consulted the weather office and saw that a slight break in the storms was coming up sometime tomorrow, possibly around noon. It would be fantastic to take Chris out and show her some of the winter sights on his sled and then drive on the trails all the way back to Frostbite Fred's when they were done and have their dinner date.

During the reconstruction at Fred's, the owners had gotten permission from the city to make an access from their property to the snowmobile trails that were located just above them on the thickly forested mountainside. Now, people could drop their trailer in Fred's lot and then go out 'motorvatin' on their sleds for the day, returning in the afternoon for a post sledding get-together to enjoy some slow-roasted meat and homebrewed ale at the public house.

Yes, owner's Mattie and Norm had all the angles covered, and business had been jumping at the place already since they'd had their soft opening a few weeks ago. With the grand re-opening this weekend to coincide with the winter festival, they were allowing whatever local yokel wandered through their doors to experience the all-new Fred's in its full, remodelled glory. And Austin didn't think anyone could get more local or more yokel than himself, being born and raised in the town as he was, and now also its mayor. His stomach began to rumble at the thought of the food they served at the pub, and at that moment, he completely understood Trip's addiction to the place. And since he hadn't had any dinner yet this evening, it looked like he might be microwaving one of Swanson's finest when he got home tonight.

The phone began ringing on the desk, and Austin creaked forward in the chair to grab the receiver as it rang for a second time.

"City of Lawless, Mayor Austin Murphy speaking."

"Wow, I'm impressed!"

"Hey, Chris! This is unexpected, but pleasantly so, I might add."

"Thanks. I can't believe you're still hard at it. I called your house, but no one was home."

"No, Alex is working part-time for Trip at the Sinclair Building doing some cleanup. He needs to make some extra cash to pay me back for the new light rack on his truck."

"That would explain it. I knew there were no practices or games until after the new year and figured someone would be home making dinner. So, then I thought I'd try this number on the off chance you were burning the midnight oil after all the time we spent decorating today."

With a laugh, Austin said, "Yeah, guilty as charged. I'm just finishing up so that we can have plenty of time to relax over the holidays. How'd it go at Geraldine's?"

119

"That's part of why I'm calling."

"Really?" Austin creaked upright and leaned one forearm on the green ink blotter that sat near the edge of the massive oak desk. He made a mental note to remember to ask Chris about his possible predate plans for tomorrow, but right now, he was curious why she'd called and asked, "What happened?"

The musicality that Christine's voice usually contained suddenly disappeared, and she said flatly, "Things. To their old tricks."

"Sorry? What do you mean, what kind of things?"

"The worst kind."

"What? Again? Really?"

"Yes, again. Really. I just got a call from Trip at the yard informing me that Willy Wilson had a run-in with something while he was out on the plow and said that I might want to get down there and see it for myself. So, I'm just heading down to the yard now and was hoping you could meet me there."

"Sure thing, Chris, I'll be right there."

"Oh, Austin, there's one more thing!"

"Yes, Chris, what is it?"

"Geraldine Gertzmeyer has had something wandering around her property as well."

"Do you think it's the same thing?"

"I don't know. I hope so. I guess we'll know more when we get to the yard."

"All right. Thanks, Chris. I'll be right there." Austin hung up and looked into the darkness beyond the banker's lamp on the mahogany desk. Visions of everything that had happened suddenly played back before him, and he felt his heart rate increase. What new horrors were now lurking in the local forests? Were his fears about what might have happened now to become a reality? He stood and shrugged into his parka, figuring he was about to find out and wondering if he might have to cancel some of his predate plans, or perhaps the entire date.

CHAPTER SEVENTEEN

With his call to Chris completed, Trip hacked at the snowy buildup that still encased the corpse. Before he went to work on the animal remains, he'd freed Spider from the building's confines. The dog had followed him out to the snowplow willingly enough, but when it caught the scent of what Trip was removing from the truck, it growled low and menacingly in its throat and backed away, keeping its distance. The dog currently sat a couple of metres away in the blowing snow, unwilling to come any closer. He looked to Trip, and he growled again.

Trip wrinkled his nose as he worked, saying, "Sorry, little guy, this thing's pretty smelly, isn't it?" Pretty smelly was putting it mildly, Trip thought to himself without amusement. 'Rank as hell' actually summed it up better, in his opinion. He was surprised the creature smelled so much even though it was frozen solid. Though not looking forward to bringing it inside, he didn't want Chris and himself standing out in the cold, freezing to death while they examined the thing.

The snow that remained around the corpse was crusted quite firmly in places, but it wasn't icy at least, and as a result, Trip didn't have to work too hard. Whatever this thing was, he knew it wasn't from around these parts, that was for sure. It was far too big for a coyote and much too ugly for a wolf. Of course, the fact that the beast was missing a leg and its skull caved in on one side didn't help it in the beauty department, that was for sure. Still, Trip wanted to be careful not to damage the carcass any further before Chris could have a look at it.

After a few moments, he finished with the beast's snow removal and climbed aboard the yard's hardtop Utility Terrain Vehicle. Spider hopped into the seat next to him as he started it up. Trip backed up slowly until the trailer attached to the UTV almost kissed the back of the Citrus Express. He hopped off and moved to the rear of the truck. With a grunt, he rolled the black-furred cadaver off the steel platform and into the trailer, where it landed with a heavy thud. "There we go! Is that better, little buddy?"

Standing on the seat with his paws over the backrest and looking at Trip, the dog gave an "Erf!", then jumped down and moved toward the trailer, sniffing as he went. He seemed a little braver, now that the corpse was out of sight and resting in the bed of the trailer.

"That's right, we'll get this critter into the shop and into the light for a moment so we can get a good look at it. Then we can throw it in the deep freeze. I'm sure this will be another keeper for Chris." Trip returned to the driver's seat of the UTV and patted the seat next to him, saying, "Okay, hop back on up, boy." The dog jumped into it quite readily once more, as if it had done so many times before. Perhaps on a hunting trip in another life, with another owner, Trip wondered.

Pulling the UTV around, he backed the attached trailer up to the rear door of the shop. While he popped out to open the roll-up door, he told Spider to stay, and the dog complied. Trip smiled, thinking he could get used to having a furry companion around him while he worked. He backed the UTV and trailer into the empty bay then went to roll the door back down. As he was doing so, he saw a vehicle pulling into the yard, but not one that he expected.

Austin Murphy stepped from his Honda Pilot and approached Trip through the blowing snow, pulling his toque over his exposed ears as he walked.

"Austin!" Trip called, then corrected himself, "Sorry, I mean, Mr. Mayor. What're you doing here?"

With a slight chuckle, Austin said, "That's okay, Trip. At ease. Austin is fine unless we find ourselves both at a city council meeting together, then you can put on your formal tux, so to speak. We've known each other for so many years now that I don't ever want you to feel you can't talk to me about anything, okay?"

Trip smiled broadly and visibly beneath his bushy white beard. Austin entered through the garage door, and then Trip finished rolling down the steel-slat door, saying, "Thanks for clearing that up. I wouldn't want to be on the bad side of the mayor," he added with a laugh. With the door down, Trip locked the chain off to keep it firmly closed. He popped the steel fire door open a crack, saying, "Just so Chris can find the entrance with all this snow, and plus it'll keep it a little cooler in here with our smelly friend in the trailer."

"I can't believe how much is coming down out there."

"I know, when we're done here, I need to go plowing the streets for a while because of what happened to Willy. I hope that break in the storm they keep talking about happens sooner rather than later." Trip reached down to scratch the head of Spider, who had plunked himself down next to his potential new foster dad.

"After I called Chris, I didn't want to bother you with anything if it wasn't a big deal."

"Well, it seems that whatever happened with Willy may be related to another incident, so this is now a big deal." He moved toward the trailer and looked down into it, then frowned as he added, "At least that's what Chris told me."

"What did I tell you?" Christine Moon entered the rear of the shop through the fire door, then turned and pulled it closed. The wind gusted ferociously on the other side, howling through the narrowing gap until the door latched with a metallic click.

"You said you have some news regarding this thing here." Austin nodded toward the quad's trailer, then added, "As well as other info."

"Well, it's more news of what Geraldine encountered, but I think both are related."

"Geraldine?" Trip asked. "Not her turkeys again, I hope."

"No, thank goodness none of her turkeys have been harmed to the best of my knowledge."

"That's good news, at least." Trip said with a nod.

"But what's the bad news," Austin asked, his face grave.

Christine arrived at his side, and together they looked down into the trailer. The remaining snow had melted off the animal's pelt, and it dripped onto the matte finish black paint covering the bed of the Arctic Cat trailer. With a slight intake of breath, while wrinkling her nose in distaste, Christine said, "Oh my."

"I second that emotion," Austin agreed.

Trip walked to the other side of the trailer and also took in the animal carcass, saying, "Is it just me, or is anyone else feeling a whole bunch of deja-vu right about now?"

"It's not just you, Trip," Christine said in a hushed voice. "It's me, too."

"Me three," Austin amended, looking at the beast before him. "This can't be happening again, can it?"

"I thought we just got off that merry-go-round," Trip added, giving his head a confused shake.

"Well, you better get ready to saddle up again, my friend," Christine said. She pulled out her cell phone and brought up the photo from Geraldine. "This photographic masterpiece is courtesy of Geraldine Gertzmeyer and her 'new-fangled' cell phone." She swiped to enlarge the picture to fill the cell phone's screen so that both men could see, saying. "Gentlemen, I present to you what's behind door number two."

"Is that the same print as the foot of this bugger here?" Trip asked, poking one of the corpses' footpads with the end of a long, metal pry bar.

"That's our sixty-four-thousand-dollar question. I've stared at this photo long enough to have it burned into my brain. Do you mind?" She handed the phone to Trip while she leaned forward into the trailer to examine the footpad of the animal lying inside.

Trip and Austin glanced at each other silently, the same hope no doubt in both of their minds.

Christine stood and looked at the two men in front of her. She held out her hand, and Trip handed her phone back. Christine proceeded to snap several detailed shots of the animal, including all four of its feet. "There, that ought to give Zelda something else to do for the evening instead of sleeping."

"Survey says? C'mon, don't keep us in suspense—is it the same creature?" Austin asked.

Christine shook her head, saying, "No, it's larger."

"What?" Trip poked at the creature again, saying, "So, you're telling me that there's something else out there once again?"

"Yes. Two somethings, actually."

126

"And you're saying this animal is larger than what was stalking around Geraldine's?" Austin asked.

"No, I'm not. I'm saying the opposite is true; the animal at Geraldine's is larger and longer. And I think I also know what it is."

"Really? Please enlighten us," Austin asked, eyebrows raised.

"Well, you know about my friend Zelda down at the zoology department at SFU, right?" Both men nodded. "So, I sent her Geraldine's picture and gave her a place to start because I'd seen a print like it and asked her if it could be a possibility."

"What? You've seen tracks like the ones at Geraldine's before? Where?"

"In the cavern. Just before… Before..." Christine paused for a moment, her voice hitching slightly, unable to go on.

Austin placed a hand consolingly on her shoulder and said, "It's all right. You're amongst friends."

Christine smiled wanly, saying, "Thanks. It's just that I seem to relive what happened up there almost every night in my dreams."

"I have nightmares too, but about what happened at the casino, on more nights than I'd care to remember." Austin added apologetically, "That was actually something I was going to ask you about tomorrow night when we were out."

"Oh, don't you worry, there will still be plenty to talk about tomorrow." She looked back to the creature in the trailer and continued, "When Ray Chance died at the cavern, I noticed tracks just like these," she said, nodding down at the cell phone's display once more. "But the one from Geraldine's looks bigger. And if that's true, then Lord help us."

"Why, what is it? What's out there?" Trip asked, the tops of his cheeks draining of their usual merry flush.

"According to Zelda, you are staring at the print of a Smilodon populator. One of the biggest of its kind, apparently—just shy of half a ton."

Austin said, "Sorry, my Latin is a little rusty. Could you help me out with a layperson version of Smiley there?"

With a grim nod of her head, Christine said, "I can. In addition to the mate of this creature still running around out there," Christine pointed to the black beast in the trailer, "we also now have another new, 'old' resident to the valley." Holding up the cell phone to display the animal print, Christine said, "Gentlemen, I give you the sabre-toothed cat."

CHAPTER EIGHTEEN

"Okay, Willy, you need to sit still, right now!" Dr. Anali Chopra commanded, pressing her hip against the examination table to stop it from moving around.

Because of Willy's subconscious fidgeting, the attractive, dark-haired doctor had been having a hard time examining his foot, despite it now being out of his bloodied boot. He willed himself to stop fidgeting and stared up at the olive-skinned doctor with wide eyes, saying, "Sorry, Doc, I get nervous in hospitals."

The doctor smiled gently and said, "That's quite understandable." She examined the puncture marks on the side of Willy's foot. The bleeding which had saturated his boot seemed to have stopped, so it didn't appear he would need stitches. According to Willy, the two wounds were where the animal's fangs had punctured his boot. She asked, "What did you say bit you?" Her emerald-coloured eyes were clear and quick, and no doubt missed very few things.

"I didn't say what it was because I don't know what it was. But what I do know is that there were more than one of them. They looked like some sort of dog-coyote-wolf thing. And man, was it pissed that I'd hit its friend."

"Well, you're quite brave, and it's clear you've been through an ordeal. However, it's not quite over yet."

"W-what do you mean?" Willy sat up on his elbows.

Placing her hand on Willy's chest to lie him back down, Anali said, "I mean, I have a couple of shots that I need to administer to you as a result of this animal bite on your foot."

Willy groaned loudly at this news.

Dr. Chopra continued, an understanding smile on her face, "I'll just clean these wounds up and then get your tetanus and rabies shots ready. I'll be right back." The doctor turned and left the cubicle, pulling the curtains closed as she did.

With a long sigh, Willy closed his eyes and tried not to think of needles as he let the emergency room doctor do her thing. He felt his leg wanting to start vibrating again, and he had to force it to be still. It wasn't like he was doing it on purpose, but as he told the doctor, he always seemed to be filled with some sort of nervous energy whenever he was at the hospital or a doctor's office. And this evening was no different. In fact, it appeared to be even more so tonight. Despite the throbbing in his foot where the animal had bitten him, he felt enlivened and bursting with energy for some reason.

The police chief and Clara had dropped him at the hospital and filled out a couple of forms for his admittance before leaving him in the hands of the emergency room staff. However, it didn't look like he would need to stay overnight, and they were going to discharge him once treatment had finished. The chief had said he'd pick Willy up and drive him home when they were ready to release him, but Willy didn't know if he wanted to bother Fred. Though it was blowing snow and cold as hell outside, he didn't care. He thought he'd probably walk home. It wasn't that far, only a couple of miles or so. And even his foot didn't hurt anymore. It must have been something the doctor did. Funny though, he didn't remember seeing her do anything to the wound yet, and in fact, had just departed to get something to clean it with.

Before Willy could mull the situation over further, Doctor Chopra returned with something to dress the wounds and two savagely long needles. "Here we are." She saw Willy's wide-opened eyes and said, "Don't worry, you won't feel a thing." The doctor smiled at him as she cleaned his upper arm with an alcohol swab.

Willy doubted that would be true and realised she probably said that to all her patients. However, he didn't say so out loud, thinking it best not to upset someone who was about to jab him twice, with a couple of needles that looked more like World War One bayonets. He closed his eyes, not wanting to see the needle approaching since he really was quite squeamish when it came to injections for some reason, and at the moment, it was more so than he ever remembered.

"Here we go," the doctor said cheerily.

Her words were followed by excruciating pain as the first needle was plunged into Willy's arm. It felt like he almost bit his tongue in half in order to stop from screaming. And then it was over.

"There. That wasn't so bad, was it?"

Willy looked up at the doctor and shook his head, unable to speak, his eyes watering.

"Good, just one more small prick." She rubbed an alcohol-soaked swab on his other arm and said, "Don't want to make one arm too sore."

Closing his eyes again, more stabbing pain ensued, and he sucked in air through gritted teeth. Though this needle was in the opposite arm, it didn't hurt any less.

"There we go," Dr. Chopra said. "That wasn't so bad, now,

was it?"

In a small, tight voice, Willy said, "No."

"I didn't think so." The doctor smiled once more and began irrigating and cleaning the puncture wounds, then dressed them with antiseptic cream and bandages. With a slight shake of her head, Anali said, "I'm sorry to say your boot was ruined from all the blood. However, since you have that dressing on, we can loan you one of our Aircast Flexi-boots that we give to people with sprains, fractures and such." She left the room for just a moment, then returned holding a grey plastic boot in her arms. "With all the snow out there, you'll need some protection for your bandages. But try not to get this dirty or scuffed, or else you'll have to buy it. Once you can find another pair of your own boots, you can return this when you get a chance." She placed his foot in a plastic baggy, then snapped the boot closed around his foot, adding, "You'll want to take the baggy off when you get home. But the bandages I applied should stay on for at least a couple of days. After that, you just need to put a light dressing on the wound for a couple of additional days." She patted his booted foot and concluded, saying, "Otherwise, you should be good to go."

"Thanks, Doc," Willy said appreciatively.

"You're quite welcome. All right, I just want you to rest here for a few more minutes before I release you. I want to make sure you don't have any reaction to the shots I gave you." She smiled again and whisked the curtains closed.

"You're the doc, Doc," Willy said as he settled back on the examination table.

Willy closed his eyes and willed himself to relax. He still felt the nervous energy, but he also knew he needed to rest. And he hadn't changed his mind—the desire to walk home was still strong. He took a deep breath, and then another, and another, and before he knew it, he was fast asleep.

And then the dreams came. He was running through a forest as fast as he could. The leaves on the trees and bushes clawed at his skin as he rushed naked through the dark green woodland. Faster and faster, he flew, unable to stop. And then he saw that he was not just running but was actually in pursuit of something. A whitetail deer leapt and dodged through the thick brush up ahead. Willy plowed through behind it, battering his way through the sharp twigs and branches as he trailed the fleeing creature. But he didn't feel the scratches at all. He looked down at his body as he ran and saw it was now covered with sleek black hair, protecting him from the brunt of the underbrush's damage.

Suddenly, he was upon the deer. He leapt onto its back and sank his fangs into the graceful creature's neck, feeling the hot blood spurt into his mouth, then down his throat and into his ravenous belly. And then he was tearing into the warm flesh of the doe's neck. Its legs buckled, and they both came crashing to the ground. Willy ripped and clawed at the deer, and then he ate and ate and ate. Everything around him was red, and it was all he saw and all he wanted.

The deer lifted its head, blood pouring from its mangled throat, then looked him in the eyes and said, "Willy, you need to wake up."

Willy roared and tore at the deer, gorging himself on its sweet flesh. He was angry at the creature for trying to distract him from eating it.

"Willy, it's Trip. Wake up, little buddy." He felt someone moving his arm slightly, and the deer faded away.

Snapping awake, Willy sat up, bewildered. "Trip? W-what're you doing here?" He felt groggy and disjointed.

"Well, after I got that beastie of yours locked up in our shed out back to keep it frozen, I got to talking on the phone with Fred Paulson. He said he was going to come back and give you a ride home. I told him I'd take care of that. Besides, I wanted them to go and have a good time and enjoy their dinner, which will hopefully put Clara in a good mood when I break the news to her."

"Break the news to her about what?"

"You'll find out when you get outside to my truck," Trip said cryptically.

"Thanks anyway, Trip, but you really don't have to run me home."

"I know, but I feel bad, this being your first night and all, and I gotta look out for the newbie."

Swinging his legs off the edge of the table, Willy sat all the way up. "Well, thanks a lot. Are you sure you don't want me to get back out on the plow tonight?"

"No, don't worry about it. When I called Larry about what happened to the Express, he came flying down to the yard. After asking if you were okay, he fixed up the light, then said since he'd had a nice nap that afternoon, if I'd approve his overtime, he'd be willing to do the run tonight. Well, since I was up before five o'clock this morning and wasn't looking forward to it, I whole-heartedly agreed to the overtime."

"That's good of Larry."

"Damn straight. Good for his wallet, too," Trip agreed. "Tell you what, I'm just going to talk to the doctor for a second and then I'll be right back."

Willy grabbed his parka from a chair where it lay folded and began shrugging it on. Trip returned by the time he was doing up his zipper and said, "All right, let's go, I'm taking you home."

"But it's okay, Trip. I don't need a ride to my place. I can walk." Even though it was the middle of a blizzard, Willy still had the urge to be outside in nature and go for a walk.

"Yeah, right. And pigs can fly." Taking Willy's elbow, Trip helped the younger man off the table and then ushered him toward the emergency room exit doors with Willy's arm across his shoulders for support. Trip added, "And besides, you're not going to your home tonight; you're coming to mine."

"What?"

"Doctor's orders. Tonight, you're sleeping in my spare room. Doctor Chopra said someone's gotta keep an eye on you after that bite to make sure you don't develop hydrophobia or a nasty infection." Trip gave him a side-eyed look and asked, "And how're you feeling right now, anyway?"

Willy looked Trip in the eye and said, "Not bad, actually, but I am super hungry. Can we stop for a burger at the Barn?"

With a laugh, Trip said, "You read my mind. Two double bacon, double cheeseburgers it is!"

The emergency room doors whisked open, and as the two men stepped out into the stormy night, Willy said, "That sounds great, Boss. What're you going to have?"

CHAPTER NINETEEN

All of Jerry's rushing around to make his appointment to pick up his Forester had proven moot since Angel had insisted Jerry drive his Lincoln Navigator instead. Jerry had to admit, the vehicle was as sure-footed as a mountain goat on most of the terrain they had encountered so far on the trip. The rear end of the Navigator kicked out suddenly as it hit a patch of slush, and Jerry Benson brought it back under control easily. The anti-skid, traction-controlled four-wheel-drive that the large, black SUV provided was almost impervious to whatever Mother Nature threw at it. Of course, there were always exceptions, but a confident driver behind the wheel in winter weather was always a bonus, and fortunately, he was one of those drivers.

Jerry recalled driving Tyler's large Dodge Ram over these very same roads in very similar weather about eleven months ago. At the time, he'd been annoyed by the truckload of loud, sloppy drunks that he'd been transporting, but now, he would take them in a heartbeat over his current situation. He glanced over at Angel Oritz and tried to imagine what Angel's brother, Manny, must have been like. If Angel was anything to go by, Manny must have been quite a piece of work.

After pushing his way into Jerry's apartment, Angel had made him an offer he couldn't refuse. Especially since the object which he used to persuade Jerry was a Glock 17 pointed at his head. So, of course, Jerry had agreed with an enthusiastic nod of his head. He smiled grimly, trying to piece together what was happening. Somehow, the man had gotten Jerry's address and seemed to think Jerry was connected to whatever Manny had been involved with in Lawless. But who had given him Jerry's address? He couldn't picture any of his friends in Lawless having anything to do with this man. And Angel hadn't been the most forthcoming person either. From what he'd been able to piece together, it had something to do with the gold in the cavern and his experience there. To top things off, after a bit more coaxing with the Glock, Jerry had divulged that he was actually on his way up to Lawless when Angel had come bursting into his apartment and his life. This news, of course, solidified Jerry's complicity, as far as Oritz was concerned, in his brother Manny's disappearance.

Glancing casually sideways, Jerry saw that his abductor was currently sitting with his eyes closed, his head tilted forward as if lightly napping. But how lightly, Jerry wondered? The Glock didn't look to be too tightly held in the man's hand at the moment.

Jerry brought his attention back to the road and saw a relatively straight stretch coming up. According to the sign, just off to the right was the entrance to Manning Park Resort. Keeping one eye on the road, Jerry turned his head slightly to the right to get a better look at the sleeping man next to him. But was he sleeping? It was so hard to tell in the dim light of the Navigator's instrument console. Jerry slowly released his right hand from the steering wheel and crept it toward the Glock lying loosely in Angel's hand.

Oritz lifted his hand slightly and rapped the butt of the Glock hard on the back of Jerry's right hand, pinning it to the console between the leather seats. "Move your hand any closer, compadre, and I'll blow your fingers off, one by one."

"Sorry, I was only looking for the seat's heat controls." Jerry tried to pull his hand back but couldn't because Angel was pressing down so hard.

"Sure you were, and I'm Jolly Old Saint Nick." He flicked off the heat to Jerry's seat. With a final firm, painful press of the handgun's butt against Jerry's hand, Angel withdrew the weapon and folded his hands once more, the pistol resting on top and pointing directly at Jerry. "Any more questions about the controls of this vehicle, you just ask. And no playing creepy-crawly with your hand, either. If I see that again, you'll be minus a few fingers, like I said. It'd be pretty tough to drive with only a thumb and pinky finger to steer by. You might want to think about that."

And think about things Jerry did. He had no idea how to get out of his current situation. Although he loved reading Jack Reacher novels in his spare time, a man of action, he was not. And he wasn't too keen to find out if Oritz would carry through on his threat to shoot some of his fingers off. Jerry decided he needed to outthink the man sitting opposite him, not out-muscle him. From what he'd seen so far, Angel seemed relatively bright and well-spoken for an ex-convict. When he'd asked the man about it as they left the city, Angel had said, "In prison, you get plenty of time to expand your horizons through reading." That was something that Jerry hoped to use in his favour if it came down to it. He'd appeal to the man's intellect—he obviously had one, but Jerry knew he'd have to be careful.

The road ahead curved gracefully through a mountain valley with a small river running next to the road. In the summer, it was quite scenic, but now, in the middle of a winter snowstorm, the only thing it was, was dangerous. According to the speedometer, Jerry was motoring along at a relatively zippy eighty kilometres per hour, twenty km/h below the posted limit. And yet some yahoo in a late model Subaru XV doing easily one-hundred and twenty kilometres per hour came flying out of nowhere from behind him, then shot down the road throwing up a whiteout of snow in its wake. "Dangerous bastard!" Jerry called out.

"Risk and reward, man," Angel observed.

"What? What are you talking about?"

"That guy there seemed to think the risk of passing you was worth the reward of getting somewhere a little sooner. Kind of like you and whatever you were involved in up in Lawless."

"Look, I told you. I was only up there with some frat brothers from college, and we got attacked by some sort of creature from hell."

Angel smirked and said, "Then I'd feel right at home with it." He adjusted his position in the Navigator's bucket seat and asked, "But why were you and your bros up there in the first place?"

"It was a yearly vacation we all took together. And unfortunately, last year, we decided on Lawless."

"So, if your friends were killed by the same thing that may have killed my brother, you still want revenge, don't you?"

"I've made my peace," Jerry murmured.

"After what you said happened to your friends, I still bet you wouldn't mind settling the score on whatever might be left inside that cavern."

"Well, I guess we're going to find out, aren't we?" A simple stone and wood sign off to one side of the road read, 'Leaving Manning Park'. The highway merged down to two lanes, and Jerry manoeuvred the Lincoln into the single lane. Up ahead, the road was barely visible in the heavy snow, winding up into the mountains once again. Jerry was stressed—this was almost too much for him to bear. He couldn't help but think that fate was getting back at him for dodging his demise in January. But if he could survive his trip to the interior that time, he would survive it once again. He was getting to be a regular Gloria Gaynor that way.

With a sigh, Jerry Benson steered the Lincoln up through a series of switchbacks, guiding the vehicle higher and higher through the winding curves. With a grim smile, he decided he'd have to add 'Getting your fingers blown off by a psychopathic killer' to the little book that he was still in the process of compiling, Darwin's Herd Thinners. The way his life was going, it practically wrote itself.

CHAPTER TWENTY

The drive from the Burger Barn on the outskirts of town to the Sinclair building wasn't a long one but considering the current shape of the roads, Alex was glad to have the on-demand four-wheel-drive his Toyota pickup provided. He'd bought the truck with the cash that he'd saved up from his part-time jobs over the last few years. First, it had been snow-shovelling the neighbours' laneways, then a position as stock boy and janitor at the Pharmasave. He had recently been promoted to cashier, and the slight boost in pay that came with it had helped somewhat, but it was still part-time and didn't provide the kind of cash he needed to fix up certain aspects of his ride. However, he was getting there, piece by piece.

He thought longingly of the new light bar that he'd bought, which now crowned the roof of his truck. Unfortunately, it was of no use right now as the snow was too heavy and became impenetrable if confronted with a light that was too bright. And at 150,000 lumens, the light rack was most definitely that. It was best used in the middle of a darkened forest, bumping along logging roads when he was out mudding with his friends.

Several minutes later, they entered the Sinclair Building, their snow boots echoing on the dusty marble floor. Across the lobby from the entrance sat the bust of Thomas Sinclair. His stern and unforgiving expression had greeted every visitor to the building over the years. But this evening, his stern expression intrigued Trudy and Alex more than they could have ever imagined.

Staring at the bronze bust, Trudy wondered aloud, "What do you think he's hiding from us behind that sour-looking face?"

"I guess that's what we're here to find out," Alex said, stepping forward and examining the bust closely. It sat on a marble column to which it seemed firmly attached, so picking it up and looking underneath it was out of the question. As well, the four-sided column was attached to the floor somehow and didn't look like it was going anywhere.

Pulling out a small flashlight she carried in her back-pack style purse, Trudy leaned in and shone the beam about the lower edge of the bronze bust. At its base lay the symbol in question. It was small, but it looked like it could be a Star of David, or... And then it suddenly came to her, and she exclaimed, "A pentagram!"

"Sorry?"

"That symbol. It's five-sided, not six like the Star of David."

"So, a pentagram. Like in the devil?"

"No, it's got the single point facing up."

"I thought it just meant the devil, and it didn't matter which way was up."

"A single point ascendant is the sign of the saviour. Two points ascendant is the devil." The small, penny-sized symbol had a single dot above the topmost point, which currently pointed upward.

"Well, you would know, Pumpkin."

"Yeah, I would." Trudy pressed her thumb to the symbol,

hoping it was a button, but nothing much happened, though it did seem to have a bit of give to it. "So, Thomas Sinclair is the saviour then?"

"I doubt that," Alex replied. Stooping down to look closer, he said, "What's that there?"

"What's what where?" Trudy questioned.

"May I borrow your light?" Alex asked, holding his hand out.

Trudy handed it over, and Alex shone the beam of the light onto the base of the bust, where it made contact with the pedestal. On the left side, at the same level as the first symbol, lay another, but this one with a slight variation. "Well, this one has the top dot rotated to the right, and now it looks like the sign of the devil." He continued around the base of the bust and discovered two more of the symbols. That made four altogether, each with a single dot rotated clockwise one more turn as they progressed around the pedestal. "What if," Alex wondered, "they need to be pressed in a certain sequence?"

"I guess that could be, but what is it?" Trudy asked. She pressed the symbol on the front, followed by the one on the left, then the rear and finally the right side of the bust, with no effect— not that she'd expected one. "Scratch the most obvious possibility. I wonder how many combinations there are?"

Twenty-four," Alex answered almost immediately.

"Well, thank you, Mister Mathematics!" Trudy said in surprise, then added, "How did you know that?"

"Because four times three, times two, times one equals twenty-four. It's a factorial equation. If there were five sides to this pedestal, there'd be one-hundred and twenty possibilities."

"Looks like somebody's been paying attention in math class."

"On occasion," Alex said with a grin.

"Okay, get at it then," Trudy said with her hands on her hips and an impish smile on her lips.

"Oh, I get the honour, do I?"

"You're the math wizard! I'd probably forget what combination I was at after the first four."

With a slight shake to his head, and a small smile playing at the corners of his lips, Alex proceeded to press the star-shaped patterns one after the other in a sequence of four. After each combination, he'd try to move the bronze bust, but with no success.

After several minutes, Alex was getting close to the end of the possible permutations that the four symbols could represent, and he began wondering if maybe his guess was wrong. However, with the next combination of symbols, he saw his self-doubt was unfounded and was rewarded with a click. Twisting the statue did no good, but when he tried tilting back the bust of Thomas Sinclair, it opened. It was just like he'd seen on the corny old Batman TV show where they had the button for the bat poles hidden inside the bust of Shakespeare. Inside of this bust was no button but instead a brass knob.

"What is that?" Trudy wondered.

"I'd say a knob," Alex offered.

"I know, silly. I mean, what are you supposed to do with it?"

"I'm no knob expert, but most people turn them." With that said, Alex turned the knob to the left and pulled as if he were opening a door. To his surprise, it did open, but not how he was expecting. The entire top of the pedestal opened when he pulled the handle up, revealing a hollow column beneath. He leaned forward and looked inside the darkened pedestal, then said,

"Huh."

Trudy looked at Alex and then back at the pedestal and said excitedly, "Well, what is it? What's in there?"

"Take a look for yourself," Alex said and stepped back so his girlfriend could take a peek.

Leaning into the pedestal to get a better view, Trudy said, "You're right, huh!" She reached inside and pulled out a dark leather pouch. It looked like something that a highwayman would have worn about his waist in which to collect valuables. It was tied closed with some leather lacing wound about its top.

"It's kind of heavy. Do you think it's more gold?" Trudy asked as she placed the satchel on the edge of the pedestal and began to unwind the lacing. After a moment, she reached into the pouch. It was indeed more gold, but not quite what they were expecting. Trudy extracted what looked like a key, but it was not like any key either of them had seen before. Its shaft was rather long and cylindrical but without any of the standard 'teeth' running along one or both edges as most keys had. One end had a rather strangely-shaped fob attached to it, which wasn't gold like the key. The material looked to be ebony or something like it. It was jet black and polished to a high shine. She turned it over in her hands. "I think it's some kind of mineral."

"May I?" Alex asked, holding his hand out.

Trudy placed the key and fob in his palm. "But what does it open, I wonder?"

"That's a question to which I have no answer." Alex held the key in his palm for a moment, but after only a few seconds, he had to place it back inside the leather pouch. Although the building was being refurbished, it was still heated, and the key and fob should have been about room temperature, an ambient twenty degrees Celsius. But instead, it was cold. So cold, in fact, that Alex thought it had been in a freezer. He reached his hand inside the pedestal, but it felt no colder inside there than it did elsewhere in the room. This was exceedingly strange. Just as he was pulling his hand out, his knuckles grazed across something that felt like paper. He gently tugged on it, and it came free from the hollow marble pedestal. "But wait, there's more," Alex said, holding it up in the air. It was rolled up and secured with more leather lacing. It wasn't paper, after all, but parchment instead.

"Oh! Let me read it, please!" Trudy said, barely able to contain herself.

Alex handed the paper to his girlfriend, and she held it out in front of herself with trembling hands. "What the heck is this? A secret code?" She turned it this way and that, puzzling over it, then offered it back to Alex, saying, "Here, you look at it."

Alex took it from her hands and studied it for a moment. "No, it's not a secret code."

"Then what is it?"

The parchment was covered in small pictures, just like what he'd been learning about in history class. "I think it's a message because these look like some sort of hieroglyphics."

CHAPTER TWENTY-ONE

Virgil Raines looked down at the outside of his front door. Deep grooves were gouged into the wooden panels. Despite the door's thickness, it looked like only a few more scrapes of its claws, and the beast would have made its way through into the house. He shivered from both the thought and the cold as he stepped down from his porch into the barnyard. The tracks he'd left just a few minutes earlier were almost filled in now. However, the prints of the creature that had been stalking him were a little fresher in the snow, and he could see where the beast followed him to his front door. When the creature had departed, it looked like it had headed directly toward the turkey barn.

He cocked the Marlin 336 and moved slowly forward into the frigid folds of the storm. He followed the animal's tracks for a few metres, but they soon disappeared, erased by the snow and wind. Unfortunately, the flashlight was doing him minimal good out here, mainly reflecting the skittering snow that surrounded him, and he clicked it off. The doors on the barn were sturdier than his front door, but he had a bad feeling that whatever was out in the snow might not be stopped by mere wooden doors.

A tremendous gust of wind battered him, almost blowing him over as he entered the no man's land between the lights of the house and the lights of the turkey barn. He stopped and peered into the swirling whiteness, completely disoriented now. With his rifle held out in front, he moved in the direction he thought the barn was located. He knew he wouldn't have enough time to aim at anything that came charging at him out of the storm and would have to fire from the hip if such a thing came to pass. After several minutes of slow progress, he saw the trees that lined the edge of his property and realised he was way off course. But then, hallelujah, faintly visible off to his right, a glimpse of brightness through the snow. Virgil grinned and breathed a sigh of relief, then began heading for the light.

The front of the turkey barn seemed untouched by anything trying to gain entrance, and he breathed a sigh of relief. Rather than going in the front door, Virgil decided to give the entire building a quick once over first to ensure that none of the other windows or possible entry points had been compromised.

Moving clockwise around the structure, things seemed fine along the left side of the barn, and the back section still appeared secure with the rear access firmly locked. He proceeded along the other side of the building and was almost to the front when he noticed one of the windows about eight feet up was pulled outward from its frame. The thing must have leapt onto the low roof of the mechanical shed next to the turkey barn and clawed the window open to gain access. Running the light over the window frame, he saw more gouges similar to his front door. "What in the hell are you?" he wondered aloud as he moved round to the entrance of the turkey barn. He readied the rifle, checking that the safety was off and then unlocked the door and pushed it open.

Chaos reigned inside the barn. Turkeys ran all over the place as they tried to hide from the thing that had come through the window. At first, he thought it was a mountain lion, but he realised after a moment it was far larger than any cougar he'd ever seen. Tan in colour, the creature was a blur of motion as it chased and brought down turkey after turkey in a bloody, feathered massacre. Virgil watched in awe as the cat prepared to take a bite out of its latest victim, a large male turkey he had taken to calling Arnold. He couldn't believe how wide the beast could open its jaws. Virgil shouted at the top of his lungs for the creature to pay attention to him and to leave his feathered wards alone. It worked—the predator stopped and stared at him with brilliant green eyes. He now had the large cat's full attention.

The beast slowly stalked toward him from the far end of the barn. It licked the blood from its muzzle and crimson-stained fangs with its long pink tongue as it advanced. Virgil blinked his eyes several times as the giant feline neared as if hoping it might disappear between blinks, but it didn't, and he chambered a round in the rifle. This was insane. He shook his head in disbelief.

Skulking toward him was a beast out of time. Massive and muscular, there was no way it was a mountain lion. He'd scared one off several months ago, and it wasn't a quarter the size of this beast. Serrated canine teeth the length of Bowie knives projected from the animal's mouth. It growled deeply then hissed at him, its short stubby tail twitching back and forth. Well-defined musculature rippled beneath its sleek pelt as it slowed its pace and lowered itself to the ground slightly as if it might launch into the air at any moment.

Still near the front door, Virgil felt the doorknob dig into his back. As the cat readied itself to leap, Raines pulled the Marlin's trigger involuntarily without trying to aim. The bullet ricocheted off of the ground in a puff of dirt, striking the wall next to the window through which the cat had entered. The predator froze and glanced to the window, startled, then it turned back to Virgil once more, another low growl emanating from its throat.

"Got your attention now, do I?" Virgil asked giddily. He chambered another round and moved toward the beast, firing again. This time, the shot wasn't as wild, and it hit the dirt just in front of the cat's paws, kicking up a small cloud of dust. All of this proved too much for the animal, and it sprung up onto the office platform overtop the mechanical room door. The sabre-toothed cat bumped his computer desk and knocked his tower pc to the ground as it moved to jump out of the window. Just as Virgil aimed another shot, the cat leapt into the stormy night.

Raines stepped back through the front door and into the blizzard. He closed the door, then pushed through the snow around the side of the building toward the mechanical room. There was a good set of fresh tracks in the snow, leading off into the forest, but he didn't know how long before they'd be covered up due to the rate at which the snow was falling. He moved into the brush a little way to see if the cat was really gone. If it wasn't, he'd take another shot at it and make sure it never came back.

The wind kicked up again, and the snow tore at Virgil as he shone the light about the ground, following the tracks. His balaclava kept blocking his vision as he moved his head about in search of the beast, and he was continually adjusting it. The brush was quite thick, and he had a hard time navigating through but soon found the tracks again and followed them. After a couple of minutes, the snow and wind proved too much, and the tracks began to disappear. Virgil moved back and forth, trying to locate the impressions again, but the snow was too heavy and the wind too quick, and they were soon erased as if the beast had never existed in the first place. He was disappointed that he couldn't track the beast and kill it. But there was still an excellent chance the animal would return for his turkeys, especially after its recent taste test.

Returning to the turkey barn, he climbed to the office loft above the mechanical room. He secured the damaged window the best he could with a few boards and an assortment of nails from his maintenance toolkit. When he was done, the turkeys had calmed down a bit, and he decided he'd better see how many casualties there were.

Blood, feathers and entrails were strewn everywhere. After a few minutes, he'd filled several large, transparent garbage bags meant for recycling with the remains of almost a dozen dead turkeys. He stacked them off to one side of the front door, not wanting to place them outside in his garbage dumpster since he didn't need to attract anything else wandering around out in this storm tonight. In the morning, he'd have to run them down to the dump.

Topping off the feed to make sure the birds had enough to eat, Virgil realised this night would be a sleepless one. He imagined he'd be out here every couple of hours to check on the birds to make sure the beast didn't come back for a midnight smorg. With a shake of his head, he dimmed the lights inside the barn and closed the door, double-checking the lock as he left.

The snow didn't seem as heavy now, and he could see a little further into the distance with his flashlight. Hopefully, the beast had fled the scene, but he still needed to ensure that the property was secure. He moved slowly through the yard toward the house, his eyes wide and unblinking. Whipping his head around to check his six, the balaclava drooped down into his eyes. He cursed and reached up to adjust it, almost wishing he'd kept his toque on instead.

Movement off to one side snapped Virgil's attention to the left. He'd let his guard down as he'd fiddle with his headgear. The beast streaked through the snow toward him, and he realised he would be too slow to bring the rifle to bear. Instead, he pivoted his arm and used the gun's stock to strike at the beast as it launched itself into the air toward him. The butt of the rifle connected with the cat's head, and it tumbled off to one side into the snow, stunned. Virgil turned to run since it was only a half dozen metres to the porch steps.

Unfortunately, the big cat was not as stunned as he'd thought, and it recovered more quickly than he would have imagined. This lack of imagination was Virgil's downfall. Mounting the three steps up to his covered porch, white-hot pain suddenly shot through his back. The feline leapt onto him, driving its two enormous canine teeth into his shoulders, penetrating both of his lungs as it did. The animal's substantial weight drove him forward to his knees, and he collapsed into the wooden stairs, his head slamming into one of the sharp corners with a hard crunch.

The cat pawed at its now unconscious prey, still quite hungry after its turkey dinner had been so rudely interrupted. With a growl, the animal clamped its teeth onto Virgil Raines' head and dragged him off into the bushes at the side of the house, eager to begin its two-legged dessert.

CHAPTER TWENTY-TWO

Celia MacKay looked down at the contents of the box and said, "They're adorable!"

"Aren't they, though?" George replied. He reached down and idly scratched one of the foundlings' ears.

"You say you discovered them in the arboretum?"

"Yup, something got in through one of the ventilation ducts from what I can see and took up residence with the coffee plants and lilies."

"Have you fed them?" Celia asked as she smiled and fawned over the babies. It had been a while since she'd had one of her own, human or otherwise.

"Nope, when I found them, I only had some pulled pork sandwich that Pattie gave me. They can't even get their eyes open yet, so I'd say they're on a liquid diet from mama for sure."

"I suppose that's true. I'll have to find something for their little tummies." She stroked one of the kitten's heads and, after a moment's silence, said, "That Pattie sure is awful nice to you."

"She knows how much I love her pulled pork, and she likes giving me samples every once in a while. You know that."

"I suppose, as long as that's all." She looked at George with concern in her eyes.

With a gentle smile, he said, "Celia, don't worry, you know my stomach belongs to you."

Seeming reassured by George's answer, she nodded her grey-haired head and asked, "Are these little guys mountain lions, cougars or pumas?"

"Those are all the same thing, dear," George advised with a sage nod of his head. "And I don't know if they are or not. They could be, but look at their tails, see how they're bobbed? Like a Bobcat's? Cougars have long tails like a lion."

"Maybe they have some Manx in them?"

"I think that's a house cat you're thinking of, dear."

"Well, in any event, I should get them something to eat. I have some milk and cream in the fridge. Maybe I'll mix a little together and see if they'll take it. I still have some bottles from when Leroy was a baby," she said proudly, referring to their adult son.

"That's a great idea." George nodded his approval and watched with a smile as his wife went off into the kitchen in search of baby bottles and cream. He looked down at the box and contemplated the infants. What were they? Were they a hybrid of a bobcat and cougar? When they mewled, he could see they currently only had their milk teeth, but their jaws seemed unusually large, enough room for some extremely large and sharp teeth, eventually. Where would he put them for the night? Not that he felt threatened by them, but what if their mama came looking for them? Of course, how would she know where they were? He supposed their mewling might attract her. However, he was several miles away from the arboretum, near Raines's turkey farm, up the western side of the valley. He didn't want to leave the kittens inside the house, but he couldn't just put them out in his unheated shed. With a nod, he decided the babies would sleep in the addition that he'd added onto their mobile home back when Leroy was only an infant, much like these kittens. It seemed like an appropriate place for them to spend the night.

Celia returned with a pair of baby bottles. "I filled them with warm cream and whole milk. These little sweeties should like it, I hope." She handed a bottle to George, saying, "Here you go, you can feed one as well." Celia gently picked up one of the large kittens, saying, "My Lord, these little angels are big-boned." She placed the cat in the crook of her arm and put the bottle in its mouth. The cat latched onto the rubber nipple and began to suck the milk and cream mixture greedily from the bottle.

George picked up the other cat and hefted it a bit, saying, "They are solid little things, aren't they?" He held the animal up in front of his face and examined the cat for a moment before nestling it in his arm. The cries from it intensified as soon as he placed the nipple of the baby bottle near its mouth, the cat no doubt smelling the milk inside. He popped the nipple in its mouth, and it began to suckle noisily.

They were silent for a moment as they fed the infant felines, the only sound, the wind kicking up and whistling around the eves of the mobile home. "Not a night fit for man nor beast out there," Celia said.

"It's pretty bad out, that's for sure. I almost missed the laneway on the way home; it's getting so thick." The bottle was empty, and as soon as George pulled it out, the kitten began to cry once more. "Man, these are hungry little guys."

"Do you think we should give them more?"

George scratched his bald head for a moment and said, "Maybe we should hold off. Let's put them down for the night, and then, if they're still complaining, we'll give them more before bed."

About a half-hour later, George and Celia had bedded down 'the twins', as Celia was calling the cubs now. George hoped she wasn't getting too attached to the animals since he would be calling animal control in the morning and have Trip Williams look after them instead.

Evening ablutions done, they were just settling in for a little late-night reading in bed when they heard a noise like fingernails drawn across a chalkboard. Celia dropped the copy of The National Enquirer she'd been reading into her lap and said, "George, what is that sound?"

The twins had been mewling up a small storm in their box in Leroy's old room for several minutes before this, and George said, "I wonder if they got out of the box?" The noise came again, and they both looked at each other.

George sighed and threw on his bathrobe, saying, "I'll go check, shall I?"

"Thank you, honey, you're the best," Celia said gratefully from the bed, the blankets pulled all the way up to her chin.

He stood in the hallway; his head cocked. The noise seemed to be coming from the addition. It sounded like someone dragging a nail down a piece of glass. However, apart from the small window, the only piece of glass in that room was the sliding glass door, currently covered with heavy drapes. When George had built the addition onto the mobile for Leroy's room, he installed a sliding glass door as a secondary exit. They had planned on using the room as a hobby room/sewing room once Leroy had grown up and moved away. Well, Leroy had grown up as they'd expected, and he hadn't lived with them for several years now. However, they'd never gotten around to turning his room into the room they had envisioned. In reality, it had just been used as a catch-all storage for the last few years. Celia was a bit of a hoarder and obsessively bought dolls and stuffies off the internet at an unprecedented rate. George had lined the wall with shelves, and they were almost all full. The way his wife was going, he'd have to build a second addition onto the mobile just for her 'addiction'.

Still inside their cardboard bedroom, the twins mewled even louder now as if excited about what lay on the other side of the sliding glass door. The squealing sound of nails on glass once again shredded their way down George's spine. Leaving the light off, he moved slowly toward the sliding glass door, his heart starting to beat a little faster in his chest as he did. The twins kicked their cries up a notch, and the scraping on the glass came again, faster and more insistent.

With one hand on the drapes, George steeled himself and whisked them aside. It was at this point that his heart almost stopped beating in his chest. With a deep inhalation of surprise, he backpedalled from the glass and stumbled over a new box of stuffies that hadn't yet made it onto the shelves. He fell backwards and landed hard on the carpeted floor, knocking the air out of himself.

"George? What happened? Are the twins all right?" Celia stood silhouetted in the doorway to the room. Another scrape of razor nails came to them, and Celia turned on the light switch near the door, then screamed and screamed and screamed.

MacKay scuttled back on his bottom to the base of the three steps that led down to the addition, shouting, "Celia! Get me my shotgun from the cabinet!" His wife fled the room and he desperately hoped it was to do what he asked.

On the other side of the sliding door, a huge cat with wickedly sharp teeth peered into the room, its breath steaming up the glass. It scraped its long claws down the glass door once more, this time pressing so hard it left white trails scored into the glass. If it kept that up, it would be into the room within seconds.

With a thud, Celia placed the stock of the shotgun onto the landing next to George, startling him. He'd just finished crawling backwards on his bum up to the top of the short flight of stairs. He stood, grabbed the gun, then turned and left the room and began moving up the hallway.

"George! Where are you going? What are you doing?" Celia shrieked.

Not saying anything, George moved to the front door of the mobile and steeled his nerves. He took a deep breath and ripped the door open, bringing the shotgun to bear on the giant cat at the same time, then pulled the trigger.

A shattering blast and blinding muzzle flash came from the shotgun as George unleashed both barrels. His aim was off, and he only succeeded in blowing a chunk out of the porch's railing that ran along the front of the mobile.

But that was enough. Startled by the loud noise at its back, the cat turned and roared at him, then bolted into the snow-filled night. George was grateful it didn't charge since he hadn't brought any spare shells and would've had to try and club the cat with the gun had it not fled.

Celia came up the hall behind him, still sobbing from fear. George closed the door and leaned against it. His wife moved into his arms, and he comforted her and told her it would be okay. Eventually, her sobs lessened. When she had calmed down somewhat, George said, "I'll go get the box of shells, and you can put on a pot of coffee—it's going to be a long night."

CHAPTER TWENTY-THREE

"So, what are you up to today? Going to do some more cleanup at the Sinclair building?" Austin asked over his bacon and eggs. It was his turn to make Saturday breakfast, and he'd gone to one of his standby favourites: an entire pack of bacon cooked on a baking tray in the oven, eight eggs, scrambled, and a half a loaf of bread, toasted. It was easy to make and nutritious, if sodium-filled because of the bacon. But it was what a growing boy like Alex needed, and boy, had he been growing. In the last eight months or so, he'd added another three inches to his height and now stood six feet, four inches tall, and was now one inch taller than his father. Most of a Saturday morning breakfast feast like this usually ended up in Alex's bottomless stomach, with Austin eating about a quarter of the food.

Over a mouthful of bacon and toast, Alex replied, "Actually, with the break in the storm, Trudy and I were thinking of doing a bit of sledding up on Gold Ridge."

"Gold Ridge? Why there?"

"Just seemed like a good idea."

"Well, you kids be careful. A lot of this snow is unstable since we've had so much recently. There could be an elevated avalanche risk. And what about the cleanup your Uncle Trip hired you for?"

"Don't worry about us. We'll be fine," Alex said, using the teenaged stock response to any questions of perceived danger. He added, "With that second storm coming in, I'll be wanting to be indoors, and I'll work like a dog to get it done over the next few days before Christmas."

"But just wait, there's more," Austin cautioned. "You were in bed when I got home last night, so I didn't get a chance to tell you then, but it looks like there's a couple of new animals running around out in our valley now."

"Well, that's where they're usually found, Dad."

"Not these animals."

"What do you mean?"

"They're new to the valley, but they're certainly not young by any means, and they're extremely dangerous."

"What? We have another Angus?" Alex's eyes went wide.

"Not quite, thankfully, but it sounds like they're going to be trouble, with one of them causing some already."

"What happened?"

Austin related the tale of the previous evening and Willy's experience on the Citrus Express. "Chief Paulson took Willy to the health centre last night." He concluded, saying. "And your Uncle Trip picked him up and took him home to spend a few days with him due to his having to get his rabies and tetanus shots."

"What? Willy got bit?"

"On the foot, after he hit one of the animals."

"Really? What did he hit?"

"We're not sure, but Chris sent photos off to her friend on the coast. And to top of all of that off, Geraldine Gertzmeyer also has something wandering around her place, which they've already identified."

"Was it another giant racoon?"

"Nope, something a little bigger. Try a Smilodon instead."

"Holy crap! A Sabre-toothed cat, seriously?

"Seriously, and it's a big one from what Chris says. So keep an eye out.

"I will for sure."

"And you might want to bring the Marlin .22 your uncle gave you for your birthday, just in case."

"That's a good idea. And don't worry, we'll be careful."

"I'm sure you will, but you know I have to worry about you since I'm the only parent you have left. And besides, your mom would probably come back and haunt me if I didn't."

"That's true. She sure did like to worry, didn't she?"

Austin smiled in remembrance of Alex's constantly concerned mother, saying, "That she did." As the boy had grown up, Patricia had been mortified over every minor scrape or bruise that he received. Of course, part of that could have been because of her medical training and the numerous years she'd spent in the nursing profession.

"Just make sure you're home before dark because that's when that second storm is supposed to hit."

"Of course, Dad. Don't worry, I won't take any risks.

***

Twisting the sled's throttle, Alex gunned the engine. Trudy clung to his broad, muscular back, and together, they shot up the mountainside toward Gold Ridge. The day was still overcast and grey, but the break in the storms had materialised just like the weather office had promised, and no snow was currently falling.

Trudy had been left in charge of provisions while he'd gathered the requisite hardware. In addition to a flashlight and first aid kit, he found a long climbing rope in the garage that his dad had received from Officer Moon. In some of the limited time off that she received, Chris had been trying to teach his dad a bit of mountain climbing before the snow had begun to fall. Since they weren't using it right now, Alex had decided they might have more use for it, considering where they were going. Not that he planned on rappelling down into darkness or anything, but he figured you never knew when you were going to need a good rope.

The day was still extremely cold, but the break in the storm had materialised like the weather office had predicted. By the time they arrived on Gold Ridge, being substantially higher in elevation, the temperature had gone from bitter to brutal. Fortunately, he and Trudy had dressed for the part of Arctic explorer, and both were well insulated from the cold thanks to numerous layers of clothing, including ski pants and thick parkas.

Alex pulled the snowmobile to a stop before a field of snow-covered scree where the cavern used to be located. There was going to be no easy way in there. Millions of tonnes of ice had come down on top of rock that had fallen during the final quake last January. But it seemed the recent tremor had added a fresh layer of ancient ice from the glacier above, which covered much of the mountain's peak.

Trudy pulled out her cell phone and brought up the photo of the map. "So, it looks like there's a spot just up there." She gestured up the mountainside a short distance.

"Yeah, I think that would be the vent that we pulled Officer Moon from. Even if it's still open, I don't feel much like trying to drop down a hole over a hundred metres deep at the moment; thanks very much anyway."

"Where's your sense of adventure?" Trudy asked.

Alex shrugged his shoulders.

"Okay, fine then, but what about this other spot here?" With one gloved finger, she pointed at another 'X' on the map near the summit.

"Let's see things with a bit more detail." Alex pulled his iPad out of his pack, which was strapped to the back of the vehicle. Its touch screen was not very responsive due to the cold, but he was able to bring the image up on the screen after a moment. After studying it for a moment, he said, "We could check that out. But after that, we should think about heading back because it'll be getting pretty late by then. My dad said the second storm front was due to be here sometime later this afternoon." Alex placed the iPad back in his pack and climbed aboard the snowmobile.

"There should still be lots of time. Let's go!" Trudy patted Alex on the back with both hands in excitement.

Twisting the throttle, Alex grinned and said, "Mush!"

CHAPTER TWENTY-FOUR

Christine brushed aside some of the snow covering the ground at the bottom of the porch steps and discovered another large spray of frozen blood. Somewhere, underneath the half-metre of snow that covered the sizable barnyard, there was no doubt more. But at least there was no snow falling. It was currently overcast, and the calm between the storms had occurred like the weather office had promised, allowing them some respite for the time being. Right now, it looked like something out of a picture postcard with a fluffy marshmallow coating over top of everything. And despite the lack of direct sunshine, she needed to wear her sunglasses when outdoors in order to see without squinting.

Margo Raines was inside the house talking to Fred Paulson, who was also in attendance at the scene today. Christine had spoken with the distraught woman herself before the police arrived and had been able to piece together a bit of what happened here. It seemed that her husband, Virgil, had never come back from the turkey barn last night. According to Margo, she'd taken a sleeping pill the night before and presumed that her husband would find his way home safely, but that hadn't happened. When she woke up this morning and discovered the empty bed next to her, she'd known there was trouble. Her first instinct was to think he was out in the turkey barn, but when she found a dozen or so dead turkeys in the barn, she decided to call the conservation office, and that's where Christine had come into the story. After Margo had swept the porch steps and found a thick layer of frozen blood, Fred had been called as well.

When Chief Paulson was finished talking with Margo, he would no doubt have the blood tested to determine if it was human. But after seeing what Willy hit last night and the prints around Geraldine's, she suspected it was. Speaking of which, there were no animal prints that she could determine in all this snow around the steps, but she hoped to check around the turkey barn in just a few minutes and maybe find some there. Sounding somewhat muted due to the heavy snow that covered everything, an approaching vehicle pulled into the courtyard behind her. She stood and turned, a smile breaking across her face when she saw the occupant of the vehicle.

Austin Murphy stepped out of his Honda Pilot into the half-metre of fresh white powdery snow. "Good thing I wore my boots," he said as he approached Christine, a smile playing on his lips as well.

"Glad you could make it. But I'm sorry to have interrupted your Saturday morning breakfast."

"Oh, don't worry about that; it ended before you called, and Alex had already rushed out the door. But thanks for your concern." Austin smiled warmly and added, "A big family breakfast was always something Alex, Patricia, and I liked to have every weekend, and the two of us like to carry it on in her honour."

"Well, I know you like family time with Alex when you can get it, and traditions are good things to continue, especially ones of remembrance. Maybe I can join you some Saturday? I promise to dress up in more than this." She laughed musically and gestured down at her dark blue uniform, then tucked a strand of long blonde hair that had come loose back under her fur cap.

Smiling again, a slight flush to his cheeks, Austin said,

"Thanks, I'd really like that." He looked around the yard and cleared his throat, and added, "With all that being said, I think meeting in circumstances like this is a tradition that we can forgo in the future, however."

"I agree," Christine said. She gestured at the blood in the snow on the steps behind her and said, "I thought you'd like to be a part of this since I believe it has something to do with what Willy hit and the beast at Geraldine's. I called Trip as well and left a message, but I forgot he's out on the plow today. At least the snow has stopped for him for now."

"That it has, but I'm sure he's got a pretty full rich day of plowing ahead of him. Larry was able to keep on top of things last night, so, fortunately, all Trip has to do is get to the side roads and other secondary routes done today.

Pointing into the nearby forest, Christine said, "Geraldine's property is only a few klicks that way. I wonder if this is going to prove to be the same predator whose print she snapped the photo of?"

"Could be a good possibility."

"Virgil's wife, Margo, said that when she went to investigate this morning, there were some dead turkeys in the barn and some prints left behind as well. Care to join me as I check them out?"

"Absolutely. But now I think that maybe I should have gone easy on the breakfast, had I known."

"You and me both," Christine replied as they crossed the courtyard to the turkey barn. "And speaking of blood and gore, I got the results back from Zelda about what Willy hit."

"Oh, really?"

"Yes, we've got dire problems."

"Well, things aren't looking too good up here, that's for sure."

"No, what Willy killed was a dire wolf."

"Dire wolf? Weren't those…"

"Extinct? Until I moved to this valley, I would have said yes. But not anymore."

The door to the turkey barn lay directly in front of them. Christine opened it and stepped through, then said, "Oh my gosh!"

Austin was close behind her and let out a soft whistle as he entered. In the middle of the floor near the door was a pile of dead turkeys in transparent garbage bags, some missing a head, a breast, or a leg. "Good Lord! How many turkeys did this thing kill?" The remaining turkeys clucked and gobbled to themselves at the other end of the barn, looking at the new strangers with curiosity.

Christine squatted down on her haunches and examined some of the prints on the dirt floor just inside the door of the turkey barn. "These look like the same tracks that Geraldine had at her place."

From behind them, a voice said, "This is getting to be a habit for you, isn't it?" Fred Paulson stood framed in the doorway, the blinding whiteness of the winter's day at his back. Like the RCMP, the Lawless Police Department had modelled their uniforms after those of their mounted brethren, and his muskrat fur hat's ear flaps were fully engaged today.

With a small smile, Christine said, "Well, animal attacks are part of my job, Chief."

Fred's white eyebrows shot up, and he said, "Actually, I mean both of you," Looking from Austin and Christine to the pile of dead turkeys, he added, "You two and man-eating creatures from out of the past seem to go together like PB & J. Last winter, it was that damned bear from hell you found, and now, Chris says we have frozen pussies from the past wandering around out here as well as the animal that bit Willy?"

Christine nodded and said, "Yeah, sorry to be the bearer of bad news." While she spoke, she had a brief flashback to her last encounter with a representative of the Lawless Police Department up on Gold Ridge not quite a year ago. Thankfully, Fred Paulson was nothing like Reggie VanDusen. His easy-going demeanour and friendly ways were a polar opposite to the ex-chief. She replied, "And speaking of which, it turns out that thing that bit Willy is called Canis dirus."

"What? We have dire wolves, too?"

"Very good, Chief!" Christine nodded approvingly.

With a slight smile, Fred said, "I still remember a few things from my high school Latin class."

"Unfortunately, we don't know how many of them there could be. Might be one, or it could be a whole pack."

"Let's hope for the lone wolf scenario," Fred replied.

"No kidding," Austin agreed, then asked, "So, which one was it here?"

"It was definitely the cat," Christine said with finality.

"Well, let's see if the tape can show us anything," Fred said.

"We have tape?" Christine asked, her own eyebrows now raised.

Fred nodded, heading toward the stairs leading up to the office. "This place is wired for sound, and video, apparently." At the top of the stairs sat an ancient Betamax hooked up to a row of four black and white monitors, two of which currently showed the far end of the barn where the turkeys were doing their sociable thing.

"Let's see if there was a tape in there." Christine eyed the A/V equipment around her with a critical eye, wondering if it actually worked properly. Well, she thought to herself, there's only one way to find out, then pressed the rewind button on the tape deck. With a clunk and a whir, the machine made a high-pitched whining noise, and the picture on the monitors began to ripple slightly as the tape rewound through the past twenty-four hours. For the longest time, the dead turkeys were the star attraction on the ageing video recorder's tape. About 2200 hours, Virgil Raines could be seen walking backwards dragging the bags of dead turkeys back to the other end of the barn where he began removing the carcasses from the bags. But then, at 2105 the night before, something came through the window of the office at their backs. It slunk through the camera's frame, then moved down the stairs to the floor below with fluid grace.

"Sweet Mother," Fred said, taking his hat off and scratching his head.

"Oh my, it's huge!" Christine watched as the big cat skulked down the stairs and then launched itself toward the turkeys at the other end of the long barn. It moved as if rippling water flowed beneath its pelt instead of sinew and bone. On another monitor, the cat flew into the frame and decapitated one turkey while ripping the leg from another with one swift motion. It then sprung into the middle of the mass of huddled birds, and chaos ensued.

A few moments later, the grainy image of Virgil Raines appeared, stepping through the entrance door. He froze, staring down the length of the barn at the cat, which was still slaughtering turkeys with careless abandon. Raines appeared to shout at the cat. It stopped its feeding frenzy and began rushing in his direction. After his first shot missed wildly, he tried again. Fortunately, this time his poor aim scared the cat badly enough that it fled from the barn the same way it came in.

The trio watched in awed silence as the ancient predator leapt up the stairs in a single bound, knocked into the computer and other electronics, then fled through the open window. On the monitor, Virgil moved back out of the barn and closed the door.

"And that's the last we've seen of him," Fred said grimly. "I've got an APB out for him, but I don't think we're going to find him in one piece, not if that blood on the front steps is anything to go by."

"I agree," Christine said. "He obviously made it back that far, but who knows where after that. And did he walk away from that injury, or was he dragged?"

Austin added, "With the amount of snow we've had, we might not find him until spring."

Christine nodded, saying, "It could have dragged him hundreds of metres in any direction."

"That's true. It is a big beastie," Austin agreed.

"How big is it, exactly?" Fred asked, preparing to put his hat back on.

With a grim smile, Christine said, "Almost one thousand pounds of pissed off pussy from the past."

CHAPTER TWENTY-FIVE

Willy had just woken up, and he was feeling ravenous. He sat upright and felt the room spin around him for a moment. Upon leaving the hospital last night, he'd felt full of piss and vinegar, ready to walk to his home last night. But after he'd eaten something at the Burger Barn, when he'd arrived back at Trip's, he'd been exhausted and only wanted to sleep. And that is what he'd done—for almost twelve hours. His muscles and joints felt a bit stiff and achy this morning, but apart from that, he felt okay. The dizziness had passed, and now his belly was growling to beat all hell.

The bedroom door was currently closed. Since he still had his t-shirt and boxers on and no one else was in the house, Willy opened it without hesitation. His heart flipped in his chest momentarily as a member of Trip's household greeted him. A large orange and white tabby cat waited just on the other side of the door. Dora was its name. At least, that's what he thought Trip had called the animal. He'd been so tired last night he was having a hard time recalling it now. The cat's greeting wasn't a warm one, however. All his life, Willy had never had any problem with animals disliking him and, in fact, felt he was almost a bit of an animal whisperer. But today, as soon as he opened the door, the cat hissed and growled at him like he was public enemy number one.

"Okay, Dora, just calm down. No one is going to hurt anyone here, I hope." It was not that he was afraid he might injure the cat but was, in fact, unsure if the animal was going to try and attack him. It stood with its back arched, tail up and ears back, spitting like a cobra.

He moved slowly out of the bedroom, the cat continuing to growl and hiss at him, but it backed out of the way as he slowly moved down the hall. "Good puss. Keep moving along. There's nothing to be angry or afraid of. It's me, Willy, animal lover."

The cat didn't seem convinced, however, and it kept up its aggressive display. Walking down the hall toward the kitchen, Willy noticed his foot was feeling much better today. He lifted it up slightly to get a better look at the side and peeled back the dressing the doctor had applied. The puncture wounds had almost healed over. Nodding his head in appreciation, he said, "Wow, that sure must be good stuff they use at the hospital."

In the kitchen, the cat moved to the other side of the room and sat down in the corner, at no point taking its eyes off Willy. After a moment, it let out a long, low, moaning howl.

"What did I ever do to you?" Willy asked but received nothing but another growl in reply. He moved to the fridge and peered inside. He wasn't sure what he wanted to eat. Usually, he'd love an egg or three, and he saw a dozen fresh eggs waiting inside. Before he'd had crawled into bed last night, Trip told him to help himself to whatever he found in the fridge. But for whatever reason, the thought of a plateful of fried eggs wasn't cutting it today. And then he saw the steak, a thick porterhouse cut, weighing almost a full kilogram.

Picking the plastic-wrapped meat out of the fridge, he sniffed at the package. It smelled bloody and delicious, and his stomach growled once more, this time louder than the cat across the room. The cat stopped growling for a moment as it heard the noise and stared at him, eyes like saucers, and it backed as far into the corner as it could get.

Willy took a cast-iron frying pan hanging from a hook over the stove and placed it on the largest element. He put the steak on the counter next to the pan then sat down at the kitchen table as he waited for the pan to heat. While he waited, his stomach continued to rumble, and the cat continued to growl.

After a few minutes, he stood once more and unwrapped the steak. He sniffed it deeply, like smelling a fine wine. Usually, he was a medium-rare kind of guy, but for some reason, today, he figured rare would be good. In fact, the longer he looked at the steak, the more he thought that uncooked and raw sounded even more appealing. He grabbed a plate from the cupboard, along with a steak knife and a fork from a kitchen drawer. With a click, he turned off the stove, then plopped the raw meat out of its styrofoam tray onto the plate.

Sitting down at the table with the platter, he gave it a good long sniff. He had never eaten raw meat in his life but felt an overwhelming urge to do so right now. Willy carved off a small piece from one corner of the steak and tentatively brought it to his lips. He touched it to his tongue and suddenly found himself pulling the chunk of meat from the fork into his mouth, and he chewed it with great relish. With that first piece eaten, he dropped the knife and fork onto the plate and picked up the steak in both hands, eschewing the cutlery altogether. He tore into it, burying his face in the slab of meat as he ripped and chewed at it with his mouth. It was so good! The blood didn't taste like it usually did. He wasn't a fan of meat that was so fresh it was almost ready to crawl off his plate, but today, he felt differently about the taste. It was almost like a fine wine mixed with dark chocolate. At least, that's how his taste buds were perceiving it today. He continued to rip and tear at the meat, and before long, he was down to nothing but the T-shaped bone in the middle.

Willy let loose a belch that sent the cat running from the room. That had been delicious, but he was still hungry. He investigated the fridge again. Cheese, bologna, leftover spaghetti and some mandarin oranges were the current choices. For whatever reason, nothing precooked turned him on right now.

He eyed the egg carton for several long seconds and then pulled it from the fridge. Taking one egg, he tapped it on the edge of the sink, tilted his head back and cracked the raw egg into his waiting mouth. He gobbled it greedily, chewing into the thick yellow-orange yoke and feeling the sliminess of the egg whites sliding down his throat. But it was satisfying, and he had another, then another, and another. Before long, the entire dozen eggs were gone, and Willy burped loudly again. Dora had been peeking around the corner of the doorway into the kitchen, but at the sound of Willy's grievous gaseousness, she darted away down the hall of the small bungalow and disappeared into a room.

"Sorry, little friend," Willy called out to the departing cat. "But don't worry! I'm not going to eat you!" Under his breath, he added, "I don't think."

With Trip out on the plow today, Willy had the day to himself. He knew he was supposed to be resting and recovering, but he just couldn't sit still. He'd tried watching a few gameshows on TV but couldn't concentrate on them. Whatever was happening to him due to that animal bite on his foot, he felt good; too good to be sitting inside watching TV, which had been one of his late dad's favourite hobbies.

At the thought of his father, Willy recalled the attack to which the man had succumbed. It had been from that hellspawn of a bear. The beast had come out of nowhere while they'd been mining near one of the largest lava tubes. Willy had been in charge of the winch, his dad dangling several feet down in the tube, pulling out sack after sack of gold ore from a thick vein that ran all the way down the shaft into darkness.

Willy Jr. had just been winching Willy Sr. up from a very successful extraction when the horror had struck. The rifle they kept handy had been back at the tent on the other side of the monster, and he'd been unable to retrieve it. He'd had no choice but to back away, leaving his father dangling. When the enormous creature arrived at the lava tube, Willy Sr. had only been partially cranked out, his head and shoulders exposed at the edge. Seeing such defenceless prey, the bear had decided to strike. As Willy Jr. had fled the cavern, he'd heard his father's single scream pierce the night before being silenced. He'd looked back briefly and watched the bear engulf his father's head in its mouth, then drag his spasming body from the lava tube. At that point, it had been Willy's turn to scream, and he'd bolted into the frigid night, never looking back until he'd eventually stumbled into Frostbite Fred's many hours later.

Now, Willy felt renewed energy and a renewed sense of purpose. He needed some retribution to make creatures like the one that had killed his father pay for what they'd done. And he knew there was at least one of the beasts left, the one that had bitten him. Throwing on his clothes and parka, he'd found a pair of Trip's boots to wear, which were a little large, but they did the job. In a closet near the boots, he found Trip's Winchester rifle and slung it over his shoulder.

Venturing out to the small barn behind the house, Willy found the other thing he was looking for, Trip's snowmobile. Living where Trip did, he had access to the forest from his back door, with the casino and Gold Ridge beyond. It wasn't snowing anymore, and the day was overcast. The break before the second storm had happened, and Willy knew he would have good weather for a little while as he tracked down and killed the creatures that had ruined his life and ended his father's. However, he needed to get something before he did that, and he needed to get it right now. Starting the sled, he revved it up and shot off into the nearby forest in search of vengeance.

CHAPTER TWENTY-SIX

It was going to be a long, grey, overcast day. Trip had started his shift on the plow bright and early at seven o'clock this morning, but it looked like he'd be hard at it until at least dinner time battling the fluffy white goodness that covered everything. Fortunately, he'd picked up an extra-large triple-triple from Timmies and a dozen honey crullers to get him through the day. He'd been trying to conserve them, but it was tough going. It was just about ten in the morning right now, and he only had six remaining. He was going to have to pace himself since he'd need the energy. Though most of the main thoroughfares were done, all the side streets and secondary roads remaining would keep his day a busy one.

Like every other vehicle in the Lawless Public Works fleet, the policy on the Citrus Express was for no passengers unless it was for training. Trip was breaking that policy now, thanks to the wiry-haired individual sitting next to him. Well, at least he was consistent—he was also violating policy to take the dog from the animal control compound in the first place. And he knew that Larry would be ticked if he found out there was a canine in the truck shedding hair all over the place.

But Spider was having a blast. He would sit attentively watching out the front window for a few minutes as they plowed their way down the road. Then, he'd move over to watch out the side window for a little while, his nose pointed toward a gap near the top. Trip had rolled that window down slightly, and the dog was enjoying sniffing the fresh air coming through the small gap. However, there was no way he was rolling it down any further since today felt even colder than yesterday. Currently, they were calling for the next storm to kick in later this afternoon, and Trip wanted to get everything as scraped down as he could for Larry this evening. He thought of Willy taking the express out, but he figured the boy should have another day or two to rest. Trip didn't mind; he found plowing to be very calming and Zen-like for some reason.

After clearing everything he could in the north end of town, he'd moved to the western side of the valley. After blowing by Geraldine Gertzmeyer's and George MacKay's place, he was now approaching the Raines's turkey farm. As he approached the lane to the farm, Fred Paulson was just pulling out with his Suburban. The chief gave a honk and a wave as he drove by, heading back into town. Up the lane, Trip spied a familiar navy-blue Dodge Ram 3500 pickup truck as well as another vehicle he recognised. He turned in and drove down the lane to see what was up.

The plow's blades were down, and he pushed back the snow as he moved up the lane. Once in the courtyard, he pulled around in a large circle, scraping things down a bit further. Trip applied the airbrake with a hiss of air and parked the truck next to Christine's Dodge and Austin's Honda Pilot. He climbed down out of the cab, then turned and reached back into it. Receiving a bonus face wash, he lifted Spider down. "All right! All right! I'm sure you must need to use the little dog's room." He wanted to let the little guy stretch his legs and have a sniff around for a few minutes while he checked things out. As soon as he put Spider down, the dog ran off with his nose in the snow, sniffing a scent he'd discovered near the house.

"Hey, Trip! Thanks for the plow. It's pretty revealing," Austin said. He stood looking at the ground that the plow's blades had just uncovered. A long streak of crimson was frozen into the ice beneath the snow.

"Holy crap, what happened here?"

"One of our new residents got a hold of Virgil Raines last night, and it didn't let go."

Stepping from out of the turkey barn, Christine said, "Hi Trip." She shook her head slightly at the frozen blood trail and said, "I wasn't sure which way Virgil had been dragged, but now I have a pretty good idea where to look, thanks to your snow removal." The direction of the blood smear indicated Virgil was dragged into the forest on the nearest side of the lot, next to the house.

"My pleasure, I guess. So, who do we have to thank for this?" He nodded at the frozen gore.

"I believe it was our friend, Smiley."

"That darn cat!" Trip said, shaking his head.

"Not anything like the one in the Disney movie, that's for sure," Austin observed.

Trip realised he'd lost sight of Spider and he whistled, then called out the dog's name.

"Spider?" Christine questioned.

Whistling again for a moment, Trip said cryptically, "I didn't want to name him Scarlett Johansson."

"Oh," Christine said, looking just a little bit puzzled.

Spider came running from around the corner of the house and let out two quick barks.

"What is it, boy?" Trip inquired.

The dog stood near the corner of the house and gave out an excited, "Erf! Erf!" as if to say, "Follow me!"

Austin observed, "I'd say your little buddy there has found something."

"What is it, little guy?" Trip approached the dog, and it ran around the side of the house once more. The snow was easily up to the little dog's shoulders, but it hopped like a bunny as it moved through the deep snow and stopped near some bushes several metres away from the house next to the forest. Pushing through the snow, Trip arrived at the spot first.

Trip called over his shoulder, "I think we've found Virgil or at least part of him." Trip called the dog to his side so Christine could move in to examine things.

"Thanks, Trip. And thanks, Spider! You are a special little guy." Christine ruffled the dog's head, and it let out a happy little 'erf', almost seeming to smile at the attention he was receiving from this pretty blonde woman.

Turning back to see what the dog had been digging at, Christine removed some of the snow with her gloved hands. "Oh my, I don't think Virgil walked away from his encounter with the Smilodon last night," Christine observed. She stepped back so Austin and Trip could see. A human leg, severed at the kneecap, lay dusted in a coating of snow on top of a pool of frozen blood.

From over near a copse of trees on the edge of the forest, Spider 'erfed' several more times excitedly.

They pushed through the snow to the group of trees. Partially covered by the branches of the pines, the snow wasn't as deep here, and it was in this place that the cat had decided to feast. Christine had to turn her head away for a moment when they arrived.

Virgil was twisted like a rag doll; his remaining limbs stretched akimbo. The leg was across the body in a very unnatural position, with one arm angling toward the house, the hand seeming to point to where Virgil wished he could have spent his evening rather than being eaten alive. The man's internal organs were gone, his abdominal cavity now only an empty hollow. Virgil's head was also MIA and could have been anywhere.

Trip suspected that the missing bits and pieces might not be found until spring, if ever. His typically rosy cheeks disappeared as the blood drained from his face. In a hushed voice, he asked, "Good God, what did it do to him?"

Recovering slightly, Christine said, "I'd say it was satisfying its hunger after being interrupted in its turkey dinner earlier."

"And Virgil became its meal instead." Austin shook his head at the sad irony.

Christine pulled out her cell phone and punched in the LPD number. "Looks like we need to get Fred back up here, and he can bring the coroner with him, too." She turned away and began moving toward her truck. "I'll get my Canon from the truck to document this as well."

Moving up the three steps to the porch, Austin paused with a sad sigh, saying, "And I'll go inside to break the news to Mrs. Raines."

"Well, good luck, guys." He nodded at Christine, then Austin, adding, "I need to get back out there and finish the secondaries." With a whistle, Trip called Spider. The dog came bounding back to him through the snow, his little tail going a million miles a minute. When he arrived, he sat obediently at Trip's side. "No time for sitting down on the job here, little guy. We need to move some snow, so let's go."

The dog looked back toward the remains of Virgil Raines and let out a low growl, then barked once.

Walking back to his truck, the dog at his side, Trip said, "I agree, little buddy. That cat's definitely bad news. I'm glad I've got you to protect me."

Spider 'Erfed' in apparent agreement and licked Trip's face as he lifted his furry friend into the Citrus Express.

CHAPTER TWENTY-SEVEN

Although she had more than enough baking to feed a small army, even after gifting some to her friend Christine, Geraldine Gertzmeyer was hard at work this morning, her oven warming the kitchen, the smell of sugar cookies filling the air.

Once the latest trays of cookies came out of the oven, she wanted to bake one more batch and then get to work on some more savoury fare. She'd picked up several items that she wanted to cook up today in anticipation of her grandson and his family's arrival. It seemed he had gotten off work a few days earlier than anticipated, and now they were driving up between storm fronts, expecting to be at her house sometime later this afternoon. Geraldine figured she'd get the lion's share of her baking duties out of the way this morning, and then she could spend more time with her grandson, his wife and their adorable little munchkins once they arrived.

After Norbert's passing several years ago, it had been hard for her around their little acreage. She'd still managed to do many things herself at that time, back when she was a youngster of only eighty-eight. But now that she was pushing the wrong side of ninety, she'd found that she needed to take things a little slower. And that meant relying on someone to take her into town for a weekly grocery shop since she had given up her driver's licence at the ripe old age of ninety. Her eyes just weren't what they used to be, and she didn't want to put someone's life at risk because of her own sense of vanity and independence. She was never a woman to rely on others and usually got things done herself. But with age encroaching upon her lifestyle more and more, she'd finally called it quits and no longer drove her car. Now, she was fortunate to have her friends to help her out.

Christine Moon had become a good friend over the last year since the young woman had come to the valley. They'd had numerous afternoon teas together, discussing life, the universe and just about everything else. Her initial assessment when she'd met the lovely young conservation officer was one of confidence, care, and kindness, and it hadn't changed since. They'd grown quite close, and the girl reminded her of herself when she was much, much younger. Everything she learned about Christine impressed her more and more. Despite the adversity from just being a woman in a male-dominated profession, the poor girl had had her fair share of troubles over the years but had overcome them all. And yet that was the thing that came through the strongest of all, the woman's dedication to her job enforcing the conservation laws to protect nature and loving what she did at the same time.

Trip Williams was another friend who had stepped up to the plate after Norbert had passed and she'd begun to slow things down. Several years back, the man had just shown up one day and had a chat with her about how things were going on the acreage. After she'd admitted that she was having more than the odd day where her spirit was willing to get things done, but her body wasn't, that had been when he'd offered to jump in.

At first, he'd come out and help feed the animals and other assorted livestock that she'd had at the time. Then, thanks to his connections through animal control for the city, he'd also helped her to eventually find homes for all of her 'children', the rescued animals for which she and Norbert had loved and cared. And so, Trip, like Christine, had been a godsend in her life. Between the two of them, they took her into town once a week for groceries. Plus, she loved to go out for lunch, and when each of her friends alternated their weeks to help her shop for provisions, she treated them out to whatever they wanted at one of the many fine eating establishments in the local area.

Thinking of the young conservation officer, it also got her pondering the prints she'd seen on her property which she'd confided with Christine about. After the most recent storm last night, she'd bundled up and swept off some of the snow that had blown onto her porch. That's when she'd seen them—more tracks. But this time, not as big as the one she'd shared with Christine. It was possibly a different animal but still sizable, like an extremely large dog. She'd taken a picture on her iPhone and meant to give a copy to her young friend. Whatever the creature was, it had been so bold as to scratch around the exterior door to her pantry, gouging some of the wooden frame as it tried to get into her goodies.

When Norbert had been alive, he'd done some major renovations on their homestead over the years. One of them had been adding a walk-through pantry in her large, country-style kitchen. Not only could she walk through into the dry goods pantry, but she could continue right through into a cool room, which Norbert had insulated for temporary storage of root vegetables brought in from the cellar of the barn. Beyond the cool room door was another door that exited out onto the covered porch that ran around the house. This made it easy to offload purchased groceries without going all the way through the house into the kitchen. It was also a wonderful place to dry age roasts she'd purchased from the butcher, letting them hang for up to eight weeks sometimes, depending on the cut of the meat.

She had also been storing her extra cookie dough in the cool room since she had no room in the fridge at the moment. Because of all the food in there, one of the room's additional features was a self-latching door that would eventually pull itself closed. That way, the door couldn't be left open accidentally and attract any wildlife lurking out in the forest.

Lost in thoughts of cookie dough, munchkins and man-eating

creatures, Geraldine moved through the dry goods pantry to access a batch of pecan chocolate chip cookies in the cool room that she'd whipped up yesterday. The dough had been relaxing for over twenty-four hours now and was ready to go. She pressed the handle on the heavy, insulated door and began to push it open.

It was at this moment that her gloriously unpredictable osteoarthritis decided to give her a blast of eye-watering pain. Geraldine cursed under her breath and began to step through into the room, then suddenly froze when she saw what was already there ahead of her.

A black hound from hell, that was the only way her brain could describe what she was seeing. A huge, black and grey dog-like creature was currently gnawing away on one of her dry-aged ribeye roasts just coming up on its fortieth day ageing in the cool room. Her inner sense of self-preservation was temporarily overridden by her sense of good food going to waste, and she cried out at the creature, "Get your drool-drippin' jaws off of my beef!"

Somehow, the animal had gotten the outer door latch open and wandered inside only to have the door close behind it, trapping itself. But by doing so, it found itself surrounded by more food than it had no doubt seen in its entire life and had settled down to feast. At Geraldine's commotion, the beast did not flinch but merely froze and then slowly turned toward her with a growl, as if it knew no fear.

Geraldine Gertzmeyer realised she had mere seconds to live if she did not act immediately. She took a deep breath to steel herself from the upcoming arthritic pain that her actions would create. But she had to endure that pain unless she wanted to feel the once in a lifetime agony of being eaten alive by the creature standing before her. She reached for the door to yank it closed, her hands already feeling the pain.

CHAPTER TWENTY-EIGHT

The storm had let up overnight, and the new day was incredibly white. Everywhere Franklin Pearce looked, a thick layer of snow covered the trees, cars, houses and roads. It was still abysmally cold outside, but at least the break in the storm had happened as expected.

Getting off shift late last night, he'd had a short sleep and then got up early so he could get down to business. Today, he was a man with a plan. He was off-duty and dressed for success, wearing a suit and tie, his hair slicked back and a shit-eating grin on his face. Overtop of all that goodness, he was wearing his winter camouflage hunting suit. Apart from keeping him warm, because the snowsuit was all white, it would help camouflage him as he went about his morning's list of priorities.

It was now a little after ten o'clock in the morning, and he'd just finished 'investigating' Roxanne Rooney's house and garden shed. That was what Franklin liked to call it, 'investigating'. It sounded so much better than 'breaking and entering'. Like many people in the Kootenays, Roxanne worked Tuesday to Saturday, taking Sunday and Monday off. This had worked out well for Franklin since this week, Saturday was his day off.

Once the woman had left for work, he'd stealthily entered

through an unlocked window and proceeded to go through everything inside of her house, and that included her lingerie drawer. It was not that he expected to find anything there, but Franklin was always of the opinion you could tell a lot about a person by going through their underwear. It always seemed to be the place that people thought no one would ever look, and they hid their most intimate objects or hidden fantasies in these drawers. At least, that had been his experience in some of the other houses he'd 'investigated' around Lawless over the last little while. And judging by some of the PVC and leather clothing along with the fur-lined handcuffs he'd discovered in Roxanne's drawers, she seemed to be a woman of hidden talents.

After going through the rest of the house, Franklin had moved to the shed and forced his way inside. That girl really needed to get a better lock on the door since he'd been able to gain entry through the oldest trick in the book. Or, in this case, the oldest trick in his wallet since he'd used his credit card to pop the lock. Once inside, he'd dug through the boxes and other assorted shed crap that the woman had stored out there but had found nothing resembling gold ore.

He'd assisted his Uncle Reggie in moving some of the gold out of the cavern before everything went south with the bear and the earthquake. Initially, the gold had been stored at the back of Reggie's garage under some tarps. Franklin still remembered his bitter disappointment when he'd gone back to the house after Reggie's disappearance, ready to claim the gold as his own, only to discover all of the ore gone. Someone had moved it, but he didn't know who. However, he had some suspects.

As part of his quest for the gold, Franklin had investigated the houses of other people involved with the cavern last winter, including Trip Williams, Austin Murphy and Christine Moon. His searches of their properties had yielded nothing, as he'd expected, and they were all just as goody two shoes as they seemed— bog-standard boring Canadians. But Roxanne's house had proved an exception as well as the most interesting thanks to the bondage clothing and 'equipment' he'd found. So now, he wanted to get to know her a little better, both because of the potential gold she may be harbouring as well as his discoveries in her drawers.

When VanDusen had gone missing at the cavern along with his gold, Franklin had made it his mission to check out everything and everyone who'd had anything to do with the operation up on Gold Ridge. He'd gone through his Uncle Reggie's personal papers, computer and emails, and had sent out several email queries. One had been to a man named Angel Oritz, the brother of the 'security specialist', Manny Oritz, who had disappeared up at the cavern as well. Franklin knew Angel had worked with his brother on occasion in Lawless over the years, so he figured it couldn't hurt to send out an email to him to see if Manny had shared any information with him. At the same time, he gave Angel a few leads, hoping his criminal wherewithal might shake things up a bit and prove helpful in locating the missing gold. It wasn't that Pearce expected any of these other people to know much about the cavern or that he'd find any of the gold going that route, but he figured it couldn't hurt to cover all the bases.

Right now, Franklin was on his way up to the Golden Nugget Casino to have a little chat with Roxanne Rooney. The road up to the resort was relatively well-plowed, with the corners sanded aggressively, as the local road maintenance department was prone to do. As a result, he'd made it up the hill in record time and had just driven by the Vegas-style mock monuments that surrounded the entrance to the resort.

Pearce pulled his Jeep YJ into the casino parking lot, then stepped out into the crisp morning. Shrugging out of his camouflage snowsuit, he stuffed it under the YJ's small rear bench seat, then pulled on a long, black leather overcoat. Along with his slicked-back hair and dark glasses, the coat perfected his subconscious impersonation of Neo from the Matrix.

It looked fairly quiet up here this morning, the only other vehicle in the lot belonging to the local retirement home. After the destruction of the casino's lobby by the monster bear, a remodelling of sorts had been done, and the entrance now sported even more glass and steel than it ever had before. The numerous sheets of tinted glass reflected the brilliant white of the surrounding winter's day perfectly, perhaps a little too much so. Despite his dark glasses, he almost needed to shield his eyes as he approached the building.

A sour smile on his face, Franklin strode through the airlock-style dual doors and took in the plethora of decorations that seemed to be everywhere inside the lobby. Though not quite at the same level of curmudgeon as Ebenezer Scrooge, he was almost as bitter about the holiday as the fictional old usurer had been. He muttered, "Bah! Humbug," under his breath as he crossed the lobby.

Whistling softly to himself, Franklin waited for the elevator to take him to the second floor and the offices contained therein where he'd find the object of his visit, Ms. Roxanne Rooney. Though he despised the Christmas holidays and all of their commerciality, he had to grudgingly admit, the resort had done a fantastic job. The lobby looked like a winter wonderland. Silver tinsel and bunting hung everywhere, with mini coloured LED lights strung amongst them. In one corner of the lobby, a massive tree sat, bedecked with all the requisite ornaments. Centred underneath its boughs, the 'Million Dollar Slots' machine was ready to take as many loonies and toonies as people were willing to pump into it.

The elevator arrived with a ping, and Franklin stepped on board. He turned to face the lobby as the doors slid shut. The front desk clerk across the way glanced over at him idly. He flashed his toothy grin that passed for a smile and watched as the girl went back to the magazine she was leafing through, the bored expression on her face unchanged. The doors slid shut, and Franklin's smile dissolved into a grim line as he thought of what he needed to do to get Rooney on board with his little plan.

The frosted glass door of the casino offices had been updated to reflect the fact that Ray Chance was no longer general manager. The new manager's name was now gilded on the front door instead, Mr. Ethan Chance. Ray's son had moved back to town to take over the business, now that his dad had drunkenly stumbled off into oblivion. Franklin had gone to school with Ethan, and he'd never met a more dishonest person, apart from himself that was. Yes, Ethan followed in his dad's footsteps for sure. He even abused alcohol like his dad, but not to the same extreme. Of course, Ethan was young yet, only thirty-five, the same as him, so he still had plenty of time to work on his vices.

"Hello, Red," Franklin said as he entered. He removed his overcoat and hung it on a coat rack next to the door.

Roxanne finished touching up one of her dark crimson nails and looked up at Franklin, smiling sweetly. "Good morning, Constable Pearce. Did you have an appointment to see Mr. Chance? Because he's not going to be in until eleven o'clock this morning."

"Actually, I'm here to see you." He smiled and removed his dark glasses.

"Little ol' me? Whatever for?"

"Well, I'm not here in an official capacity, so don't panic." He flashed his grin quickly, then continued, "Actually, I was hoping you might be close to getting a coffee break?"

Roxanne's eyes widened in askance.

"I have a business proposal for you." Franklin smiled again, using all of his teeth this time.

Red-tinted lips curving into a smile of her own, Roxanne said, "You're in luck. I have one coming up in just a few minutes, in fact."

Franklin smiled widely as he held the frosted door open for Roxanne. "What a coincidence! Well, let's head down to the coffee shop, and I'll tell you all about it. I think you'll like it. It's a real golden opportunity."

CHAPTER TWENTY-NINE

After quite a bit of cutting back and forth as they climbed, Alex
and Trudy finally arrived at the other side of the snow-capped
peak where the glacier rested on its mountaintop throne. A sizable
field of ice stretched out behind it, one that had survived several
ice ages. Numerous cracks and fissures appeared in its aged
surface as it spread out toward another peak several kilometres
away. Traversal of that area would be impossible due to the gaps
in the ice.

"Let me see the map," Alex said, removing one glove and
holding his hand over his shoulder. Trudy complied and plopped
her phone into his waiting digits. After studying the map, he said,
"Thanks," and handed it back to his girlfriend. Fortunately, it
didn't look like they were going out on the icefield. He started up
the sled and manoeuvred them toward something a bit nearer,
where the glacier met the back of the mountain.

At first, Alex didn't think they'd seriously find anything, but
as he piloted the snowmobile closer to where he thought the map
was referring, he saw that he was indeed correct, and that his
great-great-grandfather's map-making skills were spot on. The
ground sloped down quite steeply just in front of their
snowmobile's skis. At the bottom of the slope, it levelled out
against the side of the mountain next to the glacier. Quite a few

large chunks of ice were scattered around here due to a substantial portion of the glacial wall breaking away, exposing the mountain behind. Now, in the gap between the blue of the glacier and grey stone of the mountainside, the dark opening of a new cavern yawned wide before them, beckoning them inside.

***

"Who are they?" Angel asked, nodding his head. Following the prompting of Jerry's GPS receiver, they had arrived at the site of the cavern's buried entrance just moments before, only to find other people already there. It looked like the other two had come from the direction of the casino, opposite to the way they had come. Just at the edge of a small group of trees, Jerry and Angel were out of sight of the other party in question.

"I'm not sure," Jerry shook his head. At the distance they were from the pair, it was hard to determine precisely who they were. The taller of the two, a man, stood to one side of the snowmobile. A smaller person, presumably a child or woman, sat on its padded seat while the man pulled what looked like an iPad from a backpack and consulted it. After a moment, he returned the electronic device to the pack strapped to the back of the sled. Interestingly, a rifle was also secured there. Climbing back aboard, the man started the snowmobile up once more, and after a couple of quick revs, began piloting the sled up toward the backside of the mountain peak where the glacier rested.

"Well, they could be here for the same thing we are, so let's follow them. It looks like they know something we don't." Angel had learned many things over the last twenty-four hours and was always keen to learn more. His captive had been very forthcoming in divulging everything that had happened up in this neck of the woods over the last year or so. Angel was particularly interested in the part about the gold, more so than the man-eating monster that supposedly came from this now-sealed cavern. The riches contained within its depths had to have been the reason his brother had been so excited to do the job up here. And it must have been a tremendous amount of money since Manny had mentioned in the email how this would probably be his last job, and then he was retiring. With his brother now dead, and since Angel was blood, he figured that made any payment due to Manny, now payable to him. But since almost everyone involved in the scheme was now dead, it might be hard to extract payment from any of them. However, from what he understood, quite a bit of gold had already been mined from here, and he wanted to know what happened to it.

With the other sled out of sight for a minute or so, Angel started their snowmobile. He didn't have to worry about Jerry at the back causing him any problems since his hands were bound together and then tied to the sissy bar at the back of the snowmobile. Angel kept his revs low and slow since he didn't want to announce the fact aloud, so to speak, that he was following the people on the other sled. The tracks led back and forth as they climbed the mountainside, and eventually, they found themselves on the other side of the ridge, the glacier stretching out before them.

The other snowmobile was parked near the summit, just up ahead, its riders no longer in sight. Angel paused for a moment and pulled his Glock 17 from his pocket and ejected the magazine. After a quick check, he jammed the magazine home and stuffed the pistol back in his pocket. The other sled had packed down the snow enough for Angel to keep low, follow its trail and move to the top of the ridge to dope things out. A darkened entrance to a cavern lay at the bottom of the slope. Part of the glacier had crumbled away, exposing this new entrance to what lay underneath the mountain.

Angel slipped and slid back down to the sled where Jerry still sat. "All right, amigo, I am going to cut you loose. There's an entrance just down the slope on the other side. You and I are going to check it out and follow those people just ahead of us to see what they're up to. And don't forget what I have with me in case you get any ideas." Angel patted the pocket of his parka that contained the Glock.

"I don't think you need to worry about that. You should be more concerned with what might be inside there with those people."

"What do you mean?"

"I told you on the drive up here, there was a monster bear and other things that have come out of that cavern."

"Yeah, but you said your friends killed it."

"That they did. But there were other things inside there, and I don't know if they're still alive or not."

"Well then, I guess we're going to find out, amigo." Angel removed a small backpack from the back of the sled and handed it to Jerry. "Here you go, you can carry this for a little while." After Jerry had shrugged into the pack, Angel said, "You first." He nodded his head up the slope toward the other snowmobile, then tapped his pistol pocket again.

Jerry reluctantly took the lead. The snow where the other sled had driven was partially compacted but still rather hard going. Eventually, they made it to the top of the slope and gazed down into the cavern entrance. Feeling both excited and uneasy, Jerry said quietly, "This looks like it might lead to the same set of caverns that contained that gold I told you about."

Angel smiled and said, "That's the sort of good news that is going to get you out of this situation alive."

With Jerry still in the lead, they stumbled and slid down the slope to the bottom. The other people were still nowhere in sight. Outside the darkened entrance, Oritz reached into the pack on Jerry's back and grabbed a couple of flashlights they'd picked up at the hardware store. Actually, it had been Angel who picked them up at the Home Hardware store while Jerry had sat trussed up in the truck's passenger seat outside.

Oritz handed a small LED light to Jerry, and for himself, pulled out a six-cell Maglite, saying, "As much as I'd want to give you something bigger, I couldn't trust you not to bean me on the head with the thing the first chance you got. Isn't that right, amigo?"

Jerry gave a slight shrug but said nothing. He clicked on his LED light and shone it into the cavern, then moved slowly into the darkness.

"That's right, slow and steady," Angel said in a hushed voice as he trailed behind Jerry, one hand holding his flashlight and the other on the Glock in his pocket.

The inside of the cavern was vast. Jerry's LED did a good job of illuminating things in their immediate vicinity, but only Angel's Maglite pierced the gloom. In front of them, a large underground lake stretched off into darkness. "Madre de Dios! This place is huge!" Angel said, shaking his head.

Long stalactites hung from the ceiling over the lake, dripping here and there into the water. The further inside they moved, they saw some light still being provided, but it wasn't from the entrance at their back, nor was it from their flashlights; no, this light was from the lake itself. Colourful fish darted here and there, partially illuminating the depths of the hidden lake from their own internal glow. However, it was the bioluminescent algae that covered the shore and side of the lakebed that provided most of the light. It ran down the sides of the deep lake, eventually fading into blackness.

A ledge ran along the shore of the lake. To the left, part of the ledge had crumbled away into the water, making it appear a little difficult to traverse. While it may have been navigable that way, Angel settled on the easier route to start and followed the ledge to the right. At its end, they arrived on a sandy shore.

"Oh my God!" Jerry said suddenly. A human skeleton lay just up ahead. The head was missing, and the rest of the body had been

196

stripped of flesh, with only tatters of clothing remaining on the corpse. Next to the remains lay another skeleton, this one an animal. It looked like a large dog at first, but then Jerry saw the long, serrated canine teeth and knew otherwise. Shell casings lay on the ground nearby. It appeared someone had blown part of the animal's skull off with a shotgun, presumably after it attacked the person whose remains it now lay beside.

A silver flask lay in the sand several feet from the body. Angel picked the flask up and sniffed it. Wrinkling his nose, he said, "It smells like brandy." He gestured with his light for Jerry to take the lead, and they moved toward an exit from the cavern that lay directly ahead next to a small steaming stream. As they stepped through, Angel saw a thick vein of precious yellow metal swirling through the walls of the tubelike tunnel up ahead. Out loud, Angel said, "Manny, my brother, now I see why you were going to be so well paid. But don't you worry, hermano, I'll make sure I get both our shares of the action here."

Looking at the swirl of gold disappearing down the tunnel ahead, Jerry added, "Be careful what you wish for around here."

CHAPTER THIRTY

Trip got himself situated in the Express, finally ready to continue his plowing, when his city cell phone began to ring. According to the caller ID, it was George MacKay from the community complex arboretum. Trip wondered if there was a problem in the mechanical room. When he'd bumped into George at the Gas 'n' Gulp last week, he'd mentioned something about a leaky seal in one of the pumps. Perhaps it was worse than he thought? He pressed talk and said, "Good morning, George! How's every little thing?"

"Morning Trip," George replied. "Things have been interesting, to say the least."

"Really, how so?" Trip started the truck and began moving back down the lane.

"Well, you need to come to my place and see. The reason I'm calling is that this is an animal control call."

Trip's heart began to beat a little faster at those words, and he asked, "What animals are you having problems with?"

"Best if you just drop by," George replied but would say no more.

"Well, you're in luck. I'm in the neighbourhood. Just down the road at one of your neighbours, in fact."

"Really? Where?"

"Virgil Raines's place. They had some serious issues up here last night."

"Oh no! I hope everyone is okay?"

Trip didn't want to go spilling the beans too soon before the attack at the Raines farm was made public knowledge and said, "I can't say anything officially at this point."

"Oh, wow. Okay. Well, I have something that I think you'll want to see. And something to tell you that will grab you by your short and curlies."

That was not something that Trip needed to hear, considering the current situation. His short and curlies were in no immediate need of grabbing by George or anybody else. With a small sigh, he said, "I'll be by your place in just a couple of minutes, okay?"

"Great, thanks a lot, Trip. See you when you get here."

"You bet, buddy." Trip hung up the phone. Was the thing that had happened at George's place related to the incident at Virgil's?" George and Celia were only a couple of properties away from the Raines's place. Had the beast from Virgil's paid George a visit? Pulling out onto the road, he supposed he was going to find out pretty quick.

A couple minutes later, he pulled into the MacKay laneway with the Express, giving it a quick plow as he moved down toward the MacKay's mobile home. George was standing on his front porch, waiting, a haunted look in his eyes. Apart from giving Trip a quick glance and a wave as the truck pulled up to the house, his eyes seemed to be looking everywhere at once as if something were stalking him and might jump out from behind a snow-covered bush at any moment.

Killing the engine on the Express, Trip hopped down, telling Spider to stay and wait in the truck for him. The dog whined a couple of times, then lay down in Trip's still warm seat. Placing his head on his paws, the little hairball proceeded to give Trip 'the look'. It was that look that every dog owner the world over knew so well—big brown puppy dog eyes, almost tearful at their owner's departure. "Sorry, little buddy, but you need to wait here for a minute."

The dog gave a slight 'erf' and whined again. Trip closed the door, still feeling the 'you've abandoned me' vibe that Spider seemed so good at summoning into his eyes.

"Hey, Trip!" George moved to his front door and waved, saying, "C'mon inside. We don't want to stand around out here."

Trip looked around the yard as he approached the trailer. Near the steps were prints in the snow that looked way too familiar, especially after coming from the Raines turkey farm just now.

George held the door open, and Trip stepped inside, saying, "Thanks for coming so quickly, Trip."

"As I said, it's not a problem, George. I was just down the road."

"Yeah, you mentioned that. Is there any more you can tell me right now about what happened?" He ushered Trip into the living room of the double-wide mobile home.

"I can't say much, but..." Trip looked around the immediate vicinity and asked, "Where's Celia?"

"She's napping."

"So early in the day? Is she okay?"

"We didn't get much sleep last night."

"Okay, I didn't want to worry her if she overheard what I had to say."

"Too late for that; she's been worried since last night. That's why she didn't get any sleep."

"Sorry to hear that."

"Yeah, me too." George shook his head sadly.

"I can't say much, just that there was an attack at Virgil's place, and…"

George's eyes widened, and he interrupted, saying, "No, really? Was it Virgil?"

Trip nodded. "I can't say any more. Just keep it under your hat for now."

"Will do. And I think I know what did it."

"What?"

"Follow me." George led Trip down the short hall of the mobile, past a closed door where Celia was presumably napping. George entered the addition, walked down the three small steps into the room, then moved to the glass sliding door. "It was the same creature that did this." He pointed to the lower half of the door. The other side of the glass was scored by dozens and dozens of long scratch marks. George added, "I'll bet it was probably at the Raines's place looking for food so it could make milk to feed to our new houseguests."

"Houseguests?" Trip inquired, eyebrows raised.

George moved to a cardboard carton pushed partway

underneath a desk with a tan towel across the top. In a gentle voice, he said, "They just fell asleep an hour ago. They were up all night as well." George pulled the box out slightly and tugged back the covering, revealing two good-sized kittens that matched the colour of the towel. They lay sleeping deeply, their bodies intertwined, looking like one tan blob with two heads and multiple limbs instead of two separate beings.

"Oh my God. Are those what I think they are?"

Giving his head a slow nod, George said, "That they are. And I need you to take them off my hands so I can have peace of mind. Twice last night, their mama came back looking for them, but I was ready for her with my Mossberg." He looked to a corner of the room where the shotgun leaned. "I need to try to have a quick nap before heading into the arboretum to get stuff ready for tonight's reopening, and it would be nice not having to worry about getting eaten alive in my sleep."

"Well, I can absolutely take them off your hands and put them up in one of our suites at the kennels."

"That'd be great. Thanks, old friend." George patted Trip on the shoulder. "When I get into town later, I want to double-check everything at the arboretum since their mama might come back there looking for them."

"Good point. Keep me posted, George." Trip draped the towel back over the box of kittens and picked it up gently.

They moved back toward the front door, Trip's arms loaded down with the carton containing the 'kids'. George opened the front door and followed Trip out to the Citrus Express.

"Celia is in love with these two, but I'm going to let her sleep instead of waking her up to say goodbye. She can come to visit them at the yard, can't she?"

"Any time she wants," Trip replied.

George pulled the driver's side door to the truck open for Trip and then jumped back, his hand over his heart. "Holy man! That dog of yours just about gave me a heart attack!"

"Sorry about that. I forgot the little guy was in there. George, I'd like you to meet Spider."

The small wiry-haired dog gave out a small 'erf' and began wagging its tail.

Reaching in and scruffing the dog's head, George said, "Nice to meet you, too, little friend."

Trip handed the box with the cubs to George, then climbed into the truck. He reached down and took the box from George and placed them in the foot area of the passenger seat. Spider sniffed at the box with great interest and then let out a low growl. "I'll bet you recognise that scent, little buddy. But don't worry, they're not dangerous, yet." Not entirely convinced, the dog lay down on the seat overlooking the box and let out a slight whine.

With a slap on the side of the truck, George said, "Thanks again, Trip. I hope you lock them up in a safe place. Because I can guarantee to you, their mama is gonna come looking for them."

"Shouldn't be a problem, buddy." Trip closed the door and gave a quick salute to his friend, then slowly drove in a circle around the yard, giving it a quick plow so George would have one less thing to do when he got up from his nap.

Speaking of naps, the two babies were still sleeping, and Trip decided to let them be for now. He figured he'd try to get a bit more plowing done and then drop the kittens off at the yard and put them up in one of the pet suites. However, he wondered about their mother, who was searching for them, as George had mentioned. Was any place a safe place from a distraught sabre-toothed cat wanting her babies? He didn't know and supposed he was going to find out. With one eye on the forest as he drove, Trip continued his snow removal duties.

CHAPTER THIRTY-ONE

Franklin pulled the chair out for Roxanne in the casino's Gold Strike Coffee Shop and said, "Allow me."

"Thank you." Roxanne sat at a slight angle, allowing room for her to cross her shapely legs. She noted that fact was not lost on Franklin.

Sitting down across from Roxanne, Franklin said, "I'm going to make you an offer you can't refuse."

"Who are you, Vito Corleone?"

"Seriously, you won't be able to refuse it."

"Why is that?"

With a broad, white smile, Franklin said, "Because if you do, I'll place you under arrest." He waved the waitress over.

"Really? On what charge?" Roxanne raised her delicately arched eyebrows in question.

Franklin held a finger up to pause the conversation as the waitress came over, then ordered a couple of coffees and a couple of cinnamon buns for each of them. The waitress nodded and smiled, then went to place the order. "They have really good cinnamon buns here, don't they?"

"I wouldn't know," Roxanne replied with a slight shake of her head. "I'm not a fan of cinnamon buns."

"What do you mean? You've worked here for how many years now, and you've never tried the cinnamon buns?"

"Four, and no, I don't eat sweets."

"Really? I heard you had quite the sweet tooth."

"What are you talking about?"

"My Uncle Reggie kept you supplied with some pretty sweet things now, didn't he?" Franklin tilted his head slightly to the right as he posed the question.

"I don't know what you mean." Roxanne gave a slight shake of her head, her long chandelier style earrings tinkling musically.

"Oh, come on now. Let's not play any games here. We both know that you had a little business and pleasure deal going on with Reggie. He was always bragging about the little hottie that he kept on the side. And I recently discovered that hottie was you." He pointed one finger at her from his tented hands.

"Did you now? And how can you prove that? Do you have any evidence?"

"I would if I could find the gold you stole."

"What gold?" Roxanne batted her eyelashes at Franklin, raising her eyebrows in question.

"The gold I helped my uncle move from the cavern up on the hill. The very same gold that I helped him store in his garage." He paused for a moment, then added, "And if you say, 'What cavern?', I'll arrest you right now."

Roxanne uncrossed her legs, leaned forward and said in a voice from which all attempts at pleasantry had vanished, "Okay, slick, what do you want."

"I want half of what you stole from Reggie's place."

"What?" Roxanne replied a little too loudly.

The waitress came by with their orders and placed two coffees and two huge cinnamon buns in front of them. Franklin nodded and thanked the waitress. He continued speaking as he opened a couple of plastic capsules of coffee creamer from a small dish on the table and poured them into his cup. "No, not what, half. Is there a problem with this proposal? Remember, I have certain evidence that may prove interesting to law enforcement officials."

"Evidence? Well, I'm sure whatever evidence you may have would also implicate you, am I right?"

Now it was Franklin's turn to lean forward. "Listen, Red, we both know there's plenty enough gold for everyone, and there's still plenty more up there to be had, as far as I know. But after that quake, it's anybody's guess as to how to get access to it."

"Even if I believe you, and even if I had any of this gold, why should I help you?"

"Like I told you, I've got some proof." Franklin pulled a strip off his cinnamon bun and stuffed it in his mouth.

"Proof of what? That your uncle was partial to younger women? Most men are. That's not a crime. And even if there was gold, who's to say he didn't promise me some, anyway?"

"All I'm trying to do is get my fair share." Franklin flashed his toothy grin once more.

"Your fair share?" Roxanne laughed at this. "What makes you in any way entitled to your uncle's money or any share of it?"

"Because I helped him haul it out of the cavern down the hill. With him passing on, and not having any kids, that makes it mine."

"I don't think that would stand up in a court of law."

"Listen, I'll make you a proposal."

"Well, make it good. I've never had a guy propose to me before." Roxanne sat up a little straighter in her chair."

"You're ex-boss."

"Ray Chance, what about him?"

"He also had a share of the gold."

"Okay," Roxanne said haltingly. "What if he did? So did the mayor, Bob Nichols.

"I know." Franklin grinned.

"What? How would you know?"

"Since the mayor was missing and presumed dead, I knew he'd no longer have any use for the gold, just like your ex-boss. So, I entered Nichols's place to verify that was an accurate assumption."

"You mean you broke in," Roxanne said, a small smile playing at the corners of her red lips.

"It turned out to be worth my while. There was a substantial amount of gold stashed in his basement. However, I don't think that was all of it. I think he also hid some elsewhere, and I have a

208

few thoughts of where to look. And, by the way, that is so unkind. I like to think of it as, not a B&E, but more of an unauthorised search for criminal proceeds."

"Semantics," Roxanne said, then sipped her coffee.

"That may be, but apart from your ex-boss's house, the only locations I know where gold was secreted away was Nichols's place and Reggie's place. And since I cleaned Nichols out of his gold, that only left Reggie's place. As you know, that proved to be a bust. So, then I checked out your place and..."

"What? You searched my house?"

"You have excellent taste in lingerie, by the way."

"I should call the cops."

Spreading his arms wide, palms facing up, Franklin said helpfully, "I'm already here."

"Yeah, well, what if I told Chief Paulson about your little expeditions into other people's houses?"

"You have no proof."

"So why don't you just go over to Ray's house and get the gold?"

"Well, since his son, Ethan moved in almost right away after his father's death, that's why. I haven't been able to get near the place because of his security. That's why I need help with that job."

"Excuse me? You want me to help you break into Ethan Chance's house?" Roxanne lowered her voice as the waitress came by, asking if they wanted anything else. She saw that Roxanne hadn't finished her cinnamon bun and asked if she'd like to take it to go. Roxanne said yes, and the server took her bun to have it wrapped.

Franklin jammed the last bit of cinnamon bun into his toothy mouth and said, "Mmm, Delicious. And in answer to your question, yes. But not actually break in, but more of a distraction on your part. I'll take care of the illegal entry while you keep Ethan busy."

"What? How will I do that?"

"By using what God gave you, obviously." Franklin looked down at Roxanne's smooth, shapely legs jutting out from under the edge of the table.

"Are you crazy? I have to work with the guy afterwards."

"Well, you figure out the details on your end. Besides, if we get everything that's coming to us, you won't need that job after this."

Roxanne leaned forward again, saying, "What, you have someone who can move the gold?"

"I know someone, yeah." Wiping his mouth, Franklin stood and dropped a twenty-dollar bill on the table.

"I'll be by tonight to pick you up." Pearce turned and began to walk away from the table.

"Wait! Tonight?"

Looking back over his shoulder, he said, "Seven o'clock sharp," then turned and exited the restaurant into the lobby of the casino.

The waitress returned with the bill and Roxanne's cinnamon bun, asking if she wanted more coffee. Roxanne thanked her but declined. With a nod and a smile, the server removed Franklin's tableware along with the bill and cash, saying, "I'll go get some change."

Shaking her head, Roxanne said, "Keep it." With a large smile, the waitress thanked her and departed.

Roxanne Rooney sat staring at the now plastic-wrapped bun, lost in thought. She'd wanted to find someone to move the gold hidden in her garden shed. And now, she apparently had the opportunity to do so, but not quite in the manner she'd wanted. Coercion was not something under which she liked to work. But for now, she decided to go with it and see where things may lead. If Franklin had some of the mayor's gold like he said he did, and even if she shared a little of what she had, in conjunction with Chance's gold, she'd probably still come out of this deal ahead of the game. She stood, taking her uneaten bun with her and wondering what she'd wear for her upcoming 'date' tonight.

CHAPTER THIRTY-TWO

After she finished taking pictures of the scene of the attack, Christine had moved inside the barn, covering the slaughter of the dead turkeys as well. She was just putting her camera back in its case when the coroner, Bill Barlow, showed up. He stepped inside the barn, and she walked him through what had happened, showing him the security tape of the cat. Once back outside, she showed Bill the bushes and trees where Spider had found the remains.

Leaving the coroner to do his thing, Christine saw that Austin was just now coming down the steps from the house of the newly widowed Margo Raines. "How'd it go?" she asked, concern heavy in her voice.

Austin gave a brief sad smile. "It went about as well as could be expected, I'd imagine. She took it pretty hard. However, I mentioned that Alex and I could help her out with the feeding and care of the birds when time permits until she gets things figured out. She doesn't have any family in this area."

Christine shook her head in commiseration and said, "That's nice of you to help like that. I'll stop in and give her my respects as well before I head out."

Austin looked around the yard briefly and spotted the coroner's vehicle, saying, "I see Bill is on the job. Couldn't Fred make it back up here?"

"He got delayed but said he'd be back before Bill had to move the remains."

Austin nodded and said, "Sounds good. I'll just check in with Bill and then catch up with you in a few minutes."

"All right. See you in a little bit." Christine moved up the short flight of steps to the house, and Austin walked over to the turkey barn.

Just about to put her knuckles to the door and knock, Christine's phone rang. She pulled it from her parka pocket and punched the talk button. "British Columbia Conservation, Officer Moon speaking. How may I help you?"

"Christine? This is Geraldine!"

"Geraldine! How are you?" Christine wasn't expecting to hear from her elderly friend so soon. She presumed that this call wasn't just to say hi.

"Well, dearie, I was doing just fine this morning until I found something in my pantry eating one of my roasts."

"Oh, no! Are you all right? Did it do much damage?"

"Can't say for sure."

"Why's that?"

"Cause the beastie is still in my pantry!"

"What?"

"Yup, got itself trapped as it ate my food! I need you to come by and get it out of there as soon as you can so I can finish my Christmas baking! Lord knows what it's done to my cookie dough!"

"Absolutely, Geraldine. I'll be over there as soon as I can." She hung up and knocked on the door. After expressing her condolences to Margo and telling her they would find the thing that killed her husband, she went in search of Austin.

Bill Barlow and Austin stood talking near the bushes at the side of the house where Virgil's leg was found. "Sorry to interrupt, guys, but I need to borrow Austin for a moment."

"Sure thing, Chris," Bill replied with a nod and a curt smile. "I need to finish up here anyway, so he's all yours." He turned back to the remains on the ground and began snapping pictures.

"What's up, Chris?" Austin asked

They walked toward their vehicles, and Christine said, "It's not what's up. It's what's inside."

"Huh?"

"I need your help. Geraldine just called, and she has another wildlife problem, and I could use your assistance in solving it."

"Surely, anything. What can I do?"

Christine explained her plan to Austin, and he nodded along in agreement, saying, "That should work. I'll head to your yard at the conservation office and grab it now, and then I'll see you at Geraldine's." Austin jumped in his Pilot and sped down the lane, with Christine close behind in her Dodge.

***

"Careful, dearie," Geraldine said as Christine approached the inner pantry door. "I haven't heard any noise from inside there in a little while now. Either it's eaten everything it could eat in the cool room and fallen asleep, or it choked to death on the bone in my prime rib. Personally, I hope it's the latter."

"Me too," Christine said in a hushed voice. She moved next to the door and pressed her ear against it.

A loud crash came from the other side as something leapt against the cool room door and bounced off. Christine pulled away with a start. A low growl came from the next room, followed by the sound of something heavy pacing back and forth in the small windowless room, its claws clicking against the hardwood floor as it walked.

"I think it's still awake, dearie," Geraldine observed.

"I'd say you're right."

"So, what are you planning?" Just as the words came out of Geraldine's mouth, there was the sound of a heavy truck coming up the lane, followed by a honking horn.

"That sounds like part of it now," Christine said with a reassuring smile.

The pair made their way through to the front door and saw Trip in the Citrus Express plowing his way down the lane to the house, followed by Austin driving the Works Chevy Silverado.

"Well, isn't that nice! You've brought all your friends, dearie!"

"Yes, I thought we might need a little help."

Nodding in agreement, Geraldine said, "Well, you've got two of the most helpful guys in Lawless here right now."

"Don't I know it," Christine said with a smile.

Trip pulled the Express around in Geraldine's circular laneway and pointed it back down the lane towards town. Austin pulled up next in the Silverado and began backing the truck up to Geraldine's porch. Attached to its trailer hitch was what looked like a large, round piece of culvert pipe with steel mesh across both ends.

"What in tarnation is that?"

"It's a bear trap," Christine replied, walking down the front steps to greet Austin and Trip.

"But it's not a bear, dearie!" Geraldine called down from the porch.

"I know, but I think it'll do the trick just fine for our friend in the pantry."

"I think it should fit." Geraldine agreed with a nod.

"Hey Chris, Geraldine!" Austin greeted them as he stepped out of the pickup. "I thought we could use a hand." He nodded toward Trip.

"Hi folks," Trip called out as he approached from the other direction. "So, what's the plan?"

"We need to have tea and cookies since you're all here!"

Christine said with a smile, "Perhaps we can wait until we get your visitor in the cage?"

"Oh, a course, dearie. I was just thinking out loud for when you're all done."

"That sounds great, Geraldine." Christine smiled at her aged friend.

Wrapping her arms about herself with a shiver, the elderly

woman said, "I'm going to head back inside where it's warmer. Keep me posted!"

With a nod of understanding, Christine said, "Don't you worry about a thing," then moved to join the men.

When she reached the bottom of the steps, Trip said, "Before I forget, I have something for you guys."

"Really? What's that?" Christine asked.

"It's easier to show you." Trip walked them to the Express and opened the passenger side door. He lifted down the carton and showed them the sleeping kittens inside, saying, "George found these guys at the arboretum at the complex last night and decided to take them home. And then mama came looking for them."

"Oh no, are George and Celia all right?" Austin asked, concerned.

"Fortunately, yes."

"I wonder if that's what drew the cat to that part of the valley, and ultimately, the Raines's farm?" Christine wondered aloud.

"That's a definite possibility," Trip said with a nod, then asked, "I was wondering if you guys would be able to do me a favour?"

"Certainly. What is it?" Austin responded.

"Well, when we're done here, could you drop these guys off at the Works kennel? I would do it, but I need to get back on the road as soon as we're finished."

"Not a problem, Trip," Austin said with a nod.

"Great!" Trip said. He placed the sleeping kittens back in the truck and told Spider, "You can sit with these guys for a few more minutes, okay little buddy?" The dog let a disappointed whine out and settled back down on the seat. Turning back to Christine, Trip asked, "So what's the plan here?"

"Well, you remember that dire wolf?"

"I can't forget him. He's stinking up one of my storage sheds."

"Turns out we've got another one, and this one is definitely alive. It got in through the exterior door of Geraldine's pantry access and then trapped itself. Now, we need to release it and send it over to our trap."

"How are we going to do that? Just open the door and usher it into the bear trap?" Austin asked.

"Pretty much," Christine said. The bed of the trap was almost level with the porch. She stood on the edge of the trap, then climbed to the top and pulled up the trap's steel mesh entrance door until it clicked into position. "Well, I was wondering if you boys could find me some pallets or plywood sheeting?"

"I think I've got just the thing. Want to give me a hand, Mr. Mayor?" Trip inquired. Austin nodded, and together, the two men walked around to the back of the house.

While the boys looked for some wood, Christine moved back to her truck and retrieved something she hoped would work to entice the dire wolf.

Moments later, Trip came around the corner of the building with Austin following behind. Between them, they carried several sheets of plywood sheeting with a half dozen two-by-fours stacked on top.

Trip said to Christine, "I had some lumber left over from when I helped fix the front of Geraldine's house where the bear attacked. Fortunately, I never got around to taking it back home."

"Well, it's a good thing you didn't. I was hoping there was something around here." Christine climbed the steps and prepared to enter the trap to place her bait inside. Her 'bait' happened to be a battered and torn, eighteen-inch tall Pink Panther doll.

"That's your bait?" Austin asked, surprised.

"Since our friend inside the pantry is presumably full of Geraldine's roasts already, I thought it best to give it something to focus on when we open that door." The doll was one that she'd used in traps previously. Sometimes, curiosity proved stronger an attraction than hunger with some animals. She tied it to the trap trigger cage, where they would typically hang meat or other tasty comestibles for whatever creature they were currently trying to trap.

The men stood two sheets of plywood on end, then, using a DeWalt drill that Austin pulled out of the Silverado, they joined them together using a couple of two-by-fours running parallel to each other, which they also screwed to the house and porch. They left a small gap in the sheet nearest the wall on the doorknob side so that someone could reach through and turn the handle to unlatch the door. On the other side, Christine tied off one end of a section of shred-proof twine to the doorknob, and the other end was left dangling outside a gap in the opposite wall of the plywood entrance to the trap.

Double-checking that everything was secured, Austin asked, "Are you ready?" He stood with his hand through the gap nearest the wall, ready to turn the doorknob.

"Let 'er rip!" Trip said from the other side of the trap, his hand holding the twine, set to give it a good yank to pull the door open.

"Good to go!" Christine called out. She had climbed on top of the trap and stood near the open door, ready to release the mechanism manually if the animal didn't attack the Pink Panther doll once it was inside the trap.

Austin turned the knob, and Trip yanked the twine on the doorknob, and the beast charged out as if on cue. It snarled and raged and ran out onto the porch. It stood on its well-muscled hind legs and put its paws up on the plywood, growling and snapping its jaws menacingly, only inches from Austin's face. He was pressed against the other side, making sure the wood didn't move.

Up on the trap, Christine stomped her booted feet and said, "Hey you, snappy! Over here!"

The beast turned and saw Christine, then spotted the stuffed animal at the far end of the trap. It charged toward the pink doll and snatched it from the dangling chain. The door at the other end clanged down, and the beast charged back in the previous direction, trying to get its jaws through the tight steel mesh, but was unsuccessful.

"Holy crap!" Trip said. "These things are far more dangerous looking when they're alive."

"I think I need to check my shorts," Austin added, standing near the end of the trap and gazing in at the creature.

A few moments later, Geraldine came out of her house and said, "I heard some commotion. Did you get it?"

"It's all clear; we've captured it," Christine said, climbing down from the top of the trap.

Trip and Austin had just removed the two-by-fours and plywood as Geraldine shuffled toward the trap with her walker. She peered inside at the snarling beast and said, "Land sakes, you're an ugly one." It snapped and growled at her. "Oh, don't get your panties in a bunch. You probably had plenty of my food." She turned and peeked into her pantry, then added, "Consarn it all, you hairy bugger! You ate all my roasts and cookie dough! I hope you get a stomach ache!" She shook her head in disgust. "Well, you're just lucky I have enough flour, sugar and butter to make more." Turning to her friends, she concluded, saying, "Speaking of which, now that you're all done, it's time to come inside, kids. The tea and cookies are waiting!"

"I just need to make sure the trap is secure. I'll see you inside," Christine replied. With a nod, Austin followed Geraldine inside.

Before going in, Trip trotted down the front steps and jogged over to the Express, opened the driver's door and lifted Spider down. He listened for a moment. There was no sound from the sleeping kittens still nestled in their box.

"Are the kids okay?" Trip asked the dog

Spider gave a small 'erf' and licked his nose.

With a laugh, Trip said, "I'll take that as a yes." He quietly closed the door on the Express and moved to the house. Walking through the front door, he said aloud, "Hope you don't mind me bringing another friend."

Watching Trip, Christine smiled at his interactions with the dog. He really seemed to be enjoying the bond that had formed between him and the small canine. She was happy for him. Being single with no one in his life, she figured he must be lonely and hoped the little dog helped fill the void.

Turning back to the task at hand, Christine secured the secondary latch on the trap's door. The beast paced back and forth inside the metal tube, a low rumble coming from deep in its throat.

Lost in thought, she stood looking at the wolf for a long moment before joining the others inside. If this animal was the companion of the one Willy killed, they had only solved half of their current problems. The sabre-toothed cat was still out there somewhere and looking for her babies. Casting a glance over her shoulder at the dire wolf in the trap and then the surrounding forest, she stepped inside Geraldine's for a very quick cup of tea.

CHAPTER THIRTY-THREE

"Madre de Dios! This place is huge!" a voice exclaimed faintly. Two men stood near the cavern's entrance, silhouetted by the daylight at their back.

Alex watched from the shadows. He and Trudy were pressed against the cavern wall just on the other side of a small outcropping of rock along the crumbled ledge. It was just enough to conceal them for the moment. Alex held a finger to his lips. Trudy nodded with a slight roll to her eyes as if to say, 'Well, duh!'

When he and Trudy had first entered the cavern, they'd stood in awe of the vast underground lake before them. Holding hands, they'd gazed into the water's depths, filled with wonder at the colourful aquatic life that darted and dashed about beneath its surface. After that, unsure which way to go, they had decided on the left, which turned out to be a good choice considering their current situation. They had gone just about as far as they could along the narrow jut of rock and were now slightly past where the glacier rubbed against the coarse cavern wall. At first, Alex had thought the ledge and part of the wall had crumbled away, but on closer inspection, it looked like it had been blown apart. What had caused that, he wondered?

Water lapped gently against the broken piece of ledge where they stood, and it was very quiet inside the cavern. Sound carried quite well, and as a result, they were able to overhear most of what the men were saying, dozens of metres away, and for some reason, one of the voices sounded familiar to Alex, but he couldn't quite place it.

The two men moved to the far end of the lake and walked along the sandy shore. Stopping temporarily, the shorter man with the dimmer flashlight exclaimed loudly, "Oh my God!"

Kneeling to examine something on the ground, the taller man said, "It smells like brandy."

Whoever they were, Alex thought, they weren't being too wary regarding any wildlife that could be lurking around this cavern as they talked in a regular tone of voice. It was as if they didn't care if they were heard—and that made the men just as dangerous to him and Trudy as any wildlife they might find inside this cavern.

The tall man who'd been squatting down stood and waved the other man ahead to take the lead. They moved into a sub cavern, carrying on their conversation as they walked. Alex just caught the tail end of the tall man saying, "...get your share and mine." In response, the smaller said, "Be careful what you wish for around here."

And then Alex and Trudy were by themselves once more.

Trudy whispered, "Who the hell are those people? I didn't think anyone else knew where this was?"

"Nobody does, as far as I know," Alex said in a hushed voice, then added, "I wonder if they followed our tracks from the old entrance down below." There was still the mystery of the shorter man's voice bugging Alex. He could almost place it, but not quite, and it was bothering him.

Tugging Alex's hand, Trudy whispered, "They probably did follow us. So, let's get going. We don't want them to find all the gold!"

Walking along the sandy shore, they soon came upon what the men had stopped to examine on the ground.

"Oh, sweet Jesus," Trudy murmured. She looked away from the corpse, unwilling or unable to look any longer. Alex stooped down to examine it more closely, and Trudy hissed, "What are you doing? Don't touch that! You don't know where it's been!"

"Don't worry, Pumpkin, it's not going to make me dead. Whatever killed this person isn't catching." He leaned closer to the corpse for a better look. There were bite marks on the collarbone of the corpse. Alex wondered if it had been gnawed on while the person had been alive. The other skeleton next to it appeared to have been the perpetrator of the human's death. The size of a large dog, the creature's skull sported massive canine teeth stained with old blood. Alex picked up a silver flask that lay off to one side with his gloved hand and read the inscription aloud, "Money is the answer for everything - Raymond E. Chance."

"Ray Chance from the casino? Omigod!" Trudy still whispered, but her register went from her usually high pitch up to an almost imperceptible squeal.

"Well, Chris did say he was killed somewhere in these caverns. And here he is."

"Let's leave him in peace. We need to see what the other guys are up to."

"Okay, fine." Alex stood and towered over Trudy.

Trudy reached up on her tiptoes and kissed Alex briefly on the lips, saying, "Thanks for being my Indian Jones."

"You mean Indiana Jones? You're welcome, my little Lara Croft."

The opening that the men went through looked to be a smooth tube-like structure. In darkness again, Alex turned on his light and shielded it with one hand covering the lens, so his fingers partially obscured the light. He ran his other hand along the metal that gleamed from the rock. Alex breathed, "Oh wow, this stuff is…"

"Gold!" Trudy whisper-squealed.

The couple moved along the tunnel, eventually arriving at a juncture point. They could continue following the tunnel off to the right, which ran slightly uphill or take a branching tunnel running slightly downhill and to the left. Alex stopped for a moment to ponder which direction. While he did, his mind also gnawed away on the voice of the smaller man they were following. With a flash of insight, his internal memory storage units suddenly came back with an answer to the question of the voice he couldn't recall. It had been a person that had been involved in finding this gold and defeating the bear. He suddenly blurted their name out loud, "Jerry Benson!" then slapped his hand over his mouth in shock at what he'd just done.

"Alex!" Trudy hissed.

From the tube leading off to the right, they heard the tall man's voice say, "Did you hear that? Someone called your name!"

Alex grabbed Trudy's hand, and they fled to the left, down the lower branch of the tube.

***

Angel Oritz shoved Jerry Benson along in front of him and smiled as he watched the other man stumble and fall to his knees. "C'mon, let's go see who's calling your name. We'll get back to things in a second. The 'things' to which he referred was the thick vein of gold they'd discovered. The vein was constricted, however, and a large amount of rock and boulders currently blocked any further progress. However, he had something in the pack strapped to Benson's back that might help. But first, they needed to see who was calling out his captive's name in this cavern in the middle of Nowhere, BC. "Get up," he commanded, prodding the geologist in the back with his Glock. Not having a safety to worry about, the pistol was constantly ready to fire, its readiness to commit its payload solely dependent on the pressure he placed upon its trigger. And right now, he had it pressed about halfway, drilling it into Benson's shoulder blade.

Jerry struggled to his feet and began following the tunnel back toward the junction.

Angel knew that the tunnel to the left led back to the underground lake. Going with his gut, he chose the tunnel that sloped downward instead. Angel prodded Jerry again, this time in the shoulder to aim him to the right, and they began to descend further into the bowels of the earth.

The sound of rushing water came from the end of the tunnel, and it opened out into another huge antechamber, one where you could practically breathe the moisture generated by the massive underground waterfall that shot off into blackness. The path ahead of them ended at a precipice, disappearing down into a dark void. There were no other rocks or other places nearby to hide behind. "Well, they're not down here. They must be back at the lake," Angel said, then shoved Jerry in the shoulder with his hand this time, saying, "Vámonos!"

**

"I can't hold on for much longer," Alex Murphy whispered. "You need to climb up now, Trudy."

"Okay, honey, don't let go." Trudy had been hanging off Alex's back, holding partially onto his backpack and also his muscular neck, her feet dangling into blackness. With a grunt, she began to climb up Alex's back to the edge of the cliff face just above. Once back on solid ground, Trudy turned and grabbed one of Alex's wrists and heaved herself backwards to try and haul him up. It wasn't that she expected to help too much, but at least she had enthusiasm, if anything.

"Thanks," Alex said with a puff as he pulled himself back up from the edge of the cliff. He stood and shone his light at the waterfall, then toward the edge of the rockface where they had dangled.

Trudy hugged as far around Alex as she could and said, "My hero."

"Yeah? Well, you might think differently in a moment. Remember when I said there was a ledge below?" Alex queried.

With a nod, Trudy looked past Alex toward the dark void at his back.

Alex continued, "And remember I said not to climb all the way down but to hang onto me instead?"

Trudy nodded in remembrance.

"Do you want to know why I didn't want you to climb down?" Alex stepped aside for Trudy to look.

Moving reluctantly toward the lip of the rock, Trudy asked, "Why?" then peered into the darkness.

Alex shone the light over the edge and spotlighted the ledge located about three metres below, saying, "Because it's already occupied."

CHAPTER THIRTY-FOUR

The smell was driving Willy crazy. He killed the snowmobile's engine and held his head up high in the air, sniffing rapidly like a dog. Something was carrying its scent on the wind. He breathed deeply and then exhaled, his breath pluming from his mouth. Growing up, he remembered when he'd been in the forest and sometimes a scent of flowers, pine, or whatever would come to him. But it was always just a quick wafting scent, and then it was gone, not anything like this. He'd never experienced such a keen sense of smelling anything like this before. It was like his entire nose was alive and bringing new sensations to his brain with each breath. Every time he inhaled, it was like a kaleidoscope, not of colour and movement but rather of smell instead.

Starting up the sled once more, Willy gunned the engine, heading to his first destination—his house. There was something he needed to get there, and he hoped he could find it. The Wilson household was located on the outskirts of town, on the west side of the valley, easily navigable by snowmobile.

Walking through the front door, he surveyed the interior of his house. Everything was still as his dad had left it almost a year ago. Just the thought of throwing out his dad's old stuff had filled him with anguish. His dad's recliner still sat in front of the TV, an empty can of the last Kokanee in which he'd ever imbibed still on the table beside it. He was glad he hadn't thrown out or given away anything of his dad's because he needed it now, or at least one item in particular.

Willy Wilson Sr. had served in the Canadian Armed Forces for twenty-five years before being honourably discharged when Willy Jr. was just a youngster. They'd moved around from base to base when he was small, but when it came time for his dad to retire, the family had decided to move back to where Willy Sr. had his roots, the Kootenays. Well, not the whole family, actually, just Willy and his dad. His mom hadn't come with them.

Growing up, Wanda Wilson hadn't been the most caring of mothers. And when Willy had been a little older, he found out why. It turned out Wanda had a predilection for other men—no particular type, really, just about any man would do. Willy Sr. had found this out one afternoon when he'd come home early from work. He'd found his wife in their bedroom, and she hadn't been alone.

After many years of service, Willy Sr. had advanced to the rank of Master-Sergeant. Working in the motor pool, he'd always been there to fix whatever came in that needed fixing. Because of this, one of the other things he did was build things. If he needed some part or other and it wasn't available, he'd machine the part instead of waiting for it to come in weeks later. His father's hobby had almost been a natural extension of his job, and he'd continued to build things after his retirement in Lawless.

Not wanting to have a regimented life any longer, Willy Sr. never took another full-time job, and was always more than happy to pick up whatever he could get. Fortunately, Willy Sr.'s military pension covered their modest expenses, and he'd been able to buy them a small place on the outskirts of town on the west side of the valley.

Smiling sadly, Willy came back to the present. First things first—he needed to change his footwear. He'd borrowed a pair of boots from Trip, but they had been far too loose on his feet. The bite mark on the side of his foot felt like it had almost healed over now. Inside the house, in the hall closet, there was an old pair of Sorels that his dad had owned for years. Willy placed them on his feet with a small sigh of sadness; he still missed his dad so much. These boots were a little loose as well, but not as bad as Trip's pair of extra-wides.

Food was next up on the agenda. He popped into the kitchen and opened the fridge to see if there was anything inside that might appease his growing hunger. The steak and eggs he'd had at Trip's quelled his appetite for a little while, but now it was back with a vengeance. He didn't want any of the cheese or lunch meat in the icebox, no he wanted something more visceral, for some reason. The only other thing in the house was a small turkey he'd bought to cook for his Christmas dinner. He'd always loved leftover turkey sandwiches as a kid. When they'd moved to Lawless, his dad had done most of the cooking, and Willy, being a teenager at the time, had done most of the eating. His dad had always cooked a giant turkey at Christmas, and for days afterwards, they'd have turkey this, that and the other thing.

In an attempt to keep that tradition going, Willy had bought a small ten-pound bird and left it in the fridge, thawing gradually for Christmas day. Seeing the bird, his stomach roared in his belly and felt like it was tearing itself apart. He pulled the turkey from the fridge, placed it on the counter, peeled the plastic off, then sniffed the carcass. Though uncooked, it smelled very appealing. He leaned forward again, and this time, instead of inhaling, he licked the semi-frozen bird. It was like a turkey-sicle! He licked it again, then took a bite, stretching the raw skin upward in his teeth like it were plastic wrap. It suddenly snapped and retracted, hitting him in the face. Willy slurped the skin and raw strands of flesh into his mouth like spaghetti and greedily gobbled it down. Next, he ripped a leg from the bird and tore into the attached thigh's semi-frozen flesh. Several minutes later, his feeding frenzy was over, and he finally felt sated but somewhat disgusted by what he'd just done.

Willy exited the house and moved to the workshop to search

for the object of his quest. The shop Willy Sr. had built for himself on the backside of his property was almost larger than the house in front. Most days and some nights when Willy Jr. had been younger, his dad had been out here tinkering on one thing or another. And it had been one fateful night in this very shop when he'd discovered that his father had made one of the most amazing things he'd ever seen.

Having watched a video on the internet many months before, Willy Sr. had been inspired and built the contraption for no other reason than because he could. So, he did, and it worked. And it was something that Willy figured he could use now, all things considered, but he just hoped it was still somewhere in the shop after all these years. It was—buried under a tarp in the back corner on a shelf. The only thing he couldn't find was the fuel for it. He tore the shop apart and eventually found some in a milk crate underneath the workbench. After filling the tank, he strapped the device and the extra fuel to the back of the snowmobile.

Back inside the shop once more, he turned around in a circle, looking to see if there was anything else he wanted to bring on his little hunting expedition. And then he saw it on the wall over the workbench, a German Luger from the Second World War. His dad had bought it from a collector, back when he'd thought he might like to collect firearms as a hobby. However, that had been the extent of his collection. The newest rifle they owned, a Remington bolt action Model 700, had been left up at the cavern when his dad had been attacked. Well, you gotta work with what you've got, he thought decisively and brought the Luger down from the wall. A box of cartridges was in a separate drawer in the workbench. He loaded the gun, then stuffed it, along with some extra ammo, into his jacket pockets.

Willy started up the snowmobile and leaned back in the seat. He stared at his house for a moment and reminisced about his dad and their life together. There was an excellent chance he might never see the old homestead again. He wasn't sure what was happening to him and found himself scared and excited, both at the same time. Although his new super sense of smell was kind of cool, he found his propensity for raw meat somewhat disconcerting, and he didn't know what other issues or side effects he might develop. Were these things he was experiencing from the rabies and tetanus shots? Or from the wolf's bite? Perhaps it was a combination of all three? He had no idea, but since he was feeling well enough now, he felt no need to see the doctor. After all, how bad could he be if he felt this good?

Taking a deep breath, he inhaled a huge lungful of the biting winter wind and felt the scent fill his nose and then his mind, almost overwhelming him with its intensity. Willy revved the sled and moved off into the forest, following the smell wherever it may lead.

CHAPTER THIRTY-FIVE

With tea and cookies now consumed, Austin and Christine had returned to the conservation office. Inside the trap before them, the wolf stalked from one end to the other and back again. Surveying the grumbling black beast, Christine said, "I think I have a shed we can lock this fella up in for now. If you could give me a hand, we'll put our boy to bed for the night."

"You got it, Chris," Austin said. He hopped into the Silverado and backed the trap inside a small metal Quonset hut which Christine had unlocked and opened. Austin unhooked the hitch and pulled the truck back out, and Christine closed the large rollup door. At one time, the building had been used to store feed and grains used to help the populations of certain non-migratory birds and other animals survive the harsh winters in the area. Christine's idea wasn't to unleash the beast inside the storage hut but rather to temporarily store the trap inside its doors with the wolf still residing within it.

Christine stood at the back of the trap while the beast prowled back and forth inside. Reaching into a plastic baggie she'd pulled from her parka pocket, she said to the wolf, "Not that you need anything else after the pig you made of yourself at Geraldine's, but I don't want you to starve either. You're lean enough already." She dropped several large chunks of high-protein jerky through a feeding portal in the trap's steel mesh door. The jerky was kept on hand to feed larger captive predators until they could be relocated. As the animal gobbled them up, Christine said to Austin, "I'll arrange for proper transportation down to the coast for our friend here sometime in the next few days once we get the cat situation figured out. Hopefully, we'll be able to trap it as well."

"Or maybe it'll get itself locked inside of something like the big bad wolf here did." The wolf finished its jerky and lifted its head, growling deep within its throat at Austin. He backed up a half metre out of reflex, saying, "Hey, you've only got yourself to blame for your current situation."

They left the shed and locked it up, then walked toward Christine's Dodge pickup truck. She opened the passenger side door and looked inside. "Speaking of current situations, we need to do something with these kittens."

"And their mama, too," Austin said, staring at the kittens. They were still sound asleep and intertwined like a fuzzy, tan blob with ears. "How concerned should we be with mama cat and the winter solstice fair going on this weekend, I wonder?"

"Well, I've been thinking about that, and an extra degree of caution might be in order. However, despite the cat's size, I believe it would be skittish around that many people with all the noise and lights. So, that should keep it away from much of what's going on at the community complex, at the front at least. And since we know the cat is looking for its babies, we can use that to our advantage. Of course, the obvious choice would be to use them as bait." Austin raised his eyebrows in surprise at that remark. Christine saw this and smiled, then continued, "But of course, that's wrong. We can't leave them inside a trap to entice her since they might die of exposure waiting for mama to arrive."

"Or, they might be just a little too enticing to other predators wandering around the area as well."

"Yes, there's that as well. But I think we can attract their mother without putting them or anyone else at risk. So, since we need to keep these guys somewhere safe, we'll put them into protective custody in your kennel at the Works building. It's made of cinder blocks, so I don't think their mother will have much luck trying to get in there."

"I agree. I can run them over to the Yard and put them up at the hotel right now if you'd like?"

"That sounds good, but before you go, I'd like to do something."

Austin nodded, saying, "Absolutely. Let me know what I can do."

Looking down into the box, Christine said, "You can. Do you have another towel for these guys?" She stroked the kittens gently as she spoke.

"I might. What happened? Did they soil the one in the box?"

"No, but I want to use the one they're sleeping in for my little theatre production," Christine responded enigmatically.

A questioning look in Austin's eyes, he replied, "Okay, I'll go get something. Be right back."

Christine extracted two baby bottles from a cardboard carton on the floor behind the Dodge's passenger seat. She'd stopped at the Gas 'n' Gulp and picked up some baby formula on her way back to the conservation office. The bottles were courtesy of George and Celia MacKay. She poured some of the nutritious liquid into both bottles and capped them. Petting the kitten's heads, she let them smell the bottles but didn't give any formula to them, and only passing it beneath their small whiskered noses. But it was enough, and they instantly began mewling hungrily.

Austin arrived back with a large, fluffy white bath towel. Christine placed the baby bottles next to the box and took the kittens out, holding one in each arm, then asked, "Would you do the honours and change their bed?"

"Certainly," Austin replied. He took the tan bath towel from the box and replaced it with the clean white towel. Christine placed the two babies back into the carton, and they began mewling once again.

Extracting her cell phone from her pocket, Christine said, "I'm going to use an ASMR application to make a looping MP3 for playback via Bluetooth transmission on my iPod."

"You lost me at ASMR," Austin said, a tilt to his head.

With a smile, Christine replied, "Autonomous sensory meridian response." She held up the phone to show Austin the big red 'record' button on the ASMR app.

"Could you drop it down one more notch?"

"Well, you know that tingling feeling you get on the back of your neck from your scalp down to your shoulders when something or other triggers an emotional response?"

"I do."

"Well, that is an autonomous sensory meridian response. It can be triggered by things like whispering, water flowing, and other subtle and interesting sounds. People actually listen to recordings of these sounds to provoke that response. Anyway, this recording software helps enhance whatever you are recording, depending on what you set it at. And right now, I want to record this." Tapping a red button on the phone's screen, Christine put her fingers to her lips and then held the cell near the kittens. In her free hand, she picked up one of the baby bottles and waved it near the cubs, and they renewed their excited mewling. After recording a couple of minutes of this sound, she pressed the stop button on her phone. "Oh, you poor little things," Christine said, putting her phone away. She could no longer bear to taunt the small creatures or their poor little rumbling stomachs with the bottle, and she picked up the other bottle and gave one to each cub. She smiled as they suckled greedily from the rubber teats.

"So, what was all that for?"

"I'm going to take that ASMR enhanced sound and make it into a compressed MP3 recording, which I will loop on my old iPod Touch and send over Bluetooth to a portable speaker inside the trap. Wrapped around that speaker will be this." She held up the tan towel that Austin had taken from the kitten's box. "The scent of the babies on this towel will be quite strong since they've been nestled in it for the last twelve hours or so. That, combined with the recording, should be enough to entice their mother to come to their rescue."

Austin nodded slowly. "That's really a great idea. And no one is in harm's way."

"Exactly." She looked down at the box. One of the kittens was already finished its bottle of milk, and Christine removed the bottle from its mouth, not wanting it to eat the nipple.

"Okay, so where do you want to put the trap?"

"I was thinking near the back of the arboretum where George said he found them. If she was somehow accessing that area when she gave birth to the cubs, she'll hopefully come by and see if they are still there because she's obviously looking for them." The second kitten had finished its milk and was now pawing at its sibling, trying to push it away. Looking for more, the other cat was attempting to wrestle away possession of the empty bottle from its littermate.

Austin took the empty bottle and said, "I think it's time to put these babies to bed."

***

George MacKay stood outside the Lawless Community Complex, studying the side of the building and its access panels, looking for possible routes the large cat may have used to access the arboretum. As far as he could see, everything looked to be secure. Just as he was about to go back inside, the Lawless Public Works pickup truck pulled up next to him, an empty bear trap attached to the back of its trailer hitch.

"Hi, George." Christine gave a small wave as she stepped down out of the truck's passenger side and proceeded to the trap at the back.

Austin Murphy came around the hood from the driver's side and gave George a nod, saying, "How's the search going? Have you found a point of access yet?"

"Hey, Austin. It's going okay, but I can't seem to see a spot where she could have been sneaking into the arboretum unless she was coming in through some other section to get there." He nodded toward the trap. "Is that thing going to work?"

"It should if everything goes according to plan," Austin replied as they moved to the entrance of the trap. Inside at the back, Christine switched on the Bluetooth speaker, wrapped it in the kitten's tan towel and placed it into a cardboard box situated just behind the trap's pressure plate trigger. If anything of substantial weight stepped on the plate, it would spring the trap door at the front. Christine moved back out of the trap and switched on a battered iPod. The sounds of the mewling babies hungry for their mother's milk came from the cardboard box, and it sounded quite convincing.

In surprise, George exclaimed, "Oh no! You're using the kittens as bait?"

Reassuringly, Christine said, "Don't be alarmed. Nothing quite so dramatic as that. You'll be happy to know that the twins are in their own little suite at the Works Animal Control compound. They are curled up together, bellies filled with formula, and happily napping. This is what's making the sound," Christine tapped the iPod with her finger as it played back the recording of the kittens.

George said, "Oh, that's a relief! Celia wouldn't be impressed if that had been true," he laughed.

"Those kittens are two of the most amazing scientific finds of this century, next to their mother, of course. We wouldn't want to risk them at all." Christine placed the iPod in a small storage pouch located on the outside of the corrugated steel trap.

Austin said, "Well, I suppose that about does it here."

George nodded, saying, "I guess I'm going to get back inside since there's nothing I can do out here. People have been looking forward to getting inside the arboretum for months now, and I'm sure it's got a lineup."

"Sounds good, George. With the trap running interference out here, things should be okay. Plus, I'll have Alex keep an eye on it." Austin looked toward Gold Ridge, then added. "Whenever he gets back down the mountain, that is."

"He's out sledding?" George asked.

Nodding, Austin said, "He's out with his new girlfriend. Said they wanted to go up on the ridge today."

"Doesn't he know there's another big storm coming? The weather office is forecasting it as being one of the storms of the century," George replied.

"Yes, he does for sure." Austin looked up to the grey sky. A couple of tiny snowflakes slowly traced their way through the cold air, a precursor of things to come.

Shaking his head. George said, "Well, I hope he makes it back in time."

"Me too," Austin said, worry evident in his voice.

CHAPTER THIRTY-SIX

Trudy looked over the edge, and her eyes widened, then took a large intake of breath as if to scream. Alex saw her reaction and whispered in alarm, "No!" He quickly placed his hand across her mouth and felt as Trudy exhaled what would have been a shrill and high-pitched shriek.

Just below where they had been clinging to the cliff face sat a person. The top of their short-cropped, grey-haired head was directly below where their feet had dangled. Alex moved slightly to the side to try and see their face, but the person didn't follow the light with their head because they had long ago lost the ability to do so. Their clothes hung loosely over their emaciated frame, and grey skin stretched tight over their bony hands, which were resting casually on their knees as if enjoying the view. Next to them on the ledge was a non-functioning flashlight.

"Oh my God! Who's that?" Trudy whispered so loudly she was almost yelling.

"If I had to make a guess. I would say that's the ex-mayor, Bob Nichols."

"Eww! What's he doing down there?"

"I think he hid down there and then couldn't get back up. Looks like a little bit of a stretch. Glad I didn't try to lower us down there."

"That's horrible!"

"It sure is." Alex shook his head slightly. He shone his light carefully about the cavern looking for any other exit but could find none. Moving slowly back toward the tunnel, he shielded the light with his hands once more. There wasn't any sound up ahead, but it didn't mean someone might not be lying in wait just around a corner somewhere. They proceeded cautiously, Alex in the lead and Trudy trailing behind, holding his free hand.

***

Jerry Benson knew he would have to do something drastic to get himself out of this situation. The man holding him captive was obviously crazy, and that made him even more dangerous. Angel seemed obsessed with his brother and his disappearance and appeared willing to do anything to exact his revenge from anyone and everyone involved in the operation that had been run up here.

They stood on the shore of the underground lake. Angel said, "I could've sworn I heard someone say your name."

"Things can sound different underground. It could have been some rock settling somewhere," Jerry offered weakly. In fact, he had heard someone blurt out his name when Angel heard it, but he'd pretended to not notice.

"Rock settling somewhere? Do you really think I'm that stupid?" Angel shook his head with suspicion. "I never heard no rocks that sounded like a human voice before."

Jerry didn't reply and only shrugged.

A quick check of the immediate vicinity hadn't revealed anyone nearby, and they retreated to the lava tube to continue their exploration.

Standing next to the thick vein of gold that covered half of one of the tunnel walls, Jerry racked his brain, wondering who else was in this cavern that would know who he was? The only people in town that knew him were limited. In fact, he hadn't even told Austin or Christine that he had booked a cabin in the area, wanting to surprise everyone and all. He smiled ironically; it seemed the surprise was on him, being kidnapped and all.

Oritz moved to the rocks and boulders that were blocking the tunnel. They looked dense and immovable, but he nodded and said, "I think I have a remedy for our little problem here." He turned back to Jerry and said, "Turn around."

"What? Why?"

"Just do it or else."

Jerry reluctantly turned and felt Angel open the pack strapped to his back and rummage through it. After a moment, Oritz said, "There you are." He pulled a grey, rectangular block of what looked like modelling clay from the pack. Watching Angel work, Jerry could see that it was anything but modelling clay.

Moulding the clay around some of the larger rocks, Angel said, "We should only need one pack. After all, we don't want to bring the whole place down on our heads." Placing a small electronic relay into the plastic explosive, Oritz said, "All right, hustle your ass back down around the corner. Things are gonna get loud."

Taking the lead, Jerry moved back toward the entrance to the lake with Angel directly behind him. In the cavern once more, Oritz pointed with his light to a spot on one side of the lava tube's entrance and said, "Stay," and Jerry did as instructed. Leaning against the opposite side, Angel pulled a small device from his pocket and then turned it on. He made the sign of the cross and prepared to press the red button on top.

***

The passage was black up ahead. None of the bioluminescent light from the nearby lake leaked into the tunnel where they were currently located. Alex still had his hand covering most of the flashlight's beam to keep from announcing their presence to anyone else.

Back at the junction, there was no sign of Jerry or the other man. Alex's mind was racing. What was Jerry doing up here? The last he'd seen Benson, the man had been departing for the coast and vowing never to return to the valley. And yet now, here he was with some other guy.

They moved up the tunnel in which the two men had been working to see what was happening. One of the largest boulders in the tube's rock blockage seemed to have a red light flashing on top.

Trudy asked quietly, "What's that thing?"

Alex leaned in to examine it more closely. He'd seen enough movies to know that an electronic relay of some sort stuffed into a piece of grey plasticine meant only one thing. "Bomb!" he hissed. He grabbed Trudy's hand and quickly pulled her back the way they had come.

Running as fast as they could toward the junction, they expected an explosion at their back at any moment. Just as they turned the corner toward the waterfall tunnel, there was a flash of light and a huge blast. A shockwave of hot air came rushing toward them and engulfed them momentarily.

Trudy's eyes were wide, and she looked ready to panic. Alex held her in his arms for a moment, her face buried against his chest as he tried to calm her down. After a moment, they moved slowly back toward the site of the explosion. Rocks were everywhere, and part of the tube they were in had collapsed. One

244

section was still big enough for someone to squeeze through near the top, thankfully. Alex moved to this gap and peered through, just able to see the junction up ahead.

The two men slowly moved toward it, flashlights drawn. It seemed that Jerry was in the lead with the other man behind, prodding him to keep moving along.

***

Angel stuffed the detonator transmitter back into the pack on Jerry's back and gave Jerry a shove, saying, "Let's go see what happened," and they moved back toward the rock blockage.

"Yes!" Angel exclaimed with a grin when they arrived. "All right, Benson, let's see what other surprises this place has in store for us." Chunks of rock were everywhere, and dust and smoke still wafted through the air, making it hard to see, but the way up ahead appeared to be clear.

Jerry sneezed and wondered what they would find on the other side of the blockage. He was still at a loss for words from the amount of gold that he'd seen on this side. Moving forward, he was stunned to see that the mass of gold continued on the other side as well. He shone his LED light along the vein in the wall as he walked, marvelling at its purity. It swirled away into the distance and around another bend of the tube up ahead. In all his years of geology, he'd never seen or heard of such a vast deposit of gold.

At the bend of the lava tube, it jutted off to the right and then opened into another, larger chamber. Jerry felt the Glock drilling into his back once more, pushing him forward. He moved reluctantly, shining his light into every possible nook and cranny as they moved. Apart from the aquatic creatures in the lake, he hadn't yet seen any examples of the wildlife that called this cavern home. But with something like the recent explosion, if there was anything around that was hungry and curious, Jerry was quite sure that the noise would have been the equivalent of ringing the dinner bell.

They moved into the cavern, and Angel shone his high-intensity light about the vast space. More rocks and boulders were scattered everywhere. In the far corner, near another dark tunnel, one of the boulders seemed to move as Angel's light skipped over it. But Jerry saw it, and he moved slightly forward, shining his own dim light onto it, saying, "What's that over there?"

"What's what?" Angel moved his light back to where Jerry was pointing his LED. Benson was right, something was moving about over there, and it seemed to be coming their way. Whatever it was looked huge.

Jerry began backing away toward the lava tube.

"Where the hell do you think you're going?" Angel spotlighted Jerry with his torch and the Glock.

"Somewhere other than here. I don't want to be here when whatever that is gets here." He had a suspicion about what it was and was afraid he was about to have his worst fears realised. Disregarding Angel and his Glock 17, Jerry kept backing up, then suddenly turned and ran, saying, "You're on your own, amigo!"

Angel turned back to the thing moving toward them across the cavern floor. It was big, grey, and made a low, susurrating growl. His eyes widened as it came nearer, and he began to back up as well now. The grey beast began to move faster as if it had caught his scent and discovered something it liked. And then Angel saw it for what it was. A bear, but not just any bear, this thing was gigantic. Muscular, lean and exceedingly mean, a white scar ran down the side of the creature's head where something had attacked it at one point, or perhaps some rock had fallen on it. Whatever had happened, it seemed to be moving fine right now and was rapidly getting closer.

"What part of hell did you come from?" Angel questioned. He began to fire the Glock at the approaching monstrosity when it suddenly broke into a full gallop and charged hungrily toward him.

And then, Angel Oritz did something for the very first time in his life, something he had never ever thought of doing before; he turned and fled.

CHAPTER THIRTY-SEVEN

The city of Lawless had done well for itself over the years. There had been boom times and bust times, but it had survived them all. The big quake back in January had been only one of many trials and tribulations that the small mountain town had endured over the years. From the gold rush of the 1890s and early 1900s to the Dirty Thirties. The ski hill had helped the town weather the worst of the great depression, but it had still been a tough time for the area.

But things had begun to come back after the Second World War and into the '50s and '60s. The ski hill had been at the height of its fame, having had a local athlete who trained on its runs win a gold medal in the 1968 Grenoble Olympics. After that, the ski tourist trade had boomed. But in the late 1990s, global weather trends began to impact the hill, and it wasn't long before the town faced dire financial straits. Fortunately, it was something that the casino would later alleviate.

Austin Murphy had experienced many of the town's ups and downs before ascending to his current, lofty position of mayor. He'd been fortunate to have gotten on with the City of Lawless Public Works just after he'd gotten out of high school. It had been a great job, learning the inner workings of the small mountain city. Though he had been promoted after winning the recent civic election, he still missed working at the yard and his camaraderie with Trip, as well as Larry and Clara. He knew he would find similar feelings for the new people at city hall with whom he now worked. Fortunately, he knew many of the staff in passing already from his interactions with them as the head of the works department. With the City of Lawless taking an almost three-week hiatus, he wouldn't have the opportunity to get to know them better until the new year. However, that was fine with him. He knew he was needed for other duties at the moment anyway.

Before they'd departed the complex, while there was still enough light left, Christine had wanted to double-check the perimeter around the recreational building for any signs the cat might be nearby. However, she couldn't find any disturbances in the snow caused by the large feline. Because of the festival, many people had wandered through the area, making it quite hard to track a specific print.

While Christine had done that, Austin had unhooked the trap. Once they'd departed, he'd dropped Christine off at her house to get ready for their date, telling her he would return a few hours later to pick her up. On his way to his own house to shower and change, he promised her he'd check on the wolf as well as the kittens in their suite at the Works building.

Austin wanted Christine to feel unpressured for the date and figured if he could help out in some small way, such as checking on the animals in their care, he would do it. Besides, he was still feeling quite nervous about their little get together, and his butterflies had returned. However, when they met for their date, he figured he'd just be himself and see how that went—so far, it seemed to be working out. In the meantime, keeping busy checking the animals would help take his mind off things until the time drew closer.

Pulling into the conservation office, he saw something out of place—snowmobile treads tracked across the deep snow of the unplowed lot, running from the property's entrance to the main office, then departing again. Austin double-checked the doors and windows of the main building, and everything currently seemed secure. He studied the trail left by the snowmobile for a moment. From where it had parked, a set of boot prints led to the storage shed that he and Christine had temporarily stowed the bear trap containing the beast. Approaching the side door of the small Quonset hut, he could see that it had been tampered with and the lock forced. Austin pushed the door open and saw they had a problem. The bear trap no longer contained the dire wolf and now sat wide open.

The wolf's tracks led out the side door, followed by the person who had freed it. But who would have gone to the trouble of doing this? PETA? Freedomites? He didn't think so. As far as he knew, there were no wild-life activists or anti-government protesters in the area who were aware of the dire wolf's existence. So that narrowed the list of possible suspects. In fact, it pared things down so dramatically, there could only be one other person who may have done this: Willy Wilson Jr. In fact, no one else would even know that the beast existed. But how had he found out it was inside the shed?

And more importantly, Austin wondered, why did he do it? What would he have had to gain by unleashing this creature on the local population? Austin shook his head, trying to comprehend the logic of Willy's decision. Did he know something they didn't? If so, why hadn't he informed Trip at the very least of what he'd done and why? No, Willy was obviously having some sort of psychotic episode brought on by either the medicine he'd been given at the hospital or by the bite he had received somehow interacting with the drug? Austin was no doctor and didn't really know for sure. In fact, the only thing he did know was that they now had another problem back on their hands again. The cat would have been enough to deal with on its own, but with the wolf on the loose, things had just gone from semi-straightened out right back to complicated once more. He was about to call Chris with the bad news when his phone rang in his hand. It was Trip calling.

"Hey, Trip. What's shakin'?"

"Austin! Glad I caught you. I need to double-check something; you dropped the kittens off here at the Work's yard and put them in one of the suites, right?"

"Yes, a couple of hours ago, at least."

"Well, we've got more problems then," Trip said despondently.

"I was just going to call Chris to let her know the same thing."

"Really? What happened?"

"It's the dire wolf in the trap. It's gone; somebody let it out. The lock had been forced in the building where the trap was stored."

"What? Well, I think somebody may have done the same to the kittens up here then, cause they're gone."

"What do you mean, they're gone?"

"As in no longer here. Just an empty box."

"Do you think they crawled out of the box?"

"They couldn't even stand yet, so I doubt it."

"Was there any sign of a forced entry at the works yard?"

"Well, no."

"But if you say there weren't any signs of a B&E at the Works, then it could only be one person I can think of, and it's not Larry or Clara. Being Saturday, Clara wouldn't have stopped by, and Larry isn't working until tonight. So, there's only one other person who has keys to the shop."

"I know, Willy. But why would he take the cats?"

"And why would he unlock the cage and let the wolf out as well? I think that for us to have any answers to those questions, we'll need to ask Willy himself."

"We'll have a hard time doing that."

"Why's that?"

"I don't know where he is. When I discovered the cats were missing, I swung by his place and then my place. Not only is Willy not at either place, but I just discovered he took my snowmobile as well!"

"That would explain the sled tracks here at the conservation yard. He must have come by here around the same time he took the cats."

"I'll call Fred and let him know about this so he can stay on top of things." Trip said.

"Thanks. But now it looks like we're back to square one, almost. Chris has set a trap up at the complex where we think the big cat was entering the arboretum. Hopefully, that will work out. I just have to contact Alex. I wanted him to keep an eye on things there tonight, but he's out snowmobiling."

"What? Doesn't he know there's another storm coming?"

"He does. And he said he'd be back before dark."

"It's almost dark now, Austin."

"I noticed. I've texted him and tried to call him, but he must be out of cell range."

"All right, then, what now?"

"I think we'd best carry on with the festival like we planned."

"Okay. Let me know and I can watch the trap if you don't hear from Alex soon."

"Thanks, old friend, you might need to do so. I'll call Chris and get her up to date as well."

"Sounds good. Catch you later."

Austin said goodbye to Trip and hung up. He stood staring at the disconnected cell phone in his hand for several seconds, lost in thought. Where was Alex? And where was Willy? And where were the cat and the wolf, for that matter? Things seemed to have gone from not bad to exquisitely shitty in a matter of only a couple of hours, and he suddenly didn't look forward to what the coming evening might bring. Well, he thought with a sour smile, at least he now had something to take his mind off his upcoming date.

CHAPTER THIRTY-EIGHT

His LED light strobing back and forth on the walls of the tunnel as he fled, Jerry made his way toward the main entrance of the cavern. He knew that running to the sled outside would be a no-win scenario. Number one, he didn't have the keys, and number two, if he made it there and Angel survived, he'd most likely be shot in the back. And number three, if Angel were eaten, then he'd be next as the bear came rampaging out of the cavern and found Jerry stumbling about in the deep snow. He needed to come up with something else, and he needed to come up with it fast.

The cavern containing the underground lake was just up ahead, and he lunged through its steamy entrance. He couldn't believe it; here he was not quite a year later and running for his life again, this time from the offspring of the beast that had killed all his friends. And this creature was enormous in size, possibly even larger than its mother before it.

Christine had mentioned that there had been two bear cubs in the cavern, one of which may have died as it attacked Reggie VanDusen. Over the last eleven months, this other creature had been trapped behind the blockage, hibernating and waiting. Judging by the scar he'd seen on the new animal's head, this bear may have been injured by falling rock during the quake that had brought down the front of the mountain and part of the glacier. It must have been literally starving to death because it had been unable to get to the food in the other areas of the cavern, such as the underground lake with its bounty of aquatic life.

Jerry kept running until he was once more approaching the ledge at the back wall of the cavern. Behind him, he heard shouting as Angel Oritz came flying into the cavern, the giant beast from hell in hot pursuit. When he heard Angel firing his pistol at the beast, he'd flashed back to January and Tyler with his .357 magnum shooting into the fog. That had done his friend little good, and Tyler had ultimately been flayed alive by this beast's mother. Because of this, he didn't have high hopes for Angel either.

The lake lay off to his right. Its light-infused living water looked very inviting. But it was not that he wanted to soak in its warm depths but instead use it as a place to hide from the creature. If he were treading water in the middle of the lake, he hoped he would be safe. Although he knew some bears were good swimmers, especially grizzlies, he hoped that wouldn't be the case with this creature. Grizzlies had plenty of body fat that allowed them buoyancy, and thanks to their naturally oil-covered coat, their fur did not take on hundreds of pounds of water while they swam. Jerry wondered if that would be the case with this ancient predator? He made it to the ledge and raced along it, shooting past the exit without even looking at it and not stopping until he was well past and in darkness again. Gasping for breath, Jerry stood looking into the lake, assessing the situation.

There were literally thousands and thousands of fish swimming in this lake, most of them bioluminescent like the algae that covered most of the lakebed. Jerry paused for a moment, and he had to make a choice, and he had to make it now.

Angel burst into the cavern, his light flashing wildly as he ran. Just behind him, barely visible, was the beast. It let loose a thunderous roar, and Oritz shrieked. The creature had caught up to him. With a swipe of its razor claws, it shredded the back of his parka and the tattoo-covered skin beneath. It had almost been enough to knock him off his feet, but he'd managed to stay upright and kept running.

Witnessing this was enough for Jerry to arrive at a decision. He removed his bright blue parka, and the backpack Angel had made him wear, then dropped them to the ledge, along with the flashlight. Taking a deep breath, he dove headfirst into the lake.

Oritz came pounding along the ledge behind him moments later. He'd witnessed what Jerry had just done and decided to emulate his decision. Not having the time to disrobe first, he threw himself sideways into the water just as the bear swiped for him again. Its sabre-like claws whistled through the air at his back, and Angel splashed down like a cannonballer into the lake.

Jerry was in the middle of the lake by now, having done the backstroke through the water so he could keep an eye on things around him and not be taken unawares. Unfortunately, being on his back, he couldn't see beneath the lake's surface and had been oblivious of what else might be swimming in the water with him. Something brushed against his leg as he floated. Perhaps it was one of the colourful fish, curious if he might be edible. He glanced about in the water and finally caught a glimpse of the creature, and then his heart leapt into his throat. When he'd devised his cunning little plan to dive into the water, he hadn't expected the lake would contain anything more than the fish he'd seen earlier. Of course, he should have known the large body of warm water would be no different than the rest of this cursed cavern and would contain surprises of its own.

The creature was extraordinarily long and thick, with black, oily-looking scales covering its entire serpentine body. As Angel hit the water, the beast shot away from Jerry, no doubt deciding whatever had just entered its world with a splash was much more interesting than the thing floating idly on its back in the middle of the lake.

The bear stood on the ledge near the exit to the cavern, almost filling it completely. Outlined by the daylight beyond, it roared and swept one of its paws into the water in frustration, but didn't enter, just as Jerry hoped. The monster gave another shrieking roar, then turned and lumbered off into the darkening afternoon beyond. The second storm had hit like predicted, and fresh snow had begun falling outside.

Angel floundered about in the water in his heavy winter parka, trying to keep his head afloat. The water was red around him from the bear's welt across his back. Without warning, the long black beast decided he was worthy of a taste test after all and latched onto one of his arms, engulfing it almost up to the shoulder. He beat on the creature with his free hand, screaming in pain and rage simultaneously. The beast pulled away suddenly, taking a memento of Angel as it did, and his entire arm was ripped from its socket. Oritz screeched in pain but somehow managed to keep his head above water. As his life's blood poured forth, it attracted the attention of other creatures that called the lake home—creatures just like the animal that had taken his arm off. Their thick, oil-black bodies shot through the water like torpedoes to the spot where Angel thrashed about. And then they were upon him, dodging in and biting at him, pulling and tearing into his flesh. He let out a final weak scream and was dragged beneath the surface as the half dozen black beasts converged upon him all at once.

With several powerful, panicked strokes of his arms, Jerry swam toward the ledge where he'd dropped his parka and backpack. Grunting, he began to pull himself up onto the ledge. Unfortunately, his swimming had attracted the attention of another of the black creatures, and it came shooting toward him, no doubt to check and see what other food might be available in its aquatic domain. Almost out of the water, there was a brief tug as the animal tried to grab his boot and pull him back. Jerry kicked out hard, then pulled away with a yank and tore free of the creature. He flopped onto the ledge and rolled onto his back, gasping for breath and watched in horror as the lake creatures continued to feast on Angel Oritz.

Jerry knew he had only one option now; he had to get back down the mountain as quickly as possible in order to warn everyone that the horror from the past was repeating itself. Standing, he removed his wet shirt and began putting on his dry parka.

***

With Trudy's help, Alex had started to slowly and quietly remove some of the smaller rocks blocking their way near the top of the pile. They had made enough progress so that one person could almost squeeze through when they'd heard the shouting followed by the gunfire. Alex halted the extraction and put a finger to his lips as he heard the men coming their way.

Scooting up next to Alex, Trudy jammed her head close to his, and together they peered out through the hole in the rubble pile. The smaller man ran by first with his LED light, and within seconds, the taller man flew past their startled eyes. After a brief pause, in the faint light that streamed from the lake-filled cavern's steam-filled entrance, they saw what the men were running from.

Only a few metres from where they were hiding, a massive creature pounded past their point of view, chuffing and panting in ravenous excitement. Its head scraping the top of the tunnel, the beast was incredibly lean, with teeth like daggers and a tangled pelt the colour of the rock walls. Trudy had to cover her mouth to stop from shrieking in fear

Once the beast was well past, Alex removed a couple of the remaining rocks blocking the way, then squeezed through. On the other side, he reached up and helped Trudy down from the pile of rubble. Now free of the obstruction created by the explosion, they cautiously made their way toward the lake. Alex still had the Marlin .22 slung over his shoulder and attached to his pack, and he unslung it now. After hearing the other man's gunfire, he wasn't overly convinced of the stopping power of his own low-powered rifle.

They emerged through the steam into the cavern just in time to see the monstrous bear roar in frustration and swat at the water before escaping into the world beyond the cavern. In the lake, one of the men was thrashing about. Illuminated faintly from beneath by the glowing algae, the water around him was coloured deep crimson. Thick, black, snakelike creatures nipped and tore at him, ripping large chunks of flesh from his body with every bite. Trudy buried her face against Alex's shoulder, unable to witness the man's grisly demise.

Alex, however, couldn't tear himself away. He was in shock. Was that his friend, Jerry Benson, getting ripped to shreds in the lake before his very eyes? If so, where was the other man? Holding Trudy close, he looked about the dim glow of the cavern but could see no one else nearby.

Soon, the water stilled, and the oily-looking black things swam off in different directions. Slowly, the couple made their way toward the exit. As they neared the bright portal to freedom, sudden movement hidden in the shadow on the other side caused Alex to bring the rifle to bear on the person approaching them along the ledge. Chambering a round in his rifle, Alex said, "That's close enough, mister. Identify yourself."

With his hands raised in the air, the man stepped into the light. "I'm a Professor of Geology from UBC, and my name is Jerry Benson."

Shouldering his weapon, Alex stepped forward and said with relief, "Boy, am I glad it's the other guy that got eaten and not you, Mr. Benson!"

His eyes widening in surprise at seeing Alex, Jerry said with relief, "Me, too."

CHAPTER THIRTY-NINE

His hunger was back, and God, it hurt. Willy's stomach was growling so loudly, he thought it was gnawing its way out of his abdomen as if his body were consuming itself from the inside out. He'd been out in the backcountry on the hunt for a few hours now. After departing Trip's house, he'd made like Toucan Sam and followed his nose. Fortunately, the snow had held off, and he'd had no issue tracking the scents that floated on the wind. He'd never experienced such a thing before. Although he'd had a good sense of smell growing up, it was nothing like these new, heightened senses. Everything he smelled made his brain practically overload with sensation, like seeing the scent in 3D inside his brain at the same time as he smelled it. Was this how dogs and other animals with elevated olfactory senses operated? He didn't know, but it was exciting and frightening, both at once.

The wind had died down a short while ago, and now the first large flakes began to fall from the sky, their incredible latticework crumbling to nothing as they hit the ground, the trees and Willy. The fresh snow was going to make things more challenging for tracking. After leaving Trip's, he'd stumbled across some tracks that looked promising, and they had led him to the Gertzmeyer property. As well, he could smell the scent of the beast that had made them. At Geraldine's, he'd been disappointed to discover that there was nothing of interest there, and it looked like he had missed the party. However, on the wind, he'd smelled a faint trace of the creature that had been at Geraldine's, and he'd followed it. That had led him to the conservation office, where he'd found his new hunting companion.

The shed had been locked, but it hadn't been secured well enough to stop him. He'd heard the beast on the other side of the door howling and baying as he'd approached as if it had known he was somewhere nearby. Once he'd broken the lock from the door, the creature quieted as soon as he entered the Quonset hut.

Holding his hand out, Willy walked toward the ebony and grey coloured animal. While he'd approached the cage, he had not said anything soothing or attempted to calm the animal in any way but merely walked toward it.

Willy opened the feeding port in the trap's door and stuck his hand in without hesitation. With a whine, the wolf creature moved forward, its head low. It sniffed his hand and then licked it and finally rubbed its muzzle against it. Willy spoke to the beast, talking as if it understood what he was saying as he stood in front of the trap and unlatched the door. "I'm going to let you loose. Sorry about what happened to your mate, but it wasn't on purpose." The creature whined again and pawed at the closed trap door. Willy walked to the other end of the trap and retracted the cable that raised the steel mesh door to an open position.

The dire wolf stepped down to the dirt-covered floor, then slowly moved down the length of the trap until it stood before him. At almost four feet tall, the animal was not quite able to look him in the eye. It gave another slight, obsequious whine and then moved forward and licked his face, then nuzzled his hand once more. He scruffed its wiry black and grey hair, ignoring the mouthful of needle-sharp teeth staring him in the face. Willy had no fear whatsoever and did not flinch when he made contact. Somehow, he felt a connection to this beast. Whatever had happened as a result of his bite, along with the drugs, it had somehow been enough for this animal to now trust him. He chose to not question it and had decided to get out of Dodge while the getting was good.

When he'd pulled out of the conservation yard on Trip's sled several minutes later, the beast had followed him, not directly at his side, but instead trailed him from a distance. At first, Willy thought the beast was perhaps nervous about the snowmobile, but soon he saw that it was actually doing its own thing and hunting for food as they travelled.

On the outskirts of town near the public works yard, his new companion bounded off into the forest for several minutes before returning to his side. In its mouth was a winter hare as white as the snow that surrounded them. It dropped the large rabbit at Willy's feet and looked at him expectantly. Seeing the fluffy white corpse, Willy felt his hunger return tenfold. He picked it up and tore the creature limb from limb, throwing two gore-soaked legs to the wolf. Together the pair partook of the rabbit's succulent tender flesh, the beast's muzzle and Willy's face smeared in blood when they were done. Taking a handful of snow, Willy wiped his face with it, trying to rinse away some of the gore.

With their afternoon snack taken care of, the dire wolf loped away, and Willy followed it this time. They ended up at the public works yard. "What are we doing here, boy?" Willy dismounted the snowmobile and moved toward the cinderblock building. Now he could smell what had drawn the wolf here. The beast let out a low growl and pawed at the exterior door leading into the shop.

Fortunately, he had his keys and was able to spare this lock any damage. Willy left his companion waiting outside, and it settled into the snow to wait for him. The stench of the animals almost overpowered him when he entered the kennel room. Inside the topmost cubicle, he finally saw what had drawn him here, and his first instinct was fear. But why should he fear these small cats? They were not even a week old, and their eyes were still closed. However, he sensed that when these creatures grew up, they would be trouble for him and others of his kind.

Willy gave his head a little shake. His kind? Where had that thought come from? He looked at the sleeping kittens, an urge to crush and kill them suddenly came over him, but he resisted. These infants would be just the ticket to lure their mother in so that he could kill her, and then she would no longer be a threat to the pack.

He shook his head again. What the hell was going on here? The pack? He looked back at the kittens, and then he smiled— even if it turned out their mother was already dead, these small fry would make a tasty little treat for him and his companion in the near future.

In the staff locker room, he found an empty backpack. He dropped the mewling babies inside, then slung the pack over his back. When he moved outside, the dire wolf growled at him as soon as he stepped out the door. The animal smelled the sabre- tooth kittens but couldn't differentiate that they were only babies and were currently no threat. The beast only knew that the felines were its mortal enemy and needed to be destroyed. Willy kept the pack on his back and ignored the creature. The wolf padded around him in a circle, unsure what to make of this new scent that was part of him now. To the wolf, Willy said, "You can't eat these yet, we need them."

He let the wolf take the lead and followed it at a distance. They moved to the edge of the forest, skirting along the fringe of trees, just out of sight until they eventually arrived at the rear of the community complex. Something had drawn his hunting partner here. With the snow getting heavier, it seemed to have affected Willy's new super smell, and he hadn't noticed the scent the wolf was following until they were closer to it. Though the snow camouflaged their presence somewhat, it also hid the object of their quest, the mother of the mewling kittens that squirmed inside the pack on his back.

Trailing along the edge of the complex property in the thickly falling snow, they remained mostly hidden from view. Toward the rear corner of the building near the back door of the arboretum, something resolved out of the white nothingness that surrounded them—a bear trap.

His companion must have heard and smelled them first, then Willy did as well. More kittens were mewling from inside the metal cylinder. He cautiously moved inside the large, round trap. A cardboard carton sat near the trigger at the back, and he moved toward it. Upon hearing other kittens, the fur babies in the backpack began elevating their own mewling noises. Very gently, Willy opened the box and peered inside. Wrapped in a towel that reeked of the kitten's scent, he found a Bluetooth speaker. He folded the towel back around the speaker and exited the trap. The dire wolf had remained standing attentively outside the trap as if it were on guard duty while Willy had done his investigation.

It seemed this trap would be something to keep an eye on. Hopefully, mama cat would come by sooner or later, and he would be waiting. His dad's homemade experiment in self-defence was still attached to the back of the sled, loaded to bear. Between his dad's ingenuity and his wolfen companion, he felt he might succeed in killing the cat and its kittens, all in one fell swoop.

Willy sat on the edge of the snowmobile's seat for a moment, lost in thought, his mind feeling foggy all of a sudden. The wolf nuzzled his hand, and he felt his hunger swell. The intense pain in his stomach began gnawing away at him, and he knew he would have to do something about it very soon. However, he didn't want any food from the concession stand inside, nor did he want anything from the food trucks in the parking lot out front. No, he needed something raw, and he knew just where to find it.

CHAPTER FORTY

After the bear attack at Frostbite Fred's in January, the owners, Mattie and Norm, had decided to spruce the public house up a little bit in addition to repairing it. 4k high-definition TVs dotted several walls now, replacing the projection TV they'd had previously. Fresh decor along with brand-new tables and chairs served to enhance the all-natural wood motif of the establishment. Their insurance money had covered most of the damage, and they'd paid the difference to upgrade things out of their own pocket. With a soft opening at the beginning of December to capture some of the Christmas party business, things had been moving non-stop ever since.

Jenny Smith was glad to be back to work after being laid off for several months due to the pub's reconstruction. She was happy to see familiar faces coming through the doors once more. But it felt different now, especially because of what happened. Seeing Carlene Boseman killed along with several others, Jenny had needed some personal time off due to the trauma. The rebuilding at the pub had given her that time. She was almost positive she'd been suffering from some form of PTSD after witnessing the gruesome events, and the nightmares she'd had on many nights seemed to support the idea.

But all those thoughts were dispelled from her mind when she

265

saw two of her favourite people coming through the pub's front doors. She was so surprised, she did a double-take, genuinely happy to be seeing something she'd hoped might happen. Austin Murphy and Christine Moon had just entered the pub and appeared to be on a date! At least that's what she thought was happening, seeing as Austin was in a jacket and tie, and Christine was wearing something she'd never seen the conservation officer wear before—a dress. Jenny's smile stretched from ear to ear as she approached their table, and she said, "Hi guys! It's so great to see you both!" Her long brown ponytail bounced around on the top of her head as she spoke.

Brushing the snow from Christine's shoulders as he helped her off with her jacket, Austin gave a broad smile and said, "Hey Jenny."

Christine greeted the server with a large smile of her own and inquired, "Hi, Jenny, how are you?" A look of concern had entered her eyes, and she added, "Are you holding up okay after everything?"

With a bit of a sad smile, Jenny responded, "Not too bad. I'm glad it took them a while to get the renovations done here. It's given me a bit more time to come to grips with everything." She pulled a pair of menus from underneath one arm and held them up, asking, "Are you here for food tonight, or just drinks?" Her eyes lit up as she added, "We have some new additions to the menu as well, in case you're interested."

"Yes, dinner and drinks, please, Jenny," Austin said, accepting the proffered menus and giving one to Christine. "You wouldn't believe how much I've been looking forward to tucking into some of Max's ribs and roasts again."

"It's true," Christine added. "He's been salivating and practically going into withdrawal over the last few months, ever since we decided to come here once the place finally reopened."

"That's allowed," Jenny said with a grin. "There are worse

things in life to be addicted to than Max's ribs and roasts."

Austin nodded in agreement and cracked the menu open, saying, "That's what I thought, too."

"Would you both like something to drink to start?"

"Perhaps a half-litre of the house white?" Austin suggested. He looked at Christine, and she nodded her assent with a small smile.

With a big grin, Jenny said, "I'll be back in a flash, guys."

***

Austin and Christine had decided to start their date early since they wanted to take in part of the Winter Solstice Smackdown happening at the complex. It was now just a few minutes past 6:00 P.M. and Austin's nerves were on edge for several reasons. The cat that had killed Virgil Raines was still on the loose, the dire wolf was once more on the prowl after its jail break, and he still didn't know where Alex was. He hoped that the trap he and Christine had set would be effective in catching the cat. However, the wolf might be another story. He was still in disbelief that they were having a resurgence of these creatures in the area. It appeared that the cave system they thought had been forever sealed was still somehow spitting forth more blasts from the past out of its cavernous womb. He knew that he and Chris would have to check things out up on the hill once the storms had passed.

Another part of his nerves was the fact that here he was, finally on a date with Christine Moon. They had gotten to know each other reasonably well, mentally at least. And now, here they were, getting ready to take things to the next level and out on an actual date for the very first time. It had been almost two years since Patricia had passed, and he felt he was finally ready to look at life once again with some hope. The woman sitting across from him was not Patricia, but he found himself growing fonder and more attracted to Christine each day. She also filled him with hope for the future. After Patricia, he wasn't sure if he'd ever feel anything akin to romantic thoughts toward another woman, and yet, here he was, thinking them now.

"Careful you don't drown," Christine chimed, her mellifluous voice breaking Austin out of his introspective ruminations.

"Huh? Sorry, just thinking some thoughts."

Studying Austin, Christine said, "I know. They looked pretty deep. Is there anything you'd like to share?"

Jenny returned with the wine and poured a small amount from the carafe into each of the wine glasses she'd brought with her. After she was done, she asked, "Would you like a few more minutes to look at the menu?"

'Please," Christine said with a small smile.

Austin continued their conversation, saying, "I was just thinking about life. And we seem to be going through almost the same thing again as we did in January. Except that we know each other a bit better now."

"To new friends," Christine said, holding up her wine glass.

Taking up his own glass, Austin nodded and said, "And new beginnings."

Christine clinked her glass gently against Austin's and agreed with a smile, "And new beginnings."

Just as he began to take his first sip of the house white, Austin's phone began to ring. He sighed and asked, "Sorry, do you mind?" Christine shook her head in the negative, and he pulled it from his pocket. It was Alex. He took the call, saying, "Hey buddy! How was your day on the hill?"

"Dad! Am I glad I got a hold of you. Where are you?"

"I'm at Frostbite Fred's with Christine. It's our date night, remember?" He blushed slightly as he said the word 'date'.

"It's happening again!"

Christine's brow furrowed as she listened to one half of the conversation.

"What? What do you mean, happening again?" Austin put the cell on speakerphone so Chris could hear.

"There's something loose in the valley again!"

"We covered that at breakfast, remember?"

"Yeah, but you're not aware of this."

"Why, what happened?"

"We were just up at Gold Ridge like I said we'd be. And Trudy and I found a way into the cavern, and then a whole bunch of stuff happened."

"You what? The cavern? What happened?"

Christine leaned forward in interest.

"It's a bit of a long story, so I'll tell you when we see you. Just stay at Fred's. I've got the sled loaded back on my truck, and we're only a few minutes away. I need to tell you what happened, and I have someone with me you'll want to see." Alex clicked off the line, and Austin hung up his phone. He looked across the table at Christine and realised that 'date night' was now officially over.

Christine took another sip of her wine and looked into Austin's eyes as she said, "It looks like our beginnings aren't as new as we'd hoped."

CHAPTER FORTY-ONE

Wind-whipped snow ruffled the beast's fur as it moved through the darkened forest, the last of the day's light long ago smothered by the relentless storm. Now freed from the unrelenting darkness of the cavern, the creature didn't care because it didn't need to see its prey to stalk it; it only needed to smell it. And the beast knew it was currently close to something delicious. Gnawing pain ripped through its insides, driving it forward through deep drifts, its powerful leg muscles pushing the snow aside with ease.

It was ravenous, and it couldn't remember the last time it had eaten. Another pang of hunger shot through its belly, renewing its frustration that it had been unable to catch the prey that had jumped into the big water at the cavern. Despite its size, it had remained on the shore, well aware of what entering the body of water would have meant. When the beast and its sibling had been cubs, their mother would sometimes bring them with her to the big water to teach them how to hunt. She had shown them how to grab fish from the shore and not be pulled under by the black things that called the lake home. Other times she would depart the cavern to forage for prey, leaving them safe in the cavern. But then, one day, she never returned.

The beast moved through the snow, sniffing the air as it moved, but its mother's scent was no longer carried on the wind in this valley. After its littermate had died in the bubbling water, the beast had found itself trapped and unable to retreat when the earth had started to move. It had been struck by rock that fell from above, and then it had remembered no more for quite a while. When it awoke, it found itself trapped, and so it had slept and healed and waited and hungered. Now, it had been freed by the loud noise, and it was no longer constrained by the dark place and its pitiful amounts of prey. It had a new companion to keep it company—insatiable hunger. It salivated as it imagined fresh quarry being caught and crushed in its jaws and the large, bloody chunks sliding down its throat into its insatiable belly. These thoughts compelled it onward as it hunted for something to silence its burning hunger, moving ever forward through the grey, featureless twilight of the thickening storm.

After a while, it came to a trail in the snow. The creature stopped and breathed deeply, taking in great snoutfuls of air. The prey it was tracking had recently moved through here. Despite the fresh snow which lay across the other animal's tracks, the beast had no problem detecting its quarry and could almost taste its sweet, tender flesh. Inhaling, the beast's eyes went wide, and its nostrils flared—its quarry was very close by.

Near a small stand of trees in the middle of a clearing, the prey's scent became more potent than ever, and thick ropes of saliva hung from its partially open mouth. Slowing its pace to ensure it was as silent as possible, the creature crept to the edge of the trees, inhaling the scent deeply, already tasting the bloody flesh that would soon be sliding down its throat.

The doe was sleeping in a bed of needles under a large fir tree, dry and warm despite the snow that surrounded it. It had recently discovered itself with young growing inside and found it needed to rest more. She was still several months away from coming full term with the offspring carried in her belly. Ever watchful for predators, even while sleeping, the deer's eyes suddenly popped open, her muscles tensing when she thought she heard the crack of a branch nearby. With ears turning this way and that, she listened intently, her body coiled and ready to spring away to safety at a moment's notice. After hearing nothing more after several minutes of bright-eyed alertness, the doe settled back down to sleep.

Standing only feet from the sleeping deer, the massive beast was just on the other side of the towering fir tree. It slowly inhaled the doe's scent, relishing the smell of the still-warm living creature that would soon be inside its belly. It crept around the tree, a study in predatory stealth, and soon it stood towering over the small animal. Saliva once again came flooding out of its mouth, and it dripped down onto the doe.

Though seeming to be asleep, as the first drop of saliva hit the deer's head, it sprang up as if shocked by a bolt of lightning. This time, though, its leap wasn't to safety but rather to its death as a large mouthful of razor-sharp teeth closed around its head and neck, catching it in mid-jump. The beast crushed the small animal to bloody paste in its powerful jaws and swallowed it in a feeding frenzy that only left it wanting more.

Its sensitive nose already picking up other interesting scents, the predator left the clearing. Breathing deeply again, it felt overwhelmed by the amount of quarry it smelled, and it was stealthy no longer. Other wildlife in its path fled as it approached, but it didn't care. Those creatures were not what it wanted now. What it wanted was down below—more prey than it could ever have imagined, and it wanted to taste them all and never, ever stop eating. Its breath steamed from its nose as it moved eagerly forward, hot saliva pouring from its parted jaws and melting into the deepening snow.

Despite its hunger, as the steep terrain levelled out, it came to a place that it needed to stop and investigate. It pushed inside the structure and breathed deeply of the darkness, recognising what had drawn it there. This was almost like the dark place of its home, but it also had one other thing that had attracted its attention; it was heavy with its mother's scent. The beast moved to the lowest depths, smelling the dampness of the earthen floor and of old foods it had no interest in eating. This was where its mother had slept and breathed deeply of her musk. She had spent time here, resting between hunting forays to feed the growing appetites of her cubs back at the cavern. Inhaling what remained of her scent, the animal let out a low resonant moan from deep within its chest that built and built until the dark space was filled with the sound of its anguish.

Exiting the space back to the outside world, it was quickly coated by heavy snow. With another deep breath, the creature caught the scent of prey down in the valley below. But it also smelled something else mixed in with it, hiding amongst the other scents. This was not prey but an ancient rival as formidable as itself. Memories of when they were cubs flashed through the animal's mind, and it recalled their mother fending off the creature that carried this scent, or one just like it, back home in the dark place.

Their mother had kept them safe, allowing them to grow strong and fierce just like her. Now a massive animal, the beast didn't fear its adversary but instead looked forward to encountering it. And when it did, it would rip it to pieces with its claws, then grind it to a pulp in its jaws. Soon it would drink the blood of its enemy and gorge on the helpless prey that lived in the valley below. The beast pushed on through the thickening snow, large snowflakes covering its heavy pelt and camouflaging it as it moved. It roared in a combination of anger, loss and insurmountable hunger.

CHAPTER FORTY-TWO

In keeping with its name, the Burger Barn had at one time been an actual barn. As such, it was on the outskirts of Lawless town limits. Fred Paulson remembered when this part of town was countryside, back when he'd first started with the force. When Ed and Marie Popov had bought the barn many years ago, Fred recalled driving by on patrol, watching as the old structure was refurbished. Over a period of several months of hard work, it finally opened in the fall of 1989. Ever since, the Burger Barn had been selling some of the tastiest burgers around, utilising only freshly ground chuck and cooking them to flame-broiled perfection.

From his table in the second-floor mezzanine known as the 'Hey Loft', Fred looked around the dining area, noting what had changed after the Barn's recent quake induced renovation. Fortunately, with things now securely fastened to the wall, there was no danger of anything falling on anyone's head anymore. According to Marie, almost every window had to be replaced after the January rumble, but fortunately, their insurance had covered it all. Outside, the snow had been falling for several minutes. It swirled in large, lazy flakes as it fell to the ground, mesmerising him. Fred wondered what else was skulking around out there that they didn't know about? He held his chicken-avocado bacon burger in front of his mouth without taking a bite, almost forgetting it was there.

Clara Carleton nudged Fred in the ribs and nodded toward his burger, saying, "Are you just going to hold it in your hand until it gets cold, or are you going to eat it?"

"Sorry, what's that, Clara?" Fred asked, coming out of his trance.

"It looked like you were either having a 'senior moment' or suffering the effects of some other disorder to which people like us are prone."

"People like us? You mean 'life experienced' people?"

"That's a lovely way to put it," Clara said with a small smile, then nibbled at her single cheeseburger.

Fred finally took a bite of his burger and said, "I was just thinking of what's going on out there at the moment."

"You mean the snow?"

"No, I mean that wolf and now this giant cat wandering around out there." Earlier this afternoon, he'd told Clara about what had happened up at Virgil's place, leaving out some of the gorier parts.

"Well, at least it's not like that thing we had wandering around out there in January," Clara observed.

"No, but I think between the two of them, they could be just as lethal."

Clara took a sip of her tea and then said, "I suppose that could be true."

Through the heavy snow, the headlights of a snowmobile appeared outside. It pulled up to the side of the building opposite from where Fred had parked his Suburban. A man stepped off the sled, then petted what looked like a large black dog that had been following behind him.

The door to the restaurant opened down below, and Fred watched as Willy Wilson Jr. stumbled through the doors wearing a backpack on his back. Not looking anywhere but straight ahead, the young man approached the counter, covered in snow. Strangely, he didn't bother brushing any of it off himself after coming through the doors.

"I'll be back in a second. I want to see how Willy's doing." He stood and moved to the spiral staircase that led down to the main floor of the restaurant.

***

Willy approached the counter, holding his belly.

"Hi, honey," Marie Popov said with a concerned smile. "Are you okay?"

With a shake of his head, Willy said, "I've been better, but I think I just need food right now. I'm starving."

"Okay, hun. I think we can help you out. What can I get for you?"

"Give me a Quadruple Bypass, hold the fixings, and the bun."

"On one of those keto kicks, are you?"

"No, and don't cook the meat either."

"We're not supposed to sell raw meat to our customers. If you want to cook your own burgers at home, just stop in at the supermarket and buy yourself some nice ground round," Marie added helpfully.

"But I don't want to cook them. I want to eat them."

"What, raw?" Marie asked, her eyes widening slightly, taken aback by the thought.

"Yup." Willy nodded slightly, still holding his belly.

"Sorry, hun." Marie shook her head. "No can do."

"Listen," Willy began to raise his voice, "all I want…"

"What is it you want, Willy?" a voice asked at his back.

His face flushed and a wild look in his eyes, Willy turned and saw Chief Paulson standing behind him. With a flash of anger, he said, "Food, I'm starving."

From behind the counter at Willy's back, Marie chimed in, "He wanted some raw burger meat, Fred. I told him we can't sell that to him and that he'd have to go down the street to the market to get some." As she spoke, Marie noticed the backpack on Willy's back was moving, then added, "What on earth do you have in there, Willy?"

Turning partially back to Marie, Willy snarled, "None of your business!"

"Whoa there, son. Calm down," Fred said, putting his hand on his hip near his taser from out of habit from when he used to be on the road.

"Look, I just need some food here!" Willy said loudly.

"We heard you the first time, son." Trying to change the topic to diffuse the situation, Fred asked, "How's your foot feeling today?"

Confused, Willy looked down at his foot and then back up at Fred as if forgetting what had happened to him the night before.

"It's good. All healed up."

"What?" Fred said in surprise. "That's not possible."

"God's honest truth, Chief," Willy said, still holding his stomach like his intestines were about to spill out all over the place.

"You never answered the lady, Willy. What's in your backpack?" Fred could now see that something was moving around in the boy's pack.

"Nothing, just some old junk I picked up from my house."

"Old junk doesn't normally move on its own. Mind if I take a look?"

"Yeah, I do," Willy said aggressively.

Fred moved his hand to his taser and said, "I'm going to have to insist, son." Whatever was in the backpack suddenly started mewling. He recalled the phone call he'd received from Austin about the missing sabre-toothed kittens from the works yard, and he knew he needed to stop whatever the young man was planning to do with them.

Removing the pack as if in compliance, Willy started to hold it out to Fred, then suddenly seemed to think better of it and bolted toward the door. Fred pulled his taser out of its holster and said, "Hold it right there, son or I'm gonna have to tase you."

Willy paid him no heed and began opening the door, and Fred followed through on his threat. He hated to do it to the kid after all he'd been through, especially seeing as the boy was just out of the hospital. However, something was going on here that didn't make sense. Willy was one of the nicest and friendliest kids he'd ever met, and this rebellious streak was entirely unlike him. Fred felt compelled to stop the boy before he hurt himself or others.

As the taser's barbs pierced the fabric of Willy's winter jacket, the electricity surged into his body. Dropping the backpack to the floor, he fell against the glass door, spilling out into the snowy evening beyond. He vibrated and jittered on the ground, half in and half out of the doorway. After a brief pause, he began to stand again.

That's impossible, Fred thought; the boy had just had 50,000 volts pumped into him. With a shake of his head, he said, "Stay down, son," then pulled the trigger again.

Willy shrieked this time and collapsed back to the ground, apparently unconscious, falling out onto the snow-covered patio stones near the entrance. His feet were still partially inside the Barn's doors, keeping them open.

Fred began to edge toward the door, his finger still on the trigger of the taser. The security lights over the entrance to the Barn illuminated something approaching from the side of the building, shrouded in the falling snow. Fred stepped back in surprise—a dire wolf! The beast moved to Willy's crumpled form. Was this the same wolf that had bit Willy last night, Fred wondered? The one Austin said they'd captured in a trap at Geraldine's? Or was it a different one? And why was it with Willy now and protecting him? The beast sniffed for a moment and then lifted its head and growled loudly and deeply in its throat. Still holding the taser, Fred reached to the other side of his utility belt and pulled his Smith & Wesson 5906 from its holster. The beast gave the semi-conscious boy another quick sniff, growled once more, then lunged toward Fred.

The chief pulled his trigger three times. The first bullet hit the door frame and ricocheted off into the darkness. The second hit the glass panel in the upper part of the door, and it shattered, showering Willy's body with glass shards. The third bullet found its mark, blowing a hole in the centre of the animal's chest and punching it back into the snowy night.

Clara arrived at the bottom of the staircase from the loft and moved to Fred's side, her eyes wide and unblinking. She put her hand on Fred's arm and said, "What got into Willy? And why is that thing here with him?"

Fred shook his head and said, "I don't know what's going on around here anymore." Fred knelt next to Willy's supine form and placed his handcuffs on the young man, then added, "But I suspect we'll find out once Willy comes around." He helped the boy into a sitting position in the doorframe, then picked his cell phone out of his pocket and dialled Trip Williams, who picked up almost immediately. "Trip! Thought you'd like to know we found your missing kittens and the other wolf, but you might want to bring a baggie for him; he's a little messy."

CHAPTER FORTY-THREE

Turning this way and that, Roxanne Rooney checked out the burgundy-coloured dress she was wearing. With a daringly deep 'V' neckline, it clung in all the right places, accentuating each and every curve of her taut body. "That ought to do it," she said, nodding at herself in the mirror with a smile. She fluffed her red mane, checked her lipstick and then went to put on her jacket and boots. The wall clock in the living room said it was five minutes before seven o'clock.

Franklin Pearce had just texted her, saying he would pick her up in a couple of minutes. In addition to their little coffee talk, he'd sent her an email after their meeting, outlining a few more thoughts he'd had on their evening of subterfuge. Apparently, she was going to be running interference for Franklin. Once inside the house, she was supposed to excuse herself to use the bathroom, then leave the window open. Pearce would sneak in through that, and while she kept Ethan busy, he would search the rest of the house.

A knock came at her door as she was buttoning up her mink coat. She opened the door to see Franklin standing there, his shit-eating grin on full display. He was wearing a white snowsuit and looked very much like a Norwegian winter commando. Stepping inside and closing the door, he said, "Hey there, Red, are you all ready?"

"Yeah, I think so. Let's do this thing." She moved to grab her bag hanging at the door

"Let me see what you're wearing, first."

"Seriously?"

"24/7," Franklin said, his smile evaporating.

Sighing, Roxanne unbuttoned her mink and pulled it open for Franklin to see. He smiled again when he saw she'd chosen the red one with the plunging neckline, which did everything it was designed to do.

With an appreciative nod, Franklin said, "Nice. If that doesn't distract him, I don't know what will."

Her clothing check complete, Roxanne began fastening the buttons on her knee-length coat once more. She made to grab her bag, and Franklin said, "What do you need that for?"

"What do you think? Girl things!"

"Let me see." He held out his hand.

"What?" With another sigh, she opened her bag. He looked inside and quickly rifled through things, just like a cop would, then handed it back, saying, "Looks okay."

Grabbing the bag back from Franklin, she said, "Gee, thanks." She followed him out the door, turning to lock it on the way out. Inside her bag was a small travel case with a few makeup essentials, feminine sanitary products and a flashlight. What she didn't tell Franklin was, apart from the 'girl things' he saw in her bag, things were not quite as they seemed. The flashlight in the bag was actually a Vipertek VTS-195. It looked for all the world like any regular small, tactical flashlight. But that was to disguise the fact that its actual function was that of a stun gun. It was something she'd picked up a couple of years ago and never went anywhere without it. Not because Lawless was a crime-ridden city loaded with rapists and miscreants, but it was more for the feeling of reassurance it gave her when she went out for her evening jogs (when the weather permitted). She felt very confident running down the forested paths near her home, knowing she could stop a cougar or someone's errant pitbull if need be. And if every woman's worst nightmare were to come true, she had 40,000 volts to give any would-be molesters a shocking experience they wouldn't soon forget.

The drive over to Ethan's took several minutes, thanks to worsening road conditions from the heavy snow. They parked out on the street, a couple of houses down from Chance's house. Heritage homes dotted much of Lawless, interspersed with post WW2 cracker boxes in which many of the residents in the north end of town lived, just like Roxanne. However, the South end of town was where all the newer, more expensive houses had been built, and the Chance estate had sprung up along with them several years before Ray's death.

"Okay, here we are," Franklin said, killing the engine of his Jeep. Turning to Roxanne, he asked, "You ready for this?"

Looking over at Franklin, Roxanne said, "Let's just get this over with."

"You remember the plan?"

"Yeah, we just went over it on the drive here, remember?"

"After you get in the door, just make sure you make an excuse to use the ground floor bathroom at the back near the kitchen. Leave the window unlocked, and I'll do the rest."

"Gotcha," Roxanne said with a nod and climbed out of the Jeep.

The sidewalk in front of Ethan's house was shovelled, along with the walkway up to the front door, which she appreciated, since she'd worn her sexy boots, not her walking boots. She pressed the brass-framed black plastic button next to the front door. Inside the house, she could hear a faint 'bing-bong'. After a moment, Ethan answered the door.

"Hi, Roxanne. Great to see you. Please come in." He stepped back and swept his arm into the foyer. Wearing black dress slacks and a white silk shirt, with his dark hair and pencil-thin moustache, he reminded her of Johnny Depp, but shorter and rounder.

Stepping through the threshold into the house, Roxanne took in the opulence of the room around her. Off to the right, rich, cream-coloured carpets covered the floor of the living room. Large paintings dotted the walls, and several tall art-nouveau sculptures stood in opposing corners. Two very comfortable-looking leather chairs and a matching couch were flanked by glass and chrome coffee and occasional tables. To the left, a large sweeping staircase wound upward to the second floor. Mirrors sparkled on both sides of the stairs, making it look like a carnival funhouse due to the infinity of reflections.

"May I take your coat?"

"Absolutely, thanks." Roxanne shrugged out of her mink, then slipped off her boots. She kept her bag over her shoulder.

Ethan hung the fur in a large closet off to one side of the foyer, then said, "How about a glass of wine? I have a lovely malbec from the Okanagan—Mission Hill Vineyards, I believe." Seeing Roxanne's purse, he asked, "Can I take your bag, too?"

"Wine would be great, please," Roxanne said, thinking a little alcohol would be needed to numb herself for the upcoming shenanigans. "But I'll keep my bag. It has girl things I might need later."

Nodding understandingly, Ethan said, "Of course."

She followed him as he led the way toward the back of the house and the massive country kitchen situated there. Walking by a bathroom in the hall just before the kitchen, Roxanne said sweetly, "If you'll excuse me, I just need to use the ladies room first."

"Absolutely. I'll go open the wine." Ethan moved to the kitchen, leaving Roxanne to her own devices.

Filled with more chrome and mirrors, Roxanne's eyes were dazzled from the glare inside the guest bathroom. There was a window next to a glass-walled walk-in shower. She unlocked the window, popped it open a crack, then turned and flushed the toilet and ran the water in the sink for a few seconds. Pumping out some hand lotion from a dispenser on the counter, she began massaging it into her hands. Her skin got so dry in the winter. She smiled to herself, realising if all went well, she'd be able to afford enough lotion to bathe in soon if she wanted.

The kitchen was massive. Two marble islands sat in the middle of the room, one with a sink and another with a stovetop and sizeable stainless steel vent overhead. In keeping with the metallic look of the house, all of the appliances were stainless steel as well. Ethan stood at the island with the sink, working a cork out of a wine bottle. Spotting Roxanne, he said, "Just in time."

Roxanne joined Ethan at the island and watched as he popped the cork from the bottle.

"This really is a beautiful house."

"Thanks, dear old dad had pretty good taste." They clinked the glasses together, and Ethan made a toast, "To beauty, wealth and power."

Roxanne smiled and began to sip her drink.

In a sudden flash of movement, Franklin Pearce burst into the room, white balaclava pulled down over his face, gun pointed at them both. In a gruff voice, he shouted, "Nobody moves, and nobody dies."

Ethan dropped his wineglass to the floor in surprise, and it shattered into millions of crystalline shards, splashing both him and Roxanne with malbec.

Roxanne raised her hands and backed away from Ethan ever so slightly. Franklin advanced and pointed his Glock at Ethan's head, saying, "We need to have a little discussion about gold."

From behind, Roxanne suddenly moved close to Franklin. She placed her Viper flashlight against his neck and unloaded 40,000 volts into his exposed skin. Pearce dropped the Glock, then joined it on the floor, striking his head on the tiles. Roxanne stood over top of Franklin and kicked the gun away into the puddle of wine, saying, "That's right! We want yours."

CHAPTER FORTY-FOUR

Trip sighed as he looked at the state of his kitchen. It seemed Willy had eaten most of his food, and he'd eaten it raw. At least he figured that was the case since there were no pots or pans dirtied. A dozen eggshells lay in the sink, the empty carton on the counter next to it. "Who does he think he is, Rocky Balboa?" He grimaced in disgust at the thought of cracking a raw egg and dropping it into his mouth, a dozen times no less.

With something that wasn't quite admiration, Trip noted the boy had also eaten his porterhouse steak and done a pretty good job cleaning off the bone. No knives were evident in the sink with the empty eggshells, which meant he must have ripped it off with his bare hands and teeth. Trip shuddered at this new thought.

Sitting on the kitchen floor next to him, Spider let out a small, "Erf!

"Yeah, I know, little buddy. I was looking forward to that steak, too." Trip sighed again. Despite his proclivity for eating out as often as he could afford at Fred's or the Barn when they were open, he was a pretty good cook. And with two of his favourite places closed for renovations over the last several months, he'd had to rely on his own skills in front of the stove to keep himself fed. Although, he'd done pretty well with Geraldine Gertzmeyer.

Over the spring and summer, he'd repaired her porch and doorway from the damage the bear and earthquake had caused. The old girl had been very grateful for his help fixing things up, as well as his assistance in decorating the outside of her house over the last few weeks. To show her gratitude, she'd invited him over to dinner numerous times. So, although it appeared he was a generous and helpful soul, his reasons were duplicitous. With a rumble, the co-conspirator in his duplicity, his stomach, made itself known. Somehow, despite his disgust at how Willy had eaten his food, he was still hungry.

He had just gotten back from the Burger Barn after Chief Paulson had called him, and he was kicking himself now for not picking up something to eat while he was there. After he'd loaded up his sled into his truck, along with the body of the dire wolf, he'd driven away without thinking to order a sandwich. But it was understandable. At the time, dealing with the stinking carcass of the dire wolf, his appetite had been definitely on the back burner. He'd dropped off the wolf's corpse at the works yard, storing it in the outside shed with the other wolf, then called Chris Moon to update her on all the excitement.

After all that was said and done, he'd been almost home before he realised he'd picked up nothing for dinner. But then he'd remembered the steak in his fridge, and by the time he walked through the front door, he'd been practically drooling at the thought of broiling it in the oven. But now, after discovering that Willy had chowed down on it au naturel, he realised he'd need to see what he had in his freezer.

Willy was currently back in the hospital, secured to a bed for observation. A small bonus was the present the boy had left him strapped to the back of his snowmobile, a homemade flamethrower. It was quite a nice job, actually, and he figured it must have been Willy's old man who had constructed it due to the senior Willy's mechanical expertise. Willy Sr. had been a friend of Trips, not a close one, but still, an affable man who'd been a pleasure to knock back a few cold ones with on a hot summer day. Trip had seen a few videos on YouTube over the years of people building their own flamethrowers, but Willy Sr. had taken it to the next level. The thing almost looked like the rocket pack from one of his favourite old Disney flicks, The Rocketeer. He hadn't tried it out yet since he had nothing that needed to be incinerated at the moment. For now, he had left it near the back porch door in the kitchen, meaning to put it out in his shop the next day. He'd also found the hall closet door ajar and discovered his rifle was missing too. Where it had gotten to was anybody's guess since it wasn't on the sled with the flamethrower or on Willy's person when he was arrested.

Walking through to his back porch, Trip stuck his head into the small chest freezer located there, looking for something for dinner. The porch of his small bungalow wasn't really a porch anymore since he'd framed it in and insulated it. It was now a multi-purpose room, and he used it as a laundry room, recycling area and a spot for his small chest freezer. Spider 'erfed' on the floor next to him while he rummaged around in the freezer. Standing upright, Trip looked down at the small dog, "Yeah, I'm working on it, buddy. But this isn't for you; this is for me." He held out a green and red box for the dog to sniff, saying, "It's a Delissio night."

The dog whined and let out another small bark.

"Don't worry. For you, I have something special." He ambled back into the kitchen and pulled a can of Alpo dog food from a reusable grocery bag he'd left on the counter. After picking up the sled and Willy's 'rocket pack', he'd stopped at the Gas 'n' Gulp on the way out to his house. Along with the Alpo, he'd also picked up a half dozen boxes of Whiskas Cat Milk while he was there. It was for the two furry waifs he'd brought home with him from the Burger Barn. He'd toyed with the idea of taking the cubs back to the Works yard but had decided to bring them home instead because of the trauma they had been through. After their terrifying experience in Willy's backpack, he didn't have the heart to lock them up in a little cage.

The babies were now, once more, in a towel-lined, high-sided cardboard box that he'd placed on a desk in his spare room. Their little eyes were now open, and they were able to wobble around on unsteady legs but not yet ready to stand and try to climb out of their cardboard crib. And it turned out the kittens were hungry. Fortunately, the box was a fair size, and Trip was able to fit his homemade cat feeder inside. He'd taken an old rubber glove, poked a couple of holes in two of the fingertips and made nipples for them to suckle on since they were still too young to drink from a bowl. He lowered the glove into the box and the kittens latched onto the tips greedily, draining the glove in record time. Spider had danced around Trip's feet during the feeding procedure, eager to see the babies, and he had to lift the dog up to see them when he was finished.

With the twins now taken care of, Trip sauntered back to the kitchen to see if the oven had warmed up enough to get his pepperoni pizza cooking, but it wasn't quite there yet. While he waited, he opened the Alpo and plopped half the can into a small Pyrex bowl, then placed it on the floor next to a similar bowl full of water. The dog attacked the assorted meat by-products with a zeal that Trip found particularly endearing. While he watched the dog, the small light near the stove clock that said the pre-warm finally went out. He peeled off the plastic wrap, then stuck the pizza in the oven.

When Trip turned back, Spider had gobbled down his Alpo and now sat looking expectantly for something more. "Well, that was quick! I guess now's a good time for brown pop, buddy. What do you think?" The dog barked in agreement, and Trip extracted a blue and white can of Kokanee from the fridge and popped the tab on top. The snapping sound and hissing fizz that followed made the small dog jump slightly, and he said, "Sorry, pal, I should have warned you these things can be kinda noisy."

Tonight, as much as he would have liked to head to Fred's for something more satisfying than frozen pizza, he was on babysitting duty, and he'd decided to stay home with the kids. He'd have to watch the game on his ancient rear-projection TV that he'd purchased in the mid-90s. It took the antiquated set a little while to come up to full brightness, so he moved to the living room to turn it on now and make sure it was ready to watch when the pizza was done. It didn't have the sharpest picture, but the lamps inside were still bright enough for him to see the action going up and down the hockey rink on its forty-six-inch screen.

Plopping down in his equally old La-Z-Boy recliner, Trip remembered the day he'd brought the TV home and being blown away at the size of the picture. Of course, it couldn't compare to a modern 4K, but he was okay with that. When his TV finally shuffled off this mortal coil to meet its electronic maker in circuit heaven, he'd think about getting something more current, but not until then. He sipped his beer and watched a few minutes of the current game playing of the Ottawa Senators against the Montreal Canadiens, a smile creeping through his bushy white beard.

An indeterminate amount of time later, Trip awoke to the smell of smoke, the fire alarm blaring, and the dog barking. Practically launching from the recliner, he said, "Shit!" and ran to the kitchen with Spider close on his heels. Smoke poured from the stovetop vent, and he slammed the oven door down. A cloud of acrid smoke poured out and filled the room. Coughing loudly, he pulled out the smoking pizza and said, "Oh, man!"

Spider 'erfed' in agreement. Trip moved to the smoke alarm on the wall of the kitchen and muted its incessant shriek. "Sorry about that, little buddy. Hard on the ears, ain't it?"

The dog barked again but kept dancing around agitatedly as if there was something else of import Trip was missing. "What is it, boy? Did little Timmy fall down the well again?"

He followed the dog to the spare room. The kittens must have smelled the smoke and had no doubt been scared by the smoke alarm as well. They were now mewling at the top of their lungs and moving about in the box. Just as Trip reached in to pet them and try to calm them down, he heard the breaking of glass and something crash in the back porch storage room.

"What in the hell?" He turned and trotted back to the kitchen to discover he had more significant problems than a burnt pizza. With great care, he slowly opened the door that separated the enclosed porch from the house. He flicked the light on and saw the window in the door leading outside had been shattered out of its frame, and there were deep rends in the wood all around its edges. Outside, the snow was being kicked up by the wind, and some of it blew through the gaping hole where the window used to be.

"Man, I wish I had my Winchester." Suddenly, he remembered the 'rocket pack' propped up against the wall next to the door. Trip stepped into his boots as he shrugged on his parka. He strapped the flamethrower to his back, then ignited the small butane torch situated in the nozzle. To Spider, he said, "You stay here and watch the kids, little buddy." He stepped out into swirling snow, closed the door and was swallowed by the night.

CHAPTER FORTY-FIVE

Knowing that Alex and his girlfriend, along with some unknown stranger, were joining them at Fred's, Austin and Christine ordered a new item on the pub's revamped menu—a sampler platter to feed six. It included bite-sized versions of many popular items, including mozzarella sticks, beef-rib bites, crispy onion rings and tempura fried vegetables with dip. They put the order in with Jenny as soon as Austin got off the phone, hoping it would be ready when everyone arrived.

Only a couple of minutes after the platter hit the table, so did everyone else. Alex pushed through the pub door first, then held it open for his companions. Trudy came next, a worried expression on her face. Both Austin and Christine's eyes widened when they saw who came through the door last.

"Jerry Benson? What are you doing up here?" Christine stood and hugged Jerry, saying, "It's great to see you! How are you?"

With a sad shake of his head, Jerry said, "I've been better, let me tell you." He sat down at the table with an exhausted sigh.

Christine gave Trudy a small hug as well, though she didn't know the girl as well as she did Jerry. But judging by the expression on her face, the girl looked like she could use a reassuring hug. And Christine wasn't wrong—the girl hugged her back, hard, then sat down next to Alex.

Foregoing a hug, Austin stood and shook Jerry's hand across the table, saying, "It's great to see you again, my friend! What brings you back up here?"

"A convicted felon."

"What?" Christine said in surprise.

Jerry briefly outlined his adventure so far, starting with the kidnapping from his apartment and white-knuckled trip up to Lawless and ending with his experience in the cavern and subsequent swim in the lake. "And then after I clawed my way up onto that ledge and watched Angel die, I met up with these two." He looked over to Alex and Trudy, a grateful smile on his face. "I don't know what I would have done if they hadn't been there. Most likely frozen to death trying to come down the mountain on foot. When Angel got himself eaten by the things in the lake, he had the keys to the snowmobile still in his pocket. Luckily, I had enough forethought to take off my parka before jumping in the water; otherwise, I'd have hypothermia by now from coming down the mountain." He shivered slightly. To keep him warm on the way down the hill on the snowmobile, Alex had wedged Jerry between himself and Trudy, wrapping his legs in an old blanket he'd found inside the under-seat storage of the sled.

Concluding his story, Jerry added, "The heater in Alex's pickup warmed me up somewhat on the way over here, the top half at least, but I need to get out of these wet pants as soon as I can."

At the mention of dry clothes, Alex excused himself momentarily, saying, "Hang on, Mr. Benson, I totally forgot, but I might have something in my truck you can wear." He excused himself and exited the pub.

Austin and Christine had listened intently while Jerry related his tale. When he'd gotten to the part about another Angus, they looked at each other, eyes wide, stunned by this turn of events.

Shaking her head in disbelief, Christine said, "I knew there were two bear cubs, but I thought one of them boiled to death, and the other had gotten crushed in that final avalanche."

"No, we weren't that lucky." Jerry shook his head glumly, then continued, "It looks like the second cub got caught behind a cave-in and had been trapped behind it for the last eleven months or so."

Austin said, "Well, some other things weren't as trapped."

"What?" Jerry asked. "You mean there's more?"

Christine nodded yes and said, "Much more. A couple of dire wolves and a sabre-toothed cat."

Jerry sat silent for a moment as the news sunk into his mentally overloaded grey matter. "Unbelievable."

Austin added, "And the cat had kittens in the Lawless arboretum over at the complex."

"It just keeps getting better and better, doesn't it?" Jerry said morosely.

Alex returned from his truck and handed Jerry some clothing, saying, "I had some clean sweats for the gym in my backseat, but they might be a little big." He handed Jerry a pair of grey sweatpants and a sweatshirt.

"Thanks, Alex. Anything dry will be better than what I'm wearing." Jerry took the clothes and retreated to the washroom to change.

"When we were up at the cavern, we found Mayor Nichols. But he won't be getting re-elected anytime soon," Trudy said, shaking her head and shivering in recollection.

"I knew what happened to Ray Chance but wondered about the mayor. Where did you find him?" Christine asked.

Alex replied, saying, "Down a tunnel that dead-ended in a waterfall and a huge chasm. He'd climbed down onto a ledge to hide from something, I guess, and couldn't reach high enough to climb back up."

Hearing this, Christine felt a pang of guilt for the ex-mayor's demise. But then she had to remind herself that Bob Nichols had been more than willing to have her killed, or even kill her himself by holding her as a human shield and having a savage beast from hell devour her instead of him. Although she now had some closure regarding what had happened to Nichols, upon learning that the plan she'd had to distract him had been successful, the cause of his ultimate demise unsettled her, to say the least.

Jerry returned from the washroom with his wet clothes bundled up in his arms. Alex had been right; the sweats didn't fit him. He looked like a young boy dressed up in his big brother's clothes. Due to Alex's size, the shirt and pants were way too long in the arms and legs, and Jerry had to roll them up significantly in order to walk without tripping himself. "Thanks a lot, Alex. They're a little big like you figured." He gestured with his arm to accentuate the point, and one of the sleeves unrolled, extending several inches past his fingertips.

"Yeah, sorry, but that's all I had, Mr. Benson."

"Don't be sorry," Jerry responded. "It's just great to be dry again."

For several minutes, the conversation was muted as each of them enjoyed the delectable offerings on the large aluminum platter in the centre of the round table. Once everyone had been filling their faces for several minutes, Christine said, "We need to come up with a game plan here."

An insistent buzzing noise came from Christine's purse. She opened the flap and pulled out her phone, saying, "It's Trip!" She answered the call and placed it on speakerphone. "Hey, Trip, what's up? Mind if I put you on speakerphone?"

"Hi, Chris. No, go ahead. Got some news about your cat." His voice dropped in and out slightly as his cell phone fought to find a repeater tower nearby.

"Great! Where did you see it?"

"I didn't, at least not yet," Trip Admitted. "But it's out here somewhere." His phone crackled, and his voice faded again.

"Where are you? What's happening?"

"I just got back from the Burger Barn. Chief Paulson called me to come get my snowmobile that Willy borrowed and left there."

"He must be doing okay if he's out sledding," Christine observed.

"I suppose. He was at the barn looking for raw meat to eat for some reason. Maybe if was for the companion he had with him, the dire wolf."

"What? He's hanging out with that thing now?" Austin asked, surprised.

"Well, not anymore," Trip replied, his voice fading for a moment. "Fred had to put the wolf down when it charged at him outside the Barn."

Shaking her head, Christine observed "Well, at least there's one less thing out there to worry about now."

"That's true. And by the way, I dropped the wolf's carcass off at the works yard, and locked it in the shed with the body of the other wolf Willy took out with the truck."

"Thanks, Trip," Christine said.

"No problem. I knew you guys were out on a date tonight and didn't want you to have it ruined. But after what happened at my place, I wanted to let you know what's going on."

"What happened? Are you okay?" Austin asked.

"Yeah, I'm all right at the moment. But just a little after I got home with the kittens, that darn mama cat tried to break into my house through the back door."

Austin said, "What? You brought the cubs home with you?"

"Yeah, well, I didn't want to leave them unattended at the yard again, just in case."

"Did the cat get inside?" Christine asked with concern.

"No," Trip crackled, "it just broke the window and a bit of the door frame on my back porch. So, right now, I'm out on my property looking for it."

"Be careful, compadre," Austin said. "Because there's one more thing you should know—we've got another Angus on our hands once again."

"What?"

"Yeah, sorry to be the bearer of worse news," Austin replied. "Alex saw it escape from the cavern on Gold Ridge this afternoon."

"That's just great. We're back to a deadly duo once more. Well, if either of them shows their furry faces around here, I'm gonna flambé them."

"Flambé them? They're not Cherries Jubilee, you know, Trip," Jerry added.

"Who's that? Is that Jerry Benson? Hey little buddy!"

"Hi Trip. Yeah, I'm up here, but not quite how I wanted to get here. It's a long story."

"You'll have to tell me over a wobbly pop later. Look, I gotta go, this snow is really getting thick, and it's hard to see. The tracks the cat left are getting filled in pretty quick and... Holy crap! I gotta go!" Trip's phone cut off.

The group sat around the table for a moment, looking at each other, unsure what to do.

Alex said, "Dad, I'm going to take Trudy home."

"Great." Austin nodded. "And when you're done, I need you to keep an eye on the rear of the complex, in case that cat comes back or if that bear comes sniffing around. I helped Chris rig up a trap near the mechanical room at the back of the arboretum. Just call me if you see anything."

"Okay, dad. I'll keep you posted." Alex said. With that, he and Trudy said their goodbyes and departed.

Christine looked at the two men, saying, "Okay, guys, I think we should head over to Trip's and see how he's doing. On the way, I'll call Chief Paulson to notify his men to keep their eyes peeled for the son of Angus out there somewhere."

"Couldn't hurt to call the radio station too," Austin added, standing. He pulled out several twenties and left them on the table to pay for their platter and drinks.

Christine stood as well, and as Austin helped her back into her coat, she said, "Great idea! I'll have them put out a valley-wide alert for everyone to watch their backs."

Smiling grimly, Jerry added, "And their fronts." He pulled his blue parka on, grabbed the backpack he came in with and a handful of mozzarella sticks from the platter and followed his friends out the door.

CHAPTER FORTY-SIX

Trip Williams stuffed his phone back in his pocket and brought his full attention to the task at hand. Somewhere out in the snow-filled evening, the sabre-toothed cat prowled, looking to reunite itself with its babies. But one of the last things that he wanted was for that to happen. He knew, if the large predator were able to do that, by spring, they would have three dangerous carnivores from out of time stalking the residents of Lawless instead of just one. Scratch that, he corrected himself; they'd have four. If the Angus that Alex said he witnessed leaving the cavern up on Gold Ridge was in any way as formidable a creature as its mother was, then they were in some deep shit that was only getting deeper.

Spinning suddenly, Trip looked behind himself, feeling that something was at his back, just out of sight in the grey void of snow that surrounded him. Nothing was there, at least, nothing he could see. That's what had ended his call with Austin and the gang, thinking he saw something moving around in the snow. He wanted to make sure he was ready with the flamethrower, and the phone call had proved too distracting. Now, just as then, he couldn't see more than three metres in front or behind himself, and he was getting a little freaked out.

Now seemed like as good a time as any to give his rocket pack a test so that he would at least be reassured that the weapon he carried was, in fact, going to protect him if push came to shove. The pilot light of the butane torch attached to the front of the flamethrower glowed a dull blue. At a little over fourteen hundred degrees Celsius, the falling snow around it was vaporised almost instantly when the frozen flakes neared its heat.

Holding his breath, Trip pulled the trigger. A column of flame shot from the nozzle blasting a searing hot wave of death into the frigid night. The snow in the air steamed away to nothing, and the snow on the ground melted almost instantaneously like spring thaw on steroids.

With a grunt of satisfaction, Trip said, "Well, that seems to work."

The tracks from the cat had entered his property from the forest. Living on the edge of town, he was familiar with most of the forest creatures that crossed through the small acre of land he called home. Never in a million years did he think he'd ever find himself out in a blizzard with a flamethrower hunting down a sabre-toothed nightmare from the past. "First time for everything, I guess," he muttered to himself as he turned back toward his house. Its light glowed dimly but comfortingly several dozen yards ahead. There was no way he was going to find the cat out in this storm. With a sigh, he pushed through the deepening snow back toward his house.

Spider had remained inside while Trip had done his reconnaissance. It wasn't that he thought the dog would be able to do much to protect his house but hoped the hyper barking of the peppy little pooch would be enough to dissuade the cat from coming back to the house while he was out and about. He moved up the three low steps onto his back porch and pushed open the partially ruined door.

Trip shrugged out of the rocket pack and placed it near the back door, turning off the butane torch's pilot light. The last thing he wanted to do was burn his house down in the middle of a blizzard while something outside wanted to get inside to eat him.

"Spider!" Trip called as he walked into the hallway, but there was no 'erf' in response. "Where are you, little buddy?"

Trip stood, listening intently for a moment. The wind whistled around the eaves, and snow scratched across the glass on crystalline claws. Normally, his compact little bungalow was quite cosy and soundproofed from the wiles of nature, but not tonight. The wind seemed very loud inside the house for some reason. He put it down to the broken window out on the porch being the culprit.

"Spider boy! Where are you?" He called again. There was still no answering reply from the small dog, and Trip moved cautiously down the hallway to where the spare bedroom lay. Maybe the little guy was exhausted and sleeping near the kittens, doing guard dog duty. With no response, Trip grabbed one of his golf clubs from the hall closet. He wasn't an avid golfer, but he and Austin tried to get out on the links at the local golf club whenever they could, which, some years, was not as often as they would like. He paused for a moment, waffling over which club to grab. The nine iron was a hefty club at almost one pound, but the wedge felt just a little heavier, and he grabbed it instead.

The door to the spare room was partially closed for some reason, and he tried to push it open, but it seemed to be stuck. Shoving his shoulder against it, he discovered the reason for the loudness of the storm. The room was in disarray, and the double window in the wall lay shattered all over the carpet. The gusting wind blew snow through the gaping hole in the wall where the window used to be. On the floor, the cardboard box that the kittens had called their temporary home lay on its side, the babies nowhere in sight.

In a hushed voice, he asked one more time, barely audible over the wind, "Spidey? Where are you?"

A small 'erf' came to his ears, and Trip moved to the closet.

"Where are you, little Spider buddy?" This time, the bark was

304

louder.

The closet door was open a crack due to the door frame warping over the years, and it was something he'd meant to fix since it never closed properly. He pulled it open, and there, under several jackets that had fallen, a small tan tail waggled back and forth. He squatted down and lifted the jackets. Spider gave him an excited bark and practically leapt into his arms.

Trip laughed as the tiny dog began washing his face. "What? Are you afraid of a cat?"

Spider 'erfed' loudly in his ear and licked him again.

He scruffed the dog's head, saying in agreement, "Yeah, me too."

CHAPTER FORTY-SEVEN

His mouth tasted like copper, and Franklin Pearce realised he'd bitten his tongue at some point over the last few minutes. He opened his eyes, but things were a little blurry from the tears, most likely caused by the recent electrocution he'd received. His arms were down at his sides, and he attempted to flex them but found he couldn't—he was duct-taped to a chair. A single bare lightbulb swung ever so slightly back and forth from a fixture over his head. The room around him was dark, and the pool of light from the bulb overhead was the only illumination.

"Well, well, well. Look who's awake! Welcome back to consciousness, sleepyhead!" Roxanne Rooney exclaimed in a musical tone. She stepped forward into the circle of light.

Franklin snapped his head toward Roxanne and was going to unload a string of expletives only to find his mouth was taped, too. Snot flew from his nostrils as he raged behind the tape and thrashed at his bindings a bit more.

"This thing works great, doesn't it?" she asked, turning the Vipertek flashlight in her hands this way and that as if it were a new kitchen gadget she'd picked up off of Amazon. "Everyone thinks it's just a regular flashlight until it's too late. Here, want another taste?" She lunged forward suddenly as if to zap Franklin with it again, and he flinched. "No? That's too bad. It really is a lot of fun to watch you squirm." She jabbed it toward him another time, a wicked grin on her face.

"I think you've had enough fun, Roxy," Ethan Chance said, stepping forward into Franklin's line of sight. "After all, we don't want to kill him, just yet." Chance studied Franklin for a moment and added, "He certainly does seem energised, doesn't he?"

"Must be the charge I gave him." Franklin jittered and jived as he tried to break his bonds once more.

"Ah, yes. After all, any man would feel electrified to be around you." They both laughed at the joke, and then Chance held his hand out. Roxanne handed the Viper to him, and Ethan walked forward and crouched down directly in front of Franklin for a moment. In a wash of sour wine breath, he asked, "Are you going to simmer down so we can talk here? Or is your charge feeling a little low?" He brandished the taser in front of Pearce's brown eyes.

Franklin nodded slowly, a string of snot running down the duct tape over his mouth.

"Would you mind doing the honours, my dear?" He nodded toward the captive man.

"With pleasure." Trying to avoid the mucus, Roxanne made a slight grimace as she grasped the edge of the tape at the corner of Franklin's mouth. She whisked it off with a loud ripping sound, taking several of his nose hairs with it.

"You son of a bitch!" Franklin shouted at Ethan, then over at Roxanne and added, "And you, you little wh..."

Brandishing the taser in front of Franklin's face, Ethan interjected, saying, "Hey now, let's be civil." Franklin clamped his mouth shut with a snap.

Ethan continued, "Did you seriously think that nothing was going on between Roxanne and me? You know as well as I do that this girl is attracted to money. And that's something I have, and also something I want from you." Ethan stepped back, and Roxanne moved next to him, putting one of her arms about his waist.

"W-what do you mean? What money? I don't have any—I'm a cop!"

"You know as well as I do that I mean the gold. We both know that you took gold from Bob Nichols house." Ethan picked his wine glass off a nearby table and took a sip.

"What are you talking about?"

"Oh, come on, Franky, you know what the man is talking about." Roxanne walked back to Franklin and ran her crimson-coloured nails through his dark oily hair as she spoke. "Don't go playing the victim here." Franklin tried to pull away from her fingers but couldn't.

"That's right, Ethan added, "After all, you were going to rob me, remember? It's not like I'm the bad guy here."

Franklin snorted derisively at this, causing more snot to fly from his nostrils and roll down his chin.

"Roxanne, would you wipe him down, please? He's getting rather disgusting." Ethan grabbed a handful of facial tissues from a dispenser nearby and handed them to Roxanne. Stepping forward, she blotted at the slimy snot on Franklin's face, cleaning it the best she could. She then placed them over his nose and said, "C'mon, give us a big blow."

Pearce honked into the tissue. Roxanne gave him a final wipe and said, "Now, isn't that better?" then dropped the sodden snot rags into a large Rubbermaid garbage can standing nearby.

Clapping his hands together, Ethan rubbed them back and forth vigorously and said, "All right then. Let's get down to business!"

"What is it you want?" Franklin asked petulantly.

"Didn't we already cover this? Your gold, remember? Or more accurately, Bob Nichols's gold."

"Listen, I don't have…"

Without warning, Ethan stepped forward and jabbed the taser into Franklin's neck and unleashed another charge. Every muscle in Franklin's body tensed and tingled at the same time, and he felt as if bees were crawling underneath his skin while he tried to deadlift a two-ton weight. With a shriek, he said, "Shit! All right, all right!"

Roxanne said, "See, Franky? All you needed was a little motivation!"

Ignoring Roxanne, Franklin stared at the taser in Ethan's hands for a long moment and then said, "All right. How much do you want, exactly?"

"We want exactly half of the gold you took out of Reggie's basement."

"What?"

"Look, I know for a fact that you ripped off my dad when you helped VanDusen take that gold out of the cavern. In fact, I know that VanDusen only gave my dad half the gold to which he was entitled.

"How do you know that?"

"Because Roxy here told me." Roxanne moved next to him, a satisfied smile on her face.

"She's just a gold-digging bitch! How can you believe a thing she says?"

"Hey, let's be civil, remember?"

"All right. Let's say I give you some of that gold. Then what?"

"Once we get everything distributed correctly, I propose we work together."

"Like I'd trust you."

"I don't think there's ever going to be any way we can trust each other, but I think a mutually beneficial truce might be in order." Ethan placed the taser onto a table just out of the light's circle to show he was sincere.

"And what are we going to work together on?"

"Why, getting more gold!" Ethan said with a slight laugh as if it should have been obvious.

"If you cough up some of that gold you have, I think we can all work together and walk away from this little two-horse town multi-billionaires. That is if everything we've heard about this cavern turns out to be true."

"Oh, it's true all right. As well as the other shit crawling around up there. I presume you're aware of that aspect?"

"I'm sure it's nothing a nice big gun can't take care of. You do have a nice big gun, don't you, Franky." Ethan asked, then sipped some more wine.

Roxanne smirked at this joke but said nothing.

"Yeah, I have a couple of high-powered rifles that should do the trick. I never encountered anything when I was up there, though."

"Maybe you were one of the lucky ones."

"Maybe, but…" On the other side of the room, the radio in Franklin's jacket pocket sprang to life with a shrill tone and began squawking all at once, but the sound was muffled by the parka's thick fabric. Emergencies were rare in Lawless, and anytime the radio beeped with the emergency tone before an announcement, it was something important.

"Could you grab that, Roxy?" Ethan asked gently.

"Sure thing." Roxanne walked out of the light, her gyrating hips drawing both men's eyes at once. She came back with the radio in hand and gave it to Ethan. From the radio's small grill, the police dispatcher's voice said, "I repeat, all off duty personnel, please check-in. We have a situation that needs all available manpower ASAP."

Placing the radio on the floor next to the chair, Ethan said, "So what do you say? Do we have a deal so that we can release you to go about your duties protecting the citizenry of Lawless?"

"Yeah," Franklin said, his head slightly bowed as if in acquiescence.

"Excellent!" Ethan grabbed a boxcutter from the table where the facial tissues sat and began cutting away the duct tape binding Pearce's hands and legs.

Inside, Franklin was seething with anger, but he didn't let it show. He was more than happy to go along with the proposed plan for now. Still, he knew that when the opportunity presented itself, Ethan Chance and Roxanne Rooney were going to rue the day they'd ever run an electrical current through his system.

CHAPTER FORTY-EIGHT

Austin, Christine and Jerry made their way through the blustery evening to Trip's home on the north side of town, just at the edge of the city limits. As Austin drove cautiously on the slippery roads, Larry blasted by in a spray of snow going the other way. Peering through the temporary whiteout caused by the plow's passage, Austin observed, "Larry's going to have his work cut out for him this evening."

Christine nodded, from the passenger seat of Austin's Honda Pilot, saying, "The weather office has called for another twenty or thirty centimetres by morning, but thank goodness it's supposed to clear after that."

From the backseat, Jerry added, "Until the next front blows in from the coast, probably only a few days later."

"Well, there was a mention of something else hitting just after Christmas," Christine responded.

"No big surprise there," Austin replied. "Just par for the course up in these parts this time of year."

The entrance to Trip's laneway had been filled in by Larry with the plow, but Austin's Pilot, with its freshly studded tires, had no issue pushing through the deep snow. As they drove up the lane, they could see all the lights were on inside Trip's tiny bungalow. Pulling to a stop near the front door, they made their way onto the tiny porch, and Austin knocked, but there was no answer. After a moment, he tried the doorknob, and it was unlocked.

Pulling the door open on well-oiled hinges, Austin called out, "Hello? Trip?" There was hammering coming from elsewhere in the house.

A circular saw suddenly started up just as Austin called loudly. "Trip? What's happening?" With no response, Austin pounded on one of the walls with the flat of his hand and shouted out once more, "Trip!"

The saw shut off, and Trip came out of the spare bedroom, a golf club in one hand and a hammer in the other. "Oh, hey guys! Sorry I didn't hear you knocking, but I'm glad you didn't wait outside. You never know what's lurking around out there."

Looking at the implements in Trip's hands, Austin asked, "Heading out to the links to hammer away at a few balls, buddy?"

Trip held the hammer up and said, "Just trying to fix the damage the cat caused." He brandished the golf club in his other hand and added, "And these are the only weapons I have left since Willy took my rifle—these and my rocket pack, that is."

Standing to the side of Austin in the hallway, Christine tilted her head as she asked, "Rocket pack? What, like Duck Dodgers?"

Trip said, "Something like that."

"Maybe I can use it to fly myself back to the coast," Jerry said from behind Austin's tall shoulder.

Christine and Austin parted so that Trip could see Jerry. Moving forward, he gave the smaller man a big bear hug while still holding his weapons in both hands, saying, "Great to see you, little buddy! How've you been? And what are you doing here?"

"I've definitely been better," Jerry said with a slight shake of his head as he stepped back from Trip's embrace. "I rented a cabin in the valley and was planning on popping up here over the holidays to say hi to everyone."

"That's great," Trip said.

With a shake of his head, Jerry replied, "But it didn't quite work out how I had planned."

"What happened with the cat?" Austin asked.

Trip stepped back and showed them down the short hallway to let them see the boards he'd cut and nailed across his broken window. "I had to repair the porch door too. That damned cat is a regular homewrecker." He ushered his friends into his living room and excused himself for a moment. He returned from the kitchen, held up a six-pack of Kokanee in one hand, and said, "I don't know if anyone else could use one, but I sure could."

Austin and Christine each took one with an appreciative nod. Jerry hesitated for a moment, then said, "What the heck. I'm not a huge fan of beer, but this will definitely hit the spot." Cracking his can open with a hiss, Jerry took a tentative sip, then gave a small satisfied, "Ahh," adding, "Much better than Lucky Lager."

"Hell, yeah." Trip agreed, opening his own can and taking a swig.

Jerry brought Trip up to date about what had happened to him over the last day or so, including further details on his and Alex's encounter up at the cavern.

"I thought the place had caved in from that final quake in January?" Trip wondered.

"Only the front parlour was compromised," Christine said. "The lake and other areas are apparently still intact."

"Yeah, that glowing lake is certainly pumping out a freak show from the past," Jerry added.

"How is that even possible?" Austin asked.

"I'm still not sure," Jerry replied. "But I think it has something to do with whatever is in that water and how the creatures are being thawed out. From what I figure, there is some sort of biochemical reaction going on there that is reviving these things as they thaw in the warm water. For some reason, I don't believe any of them have suffered any ice crystal nucleation from their time in the ice."

"What do you mean, 'ice crystal nucleation'?" Trip asked, his brow furrowed.

"Well, let me try to explain," Jerry said in a teacherly tone. "Whatever happened to these creatures frozen in the glacier happened so fast that the ice didn't have time to damage their soft tissues when they froze. On the other hand, in the permafrost of Siberia, where they keep pulling out mammoths, bears and sabre-toothed cats, heterogeneous nucleation occurred during their freezing. This damaged the soft tissues but still slowed the decomposition almost to a stop, but not quite, resulting in necrosis."

Christine asked, "You mean the death of the tissue, right?"

"Correct," Jerry said. "Thanks to the flash freezing or whatever happened up at the cavern, none of the animals' cells seem to have been damaged too badly. And that fact, along with whatever chemical stew is in that geothermally heated lake water, has allowed them to thaw gradually enough that they haven't suffered any damage from their freezing.

Austin said, "That could be debatable. Angus seemed

permanently pissed off when we encountered him in January. Maybe his grey matter was affected."

"There's a possibility that a certain amount of brain damage could have occurred because of the freezing," Jerry responded. "But physically, they're intact enough to be up and walking around again after tens of thousands of years. It's really quite amazing."

Finishing up his beer, Trip shook his head and said, "And now we have 'Son of Angus' walking around out in the snow, complicating things further."

Pointing down at her dress, Christine said, "Sorry to add to the complications, guys, but I need to quickly stop at my place, first, and put on something more functional."

Finishing his own beer, Austin said, "Not a problem, Chris. We'll swing by your place and then head downtown to the Smackdown. I really want to make sure everything is all right there. With that cat and now Angus the Second out there, who knows what the hell might break loose."

"I agree. Jerry and I will take my Fargo into town and, just in case…" Trip paused and held a finger up as he excused himself from the room. A moment later, he returned with the rocket pack slung over his shoulder, saying, "In case we need to warm things up for our chilly friends from the past."

***

The Winter Solstice Smackdown was in full swing. It had been the city council's idea to kickstart the town's post-earthquake reconstruction with a winter solstice party just before the holidays, one that would be a time celebration and rebirth for all to remember. A half dozen food trucks sat out in front of the complex in the parking lot, offering everything from tacos and grilled cheese sandwiches to hot chocolate and cheesecake. And of course, inside, they could partake of the pulled pork for which

Pattie at the concession stand was so well known.

George MacKay stood near the entrance of the arboretum, greeting guests as they arrived. In addition to being the person in charge of the mechanical aspects of the sizeable glass-filled structure, thanks to his background in botanicals, George also served as a tour guide and educator, pointing out various flora of interest. In addition to the flora, some smaller fauna called the facility home as well, including hundreds of butterflies and over a dozen species of tropical birds. The enclosure was kept at a toasty twenty-five degrees Celsius, allowing both the plants and the animals to thrive. Though not as large as the Bloedel Conservatory in Vancouver, it was also a triodetic dome and shared many of that structure's features. It had always been a draw to the town of Lawless, long before Ray Chance's 'Mini Vegas' was constructed up at the old ski hill.

Alex Murphy had stopped in to see him a short while ago, informing him that the prehistoric cat was still on the loose but that the trap was still primed and ready to go and that he would be keeping an eye on it out back. So, with everything secured outside, as far as he knew, there was no way for the large feline to get inside the arboretum.

The turnout had been quite good, considering the storm that was currently blustering away outside. After the latest batch of lookie-loos had wandered through, George went on a quick tour of his little tropical paradise. He planned on keeping it open until nine o'clock this evening and then call it quits for the day. After everything that had happened last night, he was exhausted, and it seemed the nap he'd tried to take this morning had not been as good as he'd thought.

Approaching the far side of the dome, George saw that the door to the ventilation access shared with the swimming pool next door was sitting ajar. The latch wasn't cooperating these days, and the door kept popping open. The room was quite warm inside, almost more so than the arboretum itself. Cautiously pushing the door open, George peered into the darkened interior and flipped the switch on the wall. The lights flared briefly but failed to illuminate. He'd been having problems with the switch and had been meaning to replace it. "Dammit! I'll have to check this in the morning." He pulled the door shut, knowing it would soon pop open again. There were several 'Caution! Work in Progress!' sandwich boards nearby, and he placed them around the door to keep any nosy-neds out of the room.

Just as George MacKay walked away, the door clicked silently open once more. From the thin strip of blackness visible within, a pair of green luminescent eyes peered out, and a deep bass growl emanated from the darkness.

CHAPTER FORTY-NINE

The Golden Fortune Cookie restaurant was one of the oldest restaurants in Lawless, dating back to its opening in 1948. Offering a fusion of Western and Asian cuisines, it was constantly in the running for the annual Best Eats in Lawless competition which it had won many times during the ensuing decades. Ming Lee and her husband Huang had emigrated to Canada after the Second World War. Initially landing in Vancouver, they moved inland and eventually settled in the rugged and beautiful West Kootenays. Most of the employees working at the Cookie this evening were their sons and daughters. Serving up another order of lo mein, Ming Lee noted that business was brisk. With the Winter Solstice Smackdown taking place, and despite the snow, the 'kids' had been run off their feet. She still thought of them as 'kids' even though the youngest of her children was eighteen next month, and the oldest was halfway through a degree in marine biology.

One of the most interesting features and another draw to the restaurant was the building situated next door. Lawless, BC was one of the first interior cities in British Columbia to have a multi-story parking garage. Thanks to that structure being located adjacent to the restaurant, Ming and Huang liked to say there was never any concern over parking for patrons of the Cookie. With a capacity for almost two hundred cars, there was plenty of room.

However, one of the stories was below ground, with the other five above.

Since gravity and grease worked well together, part of the parkade's design was to accommodate a below-ground grease storage tank shared by several restaurants in the surrounding block of the downtown, including the Golden Fortune Cookie. With a capacity of almost five hundred gallons, it could hold several weeks' worth of grease before needing to be pumped out by a collection company that hauled it off to be turned into biodiesel.

Unfortunately, the grease trap hadn't been emptied in over a month now. Even more unfortunately, the company that collected the grease had changed its schedule because of the holidays and hadn't been overly diligent in informing its customers. This lack of attention went unnoticed for several days due to general busyness with the upcoming holidays, and now the drain had begun to overflow and leak rancid grease all over the floor.

Ming Lee had been informed of the issue just today by one of her kids who regularly parked their car in the parkade's basement. At first, her son thought it was just water, but when he stepped out of his Subaru, he'd almost fallen into a large puddle of grease. It was so slick, he said, if he'd fallen in it, he didn't know if he would have been able to get back up again. This grease had been unable to drain any further down into the storm sewer because its grate was also clogged. Upon hearing this, Ming had contacted the contractor in charge of pumping the trap out. He'd apologised for the confusion, saying it would be another day or two before it could be drained and suggested they minimise their dumping of used grease down the trap until then.

***

Franklin Pearce had departed the 'taser party' at Ethan Chance's house and dropped by his own place to change into uniform before heading out on patrol. It was unexpected to be called into duty on an off day like this. The last time he'd had to do so had been during the quake that had rocked the small town. He didn't mind since it meant extra overtime pay, of course, but tonight's callout got in the way of the revenge he was planning on extracting. He was still seething about the betrayal he'd suffered at the hands of Roxanne Rooney. He had almost expected such a thing from Ethan Chance due to his previous experience with the man. But it was that bitch Rooney that really got him hot and bothered. Not in a sexual way, either. The woman was truly a gold digger, with no apparent redeeming qualities apart from her smoking body. And there was also the fact that Franklin was used to being the person in control of a situation. Being out of control and held prisoner had been something that did not sit well with him or his megalomaniacal tendencies.

The downtown core of Lawless had several back alleys running east to west, a couple of which ran the entire length of the city. In fact, a person could walk or drive the entirety of the downtown through one of these back alleys without ever seeing another living soul, except possibly for where they were intersected by one of the city's north-south avenues.

Constable Franklin Pearce was currently patrolling in his cruiser, doing a back-alley sweep. With numerous garbage dumpsters dotting the rear access of many businesses in town, it seemed like a good place for him to start his patrol. The snow was still falling quite heavily, but the alley he was navigating was not as snow-filled as some others. Thanks to the prevailing winds that blew through this part of town, it was relatively snow-free. In the last block, near a short drift, he'd seen some disturbances in the snow. Definitely not people tracks; these looked like animal prints—big ones. After reporting it to dispatch, he carried on with his patrol along the alley. The suspension on his ageing cruiser complained slightly as he exited one block with a squeak and entered the next block with a creak.

Aiming the spotlight on his cruiser into the falling snow, Pearce shook his head in wonder. The stuff was even heavier now than it had been only a moment ago and he could hardly see the Cookie which lay just up ahead.

This block held one of Pearce's favourite restaurants in Lawless, the Golden Fortune Cookie. He liked to eat there when he was in uniform since they almost always comped his meal. Frostbite Fred's out on the valley highway, and the Bonanza Buffet at the casino only gave him a staff discount of fifty percent, so he found himself naturally gravitating toward the place in town that gave him free food instead.

The rear entrance to the parking garage was located along this section of the alley, right next door to the Cookie. In fact, he was thinking of stopping at their back door to get a container of chicken lo mein to snack on while he patrolled and…

"What in the hell is that?" he asked aloud, hitting the brakes a little too hard, and the heavy cruiser slipped slightly in the snow. He peered intently, trying to see through the infinity of snowflakes, not sure if he'd just seen something large, covered in snow moving around out there or not. There was a chance that he was still suffering from the after-effects of his humiliating taser electrocution. But there was also another possibility.

Franklin had contacted Mariana at dispatch after he'd gone on duty, and she'd told him there were possibly two dangerous predators currently loose in the valley. Something similar to the situation in January, apparently. That had gotten him thinking. If more animals were loose in the valley, that could only mean one thing: the cavern was open once again. It must have been caused by the tremors the town had a week ago. Not as big as the beginning of the year to be sure, but maybe it had been just enough to nudge something open again, which would mean...

"Gold," Franklin said aloud. Maybe his new partnership would prove to be something he should nurture, for now, just to see where it went. Then, once he'd gotten access to the gold up at the cavern, he could stage the two 'mysterious disappearances' for Roxanne and Ethan he was planning. It would probably be something similar to the previous conservation officer in the valley, Carl Kuehn. After Reggie had the pleasure of dropping the man down one of the bottomless lava tubes at the cavern, they'd wanted to make it look like he'd decided on an early retirement and bugged out of town with his trailer. And so, it had been Franklin's job to steal Kuehn's fifth wheel. He'd done so, stripping it of any identification and then sold it anonymously on Kijiji for a quick buck.

A sudden gust rattled the patrol car and shredded the falling snow in front of him. He engaged the flashers and stepped out of the cruiser. The wind tore at the fabric of his uniform pants with icy claws as it scoured the alley clean. Whatever was moving around out here had been just up ahead, near the exit to the parking garage. He clicked on his heavy-duty flashlight. Up ahead, a single yellow and black striped barrier at the parkade's exit stopped anyone from entering the car park in the wrong direction. Something had moved through this barrier the wrong way, disintegrating it to kindling in the process.

Franklin withdrew his Beretta 92 and held it in his right hand with the flashlight beneath, spotlighting whatever was in front of the handgun's barrel. The lights in the garage were on a sensor that only triggered when it detected the weight of a passing vehicle. Several seconds later, once the car had moved by, they would shut off, the only illumination remaining, a series of emergency lights. The overhead lights leading down to the basement level were currently on due to something heavy having just moved through them. "Lawless Police Department!" Franklin shouted. There was no response, not that he'd expected one. As he got closer, the lights leading down the ramp clicked off.

The stench made him want to gag. Almost overwhelming, it was a tangy, rotten scent like someone had deep-fried a turd in rancid oil. His eyes watered slightly as he moved down the ramp. At the bottom level, the lights had just clicked off as something moved past the sensors.

"Police department! Show yourself!" There was no response to his request. He was getting pissed off now. Descending further into the parkade, he arrived at the sensor that controlled the lighting in this section, but it didn't trip as Franklin hadn't sufficient weight to trigger it. Fortunately, his torch and the emergency lights provided enough illumination. Edging forward, he listened intently. The wind outside shrieked through the open spaces between the garage's exterior support columns and became almost the only thing he could hear. But then, it died down, just for a moment, and he heard it: something in the darkness breathing through its open mouth like Darth Vader made real.

The basement level of the parkade had a puddle filled with what appeared to be freshly formed ice. Pearce stepped slowly forward, scanning the area with his flashlight, gun at the ready. Too late, he realised he was already stepping into a part of this large puddle. But it wasn't a puddle of ice in the middle of the floor after all; it was grease, which had been creating the stench he'd detected earlier. He turned to leave, and his foot suddenly went out from underneath him.

Even more so than ice, grease was dangerously slippery, especially on top of smooth, poured concrete. This was something that Franklin discovered as he moved to exit the puddle. He began to do a rather frenetic shuffle as he struggled to maintain his balance, but it was a losing dance, and he soon succumbed to gravity's embrace. The inch of thick, rancid grease that he'd landed in ultimately did little to cushion the blow, and he cracked his head on the floor.

"Jesus! This is disgusting!" he cursed, holding the back of his head. He tried to sit up but slipped backwards once more. His flashlight was lying off to one side, illuminating the yellow-white puddle of grease in which it lay. Whatever had tripped the lights wasn't anywhere in sight right now, and darkness surrounded him.

Franklin stretched his arm out, just able to snag the flashlight with one finger, and he slid it toward himself. He shone the light about the area and stopped on the giant paw prints in the grease. Whatever it was, its traction had been unaffected by the semi-solid oil.

And then he heard it again—the breathing from out of the

darkness, just around the corner up ahead away from the emergency lights. He moved his torch back and forth, trying to locate its source. However, he needn't have bothered since the source of the sound found him first.

Arctotherium angustidens illuminated Franklin Pearce's world as its two metric tonnes of muscle triggered a light sensor in the floor, displaying it in its full, carnivorous glory. The tremendous beast's head almost scraped the ceiling of the parkade as it stalked deliberately and surefootedly across the large puddle of grease toward him, triggering light sensor after light sensor as it moved closer. Its breath huffed from its parted jaws in great clouds of steam, saliva gushing between its knife-like teeth. With every step it took muscles like steel cables rippled beneath its matted grey pelt. It plodded toward him, small globules of snow dripping from its fur onto the layer of rancid fat that squished outward from beneath each massive foot's clawed edge. Now only metres away, its razor-sharp nails scraped across the bare concrete beneath, giving it easy purchase despite the treacherous surface.

Pearce shrieked and felt for his Beretta. It had flown from his hand when he'd fallen and was now several feet out of reach, half-buried in coagulated oil.

"Get away from me, you ugly son of a bitch!" He tried to scrabble back in the grease but found he only slipped further into it then fell backwards again.

"Heeyah! Get back!" he shouted at it, but the beast was not afraid and continued toward him. There was no place Pearce could go because he couldn't extricate himself from the grease, and soon the beast was upon him. His ears rang as it roared, and he felt its breath wash over him in a fetid wave of rotting meat and death.

The beast took one more deep breath as it inhaled his scent, and then it roared, its mouth opening wide like a cavern to hell, revealing teeth as sharp as stilettos. He kicked out at it as it lowered its head toward him, but that only served to put his feet at a perfect height for the monster to catch hold of them with its mouth. With a crack, it bit into Pearce and began jerking him up sharply into the air, shattering his bones with each savage jolt of its powerful jaws, drawing him further and further into its nightmarish maw.

Constable Franklin Pearce shrieked again and again as his body was ground to paste between the animal's powerful jaws, his screams muted by the wind howling through the parkade's support columns. Soon, the garage was silent.

The beast moved up the ramp toward the night and the swirling snow. Its hunger had only been piqued by the small appetiser of which it had just partaken. The whistling wind carried scents of a multitude of prey nearby, but they were still mixed in with another smell—that of its enemy, of which its hatred was inborn. With a thunderous roar, it moved into the night, accompanied by its two companions, insatiable hunger and unending rage.

CHAPTER FIFTY

Trip watched as the cheese oozed out of the sandwich he held, threatening to encase his fingers in molten mozzarella. He and Jerry had arrived at the complex several moments before and hadn't seen any sign of Austin and Chris, yet, most likely due to Chris wanting to change into her uniform before joining them. Since that was the case, Trip figured he had time to pick up a quick snack from one of the food trucks. After all, he hadn't had anything to eat due to accidentally incinerating his pizza. But that was okay, he'd get his pizza fix anyway, and he bought a pepperoni pizza grilled cheese sandwich instead. It was one of his favourites sold by the 'Cheesed Off' artisan grilled cheese sandwich truck. Unfortunately, Jerry had declined when Trip had offered to buy him one.

"Your loss, little buddy," Trip said, his voice tinged with disappointment. However, there was another individual amongst them that definitely wanted to take Trip up on the offer of some grilled cheese goodness. Spider jumped up and down at Trip's feet, 'erfing' excitedly. "All right, all right, keep your fur on!" Trip took one more lingering, savoury bite and gave the remaining piece of crust to the dog, who gobbled it down greedily. "Geez, you'd think I never fed you or something." They continued through the gathering of food trucks and were now inside the complex with Trip carrying the small dog in his arms.

Once inside the foyer, Trip realised he'd made a tactical error. Though the grilled cheese had been delicious, he'd forgotten about Pattie's pulled pork sandwiches that were being sold at the concession. Since he hadn't had anything for 'afters' since his grilled cheese, when he saw that Pattie's line wasn't too long, after a few minutes wait, he had a pulled pork sandwich in his hands. Jerry had the privilege of holding Spider while he ate. Both watched Trip eat for a moment. Jerry shook his head sadly, and the dog barked once.

"What?" Trip asked around a mouthful of deliciously tender pulled pork. After a couple more chews, he said, "It's dessert!" He offered the sandwich to Jerry, saying, "Sure you don't want some?"

Jerry shook his head and said, "It's all yours, friend." Spider whined and then 'erfed' once as if disputing Jerry's statement.

"You don't know what you're missing," Trip chastised.

"Yeah, I think I do," Jerry replied, adding, "A heart attack and a triple bypass."

Trip smiled and waved away Jerry's concerns, then finished the sandwich in two more large bites, keeping a small piece at the very end for the dog. He took Spider from Jerry, and within seconds, the last remnants of the sandwich were gone. Moving further into the complex, Trip gave Jerry a quick tour. The swimming pool was surprisingly busy tonight, with dozens of families visible behind the viewing glass splashing about in the heated saltwater. In addition to a water slide, the Olympic-sized pool contained a leisure section where people could float along a 'winding river' style watercourse on foam boards and pool noodles.

Next door was an NHL-sized hockey rink that was currently open to public skating. Several girls spun and twirled near one end, wearing bright Christmas-coloured red and green leotards as they practised for the local figure skating club. Nearby, a group of boys in hockey jerseys that read, 'Kootenay Lawbreakers' skated about doing high-speed sprints and then abrupt stops to see how much ice spray they could kick up. They laughed amongst themselves as they took turns while eyeing the girls out of the corners of their eyes to see if they were watching.

Inside the conference area off the concession, a holiday fair was underway with numerous local merchants and artisans selling everything from home baking and candles to hand-crafted crockery and jewellery, as well as a large selection of locally made knitwear and artwork. Jerry stood looking at the people milling about him and smiled. "You know something?" he asked Trip, who stood next to him.

Trip shook his head, munching on a small tray of butter shortbreads he'd just purchased from one of the local ladies groups who had a significant presence at the fair. "Nope, I try to know as little as possible," he replied, a raft of crumbs tumbling into his bushy beard. The dog sniffed and licked at the cookie bits, burrowing into Trip's facial hair like a four-legged vacuum cleaner as he tried to collect them all.

Jerry grinned, then said, "I really could get used to this little town. The vibe is so much different than the big city."

With a nod, Trip says, "Kinda grows on you, doesn't it? Personally, I don't know how you handle all the hustle and bustle down on the coast."

They moved back into the main foyer and then toward the arboretum where George MacKay was just saying goodbye to a group that had just finished touring through his little tropical paradise. "Hey, Trip!" George said with a wave. Trip introduced Jerry to George, who proceeded to give them a quick tour. Trip put the dog down, saying, "Now, don't pee on anything." Spider 'erfed' and ran off to sniff the base of one of the palm trees.

As they toured, George said, "Many of the plants in here are, or at least were, indigenous to this area before the last ice age, don't you know."

"Actually, I do know," Jerry responded.

"Oh? How's that? Are you a teacher or something?"

"Professor of geology down on the coast," Trip said proudly, slapping Jerry amiably on the back in the process.

Recovering from the bone-jarring back pat, Jerry nodded and said, "This is true. I'm just up here from the coast on vacation. Well, I'm supposed to be, at least."

"He's aware of our little issue with the kitty-cat out there somewhere," Trip said in a low voice, not wanting to be overheard by a family that had just entered the large glass structure at their back. A little boy with the family stopped briefly to play with Spider, who 'erfed' several times, sharing his joy with the world at finally having a playmate just his size.

"Well, I hope that trap our local conservation officer put out in the back of the building will do the trick."

Trip nodded, saying, "One way or the other, we hope to catch something in it."

"Crazy stuff," George said with a shake of his head. "I wonder if there's anything else wandering around out there."

Jerry and Trip looked at each other briefly but said nothing. After a few more pleasantries, they departed the arboretum and moved once more toward the concession. Jerry said, "What, you're hungry again?"

Trip smiled and shook his head, saying, "Not quite yet, but I want to do something." He handed Spider to his friend. They had stopped at the delivery door at the side of Pattie's Pulled Pork Paradise, and Trip knocked several times. After a moment, a slender, dark-haired woman popped her head out and said, "Hi, Trip. What's shakin'?"

"Hey, Pattie. I know you're busy, but I wondered if you could help me out."

Pattie looked over her shoulder and saw that there was currently a lull in customers, and she left her assistant, her teenage daughter, behind the counter on her own for a moment, saying, "I'll be back in a second, sweetie." She stepped out and closed the door at her back. "What's up?" she asked with a puzzled look in her eyes.

"I was wondering if I could borrow some of your pork."

"Borrow some pork? Whatever for?"

"It's for the city, actually."

"What, are you having a Christmas Party?"

"Not quite," Trip responded cryptically.

"Well, I don't know if I can spare any of the cooked pork tonight; things have been pretty brisk," she said with a smile.

"Oh, that's okay, I don't need it cooked,"

"You want it raw?"

"Yeah, but it's not for eating, at least not by us." He nodded toward Jerry, who smiled slightly and looked as puzzled as Pattie by the exchange.

With a shake of her head, Pattie said, "I can spare a little, I guess. But I don't have any more deliveries until after Christmas, so I don't want to run out."

"I understand," Trip nodded.

331

"How much do you need?"

"A couple of good-sized roasts ought to do it."

"Two? Gee, hang on for a second and let me look." Pattie retreated into the small kitchen for a moment and then came back out with two large pork roasts in vacuum-sealed bags in either hand, saying, "You're lucky, I have these two kicking around from a special request order which never came through."

Accepting the roasts with a smile, Trip said, "Pattie, you are a peach." I'll cut you a city cheque tomorrow.

"Not a problem Trip, you and your friend have a good night and enjoy your pork." She moved back into the kitchen and closed the door.

Jerry stood looking at Trip, saying, "Is that what I think it's for?" He placed the dog on the ground.

Trip nodded, saying, "Yup, it's bait. Talking to George back there made me think; maybe we can use that trap out back to catch more than just the cat."

"Really? I don't think that bear is going to fit."

Smiling, Trip said, "We only need part of it inside." He tossed one of the roasts to Jerry, then reached for the keyring in his pocket as they moved to the complex's utility/maintenance room. Spider pranced happily along beside them, still sniffing at the scent of the meat in the air from his visit to Pattie's.

Trip unlocked the door, and they moved inside the utility room. Lined up along one side were several tanks of oxygen and acetylene used during the reconstruction of the arboretum. Starting at one end, Trip tapped on the oxygen tanks with the tip of his pocket knife, listening to the tone it made before moving on to the next. All made a similar, low, metallic 'dong'. Continuing along, he eventually tapped one much higher in pitch and lifted the full container out of the collection of empties. There was a small workbench in the utility room, and he placed the cylinder on it. Several spools of various gauges of electrical wire were affixed to the underside of a shelf next to the bench. Trip unravelled several feet of wire from one of the spools. After putting some slits in the plastic that held the roasts, with Jerry holding one to either side of the oxygen tank, Trip proceeded to wrap the wire around the cylinder, saying, "I give you the Meatsicle Surprise!"

With dawning realisation, Jerry said, "I see where you're going. Can I offer you something that might help?"

"Sure, little buddy! What've you got?" Trip twisted the wire and finished securing the roasts.

Jerry pulled the backpack that he still carried on his back and plopped it on the table. He reached inside and rummaged around for a moment. Trip's eyes widened slightly as Jerry pulled out several bundles of hundred-dollar bills with mustard-coloured bands on them. "I'm really glad I didn't throw this bag away," Jerry commented, then found what he was looking for and pulled out a compact rectangular cube wrapped in tan-coloured paper and placed it on the table.

"Holy shit!" Trip exclaimed. "Is that what I think it is?" The word 'C4' was printed on all six sides of the rectangular tan block in large block letters.

"Yes, and that's the same reaction I had when I first discovered I was walking around with that stuff on my back,"

"Where'd you get it?"

"Same place as all that cash, courtesy of my ex-kidnapper—this is his bag." Jerry proceeded to pull two more items from the backpack, an electronic detonator, and a remote-control mechanism with a red button on top. "Angel used this to detonate the C4 and unleash the bear from the cavern. When he got his ass eaten by the thing in the lake, I was going to leave it behind. But after I met up with Alex, I figured since we can't walk around with a howitzer on our back this time, maybe this stuff would come in handy at some point."

Trip pulled the paper from the explosive and began moulding it around the top of the oxygen cylinder, saying, "I think we've arrived at that point."

CHAPTER FIFTY-ONE

The fire of hunger still burned brightly inside the beast, gnawing away at its insides and making it careless. The animal was no longer concerned if it were stealthy or not, and its need to feed was incessant, urging it ever forward. It feared nothing, driven as it was by this intense hunger.

Its recent meal had been bony with little meat, but the flesh had been sweet and delicious, and it wanted more. Fortunately, the wind carried the scent of much, much more. Hundreds and hundreds of scents mingled together as one, becoming a tantalising stew of things it recognised and things it didn't.

But whether the scent was familiar or not, it didn't matter—they all made it salivate anew as it moved along. After spending its life in the dim environs of the cavern, its eyesight was weak, however, and when it encountered any bright light, it could not look directly into it and had to rely on its sense of smell instead. And that was not a problem because the animal didn't need to see to know where its food was; it could smell it just up ahead, and it was plentiful.

***

About a half-hour ago, while out on patrol looking for the new inhabitants of the valley, Fred Paulson had received a call from the health centre. Doctor Anali Chopra had been on duty, and she'd informed him that Willy seemed to be in some type of acute distress.

When emergency services had initially come by to collect the boy from the Burger Barn, he'd just been coming around from his tasing and had still been quite agitated. So, the EMS attendants shot him up with some of their favourite ketamine cocktail to calm him back down.

Several minutes after Dr Chopra's call, Fred had found himself standing over Willy's unconscious form in an isolation room at the health centre, protected by an N95 mask, as well as gowned and gloved. Willy was handcuffed to the bed in addition to being restrained with straps.

"I can't understand what's going on inside this boy," Dr. Chopra said with a frown, then continued, "We had to give him a much stronger sedative since the ketamine he'd been given by EMS wore off more quickly than usual. And I'm positive the tetanus and rabies shots I gave him yesterday wouldn't have caused the reaction that seems to be happening inside his body right now."

"What sort of reaction?"

"Well, it's his organs, amongst other things."

"Are they failing?"

"I don't know if that's necessarily the case. Here, let me show you." They moved to an adjacent room with several monitors on the wall. Dr. Chopra removed her mask and pointed to one of the monitors, and continued, "I ran an EKG on him first—still am, in fact. His heart is beating like a hummingbird's. But there's no sign of arrhythmia or anything like that." The monitor showing Willy's current heart rate read one-hundred and forty beats per minute.

Fred removed his mask, eyes widening slightly as he looked at the screen. "That's a little high for lying down, isn't it?"

Dr. Chopra nodded, saying, "Absolutely. The average human resting heart rate is about sixty BPM or so. And just for reference, a well-trained athlete can have a resting rate as low as forty beats per minute."

"So that's not good then.

"If he were out jogging or doing something aerobic, he'd be 'in the zone' for a good cardio workout. But for lying in a hospital bed, he's in serious trouble."

"Do you think it's an after effect of the ketamine he was given?"

"Well, at low doses, like the one he received, it can elevate heart rate a little, but nothing like this."

"So, what's causing it then?"

"I don't know," Anali moved to a computer-coloured x-ray showing Willy's internal organs and skeleton. "Here's the thing that's strange: all of his organs, his kidneys, liver, spleen, heart, you name it, they're all enlarging."

Fred shook his head in disbelief. "What will happen to him?"

"I don't know. And his skeleton seems to be growing as well to accommodate this rapid expansion of his internal organs." After a pause, Anali said in a low voice, "It's like he's transforming."

Fred Paulson shook his head in disbelief and brought himself back to the moment. He was walking around Franklin Pearce's empty cruiser looking for prints. The light bar on top was still flashing, and the engine was running. Fred reached inside and killed the light, then shut off the engine and took the keys. Franklin had checked in and reported that he was on patrol and had found some prints, and that had been the last the dispatcher had heard of him. The fresh snow that was falling made it hard to track where the constable had gone, but it seemed readily apparent to Fred.

The barrier into the parking garage lay in pieces. Tracks emerged from the lower level—well-defined tracks that left little to the imagination. Christine Moon had contacted him with the news of another 'anomaly' roaming the valley. Looking down at the enormous prints, he knew they were in deep kaka.

Taking the mic from the shoulder of his parka, he clicked it on and said, "Mariana, this is Fred. I need you to send out an APB to the rest of the force."

Mariana DaSilva crackled back, "Affirmative, Chief. Whatcha got?"

"I found Constable Pearce's cruiser, but not Franklin himself. I'm investigating now near the parkade. Have the other units converge on the downtown. There's something wandering around out here. Something big and probably ugly."

The 'other units' out on patrol consisted of the second cruiser that the LPD owned, currently being driven by Constable Jimmy Jones. With Franklin MIA, they were down to three active-duty officers, including himself and the dispatcher. Usually, the town was relatively quiet at this time of year, apart from the odd rowdy house party around Christmas and the New Year. Traditionally, they let one officer have part of the Christmas holidays off. This year, being understaffed after the attacks in January as they were, they had not, as of yet, restocked the force with fresh rookies, and everyone available was working overtime.

"Roger that, Chief." Mariana proceeded to send out the APB using the police station's high-powered antenna. Jimmy Jones came on the radio stating he was assisting a stranded motorist at the top of the Gold Mile Pass and could be there for a little while. So that just left Fred and Mariana.

Fred sighed with resignation. He'd hoped that this new beast wouldn't roam in the direction of the downtown, but judging by the tracks in front of him, it was already too late for that. He descended the ramp to the lower level of the garage and saw his worst fears were realised. The communal grease trap had sprung a leak, apparently. In the centre of the inch-deep puddle was something that caused Fred to blanch. From all his years on patrol, he'd seen his fair share of accidents and gore. But what lay in the centre of the parking garage basement level was beyond anything he'd ever seen or even imagined.

It almost appeared that someone had been trying to make a snow angel in the grease and had been interrupted by something straight out of hell. Blood was splattered all over the fat in a Rorschach pattern of crimson disgust. Wherever Franklin's body was, it wasn't here now. However, part of him still was. Off to one side of the carnage, Franklin's dark-haired head was lying on its side in the grease, mouth open in a scream that would never end, tendons and torn flesh poking out from where the neck should have been. Either the creature had tired of chewing on someone as stringy as Franklin, or it hadn't noticed his head pop off as it ate him alive. Fred shuddered and moved back into the stormy night. He picked up his shoulder mic again and said, "I found Franklin."

"Oh, that's great, Fred. How is he?" Mariana crackled back.

"Not good. He's gone all to pieces. Tell Jimmy to get his ass down to the parkade ASAP once he's done up on the pass. I need someone to guard the parkade until Bill Barlow can get here and exercise his duties as coroner."

"Oh, my gosh. Roger that."

Fred climbed into his Suburban with a puff, feeling all sixty-five of his years on this planet weigh down on him all at once.

***

The windows inside Alex Murphy's Toyota Tacoma were all steamed up, the occupants inside managing to create their own privacy, thanks to their young lust.

He should have taken Trudy home; he knew that now. But she insisted that she could help him with his guard duties out in back of the complex. Unfortunately, the only thing he'd guarded so far had been Trudy's lips, and he'd done a lip-smackingly good job of it if he did say so himself.

"We're supposed to be keeping an eye out for that cat and bear, you know," Alex complained half-heartedly.

Trudy gave him another small avalanche of kisses all over his face, ending up on his lips once more. Coming up for air, she replied, "Those two oldies can wait. What're another few minutes when you're already over ten thousand years old!" She began kissing Alex again.

Alex had parked his truck at an entrance to a bicycle pathway that ran throughout the town, connecting it to most quarters. It was paved, and during any season but winter, it provided the residents with a smooth surface on which to bike, in-line skate, scoot, or even walk if it came down to it. Seeing as no one was using it in the middle of a snowstorm, he'd parked in front of it since it was located almost directly across from the back of the complex where the trap lay. Against his better judgement, he was about to allow himself to succumb to another avalanche of Trudy's powerful kisses when there was a sudden pounding on the side of the truck that startled them both.

Trudy let out a high-pitched shriek that pierced Alex's eardrums. "Omigod! It's the bear! It's found us!"

Shaking his head, Alex said, "Bear's don't normally knock, at least not the kind we're thinking of." He wiped his arm on the steamed-up frosty window and saw his Uncle Trip peering through from the outside. He rolled the window down. Sounding somewhat embarrassed since he'd been caught slacking off on the promised guard duty he was supposed to be doing, he said, "Hey, Uncle Trip, what's happening?"

Trip looked in at them, a somewhat quizzical expression on his face. "Looks like more is happening inside here than outside at the moment." Behind him, Jerry Benson stood looking toward them, seeming almost as embarrassed as Alex felt, and he nodded toward the man.

Alex gave a slight nod in return, saying, "Yeah, sorry. Trudy and I were just going over some of the homework assignments they gave us over the holidays."

Peering over Trip's shoulder, Jerry observed, "Must be hard to remember what you'd written down without any notes."

Trudy grinned sheepishly, saying, "Umm, we memorised them?"

Trip grinned and said, "Okay, now that your R&R is over, are you ready to help?"

"You bet, Uncle Trip!" Alex replied enthusiastically, then frowned slightly as he asked, "What's R&R?"

"Rest and relaxation. Looks like you've had plenty," Trip said, a twinkle in his eyes.

Alex straightened up in his seat. "Yessir. Ready to help."

"Good. That's what I want to hear." He looked around them at the heavily falling snow, saying, "You're so far away from the complex I'm surprised you can see anything out here with the weather getting in the way."

"I've got good eyes, and besides, I've also got these." He

turned on his wipers to clear the fluffy-white buildup from the windshield, then flipped a switch. Suddenly the back of the entire complex was bathed in blinding, white light that pierced through the falling snow.

"What have you got on this thing?" Jerry asked in surprise, looking up at the light rack. "A piece of the sun?"

Grinning, Alex said somewhat proudly, "Not quite; it's a thousand watts of power which puts out almost 150,000 lumens of light. Sure comes in handy when you're four-wheeling in the bush in the dark."

"Well, I'd imagined you wouldn't be using it out on the highway," Trips said, somewhat amazed at the intensity of the light.

With a shake of his head, Alex responded, "No sir, absolutely not." He flipped the lights off, and the darkness returned.

"Good stuff. All right, guys, here's the deal. Jerry and I have set up something in the trap in addition to what Christine had there already."

Trudy nodded, saying, "We heard those kittens crying inside and almost thought they were real."

With a nod of his own, Trip said, "Jerry and I think it's certainly going to attract something, so keep an eye out back here."

"You bet!" Alex responded with a small salute.

"Oh, and one more thing."

"What's that?"

"Don't get too close to that trap, whatever you do. If things work out, we've got a surprise inside there that will blast that bear back into the past. But I don't want you guys taking the journey with it, if you know what I mean." With that, Trip turned and moved back to the complex through the deepening snow, Jerry following close behind.

Alex and Trudy said nothing and only stared at each other with wide-opened eyes.

CHAPTER FIFTY-TWO

The weight of the Hannibal .577 Tyrannosaur rifle was reassuring. It had already been more than helpful in January when Austin had used it on mama Angus, and Christine hoped that it could once more be of use. She knew there was no way to trap the latest monster bear that had been loosed from the cavern on Gold Ridge—the animal was simply too large to fit inside the trap. And tranquilising darts were out as well since the ones she currently had on hand were not powerful enough to bring down something as large as the prehistoric bear.

Austin stood next to her as she checked the rifle over and verified everything was in working order. "I never thought we might need to use this twice in one year."

Nodding, Christine said, "I know what you mean."

"Bear in mind, no pun intended, I hit the other Angus a couple of times with this thing, and it hardly slowed it down."

"No pun taken," Christine said. "And I'm not surprised, depending on where you hit it. The layers of subcutaneous fat on the OG Angus were quite thick in some places, and not so much in others."

"Well, I hit it in the ass, actually."

"That's right, I remember seeing that before we shipped the carcass down to the coast for Zelda to examine. You did a good job with your targeting for a rookie." Christine said with a grin.

"Gee, thanks. I haven't had the practice that you've had, being a seasoned pro like you are and all," Austin replied, smiling.

"Not too well seasoned, I hope?" Christine said with a slight tilt to her head, her eyes piercing him and holding him in their mesmerising gaze.

"Definitely not," Austin replied, as a slight redness rose on his cheeks.

Christine added a case of cartridges to the T-Rex's softshell Kevlar-based carrying case, then locked the gun and ammunition cabinets back up. They exited the conservation office via the rear shop door where Austin's Honda sat parked. Once inside the vehicle, Austin asked, "So what's the plan?"

"I think we should head to the Smackdown as you mentioned earlier. With the noise and the scent of the food trucks, not to mention all of the people, I think it would be a very attractive place for Angus to head."

"You're the boss," Austin said, placing the Pilot in gear. With Jerry in tow, Trip had already gone ahead of them, stating he wanted to help patrol the event to make sure everyone was safe. And most likely to load up on some of the fantastic food from the trucks scattered about near the recreation complex's entrance.

"I feel like I'm getting ready to lead a safari out onto the Serengeti hunting for elephants with this thing," Christine said, hefting the rifle case wedged between her legs.

"Well, we certainly seem to have bigger game than usual around these parts at the moment."

"Speaking of 'these parts', I was looking through those documents you found in the safe in your office."

"Ah yes, they are certainly interesting, aren't they?" The wind had died down, and the snow was falling in large lattice-work flakes once again. Austin had the wipers on high, but they struggled to keep up at times.

"Absolutely! I was reading the newspapers that were in there regarding the disappearances that happened at the time. Do you think they had their own Angus?" Christine wondered.

"I don't know. From what I gleaned, most of the disappearances were of the mysterious kind. There was no mention anywhere of people being eaten by giant marauding bears from out of time."

"And what about the fire that burned through town back then? Do you think that was an accident or intentional in an attempt to burn something out that was afflicting the town?"

Peering through the windshield with a squint, Austin replied, "That's a good question. Or perhaps they were covering something up?"

"Maybe. And don't forget the record of money collected from wealthy donors, which I believe has been going on for quite some time now."

"Donations, to what, the 'Save the Clocktower Fund?'" Christine questioned.

"Haha. I don't know for sure. But from what I could see, it's something that has been a continuing thing in this town over many years."

"Really? How many?"

"Oh, about a hundred and twenty-five or so."

"What?" Christine asked, stunned by this development.

"I found a ledger in the office after you left."

"In the safe?"

"No, but it was hidden, just like the safe." Austin described the ledger and the list of names and monies exchanged.

"And you found this where?"

"In a secret room at the back of the closet."

"And it didn't lead to Narnia, huh?"

"Unfortunately, no. But it did lead to some more funds to help with the quake reconstruction."

"How do you mean?"

"There were over a dozen burlap sacks sitting in this secret room, filled with gold ore."

"Holy moola! That's great news! And it reminds me as well. I meant to ask about Bob Nichols."

"What about Bob?"

"Well, I realise the gold in the mayor's office belongs to the city, especially since Bob probably never declared it in his taxes."

"That's a fair statement," Austin said with a nod.

"And so, it wouldn't have to be included as part of his estate, right? Doesn't he have any relatives that might lay claim to his house and property?"

"As far as I know, he was the last of his line. Never married and a lifelong bachelor."

"So, no one has ever come around to claim his estate?"

"Nope, and since no heir has come forward and unpaid property taxes are coming due on it now, the house will be seized and put up for auction."

"Proceeds from that will also go to the city. Another nice donation by Bob since the insurance policy Lawless had on certain things only went so far, and it looked like we were going to be in the red for many years to come, covering the cost of the difference. However, thanks to Bob, it seems that might be reduced significantly, barring any more earthquakes or other natural disasters, of course."

They were approaching the Lawless Community Complex parking lot. Christine was impressed by the turnout. Despite the weather currently beating down upon the town—the lot was almost full. A smile crossed her face when she saw that the doughnut truck was here tonight since she wanted some dessert, and she loved their mini doughnuts, both the cinnamon and the powdered sugar. After that, she wanted to pop inside to check things out at the craft fair. Many local artisans and other craftspeople were selling their arts and crafts here tonight, and she figured it would be a great place to look for some of the more practical things she'd wanted to pick up as gifts for the new friends in her life. Glancing around the packed parking lot as Austin pulled in, she said, "Looks like the Winter Solstice Smackdown is doing remarkably well."

Austin agreed, "It really seems this idea resonated with the townspeople. We even had vendors coming in from as far away as Trail, Creston and Cranbrook."

"It's so great to see a small town come together like this."

"Absolutely. And partial proceeds from the Smackdown are

going to the town's reconstruction fund as well, so it's win-win."

"Where did the name Winter Solstice Smackdown come from?"

"That was actually Trip's idea. He tossed that one out when we were kicking around concepts one night at one of the council meetings. He's a big professional wrestling fan, don't you know."

With a slight shake of her head and a musical laugh, Christine said, "I never would have guessed."

"Yeah, it's not too much of a stretch considering his other sporting addictions like the CFL, NFL, MLB, NHL, NBA, PGA…"

"Okay, okay, I get the idea," Christine said with another laugh.

On the outer edge of the lot, Austin said, "Finally!" and pulled the Honda into a spot near a large pile of snow.

Since things seemed calm for now, Christine decided to leave the rifle locked in the Honda for the time being. Laying the Tyrannosaur on the backseat of the Pilot, she said, "You can stay here for now, big fella." She didn't want to walk around with a lethal weapon slung over her shoulders if she didn't have to and freak out the revellers at the Smackdown as a result.

They walked side by side toward the complex, the falling snow around them illuminated in the parking lot's floodlights, an amazing display of natural artwork. Christine stopped walking for a moment and looked up into the intricately detailed snowflakes that fluttered gently down onto her face, saying, "It's really beautiful, you know?" She stuck out her tongue and caught several fluttering flakes on its tip. While she did this, she observed Austin out of the corner of her eye. He seemed to be transfixed by her actions and she wondered what was going through his head. Over the last little while, she had started to feel something very powerful toward the man next to her.

349

"What are you thinking?" Christine asked, looking up at him, a slight tilt to her head.

"Honestly?"

"Always," she said, bathing him in her radiant smile.

After a hard swallow, Austin said, "Well, I realise we haven't even had a proper first date yet because of the interruption at Frostbite Fred's and all…" He trailed off for a moment, then looked deeply into her eyes, took a deep breath, and continued, "I was just thinking how beautiful and amazing you are, and how lucky I am to have you in my life. And that recently, I've been feeling something in my heart that I haven't felt in quite a while now." He gave her a brief, boyishly insecure smile.

Christine smiled broadly again but said nothing.

Austin smiled back and said, "Aren't you going to say anything?"

"I don't need to," Christine said, moving in close to Austin. She looked up into his eyes a moment longer, then stretched up and gave him a gentle yet lingering kiss.

"Hey, you two! Get a room!" called a voice off to one side of them. They stepped apart, embarrassed and excited, both at the same time. Tearing their eyes from each other, they turned to see Geraldine Gertzmeyer in a thick winter parka leaning on her walker. She sported a pair of novelty reindeer antlers attached to her jacket's fur-lined hood. "Looks like you two got the right idea on how to keep warm," she observed. Beside her were two small children, also sporting antlers on their heads. Smiling somewhat embarrassedly at her back stood a man and a woman, presumably her grandson and his wife.

"Geraldine! It's great to see you," Christine said, moving to the elderly woman and giving her a hug.

"Likewise, dearie!" Geraldine hugged her back surprisingly hard for such a fragile-looking woman.

Looking down at the children, Christine said, "And these must be…"

"My munchkins!" Geraldine stated proudly. She patted the little girl to her left on the head, saying, "This is Becca." Looking to her right, she adjusted the antlers on the small boy's head and said, "And this is Berty." With her head turned as far over her shoulder as her arthritic neck would allow, she nodded toward the man and woman, adding, "This is Riley and Jasmine, my grandson and his wife." She turned back, smiling broadly, and concluded, "I'm sure you can figure out which one's which."

Austin and Christine laughed and introduced themselves, shaking hands with the young couple. After pleasantries were exchanged, the group began to move toward the food trucks. They stopped once they were just outside the circle of light provided by the floodlights that surrounded the encampment of trucks.

Becca looked up at Christine in her uniform and asked with large eyes, "Are you a police officer?"

Smiling, Christine said, "Sort of."

"She's like a police officer of the forest," Austin offered.

Christine nodded in agreement. "That pretty much sums it up. Why do you ask, honey?"

The little girl pointed off into the swirling snow and inquired, "Are you going to arrest that?"

Grinning, Christine looked in the direction the girl had indicated, and the smile melted from her face. Taking a deep breath, she shouted at the top of her lungs, "Everyone get inside the complex, now!"

Covered in so much snow that it appeared a snowbank had come to life, something plodded toward the food trucks— something monstrous.

CHAPTER FIFTY-THREE

Veils of steam from the deep fryer rose into the frigid air that wafted through the open order window. Business at Mama Plucker's Chicken Wings had been brisk all evening, and it looked like tonight would be a record for wintertime sales. Arlo Anghorn smiled and rubbed his hands together to warm them up over the deep fryer's heat. Behind him, the blender was at its highest setting as the machine pureed his latest creation to smooth perfection. In addition to assorted homemade dips like his Rancho Royale in the blender, he made his own special buffalo barbeque sauce to coat the chicken wings and other things he sold at his food truck.

Thanks to a lull in traffic at the order window, he'd had used the opportunity to blend up more of his much-loved ranch dressing. With only a few seconds left to blend on the latest batch, he figured it would be his best yet. He was about to turn and switch off the blender when a woman rushed by, heading for the complex, a young child in each hand. Must have a bathroom emergency, he figured with a smile. Directly behind them was a young man helping an elderly lady in a walker shuffle along as quickly as she could. Then, suddenly, a flood of people stampeded past his window, almost all of them customers who'd been enjoying food in the semicircle of trucks just moments before.

"What in the hell?" Anghorn questioned out loud. He shut off the food processor and suddenly heard the screaming and shouting going on around him. The last of the people ran by his order window, and Arlo felt the ground start to tremble as something heavy moved about just outside the back door of his food truck. He stepped out to get a better look, and his heart suddenly skipped several beats. Slamming the door shut, he dived down out of sight against the service counter next to the deep fryer.

The painful squeal of metal bending against its will echoed throughout the truck. Claws like knives hooked into the edge of the door frame at the rear and began pulling the door and the steel sheeting that surrounded it out into the snow-filled night as if it were no more than tin foil. Another claw-tipped paw hooked around the metal on the other side, and the entire rear of the truck was suddenly torn away.

A snout filled with jagged razor teeth thrust through the rupture, trying to burrow its way inside, just as razor-claws ripped more of the sheet metal from the truck's side, bowing out the frame around the order window. At Arlo's exposed feet, the beast snapped and snarled, deafening him from the noise. Pulling its paw back out, the beast took the wall that held the order window with it, including the framework that held the deep fryer in place.

Arlo Anghorn's world was engulfed in white-hot pain the likes of which he had never felt before, and he felt it twice within only a few seconds.

The contents of the deep fryer poured over him, and he shrieked in agony as he was flash-cooked to deep-fried perfection. One of the beast's claws hooked into his blistering body and hauled him out into the freezing night, and he was dragged several yards through the thick snow, cooling the third-degree burns that covered his head and torso. Arlo lay in the snow, looking upward at the light of the arc-sodiums overhead. The one eye that could still see only vaguely registered the light but could not focus on it, its lens scarred milky white. Sudden darkness descended as a mouth so large it blocked the falling snow suddenly yawned wide over top of his supine form. New fireworks of pain shot through Anghorn's mind as the creature clamped down on the seared flesh of his abdomen and began chewing its way through his deep-fried side.

A small part of Arlo's mind heard the crack and crunch of the seared meat and skin being consumed from his body, and suddenly he was transported to his backyard, where he watched himself enjoying some crackling at one of his summertime pig roasts. And then he was gone.

***

"Run everybody! Get inside the complex now!" Christine Moon shouted once more. She and Austin backed rapidly toward the Lawless Community Complex as the citizenry around them fled in all directions. Some did as requested and ran toward the sanctuary of the steel and glass entrance of the newly renovated building. The rest scattered in all directions, with some running toward their cars and others heading toward the downtown core.

Christine watched in horror as a man was dragged from a food truck on the outer edge of the food truck encampment. The snow-encrusted bear looked like an immense pile of dirty grey slush come to ravenous life as it buried its muzzle in the man's side and ripped him apart. She pulled her 9mm from the holster on her belt and began firing. The monster paid little attention as if the slugs that tore into it were mere insect bites, burying their stingers in its massive muscles.

"Come on, Christine, that's not doing any good." Austin tugged at her jacket shoulder.

Christine stood in stunned disbelief. She'd emptied all ten rounds from her Smith & Wesson into the creature, and it had barely noticed.

The snow had stopped falling, and the wind gusted, whipping snow into a white-out as they moved toward the complex's entrance. "I need to get the T-Rex," Christine shouted over the wind.

"But if that thing decides to follow you to the Pilot, you'll be dead in seconds," Austin advised placing his hand protectively on her shoulder.

"I have to try. And I think I can use the cars in the lot as cover. And besides, you need to get inside the complex and keep everyone calm and safe."

Red and blue lights suddenly appeared through the blowing snow. Fred Paulson skidded his Chevy Suburban to a halt near the scene of carnage at the food trucks and stepped out. Running toward the man being attacked by the bear, the chief pulled his sidearm from its holster as he ran. Assuming a shooting stance behind the beast, Fred began firing round after round.

Whatever ammunition Chief Paulson had in his handgun; it was obviously more effective than Christine's. The bear took notice with astonishing speed and turned on him, swiping out one of its long limbs backwards, and catching him by surprise. The chief flew into the side of a nearby minivan, landing so hard he left a dent in its side door. He slid down to a seated position and slumped forward, looking as if he might only be napping.

"Fred!" Christine called out in concern.

Austin gave Christine's shoulder a slight squeeze and said, "There's nothing you can do for him right now. Go for the Rex, and I'll distract it!" He tossed her the keys to his Honda Pilot. With that, he moved toward the bear, shouting, "Heeyah! Pay attention to me, you big ugly bastard!"

Christine moved off reluctantly, watching the bear turn and begin plodding toward Austin, an ear-rending roar coming from deep within its chest.

The monster was as gigantic as its mother, or perhaps even more so, and it was just as ugly. No, scratch that, Austin thought; this one is definitely uglier. A scar ran down the side of the bear's massive angular head where something had injured it, giving one eye a wide-open stare where the fur had not regrown around it.

"Great, now I have your attention, even though I don't really want it." Austin backed toward the complex, still waving his arms in the air. Shaking his head in disbelief, he realised, here he was, being pursued by the offspring of the horror that had tried to gut him only eleven months before—and this time without anything with which to defend himself.

The entrance to the complex was close, and he turned and ran toward it, looking back over his shoulder as he moved. But he needn't have worried, he seemed to have the beast's full attention, and it lumbered after him, an unstoppable force of man-eating nature.

Inside the complex, the people cowered behind the steel and glass that framed the newly repaired facility. Austin slammed his shoulder into one of the manual doors next to the sliding doors of the main entrance and pushed inside. "Everyone get back from the glass! There's no telling what that thing will do. Run and hide!"

"Where should we go?" one terrified woman shouted.

"Hide in the pool or the skating rink. Just get out of sight!" Austin responded, then rushed toward the sliding doors.

Geraldine Gertzmeyer replied loudly, "Anywhere but here is preferable, dearie!" With one child in each of their arms, Riley and Jasmine moved toward the possible safety of the skating rink and its steel-lined entrance doors. Geraldine followed in hot pursuit, working her walker like there was no tomorrow because if the bear caught her, there wouldn't be.

Jogging to the doors, Austin prayed he was going to make it in time. The object of his quest was a door override switch at the top of the door frame on the left-hand side.

The beast arrived at the glass and steel portico-style entrance, moving toward the sliding doors in the centre, but they didn't open—Austin had flicked the override mere milliseconds before the beast would have triggered them. Though they were now disabled, he doubted that would stop the beast for long. He began backing away toward the centre of the lobby.

With a shatter of glass, the monstrous creature began to push its way through the sliding doors. It bellowed and shrieked, the discordant sound echoing across the foyer's multiple hard surfaces. Death had arrived.

The remaining brave souls in the lobby fled in all directions, their own screams a deafening cacophony rivalling that of the bear before them. Austin stood, transfixed as the gigantic bruin forced its way inside.

Trip appeared at his side suddenly, the flamethrower strapped to his back. "Hey, Boss! This all feels way too familiar, doesn't it?"

"Tell me about it!" Austin shouted as the beast roared and pushed further into the complex, the metal framework squealing as the remaining glass surrounding it shattered in a shower of glistening shards.

"I don't want to use this inside the building," Trip nodded toward the thrower nozzle he held in his hands.

Jerry approached, jogging in from the side entrance. He saw the bear and stopped in his tracks, his face going white.

Trip said, "Jerry and I have something rigged up outside that should warm things up for this piece of shit if we can get it out back near the trap, that is."

George MacKay came backing out of the arboretum, shouting, "Everyone get back!" Tracking him as he moved through the door, the sabre-toothed cat followed him out. "Guys, we have another problem!" George called, his voice somewhere between a shout and a shriek, his eyes never leaving the cat.

Whipping his head around, Austin saw the reason for George's concern. "Well, this is just peachy," he said, a shake of his head indicating otherwise. He moved up against the concession wall and scooted a little way toward the rear entrance, the others following his lead. The cat's attention was not on them, fortunately.

The sabre-toothed cat tore its eyes from George MacKay then locked them onto the bear, which was now almost all the way inside. It hissed at its ancient adversary, then uttered a low guttural growl.

With an ear-rending roar, Arctotherium angustidens pushed itself all the way into the complex and charged toward its mortal enemy, Smilodon populator.

CHAPTER FIFTY-FOUR

Thanks to its weight, the Hannibal .577 Tyrannosaur rifle could instil quite a bit of confidence in a person. After jogging through a half-foot of snow to Austin's Honda Pilot to retrieve it and now running back, Christine was definitely feeling the full weight of the rifle's fifteen pounds in her arms. She had come to the conclusion that if a person were ever out hunting with this thing, they'd be exhausted once the time to aim and fire it finally arrived.

The snow seemed to have stopped for the moment, and she was thankful to see that the bear was nowhere in sight. However, her gratitude for the clarity of vision was short-lived once she saw that the beast had now pushed itself all the way inside the recreation centre.

Damage to the front of the complex was horrendous. Mangled metal was bent into torturous shapes as if a twister had just blown through. Angus roared, and the sabre-toothed cat shrieked as they circled each other inside the foyer, preparing to battle to the death. Behind them near the concession stood Austin, Jerry and Trip, looking unsure what to do. Several other people cowered up against the walls in various locations around the foyer, afraid to move, lest they catch the attention of one of the prehistoric beasts. There was no way she could fire the T-Rex into the complex without the risk of hitting an innocent bystander or one of her friends in the process.

"Crap! This isn't going to work!" She slung the heavy-duty rifle over her shoulder and pushed through the snow toward the back of the building, meaning to come in through the entrance near the arboretum. Jogging around the corner, she saw Alex and Trudy standing with eyes wide open near the exit, looking inside.

"Alex!" Christine shouted as she approached the pair of teenagers.

"Christine! Am I glad to see you! Trudy and I were trying to figure out some way to lure the bear out of the complex."

Her eye's lighting up, Christine said, "I think you just did." She moved to the bear trap and opened a small all-weather storage compartment on the outside of the metal tube. Pulling out an iPod inside a Ziploc baggy, she pressed a couple of buttons through the plastic.

Suddenly, the volume of the pre-recorded kittens increased significantly. Alex and Trudy could see what she was doing—trying to increase the chances of drawing the bear toward the easy prey of the babies rather than battling their mother.

Moving to the back of the trap, Christine saw that someone had been busy wiring something up to the steel tube's exterior grate next to the hitch. A tall cylinder of oxygen wrapped in meat sported what looked like a digital detonator near the top, its red light flashing that it was armed and ready. "Nice job!" Christine exclaimed, then turned to Trudy and Alex and said, "Okay, here's what I want you to do."

***

Jerry watched in horror as the sabre-toothed cat emerged from the arboretum. Some small part of him was relieved to see the giant feline and hoped that perhaps the beast might injure or even

361

kill the bear. Then they'd be down to only one predator to worry about. However, size was on the side of the bear, and he wasn't holding his breath.

The large predators circled each other, the cat alternating between hissing like a punctured tire and uttering a series of low-frequency growls. The bear let out an ear-splitting roar as it turned slowly, keeping the cat in sight while it prowled around the bruin, looking for an opening. Suddenly it found one, and with frightening speed, the sabre-toothed cat leapt in the air and landed on the bear's back. The cat's footlong canines pierced into the flesh of the bear's shoulder muscles, and it squealed in pain and anger. The monstrous bear turned this way and that, trying to dislodge the hitchhiker it had picked up, but the cat held tight, clamping its jaws down ever harder on its ursine foe. This loosed another bellow from the bruin, and it spun rapidly around, staggering as it did from the weight of the feline attacker on its back. Together, they exploded through the wall of the arboretum in a shower of glass and twisted metal, landing in a bed of tropical flowers.

Releasing its grip so it wouldn't be crushed by the immense weight of the bear, the cat moved off a short way, seeking another opening in which to attack its primaeval adversary. The sabre-tooth paused, looking in surprise over its shoulder as if it heard something in another part of the arboretum. Taking advantage of the feline's lapse in attention, the bear decided to launch its offensive, and it lunged at the cat with rapier claws fully extended and jaws wide open. The distraction proved disastrous for the feline as it brought its attention back to the fight at hand just a moment too late. The bear clamped down on its foe and lifted the beast into the air as it squeezed its jaws. A cracking sound came from somewhere inside the giant cat, and it shrieked and howled, writhing in agony as the bear shook it like a rag doll.

A sudden tap on Jerry's shoulder made him jump what felt like several feet in the air. It was Austin Murphy.

"We need to get around to the backside of the arboretum and

distract that bear if it polishes the cat off."

Jerry nodded vaguely in comprehension, stunned by the battle he was witnessing.

Several people were still in the complex lobby watching the prehistoric life and death struggle happening before their very eyes. Austin thundered at them, "Get into the ice rink or the pool, now! Go anywhere but here!" The people were jolted from their bystander trance and scattered in all directions.

"That did it," Trip observed, then turned to George MacKay and said, "George, we need to go." There was no response from MacKay. He stood transfixed as Jerry had been, and Trip had to shake the man to get a response. "George! We need to move!" Spider danced around their legs, 'erfing' in excitement and no doubt fear.

"What?" George came back around saying, "Sure, right." He patted Trip quickly on the shoulder and said, "I'm outta here. I don't get paid enough for this!" With that, he ran out into the parking lot, presumably to his waiting vehicle.

With a shrug, Trip said, "One less person to worry about, I suppose." The dog began jumping up and down at his legs, and he stooped down to pick up his wire-haired ward.

The three men quickly made their way down the corridor from the concession to the rear of the complex. As they burst through the exit doors, they found Christine sighting the bear in the T-Rex's scope through the arboretum's glass.

"Chris! I'm glad you made it back in one piece," Austin said, relief apparent in his voice.

With a serious expression, Christine replied, "Well, I knew I couldn't fire into the complex with this thing, or I would have risked hitting someone, so I thought I'd come back here and see if I could sight it through the glass. But still, if that thing moves as I shoot…"

Trip interjected, "Jerry and I rigged up something at the trap if we can just get it over there."

"I saw that," Christine nodded. "C4, huh? Go big or go home?"

A little sheepishly, Trip said, "Something like that." Spider 'erfed' in agreement.

"At least your sidekick agrees," she said, smiling lightly.

A quick toot of a horn brought their attention to Alex, who waved out the window of his truck. Trip said, "I've got Alex working some interference if we can just get that thing toward the trap."

"What's your plan?" Christine asked, still keeping the bear in the Tyrannosaur's sight.

Trip was giving a quick rundown of the proposed plan of action when a shriek came from the arboretum. Everyone's attention turned to the tropical paradise on the other side of the glass to watch the drama unfold.

The Smilodon managed to clamber onto the bear's back once more and was biting down hard on its foe's throat. The bear stumbled this way and that as it tried to shake the sabre-tooth on its back. Reaching as far as it could to one side, the ursine giant was just able to snag the cat's front leg, and it tore the beast from its back. The big cat shrieked in pain as the bear continued to turn its mighty head, flinging the feline into the arboretum's outer wall. The glass shattered into the frigid night, and most of the cat went with it.

Though large and heavy enough to break the glass, the cat had not been flung clear of the razor-sharp shards that remained in the frame. As it broke through, only the upper half of its body made it outside. The rest of it landed directly on top of a serrated pane of glass that still stood. It sliced through the cat's abdomen, the animal's blood spraying out onto the virginal white of the snow-filled night beyond.

The bear approached from one side, and the Smilodon roared in pain and anger, looking as if it might stand and pull itself off its guillotine of glass. Instead, it let out a low growl and slumped back down, almost severing itself in half this time, its lifeblood pouring out around it.

Placing one massive paw down onto the sabre-tooth's back, the bear ground the cat's carcass into the glass fragments as it roared triumphantly. Satisfied its foe was dead, the mammoth bear bellowed in rage and hunger, then stepped through the remains of the wall and into the wind-whipped night and the prey waiting outside.

Spider jumped out of Trip's arms and moved toward the gigantic predator, hackles raised, growling so low and deep in its throat that Trip was surprised the sound was coming from his little hairball. With another surprisingly large bark, Spider leapt into the air at the beast as it advanced.

CHAPTER FIFTY-FIVE

In a blur of motion, Austin Murphy bent down and scooped up the small dog as it bounded past him to defend its master from the monstrous presence in front of it. The dog squirmed to get free, and Austin had to hold him tight. "Hold on, little fella, let your dad do his thing."

The snow had stopped falling a little while ago, and now, the wind died down as well, and it became a silent but deadly night. It was as if the storm were lulling everyone into a false sense of security before unleashing more of its fury upon them.

"Thanks, Mr. Mayor," Trip said. With the rocket pack's butane pilot light already lit, Trip pulled the trigger and a brilliant jet of liquid fire shot from its nozzle, dazzling everyone with its brilliance, including the beast. The ursine monster roared at them so loudly that Austin would have covered his ears had he not been holding Trip's wiry-haired 'son' in his arms.

Christine stepped next to them, shouldering the rifle and targeting the bear in the Tyrannosaur's sights once more, then said, "Show Angus the way, Trip."

"With pleasure." Trip pulled the trigger again, and another brilliant jet of flame shot from the rocket pack's nozzle.

Off to one side, Jerry waved his arm in the air toward the back of the lot. Suddenly, the group was silhouetted against the night by Alex's eye-searingly bright light rack. Trip pulled the rocket pack's trigger again, and a tongue of yellow flame darted forth, looking as if it had come from a monstrous beast of fire and light whose body comprised the surface of the sun.

The bear let loose another shriek of anger and frustration but stayed away from the blinding light and licking flame. It continued along the side of the building, away from the arboretum's glass and toward the steel trap.

Austin shouted, "Keep it going, Trip, I think it's working!" Spider 'erfed' as Austin spoke, struggling to be free of his arms so that he, too, could do his part in things. Austin said, "This dog is harder to hold onto than a greased pig on a Slip 'N Slide!"

Trip gave the trigger another pull. This time, the tank containing the flammable agent ran out of fluid, and only a half-hearted trickle shot from its nozzle. "Okay, that's not good," he observed.

Spider was finally rewarded in his struggles for freedom and escaped from Austin's grasp, then charged toward the bear, yipping and yapping and 'erfing' his little heart out as he nipped and jumped at the immense creature in defence of his master and friends.

Angus roared and swiped at the little dog, but Spider was small and agile and easily dodged out of the way. The frustrated bear started toward the lights of Alex's truck, straying from the direction where the trap lay, but Spider jumped in front of it, unleashing a fresh barrage of barks upon the bear. Despite the dog's diminutive size, his bark must have sounded sufficiently convincing to the bear, and it continued along the back of the building, now approaching the trap.

Trip whistled to Spider, and the dog turned and bounded back toward him, leaving the bear to its own devices. The trap was parked parallel to the building, the open end facing toward the arboretum, the hitch pointing in the direction of the baseball diamond in the backfield, currently buried deep with snow.

As the bear approached the trap that lay open in front of it, it paused as if it were listening. The Bluetooth speaker with the recorded kittens appeared to be doing its job since the bear roared anew, no doubt preparing to kill the offspring of its enemy and finish the job. Chuffing and gnashing its jaws together as it moved, the beast lumbered toward the trap. It raised its nose in the air for a moment, then roared and thrust its head inside the large tube. However, that was all it could fit because of its heavily muscled body and broad shoulders, and it would never squeeze anything more than its head and salivating muzzle inside.

Christine shouted to Jerry, "You're clear, do it!"

Jerry raised the detonator in his hand, the red light blinking somewhat more dimly than it had been, for some reason. With a triumphant shout, he said, "This is for my friend's and everyone else you and your ugly mother of a mother ate!" He pressed the button.

Nothing happened.

The red light on top went from flashing dimly to dead as Jerry repeatedly pressed the button in frustration. Unfortunately, the detonator's batteries were now almost ten years old and had finally expended the last of their energy. "Shit!" Jerry shouted, his complete and absolute disappointment evident as he uttered the single word.

Austin stepped up to Christine and said, "It's all yours. Can you hit the tank from here?"

"Cover your ears," Christine replied. She sighted the meat wrapped tank just visible outside the back of the trap, then pulled the trigger on the T-Rex—and it roared.

When the seven-hundred and fifty-grain shell penetrated the cylinder, it ignited Jerry's bonus wrap of C4 plastic explosive. The world was filled with blinding light and bruising sound, and the shockwave of the concussive blast rocked everyone back on their feet.

The bear's head had still been jammed inside the trap as it tried to reach the boxful of kittens that it thought were cowering inside. When the oxygen cylinder ignited the C4, it created a venturi effect inside the corrugated steel tube. The force of the blast was directed out the front of the trap, and it engulfed the bruin completely, rending its fur, flesh, muscle and bone from its body and liquefying them in the process. Everything that the bear had been was now sprayed across the cinderblock wall behind, its flesh, hair and gristle dripping down in thick crimson icicles.

Many of the remaining windows in the arboretum's glass wall had also been shattered in the blast. With a gust of wind, the storm kicked up again, and an icy breeze raked through the leaves of the banana trees and flowers at their base, some of them already wilting from the biting cold.

Jerry lowered his hands from his ears, as did Trip. They looked at each other, then stared wide-eyed at the destruction their little 'Meatsicle Surprise' of a bomb had wrought.

Jerry said simply, "Whoa."

"I agree," Trip said, with a slow nod of his head.

Christine approached what was left of the trap. The corrugated steel was twisted outward on both sides into unrecognisable, surrealistic shapes like the trap were a plant and the twisted metal its unfurled leaves. With her ears still ringing from the concussive blast, at first, she didn't recognise what she was hearing. "Does anybody else hear that?" she asked. She gave her head a slight shake and stuck a finger in her ear in an attempt to clear any inner-ear pressure blockages.

Austin tilted his head and listened for a moment. "Yeah, I hear it too." He looked at the trap and said, "The Bluetooth speaker is obviously destroyed, so that's not the source."

"Erf, erf!" Spider offered, dancing around slightly near the ruined wall of the arboretum. Trip picked him up and said, "Watch your feet, little dude, or you're going to get cut." He stepped through into the arboretum and put the little dog down on the ground.

With a bark, Spider darted off toward the far side of the glass enclosure, Trip in hot pursuit. The dog stopped near a small utility room and began yipping excitedly.

Catching up with the dog, Trip said, "What's got your knickers in a twist, little man?" He pushed the door open and said, "Well, hello there."

Trip was entering the ventilation access room just as Austin, Christine and Jerry arrived. He emerged moments later with the two sabre-tooth kittens, one tucked under each arm. The compact tan predators mewled hungrily, their eyes now wide open as they took in their surroundings. Both spotted Spider at the same time and hissed mightily for such small creatures.

Spider returned their hiss with a barrage of barks.

"Looks like the feeling is mutual, little guy." Jerry crouched down and scruffed the top of the little dog's head.

"So, what now?" Austin asked as he looked at the kittens in Trip's arms. "Those little guys are going to need a temporary home." At his back, Alex and Trudy stepped through into the arboretum and crunched through the glass toward them.

"Plenty of room in the 'suites' at the Works yard," Trip offered.

"Thanks, Trip, that would probably be best until we can figure out what to do with them," Christine said with an appreciative nod.

While Trudy 'oohed and aahed' over the kittens, Alex said, "Speaking of doing things, what are we going to do with the cavern up on Gold Ridge? Anything can wander out into the world from that gap in the wall near the glacier."

"We need to get up there and close it permanently," Austin replied.

Trudy said, "But what about all the gold!"

"The gold that's still inside should remain there. That cavern has been the cause of nothing but death and destruction ever since it was discovered," Christine said.

"Yeah, it needs to be sealed back up— it's like it's cursed," Trip agreed.

"After seeing the inside of it firsthand, I'd tend to agree," Jerry added. "But I have to add, the scientific discoveries that might still be up there could complicate things."

"Duly noted," Austin said. "Maybe we need to investigate things up there a little further before shutting the door permanently.

As if noticing the slight pause that had occurred in the snowfall, Mother Nature resumed her blanketing of the valley. Lacey snowflakes, the diameter of softballs, began to fall to the ground, only to be ripped to shreds by a massive gust of whistling wind—the full fury of the winter storm that was promised was now upon them.

Trip looked up into the heavily falling snow, shielded his eyes during a particularly savage gust, then said, "Storm's not supposed to let up for about three days, so we might have to put any further exploration on hold."

"Like always, something nasty blows through just before Christmas," Austin observed.

"Well, it certainly did this year," Jerry agreed.

"That's right! We still have the holidays to celebrate, if that's a possibility after everything that just happened around here?" Christine wondered, a relieved smile playing at the corners of her lips.

Austin Murphy looked down into Christine Moon's beatific face, losing himself in her piercing blue eyes for a moment, then said, "After the last few days, I'd say that anything is possible around here."

EPILOGUE

Snuggling together on the couch, glasses of wine in hand, Ethan and Roxanne had listened to the drama of the evening playing out on the police scanner that Ethan kept in his living room. Though the communications of most modern police forces were now digitally encrypted, Lawless had not caught up with the rest of the 21st century and still relied on older technology that could be conveniently eavesdropped upon.

And so, the pair had cuddled as they heard Franklin check-in near the parkade, and then they smiled at the chief's subsequent grisly discovery in the basement of that same building. After a slight pause, they'd heard the chief radio the start of the bear's attack on the complex, but after that, things had gone silent for a while. Then, Jimmy Johnson radioed to dispatch that the chief was en route to the hospital in an ambulance with a broken arm and concussion.

"Well, it looks like we won't be getting any of Franklin's gold any time soon," Ethan said somewhat glumly.

"Not necessarily," Roxanne replied, a sly tone in her voice.

"How so?"

Roxanne took a sip from her wine glass. "He was a single guy. Lived alone, as far as I know. We should check out his place a little later tonight before anyone goes to his house to settle his estate. I'm sure he must have at least twenty sacks of ore, maybe more, after he cleaned Nichols out." She tilted her head and asked, "Speaking of which, how much do we have altogether now anyway?"

"Well, including what my dad had at the house here and what you pulled out of Reggie's place, we have just about fifty sacks of ore."

"I'm still surprised how much Reggie was able to get his little hands on." Roxanne wrinkled her nose like she was smelling a dirty diaper pail as she recalled the ex-police chief and the little fling she'd had with him. Though she'd found the man distasteful, once she'd discovered how much gold he was pulling out of the ground, she'd warmed right up to him. Turning to Ethan, her grimace was replaced by a more business-like expression. "What do those sacks weigh again?"

"Each one is about twenty kilograms, give or take a few hundred grams."

Roxanne's internal computer did a few short calculations, and she suddenly said, "If we add in Franklin's share, at current rates, that's almost $100,000,000 Canadian!"

"And according to our ex-partner, there's plenty more up there, just waiting to be grabbed." Chance rubbed his hands together at the thought.

"There could be billions!" Roxanne enthused.

"Exactly. So, I think we should mount a little expedition up there after the storm dies down, maybe in the new year."

"But we don't know where it is, now that Franklin's gone. How will we find it?"

"You're incorrect. There's still someone we can use to act as a guide."

"Who?"

"Willy Wilson Jr., of course. He and his dad worked for Ray and Bob up at the cavern. Hell, it was him that probably packed most of the gold in the sacks that we already have. And he knows exactly where that place is located," Franklin said, sipping from his wine glass.

"But we heard on the radio that he's in the hospital right now, so he won't do us much good at the moment."

"Well, then maybe we should go pay him a visit soon. Just to encourage his healing, of course."

Smiling broadly, Roxanne Rooney took another sip of wine, then agreed, saying, "Of course."

FINAL WORDS

Thank you so much for reading CLAW Resurgence. This is our second visit to Lawless (not counting the prequel novelettes). And there will be further adventures to come, so stay tuned (see newsletter below).

If this story entertained you and you would like to share your thoughts with others, please leave a review; they are critical to a book's success. To make things easier, here is a direct link to the Amazon review page for CLAW Resurgence so you can leave a few thoughts while everything is fresh in your memory:

Amazon.com/review/create-review?&asin=B09HL4CM2N

Please make sure to sign up for my newsletter, The Katie Berry Books Insider, for further novel updates, free short stories, chapter previews and giveaways. To join, click here:

https://katieberry.ca/become-a-katie-berry-books-insider-and-win/

Good health and great reads to you all,

-Katie Berry

CURRENT AND UPCOMING RELEASES

CLAW: A Canadian Thriller (November 28th, 2019)

CLAW: The Audiobook (July 31st, 2020)

CLAW Emergence: Tales from Lawless – Caleb Cantrill (September 13th, 2020)

CLAW Emergence: Tales from Lawless – Kitty Welch - (November 26th, 2020)

CLAW Resurgence (September 30th, 2021)

ABANDONED: A Lively Deadmarsh Novel Book 1 (February 26th, 2021)

ABANDONED: A Lively Deadmarsh Novel Book 2 (May 31st 2021)

ABANDONED: A Lively Deadmarsh Novel Book 3 (Fall 2021)

ABANDONED: A Lively Deadmarsh Novel Book 4 (Winter 2021)

CLAW: Emergence Book Series (Spring 2022)

CLAW: Resurrection (Fall 2022)

BESIEGED: A Lively Deadmarsh Novel (Spring 2023)

CONNECTIONS

Email: katie@katieberry.ca
Website: https://katieberry.ca

SHOPPING LINKS

CLAW: A Canadian Thriller:
Amazon eBook: https://amzn.to/31QCw7x
Paperback Version: https://amzn.to/31RYPK7
Amazon Audible Audiobook: https://amzn.to/2Gj3j45
(Also available on all other major audiobook platforms)

CLAW: Resurgence
Amazon eBook: https://amzn.to/2YeDdZt
Paperback Version: https://amzn.to/39TKJeF
Amazon Audible Audiobook: Coming Soon
(Also available on all other major audiobook platforms)

CLAW Emergence: Tales from Lawless – Kitty Welch:
Amazon eBook: https://amzn.to/37aSnAn
Large Print Paperback Version: https://amzn.to/3tTsoa9
Audiobook on Audible: Coming soon

CLAW Emergence: Tales from Lawless – Caleb Cantrill:
Amazon eBook: https://amzn.to/3ldY0C3
Large Print Paperback Version: https://amzn.to/3meDVg9
Audiobook on Audible: https://amzn.to/3qkKvUe

ABANDONED: A Lively Deadmarsh Novel Book 1
Amazon eBook: https://amzn.to/3jM3GDX
Paperback: https://amzn.to/3yruNLL
Audiobook: https://amzn.to/3yNot00
(Also available on all other major audiobook platforms)

ABANDONED: A Lively Deadmarsh Novel Book 2
Amazon eBook: https://amzn.to/3BTn4a9
Paperback: https://amzn.to/3BTneyh
Audiobook: Coming Soon

Made in United States
North Haven, CT
07 July 2022

21056234R00231